I0818848

Praise for

THE SERPENT & DOVE TRILOGY

"Full of everything I love."

—**SARAH J. MAAS**, #1 *New York Times* bestselling author of the A Court of Thorns and Roses series

"Decadent and dangerous."

—**RENÉE AHDIEH**, *New York Times* bestselling author of the Wrath & the Dawn series

"A brilliant, unending roller-coaster ride."

—**JODI PICOULT**, *New York Times* bestselling author of *Small Great Things* and *A Spark of Light*

THE SHADOW BRIDE

SHELBY MAHURIN

HARPER
An Imprint of HarperCollins*Publishers*

HarperCollins Children's Books, a division of HarperCollins Publishers,
195 Broadway, New York, NY 10007

HarperCollins Publishers, Macken House,
39/40 Mayor Street Upper, Dublin 1, D01 C9W8, Ireland

The Shadow Bride

harpercollins.com

Library of Congress Control Number: 2024945850
ISBN 978-0-06-348213-5

Typography by Jessie Gang
26 27 28 29 30 RTLO 10 9 8 7 6 5 4 3 2 1

Special edition, 2026

For Pippa, who will live on forever in the pages of this book

Part One

Chat échaudé craint l'eau froide.

Once bitten, twice shy.

CHAPTER ONE

Reflection

The simple chime of a music box is all that fills the silence.

I watch the trinket from across the bedroom, figurines turning in a mechanical dance, their painted wings sparkling in the glow of a single candle. Reid lit the taper earlier this evening while I feigned sleep. At dusk, Lou tiptoed across the floorboards to draw back the curtains, hoping to let in the moonlight, but storm clouds obscured the night sky and shadows crept through my window instead. They swathe me like a cloak as the fairies dance in their halo of light.

"Are you all right, Célie?" Mila whispers from the chair by the bed.

After the grotto, she found a tear in the veil near Saint-Cécile, slipping through it to linger near me in the realm of the living. Though she speaks very little—and asks me to speak even less—I cannot decide whether I appreciate it or not. I cannot decide whether I want her here at all.

"I'm fine," I whisper back.

And the fairies continue their dance.

Lou and Reid brought the music box from my room in Chasseur Tower, along with all my other worldly possessions: beeswax candles and bottles of rose perfume, paste jewels and storybooks with cracked spines. An emerald-green quilt across my bed. A standing gilt mirror in the corner. The filmy, ridiculous nightgown I currently wear.

They meant to help by filling their home with my things.

They meant to remind me that I'm still Célie Tremblay.

They couldn't have known I once coveted the fairies on this music box as much as I loved them. I longed to steal their wings and fly to their realm, to enchant wild creatures and court my own fairy prince. My nursemaid, Evangeline, gave me the box for my eighth birthday, and for an entire fortnight, I spoke of little else until Filippa—irritated—snatched the music box from my nightstand and smashed it to pieces.

She regretted it instantly, of course, and glued the fairies back together as best she could. I never noticed the newfound cracks in their smiles. Perhaps I was too young then—too busy dreaming of grand, sweeping adventures and heart-stopping romance—or perhaps I simply didn't pay attention. I stare at those cracks now, quietly hating them.

I have dreamed so many foolish things.

Turning away, I sigh heavily before inhaling once more—an instinctive reaction, one that fills my body with air it no longer needs. *Mistake.* My stomach constricts at the sudden influx of scent, and fresh saliva floods my mouth. My head pounds. My gums throb. Though I close my eyes against the nausea, the darkness of my eyelids shifts in a sickening kaleidoscope of color, pounding in unison with the heartbeats in the living room. Two of them. My fists curl even as my teeth begin to lengthen, and the saliva continues to flow. My throat contracts without permission, and for just a second, my gaze flicks to the bedroom door. Everything stills to a knifepoint.

Lou and Reid move just beyond it.

I can hear them in the kitchen preparing dinner—the gentle clink of cutlery, the occasional brush of their shoulders as they pass each other. Lou's heartbeat accelerates slightly when Reid brushes a kiss against her temple. He chuckles when she swats his backside in turn. They're wholly absorbed in each other.

Wholly distracted.

They won't notice you, a familiar voice whispers in the back of my mind. *Not until it's too late.*

And it's true. Though I close my eyes, I can almost see the blood pumping through their bodies now, and I can imagine how it would taste—thick and rich and hot on my tongue, *decadent*, like a feast of kings. Mila wouldn't stop me. We spent my last moments together, and though she hasn't mentioned it, I know she feels partly responsible for my fate. Perhaps if she'd somehow *forced* me through that wretched golden light, none of this would've happened, but she told me to choose instead.

She said if I didn't, I'd lose my choice forever.

Ironic, that.

I swallow hard. No, Mila wouldn't stop me—couldn't stop me—but would Odessa? Tilting my head, I listen to her flick each page of her book as she pointedly ignores the sickly sweet humans. "They make my teeth ache," she said yesterday before fixing me with her signature piercing stare. "When can we go home?"

Home.

To her, that means Requiem. Michal sent her here to watch over me, to *guide* me, but she never intended to stay in Cesarine. Deep down, I know Michal never intended it either. The last words he spoke to me still haunt my dreams—or they would if I ever slept.

Please stay.

He doesn't know I heard him. I shouldn't have heard him—not as my heart stopped beating—but I did. I heard him, and I can't *unhear* him. He begged me to stay, yet where is he now? Why didn't he insist I remain with him on Requiem? And if not there, why hasn't he joined me *here*, in this miserable room, to help me through transition instead of Odessa? The questions sicken me—they're ridiculous, pointless, the least of my problems—yet I cannot seem to let them go. To let *him* go. With little else to distract me from this scarlet haze, Michal has spread like a poison across my skin, and I cannot stop scratching at him.

Why did he bite me, only to abandon me? Why did he leave me to the care of my friends—leave me to *hurt* them?

I don't realize my hand grips the doorknob until my palm starts to burn.

With a hiss, I release it and leap away, glaring at the silver chain around the knob. Lou didn't think such a precaution would be necessary. She argued when I insisted, but in the end, she honored the request by digging out the only silver jewelry she owned: an ugly, tarnished necklace that once belonged to her great-great-grandmother. In the kitchen, she now pretends to retch as Reid offers her a carrot, and I curl my injured hand into a fist.

"Hold your breath," Mila says softly.

They won't notice you, that terrifying voice repeats.

I stop breathing instantly at the sound of it, and after several seconds of hard-fought self-control, I force myself to back away from the door. Disappointment echoes faintly from wherever—or whoever—the voice comes. *You're going to starve.*

It sounds like my sister.

"No, I won't."

I shake my head fiercely at the shadow in the mirror while Mila watches with wide eyes. And why wouldn't she? I'm having a conversation with someone who isn't *here*, and none of this—*none* of it—is real. Filippa cannot be in this room with me. Even if Frederic's ritual somehow worked, even if she returned as a spirit or—or as something else, I would still see her. Mila would hear her too.

My resolve hardens at that. More than anything, Mila's silence proves that Filippa is still dead, and this is just a hallucination. It wouldn't be the first time I've heard voices, would it? I glare at the mirror. Faint cracks in its silver surface refract the light in a strange way, but otherwise, the glass stands still and silent. There is no tear in the veil, no echo of laughter. No flash of an emerald eye.

I still stare at the mirror hungrily.

I know better than to do this again. I know better than to hope.

I still stalk forward until I stand in front of the wretched thing, however, gazing at where my own reflection should be. Praying for the hundredth time—the thousandth—that *this* is the moment the dream ends. That the fairy prince will kiss me awake *now*, and the two of us will live happily ever after.

Please.

Though I stand there for several more seconds, waiting, nothing happens. I close my eyes again. Open them. Bitterness courses through me when the mirror remains empty, and I turn without thinking, seizing the music box and shattering it against the floorboards. The lullaby ends with a violent, satisfying *crash*, yet my fury doesn't abate—instead it rises up my throat like vitriol, and I curse as the porcelain pieces settle. The princess's vapid smile remains whole and intact. With an unfamiliar snarl, I stomp on it with all my might. I stomp on *all* of them—every single shard—until nothing but glittering dust remains, until my bare feet should bleed and ache. I *want* them to bleed and ache.

Before I can seize the silver chain, however, low voices sound from the entry. The front door opens with a soft swish, joined by the rustle of woolen pant legs, a silk gown. The steady beat of two more hearts. *Two, not three.* Light footsteps cross the threshold in the next second, and the door closes once more. "How is she?" Coco whispers.

"Did we miss anything?" Beau asks.

Jean Luc's voice should join theirs now, but it doesn't. He didn't come.

Hard to keep them straight, isn't it? that voice croons. *Jean Luc, Michal . . . Michal, Jean Luc . . .*

I struggle to ignore it, and the soft, wet sounds of Reid's knife pause as he murmurs, "Nothing has changed."

He'll never love you.

I cringe and glance down at the residue from the music box.

"We didn't want to wake her until dinner." Lou stumbles slightly as Melisandre winds between her feet, and a sonorous purr punctuates her next words. "She seems . . . exhausted."

Mila floats closer, lifting an arm as if to wrap it around me. To comfort me. When I tense, however, dreading the contact, she drifts to a halt, her arm falling to her side instead. "It'll go better tonight, Célie," she says softly as Coco and Beau unlace their boots. "Don't lose hope."

I resist the urge to scoff at her optimism. "And on what basis are you making that assumption? Last night? The one before that? How about last *week*?"

Mila doesn't answer. She *cannot* answer—not truthfully, anyway—and instead we both listen as Beau asks, "Has she eaten anything else?"

Sometimes they forget I can hear them. Sometimes they pretend nothing has changed.

Reid continues his work with the knife, dicing meat and vegetables with an expert hand. The scent of them—gamey, earthy, perhaps venison and peas with the carrots—drifts beneath my bedroom door and congeals in my stomach. "Not since dinner yesterday."

"And tonight?"

Reid doesn't hesitate. "Deer. We're hoping a larger animal helps."

A larger animal. I stifle the urge to retch.

"I told you"—Lou lowers her voice, at least, but I still hear every word—"her body doesn't want deer. We should've—I don't know—found a bear, or—"

"Do we have bears in Belterra?" Beau asks abruptly.

Sighing in exasperation, Coco hangs her cloak, and the scent of her *blood*—my vision tilts again. I seize a bedpost for balance as she says, "How do you not know this? You're the *king*—"

"I'm not the king of *bears*, Cosette."

Odessa snorts from the corner.

"*No*, Beauregard," Coco says in a long-suffering voice, "we do not have bears in Belterra, but if we're being honest, her body doesn't want animal at all. She needs to feed—really feed, this time. I told her we could help her hunt, but she refused."

Closing her book, Odessa says rather puckishly, "Oh? And do you have experience hunting humans?"

A pause as everyone reluctantly turns to her. Though they've done their best to avoid her presence, they never ignore her outright—because of me, I think. Yesterday, she chastised Lou for feeding Melisandre cheese—"Do you have any idea what dairy does to a cat's digestion?"—until Reid intervened, at which point she chronicled the history and mythos of red hair for nearly an hour. Coco takes a deep breath now. "Of course we don't have experience *hunting* humans, but—"

"I do, actually." Unlike Coco, Reid doesn't bother to hide his distaste for the vampire in his kitchen. Somewhere between Odessa's suggestion that Melisandre stank and that, historically, his hair meant he should've been sacrificed at birth, Reid lost his social graces. "Together, we could help Célie feed without harming anyone."

"Ah, yes." I imagine Odessa examining her nails with a polite lack of interest. "The *huntsman.* Tell me, darling, with all of your ineffable experience, how do you imagine that scene unfolding? Would the four of you—three of whom govern the whole of Belterra—descend upon the streets at nightfall in search of Célie's dinner?"

"We wouldn't *descend*—"

"And what would happen if you found it?" Her voice deceptively light, Odessa continues without acknowledging him. "Perhaps a lovely young man hurrying home from a late night at the shop—would you corner him in a dark alley and politely ask him to offer a vein? Would you enchant his acquiescence if he refused? Hmm . . . no." She taps a nail upon her chin in contemplation. "You are a huntsman, after all. Instead, you would probably incapacitate him while Célie took his lifeblood by force. Either way would result in harm. Probably even death."

I stare at my feet, unable to truly see them, and listen to the soft disturbance of air as Reid shakes his head. "Célie would never hurt anyone."

"Have you ever seen a newborn vampire feed?" Odessa's voice grows unusually grave when no one answers. *She* cannot pretend to ignore my heightened senses; she wants me to hear every word. "You might've known Célie once, but she isn't human any longer. She won't be able to control her impulses, and that makes her dangerous. *Especially* to all of you. She is drawn to you, clearly—even loves you—but all emotion strongly felt turns to hunger in a newborn vampire. She needs to be among her own kind on Requiem. I cannot *fathom* why Michal allowed you to bring her here, but—"

"Célie didn't want to live on Requiem," Lou says irritably, interrupting her as my gaze snaps upward once more. "She told us just before she died."

"And slaughtering her friends?" Odessa asks. "Is *that* what Célie would want?"

"That won't happen."

"If she smells your blood while feeding, Louise le Blanc, it will."

"Well, then," Lou says as she stalks down the hallway toward my door, "let's hope she feels strongly about deer."

A moment later, she knocks, and my knees seem to grow roots as the door cracks open. She pokes her head inside with a gentle, "Célie? Are you awake? I thought I heard—" Her eyes fall to the smashed music box and widen slightly. I swallow hard. "Is . . . everything all right?"

"My music box broke." Though I say the words quickly, feverishly, the bedpost begins to splinter in my hand because I can't—I can't hold my breath and speak at the same time. I can't prevent the scent of her magic from becoming a literal *taste* on my tongue, and—and— I choke on my next words. "But I—I think I can fix it. I think I can—"

Whistling under her breath, Lou crouches to swipe a finger through the glittering dust. Her lips twitch. "Damn. I don't think even *I* can fix such an admirable fit of temper. Good for *you*, Célie, but—it is a shame. I had plans for this creepy little music box."

I blink at her, nonplussed. "What?"

"Oh, I was going to hide it next to Reid's pillow after he falls asleep tonight." She waves an errant hand, and at once, her enchantment sweeps over me, dulling the sharp edge of my hunger. Her own stomach emits a deafening rumble in response. She pats it fondly. "He tried to scare me the other day—hid under the bed and everything, bless him. He thought it'd be enormously clever to grab my ankle as I walked past." A devious grin. "He has no idea what he started."

"Why—why would he do that?"

"I might've dyed his eyebrows blue last week." Eyes glittering impishly, she stands and dusts her hands against her pants before offering one to me. "Come to dinner, Célie. You shouldn't stew in here alone."

"I'm not alone," I say reflexively.

Filippa's laughter echoes around me again, and the hair on my neck lifts. My eyes dart to Mila, who frowns.

"Right, of course. Mila is invited too."

Though I hesitate, staring warily at her outstretched hand, Lou grins and wriggles her fingers. "Oh, come on. Are you going to make us beg for your company?" She doesn't wait for me to answer this time; she simply seizes my hand and pulls me down the candlelit hall toward the others. "Stop dragging your feet, would you? It's just *dinner*. Nothing to fear among friends." She glances back when I don't respond, and Mila's silver face reflects in her eyes. "Isn't that right, Mila?"

"Quite," Mila says with a valiant attempt at reassurance.

She doesn't hear the faint laughter tinkling from the mirror behind us, however. I resist the urge to turn, to glimpse my sister spying on me in the glass. *Yes, Célie*, she seems to croon. *Nothing to fear.*

It's just dinner.

CHAPTER TWO

The Seventh Chair

They set the table for seven, just as they've done every night.

I plaster a brittle smile on my face as we enter the open space that serves as kitchen and living room, and I ignore that seventh bowl. Just as *I* do every night. Because it doesn't matter—it *doesn't*—and Jean Luc's continued absence cannot make me feel worse than I already do.

I cling to that conviction like a raft at sea as Mila drifts to Odessa.

"Célie!" Like clockwork, Beau moves first, bounding across the settee to fold me in a tight embrace. Coco follows at his heels. Soon both have wrapped their arms around me, and my throat constricts again as I stand rigid between them, locking my jaw and leaning away despite wanting to crush them against my chest and never let go. More laughter echoes through my head at the thought. *Because I love them,* I tell my sister fiercely.

Hmm. I'm sure that's the reason.

Heart plummeting, I turn my cheek away from the line of Coco's throat.

If either of them notices, they don't say, but their eyes do dilate slightly as they pull away to grin at me. I affix my own in place, feeling slightly sick. I don't need a reflection to realize my appearance has also changed. Though my skin has always been fair, it now gleams ethereal white, and my dark hair falls longer, thicker, heavier as it waves down my back, shining like glass in the candlelight. My friends' lingering glances and sharp intakes of breath confirm what I already know: my face has become a weapon.

"We needed to step out for a couple of hours," Coco says, slightly breathless, "but everything is handled now. How are you, Célie? Did you sleep well?"

Her words sound ominous, and though I want to ask her *what* has been handled, I don't trust myself to speak. Instead I smile brighter and squeeze her hands without a word.

In truth, I haven't slept in a week.

Filippa sounds almost bored in my head. *The eternal victim.*

"Well, I certainly didn't." Beau sweeps a chair from the table for me to sit, and I force myself to focus on him. On *him*, not my sister. The real and the tangible of this room. Above us, copper pots glint merrily, winking down at the chipped and mismatched bowls of stew. The entire apartment reeks of cheer, and it should be my favorite place in the entire world. Once upon a time, it might've been.

Now it feels like a prison.

"If this arrangement continues much longer," Beau says without missing a beat, "I'm going to insist one of the witches in this household conjures a proper bed for the living room. I've had a crick in my neck for *days*." He jerks his chin toward the folded blankets and stacked pillows on the settee, where he and Coco have been sleeping since we returned from Requiem a week ago.

"You're the one who demanded we stay here—not that I'm complaining," she adds hastily to me. "I'd rather be here than at the castle, especially with Chasseurs poking around."

Still smiling, I nod and keep my mouth firmly closed. Though Lou's enchantment remains, the scent of this much blood in a room is overwhelming. Especially Lou's and Coco's. Michal once told me the blood of magical creatures tastes more potent than human blood, and now I believe him. As particularly powerful magical creatures, my two friends smell *delectable.*

"You mean the lovely Brigitte?" Beau scoots my chair to the table as Reid takes my empty bowl and fills it with—not stew. Bile rises at the sight of it. Thicker and darker and altogether more repulsive than broth, meat, and vegetables, my dinner stains the white porcelain crimson.

Seventh time is the charm, you think?

Pressure builds in my ears at the sound of that voice, and I clamp my teeth to keep from snapping at it.

"Technically, Brigitte isn't yet a Chasseur, but I don't blame her for acting a bit"—Beau searches for the right word, heedless of my internal struggle—"*perturbed* tonight. There was another disturbance at Saint-Cécile earlier this evening. Grave robbers," he adds to me in explanation. "An inconvenience, usually—a couple of bodies missing every few months—but they're getting out of hand. They've dug up half the cemetery at this point."

I frown at that, but no one else reacts much; they seem to have already heard the news. To my surprise, the voice in my head remains silent as well—but of *course* she does. I shake myself mentally, nearly cracking my teeth in frustration now. She doesn't *exist.*

Odessa chooses this moment to scoff and rise from her chair, equally disgusted by the blood in my bowl, before disappearing down the hallway to her room. Mila follows. They never stay for dinner. Instead, Odessa will slip into East End to dine elsewhere, and Mila—unbeknownst to her cousin—will accompany her.

Beau frowns after them. "Such a warm, empathetic creature, that Odessa. Such keen emotional intelligence—she puts even Brigitte to shame."

"That warm, empathetic creature can still hear you." Reid drops into the seat next to Lou, leaving the chair between us open for our seventh dinner guest. I ignore that chair. I refuse to look at it. "So I'd be careful if I were you."

"Nonsense." Beau claims the seat on the other side of me, immediately tipping it back on its hind legs and lacing his fingers behind his dark hair. "If the lady vampire fancies a nip now, Célie can kick her ass for me." He smirks in my direction. "Isn't that right?"

"What?" Distracted, I speak without thinking, and I instantly pay the price; fire rips up my throat, and my eyes water at the sheer pain of it, at the potent taste of my friends on my tongue. I can't simply ignore Beau this time, however, and I don't think a simple nod or shake of my head will effectively communicate the scope of his stupidity. "Odessa is *very* old," I gasp. "Very strong. I—I watched her rip out a vampire's *tongue* with her bare hands."

Odessa's voice echoes down the hallway. "And never forget it, darling."

Beau snorts and lands back on all fours with a *plunk* before tucking into his stew. "Don't underestimate yourself, Célie. You've trained with the Chasseurs. I'm sure you could rip out a tongue or two—preferably *hers* if she keeps pontificating about the best ways to enact a trade embargo."

"Better than hearing her describe—in lavish detail—how all of your ancestors died," Lou says wryly.

"Oh, no, she gifted me with that happy knowledge too," Beau says. "Apparently, a stag gored my great-great-great-grandfather to death while he answered nature's call on the royal hunt—"

I interrupt before either of them can gather steam, my head starting to pound once more. The blood in their veins smells delectable, yes, but the blood in my bowl smells *foul.* "That is disgusting, and I have *no* desire to touch a tongue."

Liar.

"Perhaps you just haven't found the right one yet," Coco says judiciously.

"Speaking of which—" Beau turns to Reid before I can answer, and my hands fist in my skirt as his scent washes over me anew, as Filippa laughs and urges me closer. He points his spoon at the empty chair beside me. "Where *is* your insufferable little friend? He wasn't at the castle this evening."

Though I've been refusing to think of Jean Luc, the question still catches me by surprise—or perhaps it isn't the question at all but the wording. Because he called Jean Luc *Reid's* insufferable friend, not mine, and I—I suppose that's true now. The realization acts as a cudgel. It breaks the thrall of Beau's blood.

Reid sends me a furtive look, but I pretend not to see it as he says, "He couldn't get away from the Tower. He sends his regrets."

Despite my best intentions, my eyes flash to his. "No, he doesn't."

We stare at each other for a single, startled heartbeat.

"Célie, he—" Reid hesitates, clearly torn. Though he'd rather swallow his kitchen knife than have this conversation, Reid is still Reid, and he has never lied to me before. "Give him space," he says at last. "He'll come around eventually. He's just . . . he's having a hard time with all of this."

The words—spoken so earnestly, so innocently—slip below the molten heat that simmers inside my chest, filling the yawning emptiness that I've felt since waking up as a vampire. Since waking up dead. *He's having a hard time with all of this.*

"Is he?" I ask softly.

Kill them, Filippa says, softer still.

The table seems to draw a collective breath at my expression, and the cobwebs of Lou's magic brush my skin. They cloak the raw edges of my anger, and I hate them—I *hate* them—and resist the urge to claw at my flesh, to peel away each bloody layer until I'm *me* again, until I'm *Célie.* Not someone who hallucinates about her dead sister. Not someone who inadvertently inches her chair closer to the human beside her, who calculates the exact seconds it would take to debilitate first Beau, then Coco and Reid. Lou sits directly across the table, so she'd take longest to reach. She'd be hardest to subdue too, but her *blood*—

My gums split open at the thought, and my fangs descend—saliva bursting, pooling, *spreading* until my gorge rises and I choke on it.

Oh God.

Flinging myself backward, I topple my chair, and white spots burst in my vision. *Oh God oh God oh God.* My chest heaves as I struggle to hold my breath, and they're all staring at me now, wide-eyed with alarm. Both Reid and Coco have half risen from the table, and Beau sits absolutely still, like I'm a wild animal—a predator—and he dare not move for fear of drawing my attention. *You're halfway there, Célie.*

Only Lou gazes calmly back at me. "You should probably eat now."

In my periphery, Odessa and Mila appear in the hallway, silent and watching.

"I'm s-sorry." I clutch the kitchen wall with one hand, covering my mouth with the other and hiding my teeth from the room. Fresh tears of humiliation burn beneath my lids. All I seem able to do these days is apologize, yet *Jean Luc* is having a hard time? "I'm so, so sorry. I didn't mean— I should—"

With the flick of her wrist, Lou straightens my chair and pushes my bowl to the edge of the table. With another, steam curls from the blood once more. Though she doesn't appear frightened like the others, the twinkle in her turquoise eyes has gone out, and her face seems paler than usual. I *am* endangering her family, after all. Her home. The molten heat in my chest turns to ice.

"Eat, Célie," she says.

I feel myself nod, taking a tentative step forward. Then another. The silence weighs heavy over the room as I resume my place at the table, careful to move slowly for Beau's sake. He sits straighter than before, his fingers tight upon his spoon. I pick up my own without a word, dipping it beneath the crimson surface of my bowl and lifting it to my lips.

The blood tastes as foul as it smells.

I do not grimace, however, or give any other indication of my discomfort, even as my sister whispers, *How long can you survive like this, ma belle? How long before your body takes control?*

I ignore the hallucination, just like I ignore my churning stomach as deer blood enters my system. "I apologize," I say again, calmer this time, lifting my chin and meeting each of my friends' gazes. They smile tentatively back at me, and I'm already forgiven. Even Beau relaxes in his seat, and Odessa vanishes to her bedroom once more. Mila lingers for just another second—her eyes a bit too understanding—before she follows.

The silence remains a touch tense, however. Lou still looks vaguely sick.

"Was that— Did my mother come to the door this morning?" I ask Reid after another moment.

"Yes." He pushes his empty bowl away. "She came from the Tower. She's been, ah—harassing the huntsmen about your whereabouts."

"Harassing Jean Luc, you mean."

He casts me a wary glance. "She said the time has come for desperate measures."

"What did he tell her?"

"Nothing. He agreed not to disclose anything until you're ready. For now, the kingdom assumes you're still with Michal—though Jean hasn't been particularly quiet on that front." Reid hesitates. "He debriefed the Chasseurs on Les Éternels before we sailed to Requiem on All Hallows' Eve, and they . . . well, they haven't exactly been discreet since we returned. Rumors of vampires have swept the city—probably the entire kingdom by now."

"The price of silver has soared," Beau confirms. "I'm friendly with a local silversmith, and I think he'd like to marry you."

I almost laugh at that. Almost. Instead I choke down another mouthful of blood. It tastes gamey and wrong, tainted, like rancid meat on a hot day. My stomach rolls. "I never expected Jean Luc to keep vampires' existence a secret. Still, though, it's very . . . kind of him to have kept mine."

Reid gathers the empty bowls on the table to avoid looking at me. "I told you he doesn't hate you, Célie."

Another uncomfortable silence descends. His second lie.

Clutching my hands in my lap, I stare down at my knotted fingers—sleek and pale and elegant. Completely foreign. "Of course not."

The first night I woke as a vampire, Jean Luc attended dinner. The first and only meal he took with me. When I walked into the kitchen, pale and strange, his eyes tightened. When I lifted the bowl of broth to my lips—*broth*, not blood, in a hopeless attempt to maintain normalcy—I spewed it violently across the table, my body unable to consume it. Lou and Reid produced a cup of blood without hesitation, but the *look* on Jean Luc's face . . .

Though I refused the blood—knocking it to the floor in a fit of panic—Jean Luc still left.

He left, and he hasn't come back.

As if remembering that night, my abdomen contracts painfully, and I clamp my jaws together, determined to keep the blood down this time. "My mother won't—" But my hand flies to my mouth, abrupt, as my body starts to heave involuntarily. *No.* Through sheer force of will, I swallow and lay down my spoon. I will not lose my stomach tonight. I will *not.*

Beau pats a sympathetic hand against my back. "Your mother still thinks you're gallivanting across the countryside with a handsome stranger. She cares very little about his vampirism, one way or the other. Truly, I think she's angrier about your broken engagement than his taste for blood. You're good and thoroughly ruined in the aristocracy now."

With a violent shudder, I choke at his pronouncement, losing the battle before it even started. The hateful liquid burns all the way up until I expel it across the table in a desperate heave, just like every other night this week. Just like my sister predicted.

A second of silence follows. Beau's hand stills on my back. Then—before I can do anything more than cringe away, horrified—my friends move in practiced unison. Lou waves her arm, and the bloody sick on her peonies vanishes instantly. Reid gathers my bowl almost as quickly, marching it out the front door, while Beau pulls my hair aside and Coco hands me a cloth to wipe my face. "It'll be all right, Célie," she says earnestly. "We'll figure this out."

"This is nothing, really." Though Lou smiles in reassurance, she looks even paler than before. And the peonies—they remain pink instead of white. I cannot focus on that, however, as another bout of sickness wracks my body, and Reid plunks a small wash pail in front of me.

It's all so kind.

So humiliating.

"Perhaps, er—bear next time," Beau says in a horribly light voice.

I nod without a word. Because this is my life now.

When my sister speaks again, I can almost feel her presence at my back, like she stands directly behind me. Like she has stood there all along. Her fingers seem to caress my hair, and for just an instant, Beau's eyes flick to the strands, narrowing slightly as they rustle in the too-still air. *You're going to kill them, you know. You never really stood a chance.*

And abruptly, it's all too much—my sister's voice, her touch, the overly sincere expressions of my dearest friends. "*No.*" I snarl the word, slamming my palms on the table and whirling to scream at my sister, to tell her I will not be killing *anyone*—

But she isn't there. Of course she isn't. *No one* is there, and the table cracks ominously beneath my hands as Beau lurches away with a startled cry, as Reid and Coco shoot to their feet in alarm.

"Célie?" Lou rises slower than the others, frowning at the empty air behind my chair. "What is it? What's wrong?"

Beau shudders as he too inspects the space around me. "Is there another ghost here? That—that Mila woman?"

"Mila left with Odessa," I say through my teeth.

"Someone else, then?"

"There *is* no one else." The words land like knives between us—too sharp, even to my own ears—and he blinks, flinching away from them. Shame cracks open my chest in response, and instantly, I move to—I don't know, *console* him. He keeps his distance, however. "I'm sorry." *I'm sorry, I'm sorry, I'm so sorry.* The words seem to bleed from every part of me until I'm drowning in blood—mine, yes, but also theirs. My teeth ache at the scent of it, and my ears ring as Filippa's laughter echoes in a disorienting wave through the room. "Something is happening to me—"

"*What* is happening to you?" Lou leans forward on the table, her eyes narrowing suspiciously. "If no one is here, why did you shout? What is going *on*?"

I shake my head reflexively. "I didn't—I didn't mean to—"

"What aren't you telling us, Célie?"

"N-*Nothing*—"

"You're lying."

"No, I'm—I'm not—" My teeth descend at that moment, however, and Filippa's laughter reaches a fever pitch. It deafens me, and I clench my hands against the building pressure in my head, still shaking, still trying and failing to convince myself this isn't real. *This isn't real. None of this is real—*

I hear the knife before I see it.

Spinning again, I catch the silver blade a split second before it pierces the back of my skull, and in the corridor beyond, something shifts in the darkness. Something . . . ripples. "The veil," I breathe incredulously, and before my very eyes, its shorn edges mend themselves; Filippa's laughter dies instantly. Silence descends, and with it, a sickening sense of relief. Unbidden, I glance down at my fingers, not noticing how they burn until Coco wrenches the knife away.

The very *real* knife.

I'm not imagining things this time. Though I don't know what happened to Filippa on All Hallows' Eve, this pain in my hand is real. That tear in the veil was real, which means the person who opened it must be real too . . . if they're a person at all.

Meeting Lou's incredulous gaze, I say, "I think my sister is haunting me."

CHAPTER THREE

How to Commune with the Dead

"What we need," Lou pronounces an hour later, "is a séance."

Seated at the kitchen table once more, Beau groans and drops his head into his hands as a storm builds outside the windows. Thunder rumbles in the distance. "That is not what we need, Lou. A séance is never what *anyone* needs."

"Nonsense." Pale yet determined, Lou flits around the living room, gathering every unlit candle she can find while I hold my breath, watching her with carefully clamped limbs. My head still pounds, and a halo rings my vision. "If Filippa wants to play with us, we need to learn the rules of the game, or we can never hope to win. Oh, don't look at me like that," she adds. "She just tried to kill Célie. Clearly, she isn't feeling very friendly. Don't you want to know why—to know what she *wants*?"

"*No*," he says in exasperation. "I have never wanted to know anything *less*—"

"She didn't want to kill me." I speak the words stiffly, moving my lips as little as possible. "I think she wanted to make me feed . . . properly." Though I cannot bring myself to clarify further—not with them so close to me—they seem to understand all the same; Beau blanches, recoiling, while Lou shakes her head and Coco rolls her eyes.

"How supportive," she mutters.

Lou dumps an armful of candles in front of us. "But why? What does she possibly stand to gain by our untimely deaths?"

"We are rather important." Beau gestures around the table without a shred of humility, but he's also right—between the four of them, they rule the greater part of the kingdom's population. "No sense pretending otherwise."

"Maybe it isn't about us at all." Reid straightens the candles compulsively. "Maybe it's a far simpler matter of misery loving company." Then, to me: "What makes you think your sister will answer this summons after throwing a knife at you? It doesn't sound like she wants to talk."

I clear the fire from my throat. "She won't have a choice."

Though Lou grins in approval, I tear my gaze away from them, focusing instead on the scent of the peonies in their painted vase. Sweet and rosy with a hint of citrus. Because I don't have time for this deep, unending ache in my stomach. Filippa just shattered the pretty illusion of safety my friends created for me—and with Filippa, unfortunately, comes Frederic.

The Necromancer.

I tried not to think of him. I coaxed myself into believing that his plans failed—or, at the very least, that they ended with Filippa. That perhaps he would leave us alone to re-create the life Morgane stole from them. That perhaps he and Pip would live happily ever after, and I would never need to find them.

Standing abruptly, I sweep the vase of peonies aside to make room for more candles, which Lou drops unceremoniously into my hands. Beau shakes his head in disbelief as she darts off in search of chalk. "This is demented," he breathes. "What if Filippa isn't even a ghost? What if she is something *else* now, and—and we dredge up all sorts of nastiness with this little trespass—"

Scoffing, Lou continues to rummage through the cabinets. "It's better to ask forgiveness than permission."

"No," Beau says quickly. "No, it isn't." He rises from his chair with wide, panicked eyes. "Permission is *infinitely* better when the use of candles and—and"—he lets out a groan as Lou finds the chalk, drawing five long, straight lines upon the table—"*pentagrams* are involved. What if we knock, and someone else answers?"

Coco pats his cheek sympathetically before joining Lou around the table. "That's where I come in, I think."

"You *think*?"

Lou shrugs, thoroughly unconcerned. "It isn't like any of us have done this before, and without La Voisin's grimoire to guide us—"

"Any spell in that evil little book is one we should most definitely *not* be doing—"

"You shouldn't worry, then," Lou says sweetly, "as we've just established this is a spell of our own invention."

Beau whirls to Reid for support. "You can't seriously think creating a spell to summon the dead is our best plan of action. Isn't that the reason we're in this mess to begin with?"

Reid hesitates behind Lou and Coco, peering down at the pentagram over their heads. Then he turns his apprehensive gaze to me. "You astral projected when you saw your sister in the grotto on All Hallows' Eve. Could you not, er—do it again to find her now?"

"An excellent idea." Beau thrusts a triumphant finger in the air. "Go back to the spirit realm and search for her *there*."

My body stiffens.

"Don't be stupid," Lou says at once.

"It's too dangerous," Coco says at the same time. "We have no idea what Filippa has planned for us. Until we do, Célie shouldn't go anywhere alone, and especially somewhere we cannot follow."

Only when Beau mutters his agreement do I relax infinitesimally. Because the truth is—well, I haven't stepped foot through the veil since All Hallows' Eve, and the prospect holds even less appeal now.

Thankfully, Odessa waltzes through the door in the next moment, shaking rain from her parasol and slipping a small velvet box from the folds of her skirt. Without glancing up, she undoes the clasp and angles the tip of the parasol *into* the box, sliding the entire thing down after it. Though we all gape, she doesn't provide an explanation for the phenomenon, instead absently smoothing her gown and hair. It cascades down her back like a spill of ink, untouched by the storm.

A drop of blood still clings to her bottom lip.

My stomach contracts painfully at the sight of it, the smell, but she merely wipes it away with a gloved thumb and saunters closer. "Now *this* looks intriguing. Are we conjuring someone?"

Mila darts in behind her, eyes widening in alarm. "What is this, Célie? What are you doing?"

Lou dusts the chalk from her fingers with an air of finality. "We're summoning Filippa."

Odessa arches a brow. "Oh?"

Reluctantly, I explain the situation, and when I've finished, Odessa considers the pentagram anew, intrigued, while Mila shakes her silver head in disbelief. "This is a terrible idea. Did you learn nothing from your time in Requiem? The dead do not appreciate being *summoned*—"

"We don't know if Filippa *is* still dead. Perhaps she is, or perhaps she isn't. Either way"—I seize the saltcellar on the mantel, ignoring the others' questioning looks—"we'll know more in just a few moments. Now, according to *How to Commune with the Dead*, salt contains protective attributes. Scholars would use it to form a circle around the site of their summoning—"

"—to contain occult creatures, yes." Odessa nods at the general area to which I just spoke. "I assume Mila is here?" When I nod, she claps her hands. "Good. We might need her. Now . . ." She takes the cellar from me, tipping it to one side to examine its contents. The salt should be minuscule, a sea of white specks, but I can see the sharp, translucent edges of each crystal. They remind me of glass. Of mirrors. "As *we* are occult creatures, Célie darling, and as salt does very little to deter us, we can safely forgo it. That should be drawn with blood," she adds, pointing to the pentagram. "Preferably from a Dame Rouge."

We all look at Coco, who heaves a sigh and withdraws a small knife from the cabinet behind her. "You might want to leave the room, Célie," she says grimly.

"More like the house," Beau interjects.

"Alas"—Odessa discards the salt and plants her hands on her hips in a businesslike manner—"Célie is the only one among us who can traverse the spirit realm, so she must remain." To me, she adds, "If you insist on continuing your foolish hunger strike, however, I suggest holding your breath and diverting your attention for this next part."

I scowl at her before doing just that. Apparently, Odessa has anointed herself the leader of this macabre ritual, and as no one has any better ideas—or indeed, any ideas at all—we can hardly usurp her. "Wait!" Beau's alarmed voice rings out, and I hear him clap his hand around Coco's wrist. "Are we just going to—to do the summoning here? Now?"

"When would you prefer we do it?" Coco asks, exasperated. "After Filippa slits our wrists for breakfast? We need to learn what she *wants*—"

"Célie resisted our blood before," Beau says fervently. "She can resist again! Coco, please, we shouldn't be doing this—"

"It is a *terrible* idea," Mila agrees.

I hear rather than see Coco disentangle herself. Then she drags the knife tip along her forearm, and my entire body braces at the sound—slick and wet and appalling in how my fangs react, piercing my gums in preparation to feed. *Distraction.* I search my mind wildly for a distraction. As if waiting for permission, Michal's face materializes once more.

Not you, I snarl, and I can almost feel his low chuckle down my spine.

"And"—Coco's voice cuts through the hallucination—"finished!"

The sweet scent of honey engulfs the kitchen at her words, and my eyes snap open as the wound on her forearm heals with a sharp bite of blood magic. The pentagram on the table, however, still gleams wet and scarlet. *Oh God.* Holding my breath again, I drop into an open chair and clamp shut my mouth. I count every thread of my nightgown as Lou lights a candle at each point of the star.

When Beau continues to protest—loudly—Coco snaps her fingers at him. "Sit," she says sharply, pointing to the empty chair between Reid and Odessa, who pats the seat with a satisfied smirk. Scowling, Beau drops into it without a word, but he scoots pointedly away from her before turning to face Reid.

"Thanks for the help." He speaks under his breath, too low for the others to hear, and watches in equal parts resentment and fear as Coco removes the extra chair from the table. "Have you conveniently lost your ability to speak, or—?"

Reid rolls his eyes at his brother. "What exactly did you expect me to do?"

"Oh, I don't know, maybe *anything at all*—"

"Look at Lou's face." Leaning back in his chair, Reid lowers his voice further—so low now that I shouldn't be able to hear him either, nor see the small muscles around his eyes. They spasm from exhaustion. It *is* after four o'clock in the morning. Still—though he tries to hide it—he tracks his wife through the kitchen with single-minded intensity. "Look how pale she is."

Beau's brow furrows as he follows his gaze. "She looks the same to me."

"Then you need to pay closer attention. Something is wrong. She refuses to admit it, but she seems . . . sick." With a subtle tilt of his chin, he motions toward the peonies, their petals still stained pink from the deer blood. "I feel it too—a fatigue in my muscles. My magic. It's getting worse every day."

"Your magic?" Beau searches his face anxiously. "And you think it has something to do with Filippa?"

"It started on All Hallows' Eve."

I frown between them before glancing at Lou. She *does* look paler than usual—her freckles standing out in sharper relief—but her grin looks impish as ever. When she catches me staring, she winks.

Beau heaves a great sigh. "When all of this goes tits up, I'm telling the demon to eat you first."

Reid chuckles darkly while Lou claims the seat beside him, and Coco follows, sliding into the last free chair next to me. She bumps my shoulder with a small, reassuring smile. "Right," Lou says, glancing around the table and nodding to herself in reassurance. "I think we're ready now. Should we, er—join hands? Odessa, what do you think?"

"The act of joining hands in itself is completely superfluous to the ritual, but if it calms your nerves"—Odessa extends a hand first to me, then to Beau—"I think we should."

Beau stares at her proffered hand like it might grow legs, or perhaps fangs, if he touches it. "Just take her hand," I snap at him, losing my patience and regretting it instantly at the startled look on his face. I bite down on my apology. "Please, Beau. I need to speak with my sister."

With one last, grudging sigh, he accepts her hand as gingerly as possible, completing the circle. "Fine. Let's all studiously ignore how a vampire knows so much about summoning spirits and follow her blind— EEEGH." His voice shutters on a squeak as he notices Mila, who still hovers beside me.

Of course. With our hands joined, they're all touching me now; they can finally see her.

She flashes a sharp smile. "Wonderful to see you again, Your Majesty." Inclining her regal head to the others, she adds, "And a pleasure to meet the rest of you as well—formally, that is. I know rather more about you informally than I'd like to." She swoops low to kiss Odessa's cheek. "And *you*, cousin—"

"I knew you were here all along." Odessa lifts her pert nose. "And as for how I know so much about the spirit realm, Your Majesty," Odessa says to Beau, tightening her hand when he moves to pull it away. "I *read*."

"Do your books say anything else, Odessa?" Coco throws a warning glance at Beau before he can retort. "Anything we should know beforehand?"

Odessa lifts a delicate shoulder as Mila drifts closer to study the pentagram, curious despite herself. "Such magic is not a science. Those who cannot wield it will never fully understand the complexity and nuance of such a ritual, and those who can rarely share their secrets."

"Perfect," Beau mutters.

Odessa ignores him. "In theory, Cosette, you should be able to guide your blood toward the veil, where Célie will open a door, allowing your blood to cross and using it to pull Filippa here."

"How does that work?" Lou asks curiously. "Guiding her blood? Using it to pull Filippa?"

"The same way it works when she heals your wounds or tracks your location."

"It's my intent," Coco says, lips pursing as she considers the pentagram. "My blood reacts to it, and my magic follows. But—how do I find the veil?"

They all look to me then, and I swallow the fire in my throat, my fingers knotted around Odessa's. I cannot look away from the pentagram. I cannot see anything but blood. "You . . . sense it." When only silence meets my pronouncement, I swallow again, forcing my eyes shut and willing my body to settle. *Please. Please*

please please. After several more seconds, I manage to say, "It feels sort of like a presence, an awareness, like the prickle on your cheek when someone is watching you. Here—" Without opening my eyes, I lift our interlocked hands and place them upon the table. "Let me show you."

CHAPTER FOUR

Séance

Though I remain in the kitchen—my feet planted firmly in the land of the living—that same inexplicable sense of dread threatens to suffocate me as I call my sister's name into the spirit realm. "Filippa?" Familiar ash drifts through the hole I've torn in the veil. It lands like snow upon the pentagram. "Are you here?"

Our only answer is a particularly violent crack of thunder, and Coco and I nearly leap out of our skin. Across the pentagram, Lou startles too, cursing when her knee collides with the table and knocks over a candle. Though Reid jumps to his feet to avoid hot wax in his lap, he doesn't break his connection with Lou and Beau, who jerks his head around with wide eyes. "Did you hear that?"

Lou scoffs, her eyes watering in pain. "Yes, Beau, *everyone* heard that—"

"Not the thunder," he says quickly. "There was— Someone *laughed*."

"I heard it too," Mila says.

My hands tighten around Coco's and Odessa's as I follow Beau's frantic gaze around the kitchen. "I didn't hear any laughter."

"Nor did I." Unlike the rest of us, Odessa speaks with a studied air of detachment, but her eyes shine just as bright as ours. Her grip holds just as tight. Telltale signs that—despite her bluster—she hasn't ever participated in a séance either. The realization brings little comfort. "Are you sure you heard something?"

"Of course I am! At least"—Beau glances back at the pentagram, which still gleams innocuously in the candlelight—"I think I am. I—I *might* be."

Frowning, Reid tries to clean his chair with his elbow, but the wax has already hardened into brittle flecks upon the wood. Like ice. "It feels cold." He glances up at me warily, his breath visible in the sudden chill of the room. "Is that normal?"

"It is for the spirit realm."

Odessa's gaze does not waver from the pentagram. "What else is the spirit realm like?"

Mila draws closer to my chair.

"Strange." I look fixedly at the pentagram too, waiting for any sign of Filippa—her thick black hair, once gleaming like mine, or perhaps her emerald eyes, the row of dark stitches down her cheek. "Everything in the spirit realm is the same as it is here, except . . . different."

With a scoff, Beau cranes his neck to see every nook and cranny of the kitchen, still searching for the source of mysterious laughter. "That clears things up nicely, thanks."

"Frederic upset the balance with his experiments. He broke the laws of nature. I don't know precisely how it works—I'm not a witch—but the realms began twisting before his ritual on All Hallows' Eve. I can only assume the distortion has worsened since he resurrected Filippa." I glance at Lou, who listens raptly despite swaying slightly on her feet. Reid tightens his grip on her hand, his frown reflecting my own.

Something is wrong, Célie, she told me in Brindelle Park, where the trees had blackened and died. *My magic feels sick.*

"You *assume?*" Beau asks in disbelief.

I glare at him. "If you must know, I haven't actually been to the spirit realm since All Hallows' Eve. I have no idea what it might look like now, and to be frank, I don't want to know." Then, to Lou, "What do *you* think? Have you . . . felt any different since Frederic's ritual?"

"Something is happening." Before she can answer, Coco points to where crystals of ice have started to form around the pentagram. "Should we try again, Célie? *Without* interruptions?" She speaks the last directly to Beau, who does one last sweep of the kitchen before slumping in his seat. Defeated. He does not, however, release Reid's or Odessa's hands.

"Go on, then," he grumbles.

I raise my voice over the tempest outside. "If you can hear me, Filippa . . . I received your message, and though I appreciated that knife in my back, I still have some—well, questions."

As before, she doesn't answer, and Lou's eyes meet mine in the silence that follows. Perhaps she can sense my throat closing up. Perhaps she can see the tension building in my shoulders, my knuckles whitening around Coco's and Odessa's fingers. When the former winces slightly, I force myself to loosen my grip with a slow exhale, and Lou gives a quick, reassuring smile. I try to return it. Truly, I do—I *try*—yet a small part of me longs to close my eyes, to wash away the pentagram and forget all of this.

"Pip?" I say again.

The crystals creep farther across the table.

When my sister still doesn't answer, my frustration breaks into twin waves of disappointment and relief. Both crash over me as another great boom of thunder shakes the kitchen and the candlelight flickers. Perhaps Beau was right. Perhaps this entire plan has been doomed from the start. Doomed and *foolish.* Filippa threw a knife at me, so why did I think she would reappear now? Because I demanded it? I resist the urge to sneer at myself, to sneer at our homemade pentagram and honey-scented candles. I've never been able to compel my sister to do anything, with or without magic. Indeed, our relationship has always been the opposite, hasn't it?

Aren't you a little old for pretend?

The memories of our childhood chafe now, interposed between a broken music box and a silver knife. An open window. A pang of longing at what could've been—what should've been—if only we'd been brave enough to try.

Another fork of lightning strikes, and in the brilliant white light, something gaunt flashes beneath Reid's skin. Something white, something *skeletal.* My thoughts skip at the sight of it—stomach pitching like I've missed a step—but when I blink, incredulous, his face has returned to normal. Not a skull in sight.

Enough, Célie, I chastise myself. *Focus.*

"Why isn't Coco's blood summoning her?" Reid asks. "I thought the magic would—lure her, somehow. Pull her toward us."

Expression contemplative, Odessa continues to stare at the pentagram like it's a riddle she cannot solve. She doesn't notice the ice crystallizing in her hair. The rest of us do, however, and Beau gapes at her as she says, "The blood should allow Filippa to traverse the space between us, similar to how Célie can project in her sleep. Perhaps it cannot force her to do so, however, if she is unwilling or unable."

When lightning flashes again, tendrils of my own hair begin to float weightlessly around my face. I hook a foot around the table to keep my chair on the floor. "I don't know what this is," I say, unease creeping into my voice, "but it shouldn't be happening. We should stop before—"

The candle flames shoot upward in response.

As one, we recoil, our eyes widening as the table begins to spin—slow at first, then faster and faster, until the candles fly in every direction. Instead of crashing to the floor, however, they hover overhead like the ghoulish fingers of a puppeteer, tipping to drip wax onto Reid's and Beau's heads.

"Blargh!" Beau leaps from the table, breaking the circle, and clutches his magnificent hair. "Knock it off, Lou! This *isn't funny*—"

"It isn't me!" Swaying again, Lou lifts an incredulous hand to her nose, from which a trickle of blood has appeared. Odessa nearly breaks my wrist as I lunge, crashing into the table before forcing my body to still. My lungs to cease. Panicked, Lou tries to magic the blood away, but at the flick of her wrist, the peonies wither instead. They curl and shrivel as if diseased, and Lou's knees give out. Reid catches her just as another flash of lightning illuminates the kitchen. Illuminates their *skulls.*

Though Coco stumbles forward to help, she stops short after a single step, her eyes fluttering before rolling back in her head. Beau leaps to her side in panic. "*Coco*—"

Her body jolts with the next clap of thunder, however, and she blinks, shaking her head. "I'm all right," she reassures him, wiping incredulously at the blood seeping from her ear. "At least, I *think* I'm all right—"

"What is *happening?*" Lou looks wildly around the room, struggling to rise. "Is Mila still here, Célie?"

I dare not open my mouth to answer.

"I don't know what this is!" Mila drops to her feet like a sack of potatoes, but no one hears her now except me. "This is—I feel *heavy*," she says in wonder. "Célie, the veil—it must be—"

My fingertips slip from the table's edge, and Melisandre bolts from beneath the settee to tangle in Beau's feet. With a curse, he topples to his knees in an attempt to avoid her, but Melisandre is no longer there; yowling, she rises into the air like the candles and levitates above his head. My chair already bobs amidst the copper pots.

Beau swats furiously at the candle attacking his head. "We need to close it!"

He's right, of course. I summoned Filippa, not whatever magic this is, but I cannot bring myself to move—to *breathe*—as Lou and Coco huddle near the window, cringing with each streak of lightning. Fresh blood trickles from them both now. Even Reid seems weak and unsteady as he stands on a chair to rescue Melisandre. Below him, Mila gapes at the amber hue spreading across her hands. Odessa now resembles a macabre ice statue, her beauty sharper and brighter than before, and icicles sparkle in her hair as diamonds. The table still spins. It creates a draft through which Beau struggles to regain his footing. "*Célie—*"

In the next second, however, white light bursts from the pentagram, and cold wind blasts our hair backward. "Nobody move," Odessa says sharply, but Mila's chin has already snapped toward the pentagram. Her eyes widen in horror at whatever she sees there.

"Someone is coming," she whispers.

And I can't help it now—I lean forward in anticipation, heat blistering up my throat as I lean forward and ask, "Filippa?"

No one responds. The very room seems to hold its breath as the strange light vanishes once more. As the candles flicker once, twice, before an invisible force douses the flames.

All of them. All at once.

A beat of heavy, sentient silence follows—oppressive and unnatural—like a great beast waking from deep slumber and drawing his first breath. "Fuck," Lou says tremulously. "Fuck, fuck, *fuck*—" The silence exhales then, and with it, an overwhelming scent of roses engulfs the kitchen—roses and candle smoke. The latter curls toward us like fingers in the darkness, and I choke as they wrap around my neck.

Not Filippa.

Stumbling backward in blind panic, I wrench my hand from Odessa, attempting to break the connection, to locate the pentagram. Odessa refuses to let go, however, and even with my vampiric vision, I cannot see through this blackness. The shadows remain absolute. If not for her hand in mine—viselike, as if she too hangs on for dear life—it would feel like we've plunged headfirst into absolute nothingness. Into the abyss.

"What is this?"

Beau's voice rises over the sudden scrape of chairs, the frantic *thump, thump, thump*ing of my friends' hearts. In the next second, he crashes into me, pulling me into his arms with Coco, who says quickly, "Everything is going to be all right—"

Even she sounds terrified, however, her heartbeat spiking, *deafening* in my ears. The sharp scent of her blood collides with the smoke, the roses, until my head spins in a delirious jumble of sensation. Her fingers clamp against my arm. Beau's heart beats against my cheek. So warm. So hypnotic.

"Focus, Célie." Odessa squeezes my hand to the point of pain, but I can't—I *can't*—and without my sight, the onslaught of scent is too much. I can taste the roses now, can taste the fear, the *magic*, and my fangs punch through as something fetid slithers across my skin—less scent or taste and more awareness. Like someone is watching me. No. Like someone has *found* me, and the weight of their gaze threatens to smother my consciousness until I become the darkness too. My eyes flutter back into my head. "Focus on my voice," Odessa says, louder now, as Lou and Reid lurch through the darkness in search of light. "You need to close the veil—"

"The matches are on the mantel," Reid says swiftly.

"They aren't *here*—"

Lightning forks through the windows, illuminating a gloved hand reaching up through the pentagram.

All the air in the room seems to vanish. "What is *that*—?" Coco starts in horror, but in the next second, the hand strikes, lunging toward us as an earsplitting clap of thunder rends the night in two. Tremors rock the table. A copper pot crashes to the floor. We pitch into darkness once more, and though the hand snatches at my sleeve, Odessa moves with preternatural speed, dragging me just out of reach.

The hand lands instead upon Beau.

With a strangled curse, he flings himself backward, and Coco shrieks; a rush of movement disturbs the darkness. Before I can orient myself—before I can do anything but stagger into someone who smells like Reid—the candlelight flares back to life, higher and brighter than before. Hotter. It illuminates the smeared pentagram on the table. It illuminates Coco bent over it, panting, her palm covered in blood from where she dragged it through the lines. Breaking them. Disrupting the ritual and banishing the gloved hand.

The scent of roses lingers, however—as does the darkness. It smudges the edge of my vision, mottles Reid's and Odessa's faces as they peer down at me in concern. "Célie?" Reid clutches my elbow, steadying me, as his eyes search mine. "What is it? Do you need to sit down?"

"I—" My eyes flutter again, and my knees threaten to collapse. "I feel faint."

I feel strange.

"It's your adrenal cortex." Odessa seizes my other elbow, steering me toward the table. *The veil.* It still flutters innocently above the scene, and I reach out without truly seeing its edges; I bind them clumsily before staggering into Odessa once more. When the others gape at us, she says, "The adrenal cortex produces hormones associated with stress, and long-term stress increases the appetite." To me, "You haven't properly eaten since you died."

"It isn't that," I protest weakly, and in truth, it isn't. Whatever that was—it felt familiar somehow, like I've experienced it before, *known* it before, but . . . how can that be? I shake my head, and the entire room pitches with the movement. Only once have I ever seen darkness like that. Only once have I ever lived through it.

"Jamais vu." Speaking softly, Lou stands in the narrow space between the cabinet and hearth, her arms crossed and her body folded as if trying to make herself disappear. The wind outside has reached a crescendo now; it screams against the walls, the windowpanes, as if determined to reach us, to claw its way into the ominous quiet of the kitchen. "I felt it too."

"*Never seen.*" Odessa's eyes spark with interest, and she withdraws her small velvet box again. Unclasping the lid, she sticks her entire *arm* into its depths and rummages for several seconds before pulling out an enormous tome. Beau's mouth falls open as she flicks through the onionskin pages until she finds the right one. "The phenomenon of experiencing a situation that one recognizes but that also feels unfamiliar."

Reid crouches in front of me. "Was it Filippa?"

"I don't think so." I shake my head, prompting another wave of dizziness. "She would never wear gloves like that, and it didn't—*feel* like her."

"Frederic stitched her together with bits of other people's skin," Coco says. "She might wear gloves like that now."

"What are we going to do?" Lou whispers.

She wipes the blood from her nose with the back of her hand. I still see it, though. It gleams slick and scarlet in the candlelight. Wrenching my gaze away, I turn instinctively to Mila. She hasn't yet spoken, hasn't moved at all from her spot beside the table. She simply stares down at the smeared pentagram with a hard jaw and detached expression. A cold one.

It reminds me of Michal.

"Mila."

It seems to take a very long time for my voice to reach her, but when it does, she lifts her face and says, "We need to find your sister."

"You think—you think she's responsible for this?" I swallow hard, every word demanding terrible effort.

"I think something is very wrong here, and if Filippa did in fact rise from the grave, she might know what it is." Her silver eyes flick to Reid, to Lou and to Coco—the latter two still cannot catch their breath—before returning to me. "Are you sure you want to find her, Célie?"

We stare at each other for a long moment. Though a good sister would say yes—though I *want* to say yes—the answer lodges in my throat unexpectedly. Perhaps because I don't recognize my sister anymore; I don't even recognize myself, which makes us veritable strangers. The Filippa I knew would never have thrown a *knife* at me. She never would've mocked my pain. Except . . .

And you'll never know a world without sunlight, will you? Not our darling Célie.

"I—I don't think we have a choice," I say, shaking away the bitter memory of our last conversation. "If my sister has risen, we need to know." Still, the situation has proven itself to be dangerous for everyone, and if Mila involves herself, I don't know how Filippa will react. I don't know what Filippa can *do*. "Perhaps I should go instead."

"No," say Lou, Reid, Coco, Beau, and Odessa in unison.

Despite listening to only half the conversation, they seem to have pieced together enough information to understand. "Be reasonable, Célie," Reid says.

Beau shakes his head incredulously. "Mila is a *ghost*—"

"—and vampires can still die," Odessa finishes. "You have a great deal to lose, even while pretending to disdain it."

Under different circumstances, I might've argued, but the less I speak now, the better. My vision continues to pulse scarlet. As if sensing my struggle, Mila nods, her expression hardening, her shoulders squaring as she rises to her full height. "I'll be careful, Célie."

She leaves before I can thank her—gliding straight through the window toward Saint-Cécile—and a boom of thunder reverberates through the house. Through my *head.* I clutch the table to hold myself steady while Reid grasps my elbow. I still feel odd. Disoriented.

Hungry.

Another boom of thunder follows, rattling the copper pots. Then another.

And another.

It takes several seconds to realize the pounding noise isn't thunder at all. Even Beau turns to look at the door before I make the connection. Because—someone is here. Someone is *knocking.* Frowning, I peek at the clock on the mantel as the door quakes beneath another onslaught. The hands read half past four in the morning.

Whoever this is, they aren't stopping by for tea.

Lou swallows audibly, stepping from her nook and glancing from the pentagram to the door to Reid. "Should we—er—open it?"

"Are you insane?" Beau asks, low and incredulous. "We just summoned a *demon*—"

"We don't know it was a demon." Though Reid straightens, still staring hard at the door, he doesn't release my elbow. "Whoever is out there might need our help—and I doubt a demon would knock before entering."

"I don't care who it is." Coco rubs her arms absently, as if warding off a chill. "They can come back later. After what just happened, we need to rest—"

In the end, their bickering matters very little.

Everything matters very little.

Because with one last deafening knock, the front door splinters before blasting from its hinges, revealing Michal Vasiliev—dripping wet and furious—on the threshold. "Hello, pet," he says through gritted teeth, and his *eyes*—

They're the last thing I see as my breath hitches, my heart leaps, and my knees collapse.

CHAPTER FIVE

A Fate Worse Than Death

I wake to strong arms around me.

For just an instant, my heart leaps in anticipation, and my eyes snap open to find—

Blue irises.

"Reid," I breathe, and it tastes like disappointment.

Expression fierce, he holds me in a bridal carry and watches Lou at the door, where she stands with her back to us and her hands planted on her hips, entire body bristling with indignation. I look away hastily. I focus on Reid's jaw instead. He must've caught me when I collapsed, and—and that was quite gallant of him. Quite nice. He appears to be feeling better since I closed the veil. His color has returned, and his movements feel steady.

Peering up at him through my lashes, I hold my own body perfectly still and inconspicuous. Perhaps I could simply—simply close my eyes and pretend I haven't awoken. No one would need to know otherwise. No one would ever suspect. It would be for the betterment of everyone, really, if I just stayed silent—asleep, even—while Lou handles our unexpected caller. *Yes.* I nod inwardly and squeeze my eyes shut once more. Lou seems much stronger now too, so I should probably just—

"I know you're awake, Célie."

Low and pleasant, *too* pleasant—almost conversational—Michal's voice sends gooseflesh down my nape. I shiver despite myself. The last time I heard that voice, I hovered above him, watching as he dragged his broken body to my own, as he brought his blood to my lips and whispered, *Please stay.* He turned me into a vampire that night. He broke his every conviction to save me.

Then he sent me away.

I keep my eyes firmly shut.

"Come now, pet," he says, coaxing, his eyes boring almost painfully into my cheek. He must see how I shiver at the endearment—how Reid's arms tighten around me in response—because his voice darkens slightly as he says, "You've never been a coward before. Don't start on my behalf."

"You don't get to say that." Lou's sharp voice cuts like a knife through the heavy tension in the room. Whatever ailed her during the séance has clearly passed. "You don't get to speak to her at all. We had an *agreement*, Michal, that you'd respect her wishes and leave her alone—"

"—with the provision that you'd care for her." Though he speaks to Lou, I can still feel his gaze; it remains fixed upon my face, willing me to look at him. And a small, shameless part of me wants to do just that. The larger part, however, is just as cowardly as he says—because I can't look at him now. After everything that happened between us on Requiem, I just *can't.* "A mistake, clearly," he murmurs, "as it seems you've indulged her death wish." Then, softer still, and directed at me, "When have you last fed?"

My throat closes in answer, but as always, Lou rises to the occasion, despite the feeble thrum of her heart. Every muscle in Reid's body tenses as she snarls, "She doesn't want to talk to you, and if you really think she has a death wish, I don't blame her. You'll talk to *me* now. And how dare you make assumptions about how we've cared for Célie? You have no idea what she's been through—"

"And you do?"

At the dangerous note in his voice, gooseflesh creeps farther down my spine. Though that larger part begs me to keep my eyes closed—to ignore him in hopes this entire situation will just *go away*—the smaller part knows Michal better. If he came here, he came for a reason, and he won't leave until revealing it.

Just like that, I can no longer resist the temptation. Still holding my breath, I peek at him through my lashes.

And there he is.

All my thoughts take flight at the sight of him, a portrait of fury come to life—so much larger, somehow, than in my memories. So much darker. Like an avenging angel or primordial deity. Cloaked all in black, his silver hair loose, he shouldn't exist in such a mundane place—shouldn't exist outside myths and legends—yet he does.

And he is *devastating.*

"There's nothing you can do for her, Michal," Lou says, bristling at his unspoken challenge. "You should leave before I get angry."

"Spoken like a child," Michal says, "who has never seen true anger."

Lou's fingers twitch. "I am *not* a child—"

"Then invite me inside."

"Not a chance."

Dripping wet from the rain and wreathed in night, Michal grips the doorframe with thinly veiled restraint. Arms rigid. Shoulders bowed. The wood still buckles under the pressure, however, and hairline cracks feather outward from his fingertips. He glares at

Lou with a threat of violence. "There are remains of a pentagram on your table, Louise le Blanc, and your kitchen tastes of roses and blood. Though I dare not *assume* the damage you've done tonight, Célie should not require your husband to remain upright." Those black eyes find mine then, as lightning flashes behind him. They glitter with malevolence—at me, at Reid, at the broken candles and bloody pentagram behind us. "You've been very foolish," he says quietly, "endangering yourself and everyone around you."

Heat washes through me at that. Sharp, vitriolic heat. It purges all instinct to hide. Indeed, it purges all instinct to do anything except wrap my hands around his throat. "*Me?*" I snarl, pushing from Reid's arms between one blink and the next. Only Michal's eyes are fast enough to follow the movement—which they do, narrowing to slits as I stagger beneath a wave of light-headedness. I push Reid's hand away when he tries to steady me. "That's rich coming from the vampire who *swore* never to create another because—and I quote—ours is *a fate worse than death.* Do you remember that, Michal? Or"—I lurch closer, sidestepping Coco and Beau as they too reach out to help me—"do you just not care about my fate? Did you not care about *Mila's?*"

Michal's face hardens instantly.

Too far.

But—no. I shake my head viciously. *I don't care.* I don't care, I don't care, I don't *care* if I hurt him. This is *all* his fault, and my fangs lengthen as I stumble into Lou, as she snakes an arm around my waist and smells like temptation. Like oblivion. With a violent throb of my head, I push her away too. Because she cannot touch me either—no one can ever touch me again—and I clench my mouth shut, yearning to wrench each hideous tooth from my jaw. To break them, to *shatter* them. To ground them to dust beneath my boot.

When I tilt forward against the doorframe, stars erupt across my vision, and the wood cracks beneath Michal's hands. Eyes blazing, he strains forward slightly as if trying to reach me, but an invisible force holds him back. And I relish it. I relish that control. "You left me," I whisper. "You turned me into *this*"—I gesture to my face, my body, both familiar yet not—"and you sent me away."

"I'm not the one who left, Célie," he says darkly.

"I never wanted to be like you."

"Should I have let you die instead?"

"I *did* die!" The words burst from me like a dam breaking, and I flatten my hand on my bodice, directly above where my heart should beat in my chest. Where it will never beat again. As always, Michal tracks my every movement, but this time—this time he swallows hard and looks away, as if he can no longer stand the sight of me. I can no longer stand it either. "This body—it doesn't belong to me, Michal. It is *aberrant* to me. It craves blood—just like you and the rest of your *wretched* kin—which means I can never trust it." When he opens his mouth to argue, I shake my head again, stars whirling, and speak over him. "You said so yourself—vampires lose control when they feed; it's why you were so angry with me after I healed you in that attic. You knew I put myself at risk. You knew you could've taken more than I wanted to give, and you were right." My voice rises at the last, breaks at the last, and intolerable pressure builds behind my eyes as I open my mouth to say, "*God*, you were right"—

And choke on an open flame instead.

The words blister my throat, hotter than Hellfire, and I gasp in pain, in *shock*—the only sound I can make as I clutch at my collar.

I expect to see smoke. There is none, however—no fire either—and Michal's eyes soften inexplicably as he watches me. They fill with pity. With remorse. Almost like he—like he *knows* what I just tried to say.

"What is it, Célie?" Lou's hand hovers, outstretched, as if she stopped herself from touching me at the last second. "What happened?"

"I c-couldn't— I tried to—"

Michal's fingers tighten on the doorframe. He tears his gaze away to stare resolutely over my shoulder. "Speak the Lord's name?"

Even a mention of God sends a phantom flame through me. Wincing, I stare at Michal in horrified disbelief as my own fingers wrap around my throat. As they cradle it helplessly. "H-How did you know that? What is h-h-*happening* to me?"

He still refuses to meet my gaze. His jaw, however, clenches. "Vampires cannot speak of holy ones."

"Then how did *you*?" Coco asks accusingly.

"I've had many years to practice."

The floor starts to tilt again as I consider the implications of such a phenomenon. "You mean I can n-never say H-H-His"—but fresh flames shoot up my throat, and I cry out, doubling over—"n-name again?"

"It's all right, Célie." Unable to stop herself now, Lou places a comforting hand on my back. It still reeks of blood. "You don't *need* to say his name to believe."

The others' voices quickly join hers in a chorus of bittersweet lies.

"Yes," Coco says. "Everything will be fine. This changes nothing—"

"Just breathe, Célie," Reid says. "Just *breathe.*"

But I can't breathe—I don't *need* to breathe—and I—I—I claw at my chest, at my too-still heart, and will it to beat again. *Yours will be a fate worse than death.*

Michal's words echo back to me as if from very far away, in another time. In another life.

"I'm sorry, Célie," he says now, and he means it.

I know he means it.

My chest still heaves with anger as I lift my head to look at him, tears spilling down my cheeks. And in this moment, I might hate him—this beautiful, terrible angel who plummeted to Hell and dragged me down with him. How could I have known what awaited us when I promised to stay with him? He didn't tell me—I didn't ask—and now both of us must pay the price. My sister's old adage rises through the roar in my ears as he finally, *finally*, deigns to look at me, his black eyes glinting with unspoken emotion.

You can't get something for nothing, you know.

A bitter laugh rises in my throat, following the trail of Hellfire. "You might think I have a death wish, Michal, but we both know you've already granted it. I *am* dead. I've been dead since the moment I met you."

His expression shutters at the words.

It becomes perfectly, *infuriatingly* unreadable.

"Célie," Odessa murmurs.

I didn't notice her move behind me, and my body reacts instinctively; with a hiss, I tense and half turn to defend myself, stopping short at the sight of her concern. *Concern.* My lip curls. As if she *cares* about what happens to me, as if she doesn't *long* to return to Requiem and her monstrous kin. I want to snap at her too. I want to strike, to *bite*—to goad someone into fighting back—yet I whirl to Michal instead, snarling, "Why are you *here*?"

He stares at me for a long, impenetrable moment. Then—

"The dead have risen on Requiem." Despite Odessa's gasp, he speaks the words calmly, almost coolly, and releases his hold on the doorframe. "Scores of them. Your blood spilled in the grotto during our confrontation with Frederic, animating both the isle and the waters surrounding it."

Absolute silence meets his pronouncement.

Animating. I frown at the word, but before I can ask, Beau clears his throat from where he hovers near the kitchen table. "Dead as in—er, different than how *you* are dead, right?"

Reid glares at him.

Coco, however, recoils suddenly and whispers, "Revenants."

Michal's gaze snaps to hers. "What?"

"Revenants," she says, louder now and wide-eyed. "There have always been whispers among les Dames Rouges, but no one except La Voisin ever—and even she—" Forcing herself to pause, to collect herself, Coco swallows hard and looks directly at me. "I saw the spell once in my aunt's grimoire. When I asked her about it, she shooed me from her tent and forbade me from speaking of it. I think it was the only spell she ever feared."

The first tingles of dread lift the hair at my nape. "What exactly *is* a revenant?"

"A person who has returned. A reanimated corpse. One who has died and risen again with the express purpose of terrorizing the living, particularly those the corpse in question once knew."

A cold fist of terror squeezes my heart as the two of us stare at each other in dawning realization. *Filippa.*

"Oh," Beau says in a small voice. "Is that all?"

"No." Michal clasps his hands behind his back, surveying all of us with hideous apathy. "I assume even you grasp a basic understanding of your kingdom's geography. Requiem shares the Eastern Sea with Belterra, which means—"

Understanding spills over me like ice water, and I gasp at the sheer shock of it. "My blood could've traveled here too."

Michal nods curtly. "Yes."

"The grave robbers," Lou says abruptly, turning to Reid with wide eyes. "You don't think it was really—?"

His brows snap together as he considers the possibility, and my stomach plunges to the floor. "Shit," he breathes.

"Wait a moment." Beau steps forward, and his entire demeanor shifts as he looks between us. His gaze darkens. His jaw hardens. He points a finger at the dark street behind Michal, and all traces of the frightened young man vanish, leaving someone else entirely in their wake. "Are you saying *revenants* could be crawling through Belterra right now?" When Michal nods again, Beau walks straight forward until he stands beside us. "What exactly does *terrorize the living* look like? Are these creatures—are they hurting people? Why haven't we seen one?"

No one wants to answer that, so I answer it instead. "Because you've been trapped inside this house with me."

Beau looks instantly contrite. "Célie—"

Something shuffles overhead before he can console me, however, and a split second later—too fast for even the vampires to react—a shadow drops from the roof, plunging a skeletal hand into Michal's back.

CHAPTER SIX

Revenant

Michal arches forward at the impact—his eyes widening, his skin hissing—and I move without hesitation, without *thinking*, throwing myself at the shadowy creature and tackling it into the street. We land hard, rolling once, twice, before it snarls and pins me against the cobblestones with unusual strength. With *unnatural* strength.

Oh God.

My body thrashes helplessly against its grip, and I choke and gasp as the overwhelming stench of decay washes over me. When lightning flashes overhead, however, true fear grips my heart—because I recognize this creature. I recognize its tattered choral robes and the twin crosses embroidered on its chest. Though no flesh remains except half of its putrefied face, I recognize the steely eye still decomposing there too. It—along with the rest of this body—once caught Reid and me together in the confessional at Saint-Cécile. He humiliated me there. He reprimanded Reid, his would-be son and favorite of all the huntsmen.

Now he gnashes his teeth, wild with hunger, and tries to sink them into my cheek.

The Archbishop.

With a shriek, I thrust my knees upward to force him away, but they overextend, meeting only the hard bone of his spine. And his skeletal fingers—three silver rings still gleam upon them as they scrabble at my throat, my jaw, my shoulders, blistering my skin and shredding my clothing. *He's too strong.* Though I wrench my hands free of his robes, I cannot push him away, cannot move him at all, yet I still seize his skull, determined to hold him off somehow. *He will not eat me. He will* not—but his teeth graze my collar anyway, tearing into my flesh as if it's paper.

I clamp my mouth shut, refusing to scream again. Refusing to make any sound at all that might goad my friends into—

Too late.

Someone wrenches the revenant away from me, and my fingers clutch at empty air as the creature soars backward, landing several feet away with the sickening crunch of bones. Eyes shining with cold fury, Michal kneels and lifts me to my feet. "Are you all right?" he asks, and I nod mutely, staring at his back as he turns to face the revenant. Blood still gleams on the black leather of his surcoat. Wet blood. Hot blood. My throat constricts at the scent of it, and my entire body shudders, tightens, as my mouth begins to water.

Fresh blood.

Vaguely, I realize the Archbishop's silver rings have prevented Michal's ability to heal. *He's . . . hurt.* That doesn't stop my hand from reaching to touch him, however. It doesn't stop my fingers from trembling with need. Indeed, the rest of the world—the street, the houses, even the snarling revenant—seem to fall away at the sight of Michal's blood. Inexplicably and startlingly possessive, I cannot stop myself from having it, from *tasting* it, from fantasizing about how it would feel on my tongue; even Lou's and Coco's magic pales in comparison to the rich, languorous scent that is Michal. As a human, I couldn't smell him properly. I thought he had no scent at all, but I couldn't have been more wrong. Eyes wide, I now watch in a surreal sense of slow motion as my fingertips brush his back.

As they come away scarlet.

His head jerks toward me at the slight touch, and the instant our eyes meet, something twists low in my belly. His gaze darkens in response. His mouth parts.

The revenant lunges.

"Look out!" At Lou's scream, the moment shatters in a blur of limbs as Michal whirls, catching the Archbishop by the spinal column and snapping it in two. Footsteps thunder behind us as the others race into the street. The hair on Reid's forearms lifts as he stares down at his forefather's broken body, horror-stricken, while Lou blinks rapidly, her breathing louder than usual. Panicked. *Of course.*

Reid might've called the Archbishop his father, but to Lou, the creature before us actually *was* her father—and her abuser. To my knowledge, she didn't shed any tears when Reid killed him last year. She regards him now with a pained look, like she's struggling not to be sick.

"A revenant," Odessa says simply.

Michal glares first at Lou, then at Reid. "By your expressions, I assume you know him."

"Yes." Lou nods—the smallest dip of her chin—before touching Reid's arm. He seems unable to speak. "We, er—killed him last Modraniht. It's entirely possible that he came here seeking vengeance."

"Vengeance," Michal repeats flatly. Shaking his head in exasperation, he drops the two halves of the Archbishop's body to the ground. "I suppose we should be grateful for the confirmation. We now know Célie's blood *has* reached the shores of Belterra—"

He stops short, however, as the bones at our feet begin to twitch. Frowning, he nudges the Archbishop's hand, and in the next second, it seizes his boot, swiftly digging its fingers through the leather and impaling his foot.

Cursing viciously, he tries to kick it away, but it holds tighter still, levering itself upright and snapping at Michal's thigh. Though Reid and I both spring forward, it isn't necessary—Michal parts the revenant's skull from its neck, hurling its head aside, before crushing its fingers into dust. The rest of its body keeps coming, however, except now—somehow—it seems to have recognized Lou and Reid.

It snarls and gurgles unintelligibly because it does not have a tongue.

"Get behind me." Voice sharp, I pull Reid backward as the upper half of the Archbishop's body drags itself toward Lou. She lifts her hands dubiously, stumbling backward, but Michal follows, trapping the revenant under his foot. Though it claws at his pant leg, shredding skin, Michal doesn't flinch. He doesn't let it go. "How do we kill it?" I ask desperately.

He looks to Coco. "Well?"

Her voice is an indignant whisper. "Why are you looking at me? I *told* you my aunt refused to tell me anything."

When he arches a brow at Lou next, she returns to herself at once. "Oh, don't even think about it. I've never killed an undead—*thing* before. Shouldn't that be *your* expertise?"

Michal's lip curls. "Are you not reputed to be the most powerful witch of the age?"

Lou's turquoise eyes flash with the lightning behind her. "And are *you* not reputed to be the most powerful vampire of all time? An immortal *king*?" The rain has dwindled to a fine mist now. It settles in her hair, on her skin, until she sparkles with each lightning strike—small and pale and alone in the street, but still fierce. Always fierce. Her hands remain raised as thunder continues to rumble around us. "How have you been dealing with these revenants on Requiem? We can do the same here."

Unexpected silence descends as Michal says nothing, and the two glare at each other.

To her credit, Lou doesn't cower beneath his cold perusal, waiting until he abruptly returns his attention to the revenant before allowing herself to exhale.

"We've been capturing them." Michal presses his heel harder into the revenant's spine, cracking several more vertebrae. "Our witches have been incapacitating them until we find a permanent solution."

"Gasp." Lou's eyes widen in a scornful parody of surprise. "*Shock.* The almighty king of the vampires has sullied his hands with witches? I would've thought our magic beneath you."

"You would've thought correctly."

With a scowl, Lou drops her hands, looping one elbow through Reid's and the other through mine. She drags us back toward the front door. "Fine. Good. Carry on without us, then—go home to Requiem—as you clearly know what you're doing. We'll figure things out on our end without your help." Barely discernible over the thunder, she whispers to me, "This *is* still what you want, right? To stay here?" Her wide turquoise gaze searches mine, and I stare back, helpless, before glancing over my shoulder at Michal.

He looks positively lethal, still bleeding in the rain, his eyes burning as he pins the snarling, scrabbling revenant underfoot. "Is it, Célie?" he asks, equally quiet. "Is this what you want?"

His previous words echo between us, as dark and ominous as the storm clouds overhead.

I'm not the one who left, Célie.

Lifting my chin, I nod. "Please leave, Michal."

Cold disbelief breaks across his expression at my words, replaced almost instantly with colder amusement. He glances from Lou to Reid to Coco and Beau and Odessa, to the lower half of the revenant's body, which has risen to its feet, scuttled into a nearby tree, and fallen over. Then his eyes find mine. Something shifts deep within them as he stares at me. Is it pity? Remorse?

Disgust?

Before I can name it, he lifts his foot from the revenant's spine and walks away.

My breath catches as he goes, and part of me—the worst part, the smallest part, the most wretched part of all—hopes he'll look back. He doesn't, however. No. Tucking his bloody hands in his pockets, he gives me what I want, and he leaves.

The revenant snarls and dives toward us.

"Right." Coco's foot instantly replaces Michal's, and she unsheathes a thin dagger from up her sleeve before handing it to Beau. He gazes down at the revenant with palpable disgust. "It'll need to be a powerful cage—he must've clawed his way out of his casket to find us. Solid wood."

"Odessa." I swallow hard, forcing myself to look away as Michal disappears around the bend. "Did Requiem, Ltd., send any stone caskets in their last shipment to Cesarine?"

"Hmm . . . perhaps." Odessa meanders forward as well, circling the revenant as it continues to writhe. She casts a swift, probing glance in my direction before turning to Lou. "Though I hardly think such measures will be necessary. Your great-grandmother once trapped me in a hatbox."

A hatbox.

My eyes fall to her skirts.

"You knew Mathilde?" Lou asks.

"Of course I know Mathilde. I just said she trapped me in a hatbox, didn't I?" Odessa asks. "She refused to let me out until I promised never to speak to her again—I used to visit on the weekends for access to her library. She hoarded an extensive horticulture collection in that odd little cottage of hers. She always *did* remind me a bit of a dragon," she adds thoughtfully. "We got on quite well until she forced me into that box."

Beau blinks at her, momentarily distracted. "How did you fit inside a hatbox?"

"How does a witch do anything? Magic."

The bizarre urge to laugh—or perhaps weep—strikes me as Lou lifts her hands warily. Remembering the peonies, I tense in anticipation, but when she flicks her fingers, both halves of the revenant soar into the air as intended. They dangle overhead like a macabre circus performance. I do not laugh, however. Tears sting my eyes instead as the creature snarls and swipes at the lot of us, gnashing its teeth.

"Mathilde *was* an extraordinarily gifted witch," Lou says in evident relief. Now that Michal has gone, she has allowed herself to deflate slightly. To shrink. She looks exhausted. "Even my mother thought so—and Morgane loathed Mathilde. The story goes that Mathilde tried to drown her in the toilet when she was born."

"She sounds like a charming woman," Coco says. "Now—where is this hatbox, Odessa? Did you leave it on Requiem?"

"Don't be daft. I never travel anywhere without it." From her skirt, she withdraws the same velvet box I saw earlier, hardly the size of her palm. I eye it dubiously now. After watching her pull a philosophical treatise from the little box—and shove an entire parasol into it—I have little doubt a powerful witch spelled it. As if reading my thoughts, Odessa taps it with her finger, and the box seems to fold outward, expanding to twice its size, thrice, and so on until she's forced to hold the fuchsia monstrosity with both hands. Mistaking our stunned silence for admiration, Odessa hums appreciatively and brushes the gold tasseling. "Yes, it's quite marvelous, isn't it? You should've seen the *hat*."

"*That*," Beau says, "is the ugliest thing I've ever seen."

"Oh, pot, meet kettle." Rolling her eyes, she unclasps the lid, and I inch closer, curious despite myself. We might have more pressing matters with which to deal—and my teeth still throb, my chest still aches—but this magic reminds me of a simpler time, a simpler life. Enchantments like this once seemed so special, so surreal. If I'd peered into a bottomless hatbox even a month ago, I would've felt weightless, giddy at the prospect of touching something so obviously unusual.

Now, however—as I lift a too-pale hand to touch the pea-green piping—a leaden sensation fills me.

If Odessa notices, she doesn't say, instead reaching deep into the bag and extracting several gowns before thrusting them at me. She doesn't stop there, however; her parasol follows the gowns, as does a set of glass beakers, a mahogany jewelry box filled with diamonds, a telescope, a chessboard, three pots of rouge, four silk handkerchiefs, a pair of bent spectacles, rusted shackles, a set of bloodstained knives, a broken pocket watch, and—incredibly—five smashed figs. "For my peacock," she says absently, balancing the last atop the towering pile in Beau's arms.

Without warning, she upends the hatbox completely, dumping the rest of its contents at our feet.

An avalanche of books crashes to the cobblestones, and Lou and Beau both yelp, leaping aside to avoid breaking their toes. Odessa straightens with a magnificent smile before bringing the box directly beneath the revenant's suspended body. "Right, then. Whenever you're ready, Louise."

With a bemused expression, Lou tosses the telescope and handkerchiefs to the flower bed beside her.

To Odessa's indignation, the rest of us follow suit.

"Are you *sure* that box can hold him?" Concern twists Beau's features as the revenant strains for the nearest tree branch, as its skeletal fingers catch in the dead leaves to pull itself closer.

"Do you have any better ideas?" Lou blanches as the revenant reaches for the branch in earnest now, as if it can—as if it can *hear* us talking, planning to trap it. My brows contract, and together, Beau and I each take a step backward as it snarls at Lou and Reid. Though it makes sense the creature would understand us—I am also dead, after all, and have retained cognitive function—its baleful eye seems to roll with madness.

No. That isn't quite it.

Against my better instincts, I look closer, peering up at the rotted, distended face, and realize the eye doesn't roll with madness at all.

It rolls with pain.

"We need to help it." The words escape before I realize they've even formed, and everyone—*everyone*—turns to look at me like I've grown horns. And perhaps I have. Despair wells like a fount inside me at the sight of their bright, incredulous faces, at the garbled sounds of the revenant above. Because it—*he*—is trying to form words, and that shouldn't matter, not as he tries to kill us, but it *does.* It does matter, somehow, and evil as the Archbishop might've been in life, he did not choose to become this—this mindless *beast.*

I must've said the last aloud because Beau bends to meet my gaze, grasping my shoulders to make sure I hear every word. "He already was a vicious beast, Célie. Do you understand me? The Archbishop was a cruel, sadistic man, and you are not like him. You never have been, and you never could be."

"I *know* that."

Feeling sicker still, I break his hold and step backward, unable to look at anyone. Unable to bear the confusion on their features. Of course they're confused—I hardly understand it myself. The Archbishop tormented each of them. He hunted witches to every corner of the kingdom, determined to eradicate them, to mutilate their bodies on the stake. I cannot ever defend what he did. I do not *want* to defend him, just to—to— I fist my hands in my skirt. I don't *know.* Everything has spun so wildly out of control, and I've never felt so helpless to stop it.

Turning beseechingly to Lou, I say, "Please, we can't just leave him in a box to rot. We have to—to *do* something about this before it gets worse." I gesture wildly to the pitiful creature overhead. "There are others rising too, innocent people who aren't like the Archbishop, and it's my fault—"

"It isn't your fault," Lou says at once, but I speak over her, shaking my head vehemently.

"It was *my* blood. My choice to walk into Frederic's trap without waking you and Coco, without forming any sort of plan at all except . . ." *Michal.*

I cannot bring myself to say his name aloud, to admit how foolishly I acted. My only plan had been Michal—the two of us together, as if that meant something—and in the end, we both suffered for it.

Everyone did.

"No." Coco frowns and steps to my other side. "Frederic used magic from my aunt's grimoire to conceal himself, Célie. *Powerful* magic. Michal stood a better chance than anyone of detecting it, so don't blame yourself. You couldn't have done anything to stop him."

The assurance rings false, and we all know it. I could've done more. I could've done *anything*, but I cannot convince them otherwise. Not now. The words that spilled so freely before have dried up, and I choke on them, unable to articulate the gnawing fear in my chest. Unsure if I even *can* acknowledge it. Because the Archbishop, my sister, *me*—this cannot be the end for us. This cannot be eternity.

It cannot be my fault.

"We'll lay him to rest, Célie." Reid approaches cautiously, his voice low and earnest. He does not touch me, however, and relief burns behind my eyes at the small mercy. "We'll lay all of them to rest as soon as we know how, but until then . . . we can't let them hurt anyone."

The Archbishop snarls as if to punctuate the words, and slowly, I nod.

I've been such a fool . . . so wholly absorbed in my own self-pity that I failed to notice everything crumbling around me. Lou and her magic. Filippa. Grave robbers. *Revenants.*

They are all connected, somehow. *We* are all connected.

"Very well." Odessa adjusts the hatbox, and in the next second, Lou flicks her wrist, sending the Archbishop plummeting awkwardly into its dark depths. Odessa slams the lid shut on its final shriek. She flips the clasp. Instantly, the box begins to fold inward once more, growing smaller and smaller until she tucks it back into the folds of her skirt.

Without the Archbishop's snarls, the night seems rather quiet.

Rather empty.

"Come on." With an anxious glance over her shoulder, Coco slips her arm through mine, leading me toward the house. "We shouldn't linger in the street."

CHAPTER SEVEN

A Multitude of Dreams

Coco and Beau return to the castle around six o'clock in the morning. Instinctively, I know they won't be staying here any longer—there is too much to be done, too much to learn about this new threat. We're all exhausted, however, and Lou pulls me aside after they've gone, pressing a small bottle into my palm. "To help you sleep." Without another word, she turns on her heel and follows Reid to their room, where I can already hear the rustle of clothing and blankets as he prepares for bed.

My fingers curl around the bottle.

Perhaps I haven't lied as adeptly as I thought.

Shaking my head, I follow her down the hall, turning left where she turned right and slipping into my own chamber. Farther down, Odessa's room sits silent and empty; she insisted on finding Michal after securing the revenant—"To talk to him," she said simply, refusing to provide further explanation. I try not to think about that conversation. I try not to think about anything at all.

The dull ache in my gums remains, as do the sharp cramps in my stomach. Perching on the edge of the bed, I study the bottle in my hand. The liquid within looks innocent enough: thin and clear, almost like water, with a faintly iridescent sheen in the candle-light. Thunder still rumbles in the distance, and I look reluctantly to the curtained window. The sun will not rise for another hour, and when it does, storm clouds will obscure its face. I roll the bottle between my fingers, limbs heavy.

This weather reminds me of Requiem. It reminds me of Michal, of Filippa and Frederic and the revenants, of everything I've tried so desperately to forget. And perhaps that makes me the worst sort of coward. Perhaps that makes me weak, immoral; perhaps that makes me porcelain.

Either way, I long to sleep.

Before I can reconsider, I tip the draught down my throat and close my eyes.

Diamond tights glitter on my legs as I twirl in the violet light of the ballroom. Lifting my gossamer skirt—also violet, as if sewn from clouds at dusk—I throw my head back in delighted laughter. Because the music in this ballroom is bright and lively. Because the costumes are beautiful and wanton, bizarre and terrible, some even grotesque. Because I've always wanted to be a ballerina, and thank *goodness* my mother isn't here to chastise me, to forbid me from wearing such a short, lovely hem.

Rising to my tiptoes, I execute a perfect pirouette.

"Spectacular, darling." Beau flashes an indulgent smile as he spins past with Coco, whose magnificent wings trail angel dust in their wake. His own body gleams silver and translucent in this place—probably because the poor dear has died. I blow him a kiss anyway, and the two of them float through the air to waltz somewhere above our heads.

In the room beyond this one, an ebony clock ticks loudly. Its pendulum swings back and forth, forth and back, again and again until the edges of my vision begin to blur. Until my mind begins to drowse. I look away from it hastily toward a couple dancing near—a very tall man with long and curling silver hair, a thin mustache, and powdered cheeks; in his arms, he holds a lovely young woman with a pert nose and golden ringlets. "Guinevere?" I blink at her in full color, at *them*, as the man laughs merrily and I recognize his voice. His sharp teeth.

"We came to warn you," D'Artagnan says, twirling Guinevere past in a flurry of glitter and rot. "Beware of your sister. She cannot be trusted."

I stare at him, incredulous. "How do you know that? Is she here?" When he doesn't answer, simply glides past with a serene smile, I catch his arm. "Well? Have you seen her, D'Artagnan? She looks like me, except older, and—and—"

"Perverse," Guinevere finishes gleefully.

"Wrong," D'Artagnan adds.

My fingers bite into his arm as the entire room tilts and the black-and-white checks of his doublet loom larger than life, leering at me like rows of teeth. "Did Frederic resurrect her? D'Artagnan! Is she"—I swallow hard—"is she *alive*?"

He laughs again, prying my fingers away one by one. His eyes seem to glow yellow in the violet light, and his pupils narrow to the slits of a cat as he tilts his head. "Do you consider yourself alive, papillon? Do you consider me?"

"Is she *here*?" I repeat as the two resume their dance, spinning away from me. My eyes dart around the ballroom. "Is Frederic?"

Guinevere glances back at me, tossing her ringlets over one delicate shoulder. "Frederic is the least of our concerns now."

Lou seizes my hands before I can answer, cackling maniacally and pulling me through the crowd toward our friends. Leaning forward, she whispers conspiratorially, "She said no, you know, when Beau proposed."

Reid leers in front of us as an actual skeleton. His fingers wrap around a wickedly sharp scythe.

I blink at both of them, confused—still searching for D'Artagnan and Guinevere, who have vanished—and brush elbows with a monk who walks his pet lion on a leash. A low growl rumbles in its throat at a passing courtesan, and in the corner, a hooded figure dressed like Death himself stands tall and silent, watching us. Except—I shake my head, blinking again. Except now he doesn't stand in the corner at all. He stands in the entrance to the ominous clock room, which seems rather nearer than before. Lou continues to pull me toward it.

"Who said no?" I ask her, bemused.

"*Coco*, of course." A thick snake coils around the length of her body—its iridescent scales glistening first black, then purple, then green—and with a start, I realize she wears nothing else at all. The blacks of her eyes also appear larger than usual, and shadows seep into the hollows beneath them; her hair seems to crackle with energy. She sweeps a too-sharp hand down my arm as the snake's tongue kisses my cheek. "She refused to marry him because of your dress, and honestly, Célie, I can't say I blame her. What were you *thinking*?"

Bewildered, I glance down, opening my mouth to defend myself, but the sparkling ballerina costume has vanished, replaced by a blood-flecked gown sewn from the pale linen of a burial shroud. And my tongue—I taste copper there. Hot, rich copper and something else—something *foul*, something that smells of tilled earth and dead, decaying things. Instantly, I tug my hand from Lou's, but she refuses to let me go, her nails drawing four crescent moons on my wrist. "W-Where are we going?"

"To the clock room," she says simply. "He said we all must go to the clock room eventually."

"*Who* said?" I dig in my heels, but here—in this strange interim place—I am weaker than her. "Lou, I—I don't like this anymore. I think we should leave—"

Her grip only tightens, and the ebony clock strikes midnight, ringing out across all seven rooms; the musicians cease their bright music, and the revelers grow pale and still as if in some sort of reverie.

Behind us, Reid falls dead to the floor.

Horrified, I turn to stare at him, but Lou doesn't seem to notice, her dark eyes rapt upon the ebony clock. When it quiets, soft laughter echoes through the crowd instead. It lifts the hair at my nape like a breath in my ear. It sends a chill down my spine. *No.* I pull harder against Lou, refusing to take another step—because I definitely don't like this anymore. I don't like it at all. That dread only deepens when the clock strikes again—one o'clock in the morning—and Coco drops like a marionette with cut strings.

Beau merely floats over her corpse before taking someone else in his arms. "This isn't right." I twist my wrist feverishly now, trying and failing to break Lou's grip. "Lou, did you just see—? Reid and Coco—they're—"

"Dead." Lou nods as her snake hisses softly, and its black tongue flick, flick, flicks in the air. "We must all go to the clock room eventually," she repeats, withdrawing a knife from Coco's white robes.

Then she slides the blade across her throat, opening her scar in a macabre, bloody smile.

"You'd better feed soon, Célie," she says, matter-of-fact, as the knife clatters back to the floor. Blood splatters in all directions. "When the clock strikes two, we'll all die. He said so himself. He said we must all go to the clock room together."

"*Lou.*" Desperate, I search for something to stanch her bleeding, but my fangs have already descended. My hands move as if they belong to someone else, and I have no choice but to watch as they lovingly descend on her shoulders. As they caress her skin. *I am so much paler than her now.* The thought is an errant one, almost amused, but it breaks my strange focus for the split second it takes to wrench my gaze away—to glance up and see my reflection in the violet-colored window.

Jagged stitches disfigure half my face; they stretch and twist as I grin, as I laugh with the last lethal chime of the clock. Releasing Lou at once, I stagger backward, startled, *sickened*, and Michal sweeps me into his arms instead. He presses a cold kiss against my temple. Warmth immediately suffuses my body, and I cling to him, unable to let him go.

It's going to be all right.

The thought blooms through my fear like a talisman, like I hold a shield in my hands instead of Michal's waist. Perhaps because here—in this multitude of dreams—I can sense the truth. His truth, *my* truth. If Michal is here, everything will be all right.

As if I've spoken aloud, he pulls me closer, flush against him now, and whispers, "Did you miss me?"

"No," I lie.

He grins, sharp as a knife. "Petite menteuse."

Between one blink and the next, he whisks me from the ballroom to a forest clearing, where a single tree has taken root in the moonlight. A laurel crown weaves across his brow now, and his skin gleams with internal light as he reaches up to pluck a fruit from overhead. Leaning closer, I resist the urge to inhale, to bury my face in his chest and sink my teeth into his skin. My gums throb with the effort. My fingers nearly draw blood. His presence, his scent—they're headier here, disorienting, and my body aches with hunger and—and something else. Something I dare not name. Still, however, I cannot bring myself to let him go. "A fairy," I whisper in awe. "You're a fairy king."

His chest rumbles with dark laughter as he offers the fruit to me. "And what does that make *you*?"

I do not answer.

Instead, I tear my gaze away from his cruel face to behold the fruit in his hand—an apple. At first glance, it appears the perfect shade of crimson, its skin crisp and shining, but when I blink, when I *focus*, the fruit grows fur and splits open, revealing rotten flesh at the center. I knock it away from him with a cry. "What *is* that?"

He lifts my chin with a single finger in response, forcing me to meet his eyes. "Fairy tales don't always have happy endings, Célie. Should I have let you die instead?"

My throat constricts at the accusation in his gaze, but instead of breaking away, I press closer still, finding it rather difficult to breathe. "I never wanted this." The words spill from my lips in a rush of truth, but it's too late to take them back. Perhaps it always has been. "I never wanted to *die*—"

"I never wanted to die either," Michal confesses, "but we must all go to the clock room eventually."

In the distance, an ebony clock tolls, and I stiffen, my entire body going cold at the sound. The scene tilts without warning, pitching us into the roots of the tree, and I wake with a gasp.

I wake without Michal.

Though my body shivers and aches with real hunger, it takes several seconds to realize the dream was just that—a dream. I stand on wood floors now instead of undergrowth, and the thick shadows around me are no longer trees, but a nightstand and candlestick. An armoire. Pillows. I clutch my elbows and glance around, taking deep, calming breaths I no longer need. Because I'm in my bedroom.

It was just a dream, I tell myself firmly. *It wasn't real. I'm in my bedroom, and it was just a dream.*

Awareness does little to ease the tension in my shoulders, however. No. It makes everything so much worse.

Because until this moment, I have never known true fear—not when Frederic slit my throat, not when I stabbed Morgane, not even when she trapped me with my sister's corpse. It grips my heart in an icy fist, crushing it, as my gaze lands directly below me.

Because I haven't woken in *my* bedroom at all.

I've woken in Lou and Reid's.

The last vestiges of the dream vanish in a dizzying wave at the sight of them, at the realization that I hover over their sleeping forms like a silent specter, mere inches from their bed. Mere *seconds* from—from—

Tears spill down my cheeks as Lou turns slightly, her eyes still closed, and seeks Reid even in her dreams. As his hand responds by tangling in her hair. Both breathe deeply, peacefully, unaware of the danger because they trust me. *They trust me.* I lift a hand to my mouth in horror. In shame. Though my teeth throb, I bite down hard until I draw blood, relishing the pain, the sharp, aberrant taste of myself.

If I'd woken a second later, Lou and Reid would be dead.

With one last, shuddering breath, I commit the sight of them to memory. My dear friends.

Then I turn on my heel, and I flee into the night.

CHAPTER EIGHT

Absolution

Darkness still shrouds the city as I gaze up at Cathédral Saint-Cécile d'Cesarine. The sky itself seems heavier than usual, thick with gloom and exhaustion. It rests upon the spires of the cathedral as if it can no longer bear to support itself, obscuring the beautiful stained glass and gargoyles as thunder rumbles halfheartedly in the distance.

Chasseur Tower looms directly above me.

I cannot remember making the decision to come here—or even how I came to be here at all—but now that I've seen the Tower, I cannot bring myself to leave. Stark and severe, it rises like a fist to strike at the heavens, and my eyes search the familiar stonework hungrily. They strain to see through the clouds, to count each window until I find the third from the right, directly beneath the gargoyle with wings like a bird. Through it, I might find Jean Luc.

I swallow hard, and my stomach rolls with hunger.

Perhaps he is already awake, marshaling initiates to the training yard or meeting Father Achille about the grave robbers. Or perhaps he's eating breakfast—porridge with two sliced apples—surrounded by friends in the commissary. Depending on the night watch, he could still be sleeping, dreaming, alone in his room. He never feared the dark as I did, so he wouldn't have lit any candles. He wouldn't have needed them. His room would still be dim and peaceful, a touch cold, as the Tower gradually woke around him.

I can picture it all so clearly now. This life we would've shared.

Clutching my elbows, I glance to the east, where a band of grayish light marks the sunrise. The clouds show no sign of breaking, however. Rain still mists upon the empty street. It sparkles upon the lampposts and cobblestones, clings to my nightgown until the ivory silk sticks to my skin. I suppose I should feel cold—my feet bare in November—but truthfully, I feel nothing except hunger. When another pain wracks my stomach, I bend abruptly and struggle not to retch in the street.

I need to eat.

Deep down, I know that. Of course I know that. I can even envision it, yet it is something else entirely to *do* it. Straightening, I wrap my arms around my middle, wishing their embrace alone could sustain me. Because I cannot sink my teeth into another person any more than I can sprout wings and fly.

Fly.

My eyes clamp shut at the silly, errant thought.

After my initiation into the Chasseurs, Jean Luc had twirled me round and round until it felt like I *was* flying, my pristine blue coat rippling behind me.

The two of us had crept into the antechamber by the sanctuary; we could still hear the deep rumble of voices beyond the door as the other Chasseurs lingered with Father Achille. Male voices. All males. Pride swelled in my heart at the sound of them, and I pressed my forehead to Jean Luc's. My shoulders shook with quiet laughter, and Jean Luc—he laughed too, brushing his nose against mine. "I'm so proud of you, Célie. You really did it."

My happiness punctured slightly at his words. Because I didn't *really* do it—not like he did. Too many huntsmen had perished in the Battle of Cesarine, and Father Achille had granted a temporary moratorium; any initiate who'd proven his courage during battle had been sworn into the brotherhood without a tournament. Except me. I hadn't been an initiate before the ceremony—*couldn't* have been an initiate, even if I'd wanted to be.

Before that day, the Church hadn't allowed women inside Chasseur Tower except as wives.

Giving myself a mental shake, I'd kissed Jean Luc on the cheek.

This was, after all, the start of a bright new future for the Chasseurs.

And for me.

"Thank you, Jean." Unable to help it, I brushed my lips against his other cheek before abandoning all restraint and peppering his face with kisses. "Or should I call you Captain Toussaint?"

He returned me to my feet with a sly smile. "I have something else in mind."

"Oh?"

"Look in your pocket."

Curious, I reached into my coat pocket, my fingers brushing something small and round—a ring. Instant warmth suffused me, and when I pulled the ring from my pocket—diamond sparkling in the afternoon sunlight—Jean Luc had already dropped to one knee. The sunshine cast half his face in gold, and he looked so handsome, so hopeful, that my breath caught. "Célie." Taking my hand in his, he brushed his thumb across my bare ring finger. "I've loved you from the moment I fell out of the orange tree in your garden." He laughed softly at the memory and shook his head. "You—you elbowed Reid and Filippa out of the way, and you demanded to see my bloody knee. Do you remember? I knew then—even before you pushed up my pant leg, before you rushed off to find a bandage—that I'd never seen anyone so beautiful. So *good*." My heart lodged in my throat as he took the ring from me, as he held it poised on the tip of my finger. "Would you make me the happiest man in the world, Célie? Would you do me the honor of becoming my wife?"

I hadn't even stopped to consider.

I simply nodded through my tears, and when he stood, sliding the ring onto my finger, I wondered if a person could die from happiness. A harried-looking Father Achille burst through the door in the next second, however, before either of us could say a word. "*There* you are, Captain Toussaint. Where have you been?" He shook his head irritably without waiting for an answer. "It doesn't matter. A riot has broken out around Soleil et Lune. Apparently, a handful of Dames Blanches set the entire place aflame. Louise is containing the scene, but we should've dispatched a unit half an hour ago—"

"I'll go now." Jean Luc moved to release my hands with an apologetic expression, and Father Achille ducked swiftly from the room. "Stay here, Célie. I'll be back in an hour, and we can celebrate. I promise."

I clung to his fingers with the tips of my own. "But shouldn't I—?"

"No." He shook his head curtly, his eyes already looking through me. Past me. "It's your first day on the job, and anyway, you heard Father Achille—Lou has everything under control. Our presence is more a show of support than anything." Kissing my forehead, he added, "I love you."

I love you.

I've loved you from the moment I fell out of the orange tree in your garden. I'd never seen anyone so beautiful. So good.

Slowly, bitterly, I return to the drizzle outside of Chasseur Tower, staring up at the third window from the right. That bright afternoon feels like a lifetime ago. I shouldn't be here anymore—I know that—yet I cannot go anywhere else either. I cannot endanger my friends by returning to Lou and Reid's flat, and I cannot endanger the kingdom by seeking shelter at the castle with Beau and Coco. I cannot ask my parents to keep me, not like this, and Michal—

No.

Vision blurring in the rain, I stumble forward.

I just need to—to *talk* to Jean Luc, to see him. The two of us never found real closure, and everything I've touched since leaving him has crumbled at my fingertips. *Everything*, my mind echoes wildly. Even the street beneath my feet seems to shift, to pitch with each step, and I stumble again, bracing myself against a lamppost as thunder rolls in the distance. Jean Luc has always felt so steady. He always felt so safe. Pushing away from the lamppost, I stagger toward the cathedral steps with growing desperation. Because now he hates me—he *loathes* me—but he cannot hate me more than I hate myself.

Perhaps if I could just hear him say it—if someone in this wretched kingdom could tell me the *truth*—it would absolve all the terrible things I feel. All the terrible things I've *done*. Perhaps I could move forward if Jean Luc would just treat me like the monster I am.

Or perhaps I could ask him to end it altogether.

The thought, small and quiet and terrible, creeps from the darkest part of my mind. I dare not look at it too closely, however, even as Frederic's voice slithers out to join it. *It should've been you all along.*

"No," I whisper.

In a burst of speed, I streak toward the cathedral steps—determined to reach Jean Luc before other voices join—but the instant my bare foot touches the stone, it burns like I've stepped on red-hot embers. Stunned, I jerk backward, landing hard on my backside and watching as angry red blisters split open the ball of my foot. My tears fall faster now. Thicker. I can scarcely see through them as I crawl to my knees, incredulous, and lift trembling fingers to the lowermost step.

They begin to sizzle as they near the stone. They begin to *smoke.*

Just like my throat did when I spoke the name of God.

Snatching them away, I hold them against my chest and weep as the gravity of my situation finally descends. As it passes through this fetid new skin of mine like a disease, like a plague—except *I* am the disease. *I* am the plague. Never again will I speak His name, and never again will I enter His house. I will never enter His kingdom because I am damned. I will never again walk in the sun, never again speak to my parents, never again eat chocolate with my friends or escape into dreams or even flirt with the bookseller up the street, because I am undead.

Because I am a fool, and I cannot fly. I never could.

And there is nothing here for me any longer.

Slowly, I place my scalded palms upon the cool, wet cobblestones. My brethren will be waking soon, if they haven't already. Any one of them could look down from their dormitory windows and see me—the she-devil who once haunted their hallowed halls. The demoness.

The vampire.

Even Jean Luc cannot absolve that.

As if I've summoned him with my thoughts, his deep, familiar voice drifts toward me from the alleyway behind the Tower.

I close my eyes, unwilling to believe what I'm hearing at first. It wouldn't be the first time my mind has played tricks on me. When a second voice joins his, however—this one sharp, feminine, and unfamiliar—my eyes snap open.

Jean Luc often starts his mornings with exercise.

Scrambling to my feet, heedless of my wild hair and translucent nightgown, I dart around the corner. My lips have already formed his name when I skid to a halt, frowning at the scene before me. Because there is Jean Luc, of course—dressed in the lightweight clothing he wears to exercise—but behind him stands a tall, pale woman with golden hair. I frown, ducking into the shadows before either of them notices me. The woman wears the same lightweight clothing as Jean Luc, performs the same leisurely stretches, as if she is about to . . . well, *join* him.

He never allowed me to join him before.

I peer at the woman closer, forcing myself to focus through the blurred edges of my vision. Someone has lit the two torches flanking the side entrance to the Tower. The flames flicker slightly in the drizzle. Though the woman appears to be around my age, she holds herself with more confidence, her shoulders straight and proud despite her height. Her bright hair pulled tightly away from her face. It elongates her already foxlike features, emphasizes the high lines of her cheekbones.

Though she is not traditionally beautiful, I cannot look away.

"This is getting pathetic, Toussaint." With a smirk, she pulls one long arm across her chest, stretching the muscle, before moving on to the next one. "If you want to spend more time with me, you need only ask."

Though Jean Luc rolls his eyes, a small smile plays on his lips too. "You flagged in the training yard yesterday, Brigitte. Henry almost bested you. I thought you could use a little extra time to wake up this morning."

She snorts. "I still kicked your ass."

"Language." He doesn't sound angry, however. He doesn't sound exasperated or disappointed either. No. He sounds almost . . . pleased with her.

I stare at the young woman hungrily.

Still smirking, she falls quiet and bends to stretch her legs. She watches Jean Luc from the corner of her crystalline eyes, however. Like a moth drawn to the flame. And I cannot even blame her—Jean Luc has always been beautiful. Not like a vampire, of course, but . . . like a man. I can hear the steady beat of his heart, can practically *feel* the warmth and vitality radiating from him even from my hiding place. And suddenly, I can't stay hidden any longer. Stepping into the torchlight, I murmur, "Jean."

Both he and Brigitte turn in unison.

Though his gaze widens at the sight of me—his pupils dilating, his mouth parting on a slow exhale—his entire body hardens as if preparing for attack. My own body tenses in response. He looked the same when he visited last week—like he'd never seen anyone so beautiful, and like he never wanted to see me again. "Célie," he breathes.

At the sound of my name, Brigitte glances warily between us, and the light in her eyes seems to harden. *She's heard of me.* I don't know whether to feel better or worse about that. No one in Chasseur Tower would've said anything complimentary—not that it matters what they say anymore. I shake myself internally, and the world seems to shudder with me. My thoughts remain scattered, distant. Impossible to catch.

I focus instead on the sound of Jean Luc's heartbeat.

It beats in time with the dull pounding in my head. *Tha-thump. Tha-thump. Tha-thump.* I never noticed his heartbeat when I was alive—never realized how important it would be. How precious. Though I try to ignore it, nausea spikes in my stomach again. Because now he has another's heartbeat to match.

"Who is she?" I whisper, swaying on my feet.

When my eyes flutter, Jean Luc's narrow, and he inches closer reluctantly, thrusting an arm out to prevent Brigitte from following. "Go inside," he says sharply.

Brigitte doesn't move. Instead she watches me coldly, her gaze clear and sharp and blue. "I think I'll stay here."

"*Now,* Brigitte."

Lip curling, she retreats slowly, not turning her back until she reaches the door. Even then, she hesitates, opens her mouth as if to speak. At the last second, however, she seems to change her mind, exhaling harshly before turning on her heel and disappearing inside, her long hair whipping out of sight behind her.

"Célie?" Jean Luc lifts his hands cautiously, as if preparing to steady me, or perhaps to ward me off. "Are you all right? Is something wrong?" He glances behind me. "Where are the others?"

I want him to touch me.

Please don't touch me.

"I came alone."

"Why?"

I have no answer for that. I have no answer for anything anymore, perhaps never had them at all. There is only his heartbeat. *Tha-thump. Tha-thump. Tha-thump.* Instead I say, "I think I might be dying."

"What?" His brows furrow in confusion—in alarm—and he takes another step forward. Distantly, I realize he shouldn't. He should follow Brigitte inside, should go somewhere I cannot ever touch him again. His gaze tracks over my pallid skin, the hollows beneath my eyes, the sharp protrusions of my collarbone. I do not need a reflection to see how great and terrible I look. How beautiful. "Reid and Lou—they're supposed to be helping you. They *told* me they would help you. Do they know you're here?"

Slowly, I shake my head.

His jaw clenches. "Of course they don't. What about that—that *vampire*"—he spits the word like the curse it is—"who followed us from Requiem? The insufferable one? Why isn't she with you?"

Odessa.

"It isn't her fault. It isn't any of their fault."

We let the unspoken truth swell between us: *It's mine.*

To my relief, he doesn't argue this time, doesn't lie to protect my feelings like the others do. Because he knows. Jean Luc knows every hideous thing I've ever done, and he despises each one of them. He despises *me.* Instead of saying the words aloud, however, he takes another step, and the column of his throat bobs at whatever he sees in my expression. "Why did you come here, Célie?"

"I needed to see you."

Emotions flit through his eyes in rapid succession—hope, disbelief, rage, and finally, caution. *Good.* Caution is a good thing.

Caution is necessary. "You shouldn't say things like that to me," he says, voice low.

Still I do not leave. "Why not?"

"Because it isn't true. You need—other people now." Shaking his head, he forces himself to look away, to look toward the door through which Brigitte just disappeared. When he scoffs, the sound drips with self-deprecation. It distracts me from the heady drum of his heart. "Who am I kidding? You've never needed me at all. This—*whatever* this is between us—has always meant more to me than it does to you, but you already know that, don't you? You wouldn't be here if you didn't."

"Jean, I—"

His eyes flash with fury, and the hollow words collapse before I can speak them.

"Don't lie to me, Célie," he snarls, "and I won't lie to you."

Petite menteuse, Michal calls me.

Little liar.

Jean Luc and I stare at each other through the rain, an ocean of unspoken hurt between us.

"How can you even look at me?" I ask quietly. "I—I rejected you. I left you. I wh-whored myself to a vampire, and now I—now I'm—" Unable to continue, I gesture down my terrible, beautiful body, but without a word, he closes the distance between us and seizes my hand. His feels too warm in my own. Burning hot. My eyes fall to the pulse leaping in his throat. Just like the others, he doesn't realize the danger of being near me—perhaps *cannot*—because he still thinks I'm Célie. He still thinks I'm his.

He bends, bringing his face directly in line with my own, as if to prove it.

"None of that matters. Can't you understand? There is *nothing* you've done that we can't fix together. Please." He swallows hard again, and my eyes track the movement, the strong line of his throat. He doesn't seem to notice. "Célie, this can't be it for us. After everything, we—we were supposed to be together forever."

Like so long ago, his thumb sweeps across my bare ring finger, and he stares at me like a man famished.

This isn't right. He shouldn't be saying these lovely things—not to me—and forever can no longer exist between the two of us. I am *dead*, and he—he remains in the prime of his life. Years, decades, still stretch out before him, and they should be filled with love and laughter and light. Jean Luc has never been the type to yield. He will not simply succumb to his circumstances, which means he *will* find someone to love instead of me. He will build a life with them, grow old with them, and that hideous, hopeful light in his gaze—it doesn't belong to me anymore.

"Who is she?" I whisper again, and I hate myself. I hate myself for asking. I hate myself for caring.

Jean Luc pulls my hands to his chest, cradling them in his warmth. In life. Though instinct warns me to pull away—to leave before I do something I'll regret—my feet remain rooted to the cobblestones, even as he brushes a kiss against my knuckles. "She isn't you, Célie."

"You're right. She isn't a monster."

Summoning the last of my strength, I turn to leave, but Jean Luc refuses to let me go. Grip firm, he pulls me back toward him, and—in a move that damns me straight to Hell—I allow it. Head spinning, I fall against his chest, and his scent washes over me in a delicious wave. *I should leave. I should go.* Instead I rub my cold cheek against the steady beat of his heart until it's the only sound that exists. "You aren't a monster." He tangles his fingers in my damp hair. *Tha-thump.* "I could never love a monster, and I love you."

Tha-thump. Tha-thump.

"Say something," he breathes, "please."

I've loved you from the moment I fell out of the orange tree in your garden.

My hands curl in his shirt. He feels just as he always has, except different too—softer, warmer. Better. Desperate to capture the heat of his skin, I slip my hands through the buttons of his shirt, watching as if my fingers belong to someone else. I never allowed myself to touch him like this before. I shouldn't allow it now. It isn't fair to him. Still, I inhale deeply, pressing my palms against his heart. I never allowed myself to savor the sweet, clean *scent* of him either—

Without warning, my arms snake around his waist, and I draw him closer, holding him flush against my body.

Tha-thump tha-thump tha-thump.

Transfixed, I drag my tongue along the rapid beat of his pulse. He tastes like salt, slightly bitter from his soap, but beneath it all, something richer lingers. Something darker. My entire body shudders in time with his. With a groan, he tries to pull away, his breathing ragged and his eyes unfocused. "Célie, what are you—?"

The Tower door bursts open, and Brigitte snarls, "Get away from him!"

Too late.

My fangs have already lengthened, and—though weak, though faint—I am still a vampire, and perhaps all the more dangerous for it; neither can move fast enough to stop me. Brigitte's shout still hangs in the air as I sink my teeth into Jean Luc's throat.

CHAPTER NINE

Petite Menteuse

His blood surges into my mouth, thicker and faster than expected. Hotter. It streams down his throat and shoulder, across my chest, until it paints both of us scarlet. I don't stop, however. I can't stop. Though tears pour down my cheeks, though he thrashes against me in shock and horror, spluttering incoherently, I merely thread my arms beneath his shoulders and drag him lower, closer. Easing my access. "C-Célie—" He seizes my waist and attempts to pry me away. "Célie, *stop*—"

I hardly feel his efforts. His hands could be a gentle caress. Indeed, as his blood fills my body, it becomes startling easy to hold him. To keep him with me forever. *Mine.* The thought rises like a snarl—and perhaps I *do* snarl, my teeth sinking deeper—because Jean Luc scrabbles at my nape now, my hair and nightgown, desperate to find purchase. And his *fear*—I can sense it, scent it, sharper than blood magic and just as potent, even inebriating. It floods the entire alley until I might drown in it, and my jaw clamps instinctively in response. My tongue works frantically. *Wasting it.* I am *wasting* his lifeblood, but I cannot control the flow, cannot do anything except bear him to the street and trap him between my knees, pinning his useless hands to the cobblestones. Because I need more of it.

I need *more.*

Before I can properly adjust my bite, however, my ribs erupt in agony.

"Let him *go*!" Brigitte's calloused hands replace Jean Luc's, and she screams, tearing at my arms before sliding his silver Balisarda through my ribs once more. Twice. Three brutal strokes. Though I choke, snarling and twisting away from her—delirious with pain, *burning*—my hands refuse to relinquish him. My teeth remain in his throat, even as his movements grow slower. Weaker. Brigitte lifts his Balisarda to strike again, her eyes crazed with fear. The scent only goads me further. "Get away from him! I said *get*"—she grits her teeth with effort, still swinging wildly—"*away*!" She hacks at my arms now, merciless in her assault. "Help! *Help!*"

In a sickening circle of life, however, Jean Luc's blood heals my wounds as soon as they open, and Brigitte's sobs soon join my own. "Help!" Her shrieks split the dawn like an axe. "Someone please help us! *Please!*" In one last, desperate bid to free him, she swings the Balisarda high, higher, before embedding it in my neck.

Pain unlike anything I've ever felt rends my body in two.

Because this time, she leaves the blade half-buried in my flesh, and I feel every inch of it as I turn, slowly, to face her.

Lethal purpose pounds through my chest as I wrench the Balisarda away, as I toss it to the ground and rise to my feet. Though the wound doesn't heal instantly, vanishing like the others, the skin still knits itself back together. It leaves an angry puckered line.

Too late, she realizes her mistake. Her eyes widen when my lip curls. Her breath catches when my vision sharpens, bleeding red, and—after a split-second deliberation—she darts up the alley in an obvious attempt to lure me away from Jean Luc. And I will oblige her. *Oh yes.* I will give her *exactly* what she wants, and I will relish watching that bright, cold light leave her eyes as she dies to protect him. Blood roars in my ears. Though her gaze darts frantically for a means of escape, there is none.

If she runs, I will catch her, and already my knees bend in anticipation, my entire body trembling, tightening, because I hope she does—I hope she runs.

As if in slow motion, she turns to do just that.

And I attack.

It takes less than a second for arms of iron to wrap around my chest, pinning my own to my sides. His scent engulfs me next—rich, decadent—and heat coils tight within my belly in response. *Michal.* And now *I* am the one thrashing in vain, seething and snarling against him, helpless to move until he frees me. I should've known he wouldn't leave. I should've *known* he'd interfere—

"Hello again, pet." His voice drips with apathy, and he shakes his head, heedless of my efforts to snap his shin with my heels. "We really must stop meeting like this."

"Let me go," I snarl.

"As much as I'd enjoy watching you eat your fiancé, I don't care much for the mess it'll leave behind."

"I *hate* you—"

"I know you do, Célie."

I shudder convulsively at my name on his lips. And I hate my reaction—I do. I hate *him.* With a vicious curse, I writhe and twist, driving my elbows into his ribs. Attempting to create space, to loosen his grip. My skin tingles intolerably where he touches me, and—and he cannot *be* here. I told him to *leave.* Though Jean Luc presses a hand to his throat to stanch the bleeding, the scent of his blood still entwines with the delicious scent of the vampire behind me, the scent of fear. My head spins with it all—each scent more potent than the last—until I am mindless in his arms, delirious. Until all I can hear is the sluggish beat of Jean Luc's heart and the rapid beat of Brigitte's.

Until all I can *see* is scarlet upon the cobblestones, down my front. It coats Michal's leather sleeves now too.

It makes them slick.

"Y-You're *him*," Brigitte stammers, her face white as she stares at us. "Captain Toussaint told us about you. He said you're the one who stole her away, who *turned* her—"

"I suggest"—Michal jerks his chin toward the Tower as she searches frantically for the Balisarda—"you take the good captain and leave, telling no one what transpired here. Vampires have no quarrel with huntsmen." I can almost hear his eyes flash as he adds, "Yet."

"Oh, I don't think so, *leech*." In lieu of a Balisarda, Brigitte hurls the word like a weapon. "The Chasseurs will have heard me. They'll be here any moment, and you and that *succubus* will get what you deserve—"

"Don't be foolish, Brigitte." His teeth grind as my nails claw at his forearms, shredding leather and linen and skin. Drawing fresh blood. *His* blood. The scent of it breaks over me like a wave. It further lubricates his sleeves. "As we speak, my cousin is waiting outside to compel your precious brethren to return to their rooms. It turns out no one heard your screams after all."

Brigitte trembles all over now, yet with a shout of triumph, she swoops low and snatches Jean Luc's Balisarda from the shadows near the steps. "Then I'll kill you myself," she says. "I'll drive this dagger straight through your cold, dead heart."

My gaze snaps upward at that. Unbidden, a low and guttural sound tears from my throat—a sound I've never made before—and I twist again to face her, slipping beneath the slick fabric of Michal's sleeves. For a single, glorious second, nothing stands between me and Brigitte. I start toward her too swiftly for my mind to follow, to make sense of the sudden fury licking up my spine.

Before I can tear out her throat, however—before I can *feast*—Michal appears between us. When I snarl again, attempting to dart around him, he sidesteps, and I crash into his chest, too slow to counter him. Brigitte seizes the opportunity to lunge at his back with the Balisarda, but he swats it aside with rapidly thinning patience. When it skids—useless—behind me, Brigitte regains her senses and retreats to Jean Luc's side.

I glower at her from behind Michal, hissing softly.

She drops to her knees in response, looping her arms under Jean's shoulders and attempting to drag him backward. Away from me.

A mistake.

It's like someone else has taken control of my body. All I can see is her hateful face, her hands on Jean Luc, and none of this makes sense. He doesn't belong to me—I *know* that—yet the scent of his blood, the scent of *Michal*, nearly cleaves my body in two with wanting. My spine actually bows with hunger, with *pain*, and I lunge, baring my teeth, snapping at them—

Michal's arms wrap around me once more, and he lifts me from my feet as still I strain forward, sobbing now. Vaguely, I realize he speaks low and fast at my ear, but I hear only one word. "Célie," he breathes. Over and over and over again, he says my name. Just my name. *Célie.* As if he knows I've gone somewhere he cannot follow, and he won't stop until he drags me back. "You don't want to kill them. Not truly."

"You don't know what I want," I snarl.

"Oh, but I do." He still refuses to let me go, holding me tight and fast against him. "Your senses have heightened. Everything feels sharper, brighter, *better* as a vampire, but the pain feels more intense too. Your teeth are *aching.* Your head throbs. The scent of his blood has become a heartbeat in your chest, and you can't hear anything except that frantic drum. You want to rend her limb from limb for touching him because he belongs to *you.*"

I shake my head vehemently. A liar.

A liar, a liar, a *liar.*

Just like that, I wriggle through his arms—completely out of control—but as before, he appears in front of me. This time, however, he forces me against the alley wall with a hard forearm against my chest. His slippery surcoat has vanished, leaving behind only a shredded black shirt. His collar fell open during our tussle; his cravat lies crumpled and forgotten upon the street. If possible, his disarray makes him feel all the more menacing—wilder, somehow, and darker, like a primeval god looming over me.

"Enough, Célie," he says with unnerving calm. "Unless you want to bury your fiancé and his new friend, you need to stop pretending to be human. Whether you like it or not, you're a vampire now, and vampires are a predatory species—*the* predatory species." His black eyes bore into mine, insistent and immovable, and I know—I *know*—that his patience has reached its end. "We cannot survive on morality."

The words crumble the last of my resolve.

In its wake, a flood of bitter embarrassment rushes through me instead. It fills each crack in my chest until I might drown—in my stupidity, yes, in my *recklessness*, but also in my fear. I knew I would eventually need to feed. After living on Requiem with Michal and Odessa and Dimitri, how could I not? I knew what it would require to survive as a vampire, and truthfully, the blood itself never disgusted me. It still doesn't.

Behind Michal, Jean Luc struggles to rise to his elbows, his eyes narrowed in disbelief—still seeking mine even as Brigitte tries to drag him away. He digs in his heels. I can hold his horrified gaze for only a second before looking away. Because the scent of his blood still stirs something inside me. Because my belly still clenches tight in response; my fingers still curl to claim him.

I delayed the inevitable because I didn't want to hurt anyone.

And so I do not fight Michal any longer. I simply lift my chin, and I bare my entire soul. "I don't think I can do this."

It's the hideous truth I've tried to avoid, the one my friends and family have always ignored because they love me—I am not enough. I never have been, and I never will be. At every turn, I have failed: to be a sister, a lady, a huntswoman, a fiancée. I even failed at being a Bride. Frederic won—he resurrected my sister—because I thought I could outwit him, could undo all his careful planning with nothing but hope and fairy dust. Of course I'd now fail at being a vampire too.

It seems everyone got their wish, after all, and how terribly disappointed they all must be.

I am still, tragically, Célie.

As expected, Michal doesn't pity me. If possible, his expression hardens even further, and he releases me without warning to wrench up his sleeve. "I'm afraid you don't have a choice. If you refuse to eat, you *will* kill someone—likely all of Chasseur Tower—and you'll loathe yourself more than you already do." Before I can stop him, his fangs descend, and he bites his wrist deep enough to draw blood. His scent punches through me like the blade of a knife. Its jagged edge stabs at my throat, my chest, my stomach until I hiss in delirious pain. He doesn't care. "Your options are limited now, Célie. You can either feed from me, or if you prefer, I can show you how to feed from these two. I can even teach you how to compel away their memories—"

I shake my head before he can finish, ignoring the way his blood drips down his forearm. My jaw aches. "I won't violate them like that."

"She stuck a sword in your neck."

"No, I—I took more from Jean Luc than I should've. She was just—just—"

"Célie." Michal's voice softens inexplicably as he brushes the damp, tangled hair away from my face. It brings his wrist closer to my mouth, and I clamp my eyes shut, refusing to breathe. Refusing to *think.* Because I cannot drink from Michal again. Not now, not as a vampire. To do so would be abhorrent, unnatural—intimate. So incredibly intimate. Though I cannot explain why, I know deep in my bones that something will change between us if I do.

As if to reassure me, he sweeps a tear from my cheek with his thumb. "You won't hurt me."

Don't be disgusting, Mila once said. *Vampires only drink from vampires in* very *nonfamilial situations.*

I never asked what she meant, never dreamed such a thing would ever be relevant to Michal and me. And perhaps it's the pain in my stomach—or perhaps I really am the worst sort of liar—but the consequences seem to matter even less now than they did before. I have already done the worst. I have already attacked someone I love—almost killed him in a fit of passion, or perhaps blind rage. Jealousy. Perhaps Odessa was right, and all emotions keenly felt as a vampire blur into hunger.

Eyes still closed, I seize Michal's wrist just as the bite marks begin to heal. I cannot stand to look at them. I cannot stand to look at *him*—not as my lips close around his skin, not as my teeth sink deep where his have just been. His forearm falls away from my chest at the first pull of my mouth. It snakes around my waist at the second, steadying me when my knees give way. "Easy," he murmurs, bearing us gently to the cobblestones.

But it isn't easy. It isn't easy at all.

The taste of his blood—nothing could've prepared me for it, and nothing can ever compare again. Immediately, I know I've made a terrible mistake, but if Hell itself descended upon us now, if revenants crawled from every grave, I wouldn't be able to stop. It explodes on my tongue in a heady, arcane rush of heat, of *magic*, and by the third pull, my head threatens to spin from my shoulders. My body threatens to collapse. Still I keep my eyes closed, pulling him closer, drinking him deeper until white stars burst across the darkness of my eyelids. I suspected Michal to be stronger than the average vampire, but I'd never known how *much*.

It isn't until I feel him flowing through every part of me—powerful, *potent*—that I realize he hasn't told me to stop. He hasn't pulled away. Indeed, he still crouches before me, stroking my hair and murmuring encouragement. Allowing me to take as much as

I need. To . . . use him. "That's it." Another stroke of his hand. "Good girl."

And I feel better now. I do. As my eyes flutter open, I feel fuller, satiated, almost like myself again, except . . . different.

Fluid and graceful.

Strong.

He watches me with an inscrutable expression, his hand stilling on my hair when I finally lift my mouth from his wrist. His voice, however, is hoarser than before when he asks, "Did you get enough?"

"I . . ." My own voice sounds distant, dreamier, as I stare up at him, transfixed by his silhouette in the torchlight. "Yes, thank you."

"And you're . . . all right?" he asks quietly.

His eyes search my face with that same impenetrable intensity.

Too late, I realize how filthy I must look—hair wild and tangled, feet bare, my nightgown soaked with rain and mire and blood. *His* blood. I wipe it slowly from my mouth before tearing my gaze away from him. Another mistake.

The rest of the scene trickles in slowly at first. Though Michal has positioned himself to block the street, my senses have sharpened, and I do not need to see Jean Luc to hear that his pulse has steadied. His bleeding has slowed. His breath remains shallower than it should be, and Brigitte pants as she struggles to drag him to the door. The rapid, panicked beat of her heart, the slick sound of his clothes against the cobblestones—the sharp tang of his blood, so much *blood*—no longer fills me with rage, however. It no longer fills me with hunger.

No.

My entire body trembles as I push to my feet. Michal rises

with me, still standing too close. Still shielding me from the street.

"Célie," he starts, placating, but I sidestep him swiftly. His blood rushes to my cheeks at the scene before me. It churns viciously in my stomach, threatens to rise.

The rain has stopped.

It leaves a river of scarlet in the street. My throat thickens at the sight of it.

I—I was not clean in my attack. I was not gentle.

"No," I choke, starting toward Jean Luc.

"Don't touch me." As if waking from a trance, he stops fighting Brigitte now, scrambling backward, and the scent of his fear is a living, poisonous thing between us. In the full light of dawn, I can finally see why: his shredded skin, his mottled flesh, his glazed eyes and ashen color. "Just—just get away—"

I nearly tore out his throat.

Any strength I might've felt vanishes as I leap forward, seizing his Balisarda and dragging it down my forearm. "Please—" I fling the blade aside, thrusting my arm toward him desperately. "Please take it, Jean. It'll heal you. It'll make this—all of it just—"

All of it just what? asks a nasty voice in my head. *Go away?*

Any strength I might've felt slips like sand between my fingers as Jean Luc staggers to his feet, shoving my arm away and collapsing against Brigitte, who does her best to support his full weight. That strength heats and melts into brittle despair—because something like this doesn't just *go away.* Something like this starts a war, starts a bitter crusade like the one we just ended. *No.* As if reading my mind, Brigitte sneers, her face red with exertion as she helps Jean Luc to the Tower. "We'll hunt you for this. We'll make you *pay.*"

"But I can fix—"

"You can't *fix* this." She reaches behind to pull open the door, struggling to heave him across the threshold. "Captain Toussaint is the only reason the Chasseurs haven't burned your island to the ground."

No no no—

Hysteria rising, I chase after them, addressing Jean Luc now, waving my arm beseechingly. "You could *die*, Jean Luc. Please, please, just let me heal you—"

"Like he healed you?" Voice faint, Jean Luc winces as Brigitte jerks him into the corridor. I still reach for him, determined to do *something*, but Michal's hand descends on my shoulder just as my fingers start to burn. I snatch them away, tears welling anew at the blisters. At the smoke.

"You can't follow them," he says softly.

I whirl to face him, to plead that he somehow—someway—undo all of this. "*Why?*"

Why did this have to happen?

It isn't Michal who answers, however. It's Jean Luc. Tears track down his cheeks as he stares at me from the shadowed corridor, but his expression isn't mournful. It isn't sad. Instead his entire face screws tight with disgust. "Because the Church is holy. Evil cannot enter here."

My eyes widen in hurt. In disbelief.

Evil.

"As you've refused our blood," Michal says curtly to Jean Luc, "you should know that your healers can do nothing for those wounds. I myself do not care if you live or die, but Célie does. She is the only reason I offer this alternative—summon your friends instead. Blood magic can heal you if administered quickly."

"Like we'd ever trust *you*—" Brigitte starts, but Michal swings the door shut in her face. Then he turns to me.

"Célie?" he asks, his eyes wary.

We must all go to the clock room eventually.

"Take me to Requiem, Michal," I whisper.

PART TWO

Un clou chasse l'autre.

One nail drives out another.

CHAPTER TEN

Make It So, and It Will Be

An hour later, I sit in an odd little consignment shop overlooking the docks.

It isn't much—a few dusty tomes on navigation, a bundle of rope, and, curiously, a basket of kittens—but Michal and Odessa know the owner, a portly, middle-aged man with a kind smile and a desk in his shopwindow. "Wait here," Michal told me, his hand at the small of my back as he ushered me into the shop. "I need to speak with the harbormaster."

"Does this place carry stationery?" I asked him in a hollow voice. "And envelopes?"

He hesitated in the doorway, casting me a searching look. "I believe so."

I stare down at said envelopes now. Sitting at the desk in the window, I focus on the heft and texture of the linen, the crisp corners, the shopkeeper's glistening seal. Crimson wax. My breath quivers slightly as I lean forward to blow on the viscous liquid until it hardens, until it resembles something other than—other than—

I give myself a vicious mental shake.

Blood.

This is getting ridiculous. I can still say the word. I can still *think* it.

My hands, however, seem to disagree; they snake out in a wretched blur, flipping each envelope to hide the wax, and I gaze instead at the names scrawled across the fronts in black ink. *Black like the kitten underfoot,* I think firmly. My vision narrows on those letters, on each loop and curve of my handwriting until nothing else exists. *Black like my hair, like the shopkeeper's vest. Black like—*

My gaze flicks upward, and I watch Michal through the window as he argues with the harbormaster.

Even at a distance, I can see his black eyes.

Amidst the bustle of merchants, of dockworkers and fishermen, he looks more preternatural than ever, too still and too beautiful to ever be mistaken for human. Too pale. His alabaster skin shines like a beacon in the overcast light, stark and perfect against his dark clothing. Fortunately, his surcoat hides most of his torn shirt beneath, except for the sleeves. I shredded those too. The harbormaster eyes the claw marks in the leather dubiously, pulling out a handkerchief to wipe his brow.

Michal gave me his cloak to hide the bloodstains on my nightgown.

Forcing myself to relax, I count the kittens in the basket while I wait for him to finish arranging our transport. Seven of them in all. They mewl and scramble against the wicker in a desperate bid to reach me. Ruefully, I bend to scratch each of their little heads with a pang of unexpected loss; my mother forbade animals in the house, so Filippa and I never owned a pet.

I straighten with a miserable sigh. Eventually, Filippa persuaded her into allowing me to adopt one of the horses from our stable—Cabot—and when I joined the huntsmen, I insisted on taking him with me from West End to Chasseur Tower. He probably thinks I abandoned him now. He probably takes his oats from Brigitte.

I wish Michal would hurry up.

Near the till, Odessa peruses a brilliantly inked star chart as the shop owner counts the last of his couronnes, taking careful notes in his ledger. "Lucille traveled all the way to Zvezdya to acquire that piece," he tells her proudly, "along with a compass of pure obsidian from the home of a sorcerer—the Shadow, locals call him."

"Sorcerers don't exist, Yves," Odessa says absently—though not unkindly—as she examines the chart. "I hope your daughter didn't pay an exorbitant sum because a charlatan called himself the *Shadow.*"

"Always the skeptic." Chuckling, Yves closes the till and pats her arm fondly. "Alas, your brother would believe me—and where *is* Dimitri, anyway?" Odessa stiffens near indiscernibly at the sound of her brother's name, but Yves doesn't seem to notice, his eyes glittering with mischief. I wonder if he knows to whom he truly speaks. I wonder if he knows what she eats. "Is he out romancing the locals? I know Lucille would love to see him before he leaves."

Fixing a smile on her lips, Odessa returns the chart to its shelf. "Dimitri is otherwise occupied, I'm afraid."

Otherwise occupied. It isn't a lie, per se. Disappearing with the Necromancer after his betrayal on All Hallows' Eve has probably kept Dimitri quite busy this week. No one has seen him since the grotto—where he murdered Babette, fed from Beau, and attacked his own sister in a desperate bid to take La Voisin's grimoire. In his defense, he believed it held the cure to his blood sickness.

He also almost killed us all.

Odessa stares fixedly at the tin of biscuits by the star chart, her body taut as a bow.

Thankfully, a customer enters then; he interrupts whatever Yves might've said.

As if sensing the weight of my gaze, Odessa's eyes flick to mine, and I look hastily away, spreading my envelopes across the desk: *To Jean Luc*, *To Brigitte*, *To Lou.* My fingers still tremble slightly against the last letter. They haven't stopped trembling since I wrote it. I stare determinedly at the stained crescents of my nails, the dried brown blood underneath, instead of imagining her expression when she wakes and cannot find me. *Brown like autumn leaves. Like acorns and chestnut coffee.*

Lou deserves so much more than what I've given her. They *all* do, yet I cannot bear to say goodbye in person. It makes me a miserable coward, yes—and a wretched friend—but if I return to their doorstep, if I sit in that merry kitchen with its copper pots and fat peonies, I know I'll never leave. Eventually, I'll hurt one of them like I hurt Jean Luc, and that cannot happen. I cannot put us in such a position again.

Never again.

I cling to that resolve with every fragment of my body. It becomes imperative, a life raft, and though it won't buoy me forever, it buoys me for now. It will buoy me straight to Requiem, where I must . . . atone for what I've done somehow. Where I must make things *right.*

I run my finger over the sharp corners of the envelope, thinking hard.

Three years ago—on the night of my debut into society—I stood alone at the top of our grand staircase, staring down at the beautiful peers in our ballroom. I nearly vomited at the sight of their unfamiliar faces, of my own empty dance card. My mother had refused to invite Reid to the soirée. He held no title or fortune, yet I still wanted to marry him. I'd never danced with anyone else. "You'll be fine," Filippa told me fiercely, seizing my gloved hands. "Every gentleman in this room will be clamoring to meet you tonight, ma belle. Mark my words—Maman and I will need to beat them away with a stick."

I regarded her with wide, helpless eyes. "What if they don't?"

Our mother stepped forward with that familiar air of competence and severity. "Make it so," she said curtly, "and it will be." Then she pinched my cheeks with brutal efficiency and towed me down the stairs.

Make it so, and it will be.

Nonsensical words, to be sure, yet her advice—it worked that evening. Under her sharp eyes, I held my shoulders straight and my chin high. I batted my lashes, and I spoke with confidence, feigned wit and charm. By the end of the night, my feet ached from dancing, and two men proposed the very next morning.

I've always been good at pretend.

And if it worked then, why shouldn't it work now?

I might be a monster, but I can still act otherwise—like my life hasn't just shattered into a thousand jagged pieces, like my teeth don't still ache to taste blood. Instead, I can go to Requiem, and I can start again. I can do better. I can *be* better.

"You don't need to explain yourself to anyone, Célie," Odessa says, pretending not to read Jean Luc's and Brigitte's names over my shoulder. Lost in my thoughts, I didn't hear her approach. I gather the letters with a scowl.

"I almost killed them, Odessa."

"And?" She stoops to retrieve one of the kittens who have escaped the basket, lifting it by the scruff to peer directly into its blue-gray eyes. It meows loudly for rescue. "A letter will not change what happened, nor will it change their minds. They cannot understand what transpired in that alley because they are human. Filthy little things, aren't they?" she adds, tilting her head at the kitten. "Yves sells them to sailors to catch rats on their ships, yet I think a rat would eat such a small creature, don't you?"

I snatch the kitten away from her and return it to the basket. "It doesn't matter if they change their minds. I still need to apologize."

"Why?"

"What do you mean *why*?" I straighten, inexplicably flustered, and cram my letters into the pocket of Michal's traveling cloak. "I hurt them. It's the right thing to do—"

"According to whom?"

"According to *everyone*, Odessa," I snap. "I took a vote, and *everyone* agrees the polite response to tearing open your ex-fiancé's throat is to apologize."

"And yet," she says, "you just said it doesn't matter if they change their minds. If so, one might question the need to apologize at all—unless, of course, the apology is for *your* benefit instead of theirs." She pauses as I blink at her, stunned. "Well? Do you truly think they wish to hear from you?"

"Must you always twist everything I say? It's *exhausting*—"

"Just something to think about." She shrugs and plucks a book from the shelf before stopping short, turning with a beleaguered sigh. "Though while we're on such an uncomfortable subject . . . I *might* need to apologize for the role I played in all this." She waves a hand toward my bloodstained nightgown, her garnet bracelets clinking around her wrist.

I wrap the cloak tighter around my waist. "You didn't do anything, Odessa."

"You're right, of course, but alas, that is precisely the issue—I didn't *do* anything, and Michal tasked me with guiding you through your transition." A pause. "He trusted me, and I allowed you to starve."

"You didn't—"

"I knew animal blood could never sustain you. I knew you'd eventually need to imbibe from the source. Everyone in that wretched house could see you withering away, yet we did nothing to stop it. I failed as your mentor—not that I asked for the job," she adds, lifting her chin in a haughty, defensive sort of way. "I would've much preferred to stay in Requiem. Newborn vampires aren't my particular cup of tea. Too impulsive, you know."

I do know. Rather than tell her that, however, I finger the clasp of Michal's cloak and stare fixedly at the basket of kittens. A cream-colored tabby blinks back at me. "Yes, well . . . I won't be starving myself anymore, which means you're officially relieved of your duties. I know better now."

"Right." She hesitates again, and I cannot help it—I glance up at her, frowning. She has the air of a woman preparing herself to do something extremely unpleasant. "Except . . . I'm not sure you do, darling—know better, that is."

"What do you mean?"

"Well . . . have you learned about the birds and the bees?"

Spluttering, I nearly knock over the desk as I jolt forward. "*What?*"

"The birds and the bees." Her hand grows more agitated, and she lowers her voice. "The analogy doesn't apply to vampires, of course, as we cannot reproduce, but the mechanics remain the same—"

"*Odessa.*" Hissing her name, I glance at Yves, who remains deep in conversation about the benefits of using a True Lover's Knot over a Double Dragon. "*Why* are we talking about this?"

"Well, darling, I assume that lovely flush in your cheeks isn't simple coincidence—not when you smell so thoroughly of Michal."

Oh no.

"I smell of Michal?" I ask faintly.

"Yes," she says slowly, placatingly, and if I hadn't died in that grotto, I'd want to die all over again. The heat in my cheeks burns deeper as—unbidden—my eyes flick to the window. To Michal at the docks. He still speaks with the harbormaster, but at that precise second, his gaze snaps upward, finding mine. I turn sharply, and this time, I *do* upset the desk. Its leg skids into the basket of kittens, who tumble out in a heap of orange and gray and black. *Oh no no no—*

Limbs blurring, I right the basket and scoop them inside before they touch the floor.

Odessa sighs again.

"Célie." She looks as if she'd rather stick pins in her eyes than continue this conversation, and I agree. I wholly and *thoroughly* agree. "You have nothing of which to be ashamed. If consensual, the act of blood sharing is completely acceptable between vampires. I only ask about your sexual expertise in case you *felt* things during the act—things you might not understand. Vampirism tends to amplify sensation, emotion . . . all of it, really."

"The *act*?" My voice rises to a squeak, and both Yves and his customer glance in our direction now. Odessa waves them away with a pained smile. "With Michal? But we didn't— I'd *never*—"

"There isn't a word to describe how little I want to hear the rest of that sentence. I am simply ensuring you know how intercourse works if the opportunity presents itself." She clears her throat delicately. "You *do* know how it works, then?"

I stare at her, incredulous. Though I've never—well, *performed the act*, I've read more than enough books to understand the mechanics. I'd rather combust than tell her this, however, so I simply snap, "Yes, Odessa. I know how it works."

"Excellent." She lifts her chin, smoothing her bodice in palpable relief before adding, "That said, if you have any questions—"

"I don't—"

"—or if you ever *have* any questions—"

"I *won't*."

She rolls her eyes just as Michal enters the shop with a carefully neutral expression. It gives him away entirely, and I want to die all over again because he must've overheard this *ludicrous* conversation. I stifle a groan. Of course he did. He's a vampire, which means he overheard everything, and I—I stare fervently at the kittens, cheeks blazing, unable to meet his gaze as Odessa says, "She's all yours, cousin." Then, sweeping past us to the door: "I'll be on the ship. *Do* hurry up, won't you? This city is tedious at the best of times, let alone after a week of listening to Louise le Blanc and Reid Diggory demonstrate *their* understanding of certain mechanics—"

"Odessa!"

She merely lifts a shoulder, however—unconcerned—and disappears.

Michal and I stand in awkward silence for several seconds. Or rather, *I* stand in awkward silence while he stands in what I assume is his best impression of a marble statue—tall and cold and perfect—waiting for me to speak.

"Well?" My voice comes out higher than usual, almost shrill, and I clear my throat hastily. "Did the harbormaster agree to rearrange his departure schedule? Can we leave?"

"Yes." Michal opens the door, gesturing for me to precede him—which I do, wrapping his cloak tighter to hide the bloodstains down my front. He doesn't touch me this time. His hands remain clasped firmly behind his back.

"And did—" I clear my throat and start over. "Did you happen to keep my trousseau? Do I have—er, clothing on Requiem?"

"Everything is exactly as you left it." His gaze drops to my feet, where his too-long hem hides my bare toes. "Though the harbormaster has agreed to wait if you'd like to collect your things from West End. We can retrieve them before we—"

"No." I shake my head instantly. "My parents can never see me like this."

He gives me a cool sidelong glance. "Never," he repeats.

"Well, not *never* never. Just not—not right now."

He looks away again. "I see."

"No, you don't." Even to my ears, the words sound a touch desperate, but they spill between us before I can stop them, perhaps because I still can't read his expression; I can't discern what he's thinking behind that impassive stare, only that he *is* thinking something, and I want to know what it is. Is it amusement? Judgment?

At *that* thought, an inexplicable need to defend myself rises. "My parents think I've eloped, or otherwise whored myself to a man who is not my betrothed. They think I've been compromised. To them, it's the worst thing that could've possibly happened to me, and I—I don't want to prove them wrong. Not yet, anyway."

Another beat of silence. Then—

"As you wish."

He dips his chin without another word, continuing toward the ship, but I snatch his shredded sleeve before he can outpace me, irrationally agitated by his lack of response. It shouldn't matter what he thinks. I shouldn't *care*, yet I can't stop myself from saying, "If you have something to say—"

He arches a brow at my hand on his arm. "Oh, I have many things to say, pet, but you aren't ready to hear them."

"I told you not to call me *pet*," I snap, "and you don't get to decide when I'm ready to hear things, Michal. I'm not a child. I can handle a few unpleasant words from *you*."

Despite my bravado, warmth still creeps into my cheeks beneath his full, undivided attention, and when I rescind my hand—flustered—he says, "Fair enough." He still doesn't touch me, however. Instead he leans low, his black eyes glittering with something that looks suspiciously like hurt. "How about this? A sadistic witch tortured and killed your sister last year. Your parents know the worst that could happen, and it isn't you whoring yourself to me."

He turns abruptly on his heel then.

He leaves me standing there gaping after him like a fish.

It takes several seconds for me to clamp my mouth shut, to bite my tongue and remember I did *ask* for those unpleasant words. I wanted to know exactly what he was thinking, and he kindly obliged. Now I have no choice but to chase after him and demand an explanation—for his callous regard, yes, but also for that strange look in his eyes. That slight crack in his wall of ice. "What does that mean? You can't just *proclaim* these things and flee into the night, Michal—"

"It's dawn."

"Flee into the dawn, then." Though I dare not catch his sleeve again, I hurry to step in front of him, blocking his path and searching his face for—well, I don't *know*, exactly. "Do you think I should visit my parents? Do you think I should tell them what happened to me?"

"It doesn't matter what I think."

"What if it did?"

The question surprises even me, and I blink up at him, alarmed by my own nerve. This is Michal, after all—ancient and powerful, the cruelest of vampires—and we've never exactly been open with each other. Not like this. I resist the urge to squirm beneath his appraisal.

"We aren't friends, Célie Tremblay. You've made that very clear."

I swallow hard. "What if we were?"

"*That you would even* think *of friendship while you plan to maim and murder my loved ones proves you are quite incapable of it.*" He recites the words as if verbatim, his voice flat, and with a shock, I realize they belonged to me. He—he memorized them. As before, he waits for me to respond, and as before, I have no idea what to say. Did I ever apologize for accusing him of murder?

Did I ever thank him for defending me in the aviary? In this very harbor?

"Things have changed since then," I say instead.

"Have they?"

"We aren't—" I clear my throat, forcing myself to hold his cool gaze. He warned us about the revenants this morning. He didn't need to tell us—didn't need to sail all this way—but he did, inadvertently saving Lou and Reid from the Archbishop in the process. He saved Jean Luc too, despite those chilling last words: *I myself do not care if you live or die.* I exhale a slow, measured breath at the thought of him in the alley, biting his wrist before offering it to me. Stroking my hair as I fed. "We aren't enemies anymore, Michal."

"And that makes us friends?"

"I don't know what it makes us."

We stare at each other for a long second, neither willing to give anything else—and it's enough. For now, not being enemies is enough. As if reading my thoughts, Michal gives a terse nod. When he steps around me, however—his gaze sliding back toward the ship—his entire body stills.

"What is it?" Instinctively, I freeze too, and the hair on my neck lifts as Michal's lip curls. I glance around us. "Michal? Do you smell something?"

He shifts slightly in response, turning his face into the wind. My body does the same, as if it senses something beyond my awareness. Something dangerous. "Do *you*?" he asks.

"I—" Another gust of wind blows past at that second, and with it, the faint scent of decay brushes my cheeks, sweeps down my nose. I recoil instantly, whispering, "Revenants."

Michal nods. "What else do you smell? Focus on the scent."

"But I can't—"

"Yes," Michal says, his voice hard, "you can."

Make it so, and it will be.

Closing my eyes, I inhale deeper now, try to catch that faint tendril of miasma and follow wherever it leads. There are so many smells here, however—too many smells, an overwhelming amount—and it takes several seconds to ground myself beside him, to sift through the salt and sweat and stink of the harbor. And then—

There.

My eyes snap open at the first waft of that scent on the breeze: sharp and metallic and heady. My fangs descend without warning. "It's blood," I tell Michal in dawning realization. "I smell revenants and blood."

CHAPTER ELEVEN

Death of a Thief

We follow the trail to the end of the harbor.

Around the corner of the last building—tucked between a grubby pub and the open sea—three revenants hunch over a terrified couple. Even moving at full speed, trying and failing to keep pace with Michal, I categorize each detail of the scene in rapid succession: the revenants' bloated bodies, their privateer uniforms, the water dripping from their mottled skin.

Drowned, I realize in alarm.

My blood must've resurrected them at the bottom of the ocean.

Michal rips the first revenant away from the man—badly injured, bleeding profusely from bites in his stomach, his thigh—while I dash for the woman, who cowers behind a barrel of crème de menthe and clutches her wounded arm. If possible, her eyes widen even further at the sight of me. "Oh God," she whispers.

Too late, I realize that Michal's cloak has fallen open to reveal my bloody nightgown, that my incisors remain long and sharp.

His shout spurs me into action.

"Get out of here, Célie! Take her and go!"

Covering my mouth with one hand, I seize the woman after thrusting the second revenant away; bile rises in my throat at how its flesh bursts under my palm. *Don't breathe.* I repeat the words in a manic stream of consciousness, whisking the woman away from the waterfront. *Don't breathe, don't breathe, don't breathe—*

"You," the third revenant gurgles.

Something like recognition sparks in its watery eyes, and it catches my hair before we round the corner. It wrenches us backward as pain radiates across my scalp. I gasp—breathless with it—and at the scent of the woman's injury, fresh pain sears my throat. It doesn't hurt like it did before, however; Michal's blood still courses through my system. It dulls the ache. It strengthens me, and with a curse, I reach backward, grasping the revenant's swollen wrist and twisting with all my might. It releases us instantly, and I bolt through the harbor before it can recover. Though the woman screams anew—screams loud enough to wake every corpse in the kingdom—her arms clamp viselike around my neck.

I don't realize she's clawing at me until I release her several streets away.

"Vampire!" Her shrieks rend the quiet of the garden path—somewhere deep in West End, judging by the ornamental shrubbery around us. She clutches her elbow in blind panic, shaking her head and backing into a trellis of dead roses. "It's a vampire! Please, someone help me! Please, please," she whispers to me, quieter now. "I have ch-children." As if she were realizing a grave mistake, her eyes grow even wider, and she searches for something—anything—she can use as a weapon against me. My stomach pitches at the familiarity of the situation, at the cruelty of this particular jamais vu. How many times have I felt this same terror? How many times have I been unable to defend myself? "But don't take them either! We—we wouldn't t-taste right, and—"

"I would never hurt you." My hands tremble as I lift them

between us, as I slowly move to refasten Michal's cloak. Hiding all evidence of my lie. "This isn't what it looks like—"

She doesn't pause to listen, however. She doesn't care to hear my explanation. The instant my fingers touch the clasp, she flees back in the direction from which we came—toward her injured husband, probably, or perhaps her children.

I watch her go with a horrible sinking sensation.

She feared me just as much as she feared the revenants. Perhaps more.

"I wouldn't let it bother you," says a voice to my right, and when I turn, startled, all concern for the woman flees with her, vanishing up the path. Because that is Frederic stepping out from the hedge, and the sight of him steals the breath from my lungs. "Hello, little sister." He bares his teeth in a savage smile. "Did you miss me?"

Cold fingers of dread creep down my spine.

The last time I saw this man, he'd cleaved the very world in two for love. That overbright look in his eyes now, however—that isn't love at all. No. That look is hatred, and the full force of it sends me back a step. Why would he possibly risk coming to this dead rose garden in the middle of the day while the Chasseurs still search for him?

"What are you doing here, Frederic?" I ask warily.

"What do you *think*?"

With the jerk of his head, he gestures behind him, and there—

There stands my sister.

It turns out Mila didn't need to find her at all. She found me.

The ground seems to tilt at the sight of her, an apparition pulled straight from my darkest nightmares. Except she isn't an apparition anymore. No, Filippa Tremblay is just as solid as I am, just as *real*, and the black stitches down her cheek—those are real too. I stare at her in horror. My eyes are sharper now; they see all the things I missed while trapped beside her in the grotto.

They see how . . . unnatural she looks.

Though I knew Frederic stole her body from the catacombs, reversing the blood sickness Morgane inflicted and sewing her remains with bits of other people, I hadn't realized the extent of the damage. I should've known better. I should've *prepared.* Her flesh had been rapidly decomposing when Morgane forced me into her casket before La Mascarade de Crânes. Even Frederic's magic could only do so much to preserve her.

Now she stares back at me with the face of a chthonic deity: half hers and half not. To the left of the stitches, her skin remains her own, ivory and smooth, with her emerald eye intact and her eyebrow black as her hair. To the right, however, her skin is too pale—as pale as my own—with an eye that once belonged to someone else. The iris isn't emerald but deep brown. Almost black. And her eyebrow there—it's several shades lighter than it should be. *Also stolen.* She wears a gown of pure white with sheer sleeves as if she cannot feel the cold, and at her crown, a delicate silver hairpiece nestles. The diamonds look like ice. Like snowdrops in a winter palace. *No gloves*, I realize abruptly. *I was right.*

Unbidden, my gaze next falls to my sister's stomach.

"She's still dead," Filippa says.

Her voice holds no inflection. No emotion.

I wince at the sound of it. Three simple words. Three perfect blows. Despite all Frederic's careful planning, my blood failed to resurrect their daughter too, and—and what does that *mean*?

Was it truly my sister tormenting me, or did I imagine her voice in my head? If the former, how? And if the latter . . . *why*?

Why has any of this happened?

Swallowing hard, I glance around for Mila before accepting she isn't here—I am alone—and force myself to return Filippa's hollow gaze. I resist the urge to approach her, to console her, because she wouldn't want it. She wouldn't want my questions either. Even undead, my sister is still my sister, and her grief isn't mine. As if sensing my thoughts, she shakes her head and clicks her tongue reprovingly before I can apologize. "The world doesn't live and die at your fingertips, ma belle."

At that, Frederic grimaces before stepping forward with a resolute expression. "This time it did." The wind ruffles his unkempt hair—dirtier now than I've ever seen it, and longer too. Shadows have crept beneath his eyes. Combined with the sickly pallor of his skin and the dark stubble along his jaw, he looks . . . haunted. "You aren't supposed to be here, Célie."

In his hand, he holds La Voisin's grimoire.

"Oh?" My nape prickles at the sight of it, and I shift away from the trellis to keep the path behind me clear. I can outrun Frederic now. If he attacks, I can flee to Michal's ship, and this time, he won't be able to follow us to Requiem—not until Yule next month. The protective enchantment around the isle won't lift until then. Still, it seems a wasted opportunity not to press for information first: about the revenants, about how to lay them to rest. "And where should I be if not here?"

My gaze falls to the grimoire.

"You should be *dead*." Spitting the word, Frederic lifts the evil little book between us and shakes it with frenetic energy. "The spell called for Blood of Death. It *required* your death—"

I gesture with forced calm to my sharp teeth, my terrible and beautiful face. "It might've escaped your notice, but I *am* dead."

"Not properly," he snarls, stabbing a finger at my sister, "or Frost would still be growing in her belly, and *she* wouldn't be so—so—" He seems to struggle with the words, his knuckles white against the grimoire. "She wouldn't be so *different* now." As if unable to resist, he pulls Filippa to his side, lifting his hands to cradle her face. The grimoire presses directly against her stitches. "Look at me, darling," he says softly, feverishly. "Please look at me. Just *look* at me, Pip, and everything will be just like it was before. We'll be together. We'll be *happy*."

Filippa gazes back at him, strange and unblinking. "I am looking at you." A pause. "Darling."

Frederic's expression crumbles. Whatever he hoped to see in her mismatched eyes is clearly no longer there, and after several more seconds, he releases her with a pained sound, his fingers lingering above her cheeks as if he still longs to touch her.

I might've once felt sick at his loss.

"She won't look at me, Célie." Though he speaks to me, he still stares at her like a starving man. "The Filippa we knew loved us. She would do anything for us, but this one—she won't—she says that she feels cold, empty, hungry, and I can't do anything to help. I can't *help* her because you're still alive. Don't you understand?" He drags a hand through his ragged hair before plunging it into his coat, withdrawing a crooked knife, and whirling to face me. Emotion chokes his voice. "None of this is right. None of this is what *should've* happened—"

"You expected differently?" I cannot keep the note of derision from my own voice. I should run. I should flea into the mist before he attempts to use that knife, but his movements are clumsier now. Slower. If I wanted, I could crush him with my bare hands, and part of me longs to do just that.

This man has taken everything from us—our innocence, our dignity, our peace. Like a thief in the night, he stole my very life, slitting my throat and draining every last drop of my blood, forcing it into my sister to steal her death too. I cannot feel sympathy for him; I cannot feel anything but disgust. "After Morgane tortured and killed her, after *you* punched a fist through the veil—dragging her back here, violating her body and soul—you thought she would remain unchanged?"

"I didn't *violate*—"

But I scoff, unwilling to hear any more. "The spell worked exactly as intended, Frederic. You woke her up. You woke all of them up, and now they're crawling out of graves across the kingdom, exacting vengeance on those who've wronged them. Perhaps next they'll come after *you*," I add with relish.

"They already *have*, little sister!" He thrusts the knife and grimoire into the air for emphasis. "You still don't seem to understand. Those revenant witches—they would've *eaten* me if not for—for—"

His eyes flick to Filippa, who stands calm and regal in her glittering gown, not a strand of hair out of place. My frown deepens as realization trickles in from my subconscious. Despite her macabre stitches and eerie eyes, she doesn't hold herself like the other revenants; she doesn't act like them either. The Archbishop tried to take a bite out of my cheek, after all, while the three at the docks did their best to devour everyone in sight. None of them spoke.

None of them slipped inside my mind and . . . reasoned.

Frederic's heartbeat quickens at the small smile on Filippa's lips.

"You've eaten," she says to me. "It suits you."

I regard her warily. "How are you talking to me, Pip? How have you *been* talking to me?"

"I've eaten too."

Frederic swallows hard at that, his hands twitching around the knife and grimoire. "She's been insatiable, Célie. *Insatiable.* It's all I've been able to do to keep her from—"

"To keep her from *what*, Frederic?" My voice grows louder as realization surges from a trickle to a flood. *Please no.* "What have you done?"

He lifts his chin defensively. "What I must."

And now I really do feel sick; it takes little effort to imagine my sister's mismatched face instead of the Archbishop's rotting one, her teeth on that man's thigh instead of the privateers'. It could've been her instead of them at the harbor. It *has* been her. With Frederic's help, she's been . . . *eating* people, truly eating them. Consuming their flesh.

Like you've consumed their blood?

Bile rises in my throat—at the comparison, yes, but also because I cannot tell whether it was her voice or mine inside my head. Pressure builds behind my eyes. "What have you done?" I whisper again. Because none of this is right—not her, not magic, not the witches, and not the revenants either. *Not me.*

Another sunken smile. "I made a friend."

Frederic's gaze darts between us in confusion. He still holds the knife and grimoire half-raised as if unsure how to proceed now that Filippa has joined the conversation. "A *friend*?"

She ignores him.

Gritting my teeth, I step forward, just as heedless of Frederic and his knife. Heedless of anything except the flat black of my sister's stolen eye. I want to shake her, to slap her, to rattle any kind of emotion from the horrid emptiness of her expression. My sister has always been secretive and withdrawn, but she has never—*never*—been unfeeling. She has never been cruel. "Who is it, Filippa? *Tell me.*"

"Pray you never find out."

But Frederic's patience has finally reached its end. Shaking his head, he snaps, "Enough of this. We came here to finish the ritual, and there will be no loopholes this time, no ambiguity and no escapes. You will die to resurrect your sister, and she will *finally* return to me." Lifting the knife and grimoire abruptly, near overwrought with purpose, he lunges toward me, and my knees bend in preparation to bolt, to find Michal and flee. To lose this particular battle as a means to winning the war.

And then, quite suddenly, Frederic stops.

The entire garden seems to still with him—to suck in a collective breath—as together, we look down at his chest. At the unfamiliar, black-gloved hand now protruding from it.

Oh my God.

Blood spurts from Frederic's mouth.

"Pip," he whispers, his eyes wide and unseeing—searching—but Filippa says nothing in return. She says nothing, and a single tear tracks down his cheek as he collapses to his knees, falling forward without another word.

Dead.

Frederic is dead.

CHAPTER TWELVE

Mon Mariée

A terrible ringing starts in my ears at the sight of Frederic's body, at his parted mouth and sightless eyes, because—because he can't be dead. He simply *can't* be. I retreat a small step, shaking my head in staunch denial. If Frederic is dead, all of this—it really *has* been for nothing, and how will we ever reverse his magic? How will we right all his terrible wrongs? How will Filippa—? *No.* I grip the trellis for support, refusing to accept the wreath of blood around him. Refusing to acknowledge the sting of my teeth, the burn of my throat.

The scent of roses.

Roses.

My fingers tighten on the wood. These withered blooms behind me cannot possibly be responsible for such an overwhelming scent. It seems to envelop me, to caress my cheeks with phantom hands, mingling with candle smoke and something else—an awareness, or perhaps a memory. It crawls across my skin like ice until I shiver with it, until familiar darkness blooms at the edges of my vision.

Whoever killed Frederic, I know him. I *recognize* him.

And when I look at him for the first time, my knees nearly give way.

"You're welcome for that," he says wryly.

At the sound of his voice, even the wind stops to listen, the autumn leaves floating eerily between us. My sense of dread only deepens at Frederic's heart in his palm—because it no longer resembles a heart at all. Now it resembles a withered black husk. Dropping it in distaste, the man dusts his gloved fingers on the leg of his pants. "Honestly, Filippa, I've only had ears for a week, and I wanted to stick them with something sharp every time he spoke. You owe us a very long explanation."

My mouth parts in shock at his callousness, and the ringing in my ears reaches a fever pitch.

"The *Necromancer*, he called himself." With a grimace, the man drops to his knee beside Frederic, plucking up the grimoire and wiping its cover on the grass. "Even his blood smells foul. Not like yours," he adds in an offhand voice, casting me a cursory yet appreciative glance. "I couldn't smell you before, but now I understand what all the fuss is about." Pausing thoughtfully, he extracts several glass vials from his cloak. "Though I suppose I'm really smelling *myself*, aren't I? Our scents are intertwined." To Filippa, he adds, "You might want to leave for this next part, darling. Go check on our little friend."

Without waiting for her to respond, he seizes Frederic's knife with quick efficiency, testing its heft in his palm before raising it high overhead. My eyes widen as I realize his purpose a split second before he strikes. With a cry, I leap forward to stop him—to snatch at his wrist—but he clicks his tongue reprovingly. In an instant, figures detach themselves from the shadows around us. Though the roses hide most of their putrid scent, they cannot disguise all of it. I freeze mid-step, eyes widening.

Revenants.

Everywhere.

"Ah, ah, ah," the man says with a wink. "We mustn't touch."

And without further ado, he drives the knife deep into Frederic's throat, collecting the blood that spurts in a sickening fountain. The scent of it doesn't provoke my fangs, however; instead I fight the urge to retch from the poisonous stench. "Not very pleasant, is it?" The man stoppers his first vial, then his second, examining each one in the overcast light. "Still, the blood of a Dame Rouge . . . who can afford to waste it?"

What is *happening*?

"F-Filippa?" Horrified, I retreat to the trellis once more. "Who—?"

Still cradling her stomach, Filippa stares at Frederic's blood for a long moment. Then, quite abruptly, she turns on her heel. "Remember our deal," she says flatly over her shoulder, and the man inclines his head in response. Thorns prick at my blistered palm as she just . . . leaves me here, and the fount of Frederic's blood slowly subsides.

The man before me whistles a merry tune, and I—

I've had enough.

Michal should be here by now. My panic spikes at the thought of why he hasn't found me, but I ignore it. I just need to locate him, and together, the two of us will find a way to handle the revenants. We'll deal with my sister too, perhaps bring her to Requiem for—for some kind of treatment. Surely *How to Commune with the Dead* will hold answers, or else Odessa will, or even—

My eyes fall to where the grimoire lies beside the man.

I saw the spell once in my aunt's grimoire, Coco said. *When I asked her about it, she shooed me from her tent and forbade me from speaking of it. I think it was the only spell she ever feared.*

A spell from that evil little book started all of this. Perhaps it holds the remedy too. Slowly, silently, I ease two fingers from the trellis, refusing to blink as the man continues his work at Frederic's throat, intent and distracted. I might not get another opportunity like this one. If he leaves with the grimoire, we might not ever see it again. I can survive the burn of my sister's cross; I can snatch up the grimoire before he plunges the silver into my chest.

I lift a third and fourth finger from the trellis, a fifth and sixth, holding my breath.

"A valiant effort." Without looking at me, the man pockets the last of Frederic's blood—along with the grimoire—before rising with a darkly satisfied smile. "But you're far too clever to provoke me."

"Who are you?"

"As if you don't know." Gesturing down his powerful body with a dismissive wave of his hand, he adds, "Though this part is rather new. Do you like it?"

A sense of paralysis seems to overwhelm me at the question. "I—I don't—"

"That's because you aren't giving me a proper look." He stalks closer, suddenly impatient, and lifts my chin between his thumb and forefinger. "Go on, then. Drink your fill. I can wait."

Roses snarl in my hair as I jerk away—because his words are too casual, too careless, to match the sheer violence in his wake. It frightens me. "Who *are* you?"

"Don't play coy, mon mariée."

His eyes bore into mine. At his feet, the grass has started to shrivel, his presence creeping outward across the entire garden. A bird falls dead from the tree beside us, and my body—it feels strange too. An awareness presses against my skin, raising the hair on my nape.

Mon mariée.

"No." I shake my head instinctively at the words, holding tighter to the trellis—nearly leaping from my skin when the wood cracks beneath my fingers.

Mila told me I'd been touched by Death, yes, but she hadn't meant *literally.*

She meant it as a metaphor, an explanation for my affinity with the ghoulish and the ghastly after surviving Morgane's torture—unwanted yet useful, especially during Frederic's twisted experiments last month. He broke the very foundation of magic when he began tampering with life and death, and—and— *He broke the very foundation of magic.*

In sheer desperation, I contort myself around him, darting beneath his arm and trailing dead roses in my wake.

"That isn't possible." I lift my hands placatingly as he turns to follow me, grinning again. The priests of my childhood never taught about Death—not as an entity, a deity in its own right. There was only God, and angels, and demons, sometimes even the Devil, but never Death. "You aren't— You can't be—" At the last, my voice turns decidedly pleading because—because Death cannot have a body. Death cannot be standing in this garden with mercurial gray eyes and dark windswept hair, and he certainly cannot have a *dimple.*

He called me his Bride.

Oh God.

As if he senses the direction of my thoughts, his grin widens, and his eyes seem to . . . swirl, somehow, like liquid silver. He brushes his hair away from them in a deceptively human gesture. Most would call the strands black, but they're deeper than my own, almost blue like a raven's wing.

"You *do* like," he says shrewdly. "How interesting."

Still backing away from him, I nearly trip over Frederic's corpse. "H-How are you here?"

"Isn't it obvious?" He nudges Frederic with his foot, and even though I despised Frederic—even though he deserved much worse than a quick and simple death—nausea rises at the sight of a boot on his cheek. At the smear of dirt it leaves behind. "This disgusting little insect upset the balance. He tore a hole through the veil when he stole Filippa from me—a permanent one this time. Not like the little cuts you leave behind." Death presses harder with his foot, his eyes flicking to mine. "I detest nothing more than a thief, but you'd know all about that, wouldn't you? Vampires are the greatest thieves of all."

Exhaling a harsh breath, I stumble to a halt and force myself to square my shoulders, to extend my hand. "Just give me the grimoire and I'll be on my way. I'll even"—I nearly choke on the words—"dispose of Frederic's body for you. The Chasseurs will never need to know what happened here. They'll never need to know about *you*, which means you'll be free to—to leave this place and forget all about us."

Please leave this place and forget all about us.

"A tempting offer"—tilting his head, Death listens to something I cannot hear—"but your merry band of men sounds a bit preoccupied at the moment. Something about vengeance and vampires and tits for tats." At that, my stomach plummets to somewhere between my feet, and I strain to hear beyond the garden. Death's presence seems to have silenced our immediate surroundings—as if all fauna fled with the wind, or died like the bird—but to the east . . .

Those could be shouts.

Chasseur Tower is to the east. The harbor too, which means . . .

Michal.

Fear twists like a knife in my chest at the possibility, and unbidden, my fangs descend. Death doesn't seem threatened by them, however. Instead his smile widens, and he laughs at me.

He laughs at me.

I look past him, chest tightening as the disturbance in East End reaches a cacophony. The shouts seem to be moving closer. And is that—steel on steel? Horse hooves? Though I concentrate with all my might, I cannot distinguish the individual sounds. Even so, *something* is happening over there, and all signs point to Michal and Jean Luc, perhaps even Brigitte. I clamp down on a scream of frustration. How absolutely *idiotic* of me to assume she wouldn't follow through on her threat in the alley.

"If you won't give me the grimoire"—I attempt to wriggle past him once more—"get out of my way."

Before he can answer, however—before either of us can do anything—the shouts pitch abruptly louder, and Michal's voice detaches itself from the rest, speaking calmly, quietly, despite what sounds like a horde of huntsmen at his back. "Where are you, Célie?"

My heart leaps to life in an instant, and I don't stop to think, to examine my profound relief, instead shouting at the top of my lungs, "I'm here! Michal! I'm over here!" Instead of wriggling, I now shove Death squarely in the chest, and he yields a single step.

When I wave my arms, rising to my toes in case Michal cannot see me, the man before me grins in wry amusement.

"Please, Célie, you must stop this incessant flattery, or I'll have no choice but to take you with me." He steps in front of me again. "Your sister won't like that."

Hardly hearing him, I wave my arms anew just as Michal rounds the corner, and my mouth dries at the sight of him, whole and unharmed and *furious*, moving faster than I've ever seen him. Lethal in his focus on the garden. On me. Several streets behind him, Brigitte shouts terse commands to the huntsmen, and in front of *her*—

My mouth falls open, and my vision narrows on Dimitri's face.

Dimitri.

He moves in a blur of amber skin and crimson velvet, laughing openly as he goads Brigitte, sidesteps Henry, trips Basile with a carefully placed foot. *He's distracting them*, I realize in disbelief. *He's—helping us. Why is he helping us?*

I cannot dwell on my confusion, however, not with literal Death standing before me. "My sister?" I ask him distractedly. "What are you talking about? She won't like *what*—?"

"I made a promise, my sweet, to exhaust every option, and my word is my bond."

He lifts an almost affectionate hand to brush a strand of hair away from my cheek. I recoil instantly—from both him and his bewildering words. "Good luck, mon mariée. I daresay you'll need it. How does that expression go—something about friends like these and enemies?" He clicks his fingers. "No, no. It's about keeping your enemies close. Yes, that's the one."

My face snaps toward his at that.

But with a polite bow in my direction, Death turns away, thrusting his hands into his pockets, strolling up the street, and whistling that same merry tune. Disappearing through the veil between one step and the next.

CHAPTER THIRTEEN

Taboo

Michal doesn't speak as I follow him through damp alleys and side streets. We avoid the main roads to the harbor, doubling back and circling around Dimitri and the Chasseurs, but before we can board the ship, I whisk into the consignment shop and thrust a handful of couronnes at Yves. Ignoring his baffled expression, I seize the basket of kittens and dart past Michal without offering either of them an explanation.

These kittens deserve better than a life at sea.

They're *cats.* They loathe water.

Undeterred, Michal follows when I flee across the gangplank, his expression rather frightening as I heft the basket of kittens higher. Though he says nothing, his silence reeks with the promise of a rapidly approaching conversation, and quite frankly, I don't care to have it just now—or perhaps ever. I don't care to answer his questions about Frederic and Death either, and I *especially* don't care to talk about my sister.

Filippa.

Her name is a knife in my ribs as I hasten belowdecks, the blade digging deeper with each step.

Filippa. Filippa, Filippa, Filippa—

"Célie."

Gritting his teeth, Michal reaches for my arm at the bottom of the stairs, but I jerk away from his touch, pushing forward blindly with my basket of kittens. "Everything is fine," I say in a horribly light voice. "Nothing even happened, really—"

Michal snarls in an uncharacteristic display of emotion. "The hole in Frederic's chest says otherwise, and I *saw* your sister—"

"What do you mean you saw her? She *left*—" I cringe at the slip, cursing myself mentally. Filippa must not have left at all, but how had Michal seen her? Why on earth had she sought him out? "Did she . . . say anything to you?"

"Regrettably, Brigitte's axe occupied most of my attention. Your sister made sure to watch."

I choke on a laugh, unsure how else to respond, to deflect—not if he saw Filippa. Not when he *did* see Frederic's broken body and hear Death's parting words. Michal has never been stupid. The three of them appeared within moments of each other in the same location; he'll have pieced together some sort of connection, even if he doesn't understand it—not that I understand it much more than he does at this point. There are simply too many pieces on the board to make sense of anything. Revenants. Frederic. Filippa and Death, even Dimitri—

Dimitri.

I stumble on the ornate carpet at the sound of his voice overhead. If I focus, I can just hear the whoosh of his body as he vaults over the bulwark and lands lightly upon the deck. "What is *he* doing here?" I snarl, whirling to face Michal and clinging desperately to my spark of anger. Anger is good. Anger is actionable.

Above us, Dimitri's footsteps falter. *He can hear me. Excellent.*

"He stopped Brigitte from sticking said axe in my back."

"Well, isn't that convenient?"

"You would've preferred the alternative?"

"Of course not, but where has he *been*, Michal?" Scoffing, I turn away again to storm down the corridor before answering my own question. "I'll tell you where—cozying up to my murderer to get a peek at his grimoire. It would explain why he hasn't sought us out until now."

"Would it?" Michal's eyes flash when I glance behind. "I didn't see the grimoire among Frederic's remains, Célie. Do you know where it is?"

Yes, I want to say, but something stills the word on my tongue. I dart up another corridor instead, praying he'll lose patience and abandon this very unpleasant conversation. "The grimoire is . . . gone," I say when he doesn't miss a single step. "We'll need to—to find some other way to manage the revenants—"

"Who was the man, Célie?"

But Odessa glances up as we pass the open ballroom doors. "There you are," she says from her desk. "Is that my brother I hear upstairs?"

At that, Michal finally stops short, seizing the doorframe with one hand to lean back and stare into the candlelit room at his cousin. She sits stiffly, gazing down at an open scroll without truly seeing it, her fingers white upon the parchment. "Yes," Michal says carefully. "He returned half an hour ago."

"He helped you escape the Chasseurs." It isn't a question, and she still doesn't lift her eyes from the scroll. She must've overheard our conversation in the hall, or perhaps she could hear the chase itself, which means—

Michal's eyes narrow. "Thank you very much for *your* help, by the way."

"You had the situation in hand."

"Did I?" Michal's scowl deepens as I skirt around him and hurry toward Odessa, who appears in desperate need of an ally. Dimitri, I notice, hasn't yet sought out their grand reunion. Probably a wise decision. He *did* snap her neck last month. "It felt a bit tenuous for a moment—probably as a revenant sank its teeth into my spine, and the huntsmen swarmed like ants."

Odessa's dark eyes simmer with anger as she finally looks up. No. With *hurt.* My chest twists at the sight of it. Odessa loathes emotion, and she strives to avoid it at all costs; of course her twin's disappearance affected her more than she showed. I should've realized it sooner, should've tried to—help, somehow, if she would've allowed it.

"What about the harbormaster?" Hastily, I plunk the basket of kittens onto her desk as the ship pitches beneath us. Through the wide windows of the ballroom—she tied open the heavy drapes to let in the dim morning light—the horizon begins to move. "He knows which ship is ours. He could tell the Chasseurs—"

A kitten with silver fur escapes the basket at that second, however, plunging into Odessa's lap. Her lip curls in distaste as it begins to meow and climb the bodice of her deep wine-colored gown. "He won't."

"How do you know?"

"Because I persuaded him otherwise." Nose wrinkling, she detaches the silver kitten and shoos it away while I try not to envision her persuasion tactics. "Why are there kittens on my desk, Célie?"

"You said sailors use them to catch rats on ships." I gesture around us, acutely aware of Michal's heavy gaze upon my face. "This is a ship, is it not?"

"You aren't a sailor," Michal says tersely.

I frown at him. He has every reason to be upset, of course—what with revenants and huntsmen attacking him all morning—yet I am *trying* to distract his cousin. "I don't need to be a sailor for cats to eat rats," I tell him coolly. "And I couldn't just leave them to rot in that shop—"

"So you'll leave them to rot on Requiem instead?"

A muscle flexes in his jaw, and while there is nothing inherently menacing in the gesture, I resist the urge to take a step back. I've never before seen him look so—well, *combative.* Not with me. The ever-present ice in his expression seems to have cracked since chasing after me, revealing something that looks suspiciously like agitation.

I am not, however, in the mood for an agitated Michal.

"They won't *rot.*"

Squaring my shoulders, straightening my spine, I dare him to argue. Because he isn't the only one growing steadily agitated; just the sight of him—his shoulders blocking the door, his eyes narrowed, and his hand still clenched upon the frame—sets my teeth on edge.

I hate being this aware of him. I hate being this aware of *myself* whenever he's near.

He apparently feels the same.

Patience snapping at last, he releases the doorframe and steps aside, gesturing Odessa into the corridor beyond with a curt swipe of his arm. "Go. The longer you delay your reunion, the harder it will be."

My eyes widen at his tactlessness. "But she doesn't want—"

"I know she doesn't," he says, his voice clipped, "but what we want and what we need aren't always the same things. Odessa"—he captures her gaze and holds it—"I haven't had the chance to speak with him at length, but he seems different now. He seems . . . better."

Her brow furrows. "Better?"

Michal nods. "Like before."

Odessa's expression empties at that—as if Michal's words have triggered some sort of defense mechanism—and she lifts her gaze to the paneled ceiling, where Dimitri hovers above deck. Where he waits. Instinctively, I realize Michal is offering Odessa the chance to speak with her brother first, to pass her own judgment before Michal and I enter the conversation. To pass *the* judgment.

I frown between them, unsure how I feel about that.

Dimitri snapped her neck, yes, but she didn't die. Not like I did. Still, it feels selfish—heartless, even—to point out such a thing when Odessa so clearly needs to work through his betrayal. Dimitri is her twin. No matter what he does, he will always be her twin; she will always love him, and . . .

How very difficult that must be.

At last, Odessa looses a slow and steady breath before nodding. "I'll speak with him."

Sensing her nerves, I snatch up the basket of kittens and thrust it into her arms. "Just in case you need some, er . . . armor."

She stares down at them without reacting for several awkward seconds. "They're kittens, Célie."

Heat creeps into my cheeks. "Right. I— You're right, of course." When I try to take them back, however, her fingers tighten on the basket, and she refuses to let it go. I drop my hands at once. Without a word of explanation, she lifts her chin, straightens her shoulders, and stalks across the room to do battle—but not before throwing a quick, appreciative look over her shoulder at me. "Thank you," she says quietly.

Michal closes the door behind her with an ominous click.

A jittery shiver erupts across my skin at the sound, and I descend into her chair with as much poise as I can muster. "What happened to the man with the revenants? Did he survive the attack?"

Michal doesn't answer right away. Instead he shakes his head as if disgusted and stalks forward. "No," he says at last.

My heart contracts painfully at such a simple, devastating word. "And the revenants?"

"Pulled apart and tossed to sea."

I remember the Archbishop with his corpse cleaved in two, each half still trying to slaughter us. "I don't know where the woman went, but hopefully she'll have time to gather her children and flee before the revenants find her again." I glance up, hoping he'll reassure me, but his expression remains scathing. A fresh pang of hunger shoots through me as our eyes meet. "Because they'll piece themselves back together and go after her, won't they? Coco said revenants rise from the grave with the sole purpose of terrorizing the living."

They also somehow recognized *me*, but it feels counterproductive to bring that to Michal's attention.

Still, he seems to sense my reticence, and the silence in the ballroom deepens until I can practically feel his anger burning my skin. At last, unable to stand it, I open my mouth to say something else—to ask about Brigitte and Jean Luc, perhaps how they found him—but he shakes his head, the warning in his voice clear. "Who was the man, Célie?" he repeats.

And here we are.

Swallowing hard, I knot my fingers in my lap and inspect my knuckles. *Just tell him.* The impulse to lie wages war against my better judgment, and I unclench my hands abruptly, tugging on a frayed thread at the sleeve of his cloak instead. *Just tell him, and he can help you. He* wants *to help you.* It makes little sense to keep Death a secret, yet a seed of unease still cracks open in my chest as Michal draws to a halt in front of the desk—because Michal will help me, yes, but as before, he might also hurt my sister.

No. He *will* hurt my sister.

If he learns Filippa might be a threat—that she made some sort of deal with Death—he won't hesitate to send her back to the grave. *As he should*, says that nasty voice of reason. *As you should.* But it isn't that simple either. Something more lingers in the shadows of my mind, half-formed and impossible to grasp. It compels me to stay silent.

Leaning forward, Michal plants his palms wide against the wood on either side of me. "Well?"

We stare at each other for a split second. Then— "He didn't tell me his name," I say quietly, inching back in my seat and holding my breath. "But I think he—I think he stepped through the veil after Frederic tore it open. He said something about a—a permanent hole this time. A door."

To my dismay, Michal doesn't seem surprised by the revelation. "He didn't smell like a revenant."

"No, he didn't, but—Filippa doesn't either." I wince again, cursing myself for linking them even in theory. I just—I can't *think.* My throat burns anew at Michal's proximity. Indeed, he stands close enough now for me to see the flicker of disappointment in his eyes before a bitter smile twists his lips. He knows I'm withholding something.

"Still a liar, I see."

"Because you're such a beacon of virtue."

He laughs softly.

"As you insist." Deceptively casual, he straightens, and the hair on my neck tingles in anticipation as I straighten too. Whatever Michal is about to do, I'm not going to like it—I'm *not.* My fingers curl into my skirt as his slip beneath the desk.

"And it seems you *do* insist," he says silkily. "From the moment we met, you decided I am the villain in this story, and nothing I do will ever change your mind, will it?" Though he tries to hide it now, his hurt still shines sharp as broken glass in his expression, and my stomach twists with inexplicable guilt. "Fine then, Célie. You win. We aren't friends. Shall we have a game instead? You've always liked a question for a question, and far be it from me to deny you anything. I'll go first, shall I?"

Before I can answer, he flicks the table aside like it weighs nothing, and it skids across the lacquered floor, scattering Odessa's scrolls in a flurry of parchment. Leaving only empty air between us, and then—when he steps into that too, deliberately closing the distance—nothing at all. Jolting at the sound, I swoop to gather her papers, guilt spiking instantly to indignation. "Michal! Have a care! These belong to Odessa. You can't just—"

"There you go again"—he looms over me as I kneel, entirely too close, too *tall*—"telling me what I can and cannot do. Why is that? I wonder. No one else claims such a privilege."

I glare up at him from my knees, refusing to scramble away. "Perhaps you shouldn't frighten everyone around you into submission.

It isn't *quite* the boast you think it is, and furthermore, you aren't particularly good at it anyway. I'm not afraid of you." Unable to stop myself, I lash out for emphasis—to prove my point, to knock him back a step—yet his legs could've been made from tempered steel.

That wretched twist of his lips deepens to a smile.

"No, you aren't afraid of me." Crouching slowly, he pries the scrolls away and casts them behind us. His own hands are so much larger than mine. So much stronger. My mouth dries when he poises them so gently around my delicate, useless fingers. "You never have been. Now answer the question."

"I didn't agree to play this silly game."

"I can think of a different one." His eyes fall to my lips. "We don't need to be friends to play it."

I snatch my hands away, cheeks blistering and teeth throbbing. "This isn't the time for games at all, and—and *someone* needs to tell you what to do, clearly."

"And that someone is you?"

"I—I don't know." Now I *do* scramble backward because Michal—he's shifted closer, somehow, without me noticing. His knee nearly brushes my hip, and one hand winds languorously through the ends of my hair, his knuckles brushing the curve of my spine with each pass. Everything inside me tightens at that touch. Though I try to shake my head—to tell him no, I am not that someone, not *his* someone—instead my neck tips back without my permission. My mouth parts on an exhale, and my fangs—

Oh God.

My *fangs.*

Humiliated, I lift a hand to hide them, jerking backward into the desk, and one sharp point pierces my lower lip upon impact. It draws blood. *His* blood. Or—or is it my blood now? I don't *know*, but a wave of delicious heat crests through me at the taste of him. I shouldn't like it. I shouldn't relish the thought of his body in mine, the thought that I've—*claimed* some small part of him, yet I do. And I have no choice but to watch helplessly as he rises with that terrible half smirk because he knows.

He *knows.*

"How ironic." He extends a hand, and when I take it, tentative, he hauls me to my feet—then tugs my fingers from my mouth, baring my fangs to his gaze. He stares at them without apology. He stares at the blood on my lips. "Here we are, the wicked and the righteous, yet I am the truthful one, and you are the liar."

My stomach contracts near painfully when he presses his thumb to my lip, coaxing another bead of blood to appear. My voice becomes a whisper. "Why is this happening to me?"

"You've been taught not to listen to your body. You've been taught not to trust it. As a vampire, however, ignoring your anatomy is not only tragic, but also dangerous."

But that's ridiculous. *All* of this is ridiculous, and— "I can't just *feed* on people whenever the urge strikes, Michal. I'm not like you. It isn't right."

"Why isn't it right? I never said to kill them."

"Because I *will* kill them! You saw what happened in the alley. I—I completely lost control. If you hadn't arrived when you did, I would've torn out Jean's throat, and I would've done *worse* to Brigitte. I wanted to do worse."

He presses harder with his thumb. "And a great loss that would've been for all of us."

"You're unbelievable." I resist the sudden urge to snap at him, to catch his thumb between my teeth and *bite* because—because that would be disturbing. Because people can't just bite each other in the middle of a conversation. "You just said we shouldn't kill—"

"What I said is the kill needn't be inevitable. If you want to rend every Chasseur's head from their shoulders, I'll wholeheartedly support that endeavor—I'll even help—but only the sickly and the starving lose control while they feed. So . . . yes, in this instance, I'll concede your point. If I hadn't arrived to pry the good captain from your arms, you would've killed him." A pause as he lifts his thumb from my lip, as he glares at the brilliant scarlet he left behind. *He hates it too,* I realize in a bolt of clarity. *The effect I have on him.*

Lip curling, he wipes my blood on his pants. "You probably still will."

"Excuse me?" I recoil instantly, my eyes narrowing in disbelief. "What did you just say?"

"Feign ignorance all you want, Célie. You're a vampire now. Everything we felt as humans, we feel deeper as vampires—anger turns to rage, pleasure to bliss. That means we're often drawn to the blood of those with whom we feel an emotional attachment. You proved that today." Clasping his hands behind his back in that infuriatingly superior way, he steps away from me. "If you want to protect your loved ones, learn how to feed—or don't. I don't particularly care what happens to your darling Jean Luc either way." He shrugs, his black eyes glittering with malice. "And you still owe me a question."

A question.

A snarl tears from my throat, and the sound is so foreign, so inappropriate, I can almost pretend it isn't mine. "Are you *jealous*? Is that what this is? I followed Jean Luc instead of you?"

"Don't flatter yourself, pet. You broke Toussaint's heart and nearly ate it this morning—I think we can do better, don't you?" Then, harsher still, "Three questions."

"Like hell." I stab a finger at his chest. "This isn't a game to me. Just because you're too *repressed* to say how you feel without guise doesn't mean I'm going to indulge you." He snorts derisively at that—as if I've said something hilarious—and I nearly scream with frustration, shoving him with two hands now. "What exactly are you suggesting, Michal?" When his cloak tangles at my feet, I hurl it behind me, searing with heat as scarlet washes across my vision. It smells like him. It smells like *us*. "And how can I learn to feed when I'm always *starving*? I just fed from you this morning—I drank more than I should've—yet even *looking* at you now, I want to—to—" I cannot finish the sentence, choking on the words, and he shakes his head in disappointment.

"Still refusing to listen to your body." When I shove him again, his eyes flash, but he refuses to yield a single step. "Four questions."

"You want me to listen to my body?"

"I do. Five."

Blood roars in my ears. Forget rending the Chasseurs' heads from their shoulders—I'm going to tear Michal into little pieces and scatter him across Requiem. Vision narrowing on his horrible, *beautiful* face, I lunge, but he sidesteps easily, catching my elbow and spinning me in a smooth pirouette. I slam my fist against his chest instead. To my astonishment, he doesn't try to stop me. No. He *steadies* me as I stagger backward, cursing and clutching my hand. "You want to hit me," he says, eyes blazing. "Good. Do it again."

"What do you—?"

"Hit me, Célie." He seizes my fist and wrenches it toward his chest. When I splay my fingers in protest, piercing his skin with my nails, he captures my chin in a brutal grip. If I were human, it might bruise, but I'm not human—and neither is he. Leaning low, he bares his teeth and snarls, "I can take your blows. I can take your bite too if you'll let me. What I'm *suggesting* is you feed from me until you learn how to control it."

I claw at his wrist, his chest, unsure whether I'm pulling him closer or pushing him away. "Why would you do that?"

The question acts like a bucket of ice water over Michal's head.

His body stiffens, and he hesitates, drawing back slightly to look at me. His eyes search mine for a split second, fraught with—*something*, but they shutter again just as quickly. And I hate it. I *hate* this newfound hesitation. Because Michal has never hesitated before. Michal has never recoiled from me. Indeed, when his hand falls from my chin, I want to strike him anew, to seize his shoulders and *shake* him until he tells me why he's acting so—so—

"You cannot hurt me," he says simply, his expression cool and unaffected. Too cool. Too unaffected. "Not like you can the others. *That* is why I'm offering my blood—because you must learn how to feed, or you'll never forgive yourself." And then, incredibly, "Six questions."

I stare at him in disbelief.

And in the instant it takes for those words to penetrate, I know exactly what I want to do. "You presumptuous *ass*," I hiss angrily. "You want to teach me how to feed? Fine. *Fine.* Let's go."

Shoving him aside, I storm out of the ballroom and up the wide, sweeping staircase in search of someone—anyone—with whom to prove him wrong.

Across the deck, Odessa and Dimitri rise from an enormous crate at the sight of me. I seem to have interrupted them mid-conversation, but Odessa's face has softened since she left us; the anger simmering in her eyes has slightly cooled. It's all the permission I need.

The time for answers and explanations will come later, but for now, a wave of recklessness crashes through me, and I march over to Dimitri without preamble. "Hello again, Dima. Michal says I need to learn how to feed."

Bemused by the abrupt greeting, he glances at Odessa, but he still accepts my hand without hesitation. He even presses a chaste kiss to my knuckles as Michal arrives, dark and silent as a shadow. "Nice to see you too, Célie darling. And how has my most delectable friend been faring since we parted?"

"She's been *starving.* Thank you for asking."

"Ah, yes." Dimitri grins, his gaze sweeping down my new figure. The impact is only marginally ruined by Michal's overlarge cloak and my stained nightgown, but he kindly ignores both. *Odd.* The blood down my front hasn't yet dried, but his body remains at ease. "We turned you into a vampire without teaching you how to act like one. Quite rude, wasn't it?" Flicking an arch glance around the deck, he lowers his voice conspiratorially. "Though between the two of us, there might not be much to teach. Everyone on this ship looks approximately four seconds away from begging you to eat their heart."

"Including you?"

Dimitri blinks in surprise before grinning wider, revealing his dimples. A devilish glint enters his eyes. "Don't tempt me with a good time, darling."

Michal scoffs.

Good. Though my cheeks warm, I force myself to stay still, to see how far I can take this. I've never acknowledged Dimitri's flirtation before—let alone indulged it—because the stakes around us have always been too high. Furthermore, he never actually meant it. He doesn't mean it now either, but he also doesn't seem able to resist playing with me. He loves a game, Dimitri, especially one that irritates his cousin, and I *do* need to eat. Wouldn't it be better to feed from someone I cannot accidentally kill? "You'd consider it, then?" I ask him.

I ignore the flutter of nerves in my stomach. Once upon a time, I flirted often—with Reid, with the local bookseller, with the handsome young men of society. Truthfully, I even enjoyed it. The thrill of a moment, a simple connection.

There is nothing simple about my connection with Michal.

Chuckling, Dimitri leans back against the crate. "Would I consider giving you my heart?"

Here goes nothing. With a delicate touch on his arm, I meet his gaze directly, and I smile—a brilliant smile, a glowing one; a smile I've never before given Dimitri. In truth, I haven't smiled like this for a very long time, and it feels strained and unnatural on my face. He doesn't seem to notice, however. His eyes widen infinitesimally at the sight, and he blinks, his pupils dilating as my fingers slide from his forearm to his hand. "Your blood," I say softly.

Immediately, I know I've said something—not *wrong*, perhaps, but odd.

Odessa—who'd been watching us with curiosity—looks away swiftly, and even Dimitri stiffens slightly. His hand remains clasped around mine, however, even as he leans forward and lowers his voice. "You're asking to feed from me?"

"Should I not?"

It isn't Dimitri who answers. "Of course you should," Michal says smoothly, "if that's what you want." I feel rather than hear him move directly behind me, his black eyes sliding down my body like shards of ice. I repress a delicious shiver. "*Is* that what you want, Célie? To feed from my cousin? I am sure he wouldn't refuse you—not after that smile."

In front of me, Dimitri carefully withdraws his hand.

Though I glare up at him—no longer demure but silently beseeching him to *stay*—he avoids my gaze, avoids Michal's too, and looks anywhere but at the two of us.

His lips, however, twitch.

Traitor.

Seeing no alternative, I spin on my heel to face Michal and crash right into his chest. "*Excuse* you—" Taking a hasty step backward, I collide with Dimitri instead, and he seizes my elbows to prevent us both from toppling over the crate. Michal's eyes darken at the touch.

And that—that is just unacceptable. "And what if I *do* want to feed from Dimitri?" That sense of recklessness crests higher, and I lean back against Dimitri's chest, trapping him against the crate as he exhales an incredulous laugh in my ear. "Why are you all acting like it's such a—a taboo request? *You* offered blood to me this morning, and no one batted an eye about that." I crane my neck to glare at Odessa, who no longer pretends to admire the horizon and watches us with rapt interest. "And you said blood sharing is perfectly acceptable between vampires."

"Did I?" she asks mildly. "I don't remember."

When Dimitri places light hands on my shoulders—as if unsure what else to do with them—Michal grips the mast beside him. His lip curls over his teeth. His very *sharp* teeth. "You're testing my patience, pet."

"I can feed from whomever I wish," I snarl.

His eyes flash, and beneath his hand, the mast begins to splinter. "So *do* it."

"I will!"

"I'm waiting."

With another snarl, I whirl again, spinning in Dimitri's arms and slinging my own around his neck. "Do you want to do this or not? Just tell me if you're too frightened, and I'll find someone else. I'll proposition this entire *ship* if I must—"

The mast gives an ominous *crack*.

Snorting with laughter, Dimitri glances between Michal and me in wild disbelief—like he's never seen anything quite like this. Like *us*. It only makes me angrier. "Well," he says, "when you put it like *that*—"

"Don't be an idiot, Dima," Odessa says sharply, half rising from the crate. "Can you not see they've started to—"

"Do not finish that sentence," Michal snarls.

"*What* sentence?" I storm toward him before realizing what I'm doing, not stopping until our chests brush, until I'm forced to look up, up, *up* to meet his gaze. My breath hitches at what I see there—derision, yes, but also knife-sharp longing—and my thighs clench in anticipation. He sees it all, of course. He always sees it all. "What is she talking about?" I ask softly, adopting his lethal calm. I do not mean to do it. I cannot help myself.

His eyes fall to my lips, and his jaw clenches. "Nothing that concerns you."

I seize his tattered shirt, resisting the urge to shake him, to climb his body until I can *feel* his muscles tense and flex beneath me. The strength in his fingers alone has nearly snapped the mast in half. "If you don't tell me, I swear to—"

"To who?" He bends with a vicious smile, hooking my chin with one of those fingers and ever so gently prizing it upward. "Not to God, surely?"

I rear backward in outrage. "What is *wrong* with you?"

His touch vanishes in an instant, and he retreats several paces away. "So many things, Célie." A bitter laugh. "So very many things."

Humiliation floods my face at the abrupt absence of him. And in this moment, I hate all of it—the distance between us, the loathing in his voice, the blood in my cheeks. *His* blood. I hate that it flushes my skin. I hate that it sustains my body. Most of all, I hate that despite everything, I never would've fed from Dimitri, and Michal seems to know it.

"An egregious oversight on his part not to have informed you," Dimitri says with a bemused grin, his dimples flashing, "but vampires don't share blood with other vampires outside of *very* intimate situations." He pauses meaningfully as if waiting for me to respond. When I don't, he glances between us and says, "Sex, Célie. I mean sex. Or love, I suppose, which must mean my cousin—"

Shaking his head, Michal stalks past his cousin to the stairwell, and—without so much as a word—shoves him overboard.

Dimitri hits the water with a deafening splash.

Smirking despite herself, Odessa peers down into the churning waves as Dimitri curses, still laughing, but she waves him off with a flick of her wrist before turning back to me. "He'll be fine. He can swim. And as for you—" She pats the crate, motioning for me to sit. "I wouldn't fret about any of this. Vampires do not possess long memories—after the first five hundred or so years, no one will even remember this little debacle—"

"Odessa," I manage quietly. "Please shut up."

CHAPTER FOURTEEN

Unexpected Visitors

Dimitri still wears an enormous smile when we reach Requiem.

In some ways, the isle looks exactly as I remember—the roads steep and narrow, the markets teeming with all manner of unusual wares, the castle looming above like a specter as a nondescript carriage winds down to meet us. A veritable feast of the senses, even to a human being.

As a vampire, however, it's an onslaught.

Dozens of hearts beat an erratic rhythm beneath the din of voices, of footsteps, of *breaths*, and I can somehow scent each one. I can *see* the latent hair follicles beneath each loup garou's face, the clawlike protrusions between their knuckles as two struggle to lift the gangplank. Likewise, the skin of a passing woman—a melusine hawking oranges to the disembarking crew—gleams like pearls in the torchlight. I stare after her, transfixed. She smells of salt. Of slippery, slinking things, and for some *maddening* reason, my teeth begin to ache at the scent, followed by that twist of disgust. I cease breathing immediately.

I avoid looking at Michal while we wait for the carriage.

Vampires don't share blood with other vampires outside of very *intimate situations.*

The words clang like a bell in my ear, echoing over and over again until my head rings. Not only did I proposition Dimitri in front of *everyone*, but I also fed from Michal.

I fed from him, and I liked it.

I'm not the only one changed since the last time I came to Requiem, however.

While Frederic's experiments had already started . . . twisting things on the isle before All Hallows' Eve—and everywhere else—he hadn't yet broken them. The ground might've oozed blood when I first trekked to the castle, but it hadn't trickled from the gables at the market like macabre tears. The shops and stalls themselves might've sold unusual goods, but at least those goods had been vibrant, scintillating—not strangely subdued, as they are now. Almost faded, like a veil of shadow has fallen over them. Or perhaps over my vision?

Due to a witch's trick, darkness has always plagued Requiem, but this . . . it feels different.

It feels almost like the *spirit* realm.

Frowning, I cast a glance up the street, but that eerie shadow remains. It clouds the faces of anxious passersby, the vagrant cats, the very cobblestones upon which they all walk. It drains the color from everyone and everything. The entire island. And the *air* here—

My frown deepens as I inhale tentatively. Though my throat burns anew at the scent of blood, it doesn't consume me like it would've before drinking from Jean Luc and Michal. No. Altogether more concerning is how the air *feels*—thinner than usual, and cold.

Much too cold.

It condenses into little white clouds from the mouths and noses of everyone in the market. Even Michal, who stands with his hands clasped behind his back—shoulders proud—and surveys the scene with his signature disdain. His cool gaze belies the tightness around his eyes, however.

Something is wrong here. Something is very wrong.

Silver flashes in my periphery, and my gaze snaps to where a translucent hem vanishes behind the nearest cart. My unease deepens as confusion builds, and I search the street for any other telltale signs of ghosts—because this isn't *quite* like the spirit realm either, rather an unnerving amalgamation of the two. I shake my head to clear it. The veil separates the realms; they simply cannot mix, and anything else would be impossible.

Then you need to pay closer attention.

Reid's words drift back to me, and I remember the blood dripping from Lou's nose when I opened the veil in her kitchen.

Swallowing hard, I shift closer to Michal as other figures gather in each nook and cranny of the street—crouching on rooftops and looming in alleyways—still and silent and predatory in their intent. I can see them better now than I did before. I can feel their attention on us like a honed blade pressed to my throat.

As if vultures to a carcass, the vampires have come.

The villagers can feel them too; sailors and merchants alike skitter away from their glowing eyes, ducking into pubs and shops as if instinct warns them to seek shelter. "I thought you quelled the last coup d'état?" I murmur to Michal. "Why is everyone so tense?"

Odessa's eyes cut to his with a darkly accusatory gleam. "This is not civil unrest." Thunder rumbles in the distance, punctuating her words, and those brave enough to remain in the street cast us furtive glances. "The villagers are frightened. The vampires too," she adds with a sniff. "They must sense the veil has torn, even if they cannot name their fear. They can certainly *see* its effect on the isle."

"They can see it?" I ask quickly. "The blood and the—everything else?"

Odessa tenses further, as if she wishes I hadn't spoken, but it is Dimitri who answers. "I assume they can, as I can see it too." He shudders and glances across the street, where the—the *skeleton* of a cat watches us, its spindly tail flicking. "Though it's a feeling too, isn't it? A *scent*."

My brow furrows as I tear my gaze from the cat, inhaling again. Beneath the thin, cold air—the electric charge of the storm—trace notes of another scent linger. "Do I smell something . . . floral?" I focus on it, following the scent through the brine and algae and sweat of the harbor, past the silk shawls and leather boots of a merchant up the street. *Roses.* My stomach clenches like a fist.

He tore a hole through the veil when he stole Filippa from me—a permanent one this time. Not like the little cuts you leave behind.

"And something else . . ." My voice trails away as I struggle to place the second, stronger scent. "What *is* that?"

"You smell it too?" Odessa sounds mildly impressed as I crane my neck toward the castle, trying to locate the source of that irresistible aroma. A peculiar sensation jerks through my belly in response, like a hook pulling me closer. "How interesting."

"Why is that interesting?"

"Because not everyone can isolate their own scent."

A flush creeps up my neck. "Are you telling me that scent is—"

"Yours," Michal says abruptly. "You smell like Death." At my appalled look, he shakes his head. "Not the literal scent of rot, Célie. You don't smell fetid. You smell . . ." He trails off in search of the right word before waving a hand. "Well, like *that*, and the scent has only strengthened since your transition."

"Excuse me?"

He doesn't clarify, however, instead gesturing to Pasha and Ivan, the two vampires who accompanied me on All Hallows' Eve. The former boasts sweeping black hair and frost-white skin, while the latter has shaved his dark head completely; both regard me with utter contempt in their pale blue eyes as they melt from the shadows to join us. It seems vampirism has not elevated me in their esteem.

Their reaction to my presence, however, pales in comparison to their reaction to Dimitri. Glaring openly, they move to stand on either side of him—to *loom* on either side of him—and a muscle jumps in Ivan's jaw while tendons flex in Pasha's throat. They must've heard of Dimitri's involvement on All Hallows' Eve, or perhaps of how he snapped Odessa's throat. Either way, they seem keen to make their displeasure known.

Dimitri appears not to notice, sliding his hands into damp pockets and addressing them each quite cheerfully. "Hello, Ivan." He inclines his chin. "Pasha."

Neither responds, and after a moment, Dimitri pretends to tug at his collar with a rueful grin. "Not winning any popularity contests these days, are we, Célie?"

Odessa's lips purse as she gazes past us toward the castle. "Worry not, little brother. They'll forgive you eventually." She says nothing of them accepting *me*, however, and her omission feels intentional.

"Pasha and Ivan have volunteered as your personal guards." Voice harder than before, Michal continues as if none of us have spoken, and I scowl at the obvious lie as a fat drop of rain lands upon my head. *No.* I wipe at the icy precipitation, examining it on my fingers. *Sleet.* "You may use them or not, but each shall remain at your disposal."

Odessa's eyes darken inexplicably. "Should that really be the priority right now?"

"Enough, Odessa."

"Is it?" Furrowing her brow, she speaks in an incredulous whisper, but I still hear her. Everyone still hears her. "Célie is a vampire, Michal. Should we be allocating much-needed resources to her protection when she can protect herself? There *are* still revenants terrorizing the isle, aren't there?"

Apprehension prickles my neck at her words. Though Michal has long deserved a thorough setdown from Odessa, I've never seen her openly contradict him. But I suppose there must be a first time for everything? Perhaps—perhaps this will be that time. Here. Now. About *me.*

I glance at the rather hostile vampires all around us before searching anxiously for the carriage. As if reading my mind, Michal says, "We'll discuss this later, cousin."

But Odessa refuses to let the matter drop, catching his sleeve. Hardly moving her lips at all now. "Is what Dima said on the ship true? Have they *eaten* two of us already?"

Oh God.

"How would Dima know? By his own account, he has not been on the isle."

Dimitri's grin vanishes at Michal's tone. "Margot wrote to me. She's been . . . frightened. A revenant attacked her shop last week. It climbed right out of an unmarked grave in the garden."

My stomach pitches at the thought of the soft-spoken Margot Janvier and her quaint fleuriste being ravaged by a corpse. "Is she all right?"

"Shaken but unharmed," he murmurs. "Her neighbor is a witch, and they trapped the revenant in a flowerpot."

Odessa presses onward before I can express my relief. "So?" she asks Michal. "Is it true?"

"And if it is?"

"If it *is*," she whispers, "I would urge you to reconsider assigning Pasha and Ivan to babysit Célie." She flashes me a vaguely apologetic glance. "Our priority should be ridding the isle of these abominations and protecting our people—as well as closing the *doorway* Frederic tore through the veil."

She heard me on the ship, I realize.

"They aren't coming through that one." Michal speaks almost absently, surveying the street overhead rather than looking at her. It feels almost . . . disrespectful, like he cannot be bothered with this conversation, but that also cannot be right. This is Michal. Everything bothers him, especially things regarding his precious isle. "They seem to be tearing through the veil near their graves—not that any such limitation exists once they're in our realm. The revenant at the fleuriste's fled halfway across the city before they trapped it."

Odessa stares at him in horror. "Are you saying a new door is created with each revenant?"

He lifts a shoulder. "I assume they're more like windows, but alas, I cannot see them—not like the other."

My brows contract at that. Michal shouldn't be able to perceive the veil, and neither should anyone else. "You can actually, er—*see* the door Frederic created on All Hallows' Eve?"

"Not the veil itself, no."

My frown deepens. "Then how do you—?"

Odessa seems much less concerned with the particulars.

"Never mind all that," she snaps, waving an agitated hand at the peculiarity around us. "Do you have any ideas on how to *mend* all these wretched holes?"

At last, Michal's eyes reluctantly meet mine, and in them, I see his answer. *Me.* I am the Bride, after all, and the only one with any real experience tearing and mending the veil. He flicks his gaze away. "I have plenty of ideas, Odessa, but none I am going to discuss here."

"Odessa," Dimitri says quietly when she opens her mouth to argue. Her teeth snap shut in a furious smile.

"Very well." Then, speaking through them as if unable to help it— "Revenants aside, Michal, the outside world now knows of our existence after All Hallows' Eve. The huntsmen know of our island, and they know of our weaknesses too."

"Jean Luc isn't stupid." Though every vampire in the harbor can still hear me, I lower my own voice and hasten to reassure her. "The Chasseurs would never come to Requiem—"

"They came for you once. They could come again."

I blink at her, shocked. She never mentioned any of this while in Cesarine, or even on the ship during our return journey. Perhaps if she'd voiced her fears, we could've assuaged them in private, but she never said a word. My frown deepens. "I don't—" I shake my head to clear it. "Jean Luc is just angry with me right now. He lashed out this morning, but after he calms down, he'll realize this is a fight he does not want and cannot win." I squeeze her elbow and force an encouraging smile. "The Chasseurs will not come here again. I promise."

For a split second, she looks like she wants to argue—with me or with Michal, I do not know—but she returns to herself just as quickly. *Like the flip of a coin.* My unease deepens at the abrupt shift in her expression.

It's a familiar one.

A *familial* one.

And it takes all of my resolve not to linger on the comparison between her and Dimitri.

"Forgive me, darling." With a sigh, Odessa lifts the hood of her cloak to cover her hair, and raindrops cascade around her shoulders like tiny jewels. "I meant no offense. I left my parasol in the witch's flower bed," she adds defensively to Michal, who still glowers, "and you know how I loathe being damp."

He rolls his eyes and returns his attention to Pasha and Ivan. Though I open my mouth to question her further, Dimitri shakes his head in warning, and I close it once more.

When the carriage at last rolls to a halt in front of us, I almost believe the altercation never happened. Neither Michal nor Odessa mentions the scent of Death or threat of invasion again. Unsure what else to do, I follow their lead and step up beside the wild-eyed horses. They toss their great heads in agitation as thunder cracks, followed immediately by another fork of lightning.

The dazzling light illuminates a gilt crest upon the carriage door as Michal opens it. Wreathed in flames, what appears to be a *cross* lies opposite a horned dragon upon the black lacquer. "Is this your coat of arms?" I ask despite myself.

He gives the crest a distracted glance before handing Odessa into the compartment. Something in her bearing still feels . . . off, somehow. Strained. I cannot explain it, but she takes great care to avoid my gaze as she settles upon the bench. "My father was a cleric," Michal says shortly.

"What?" Blinking in genuine surprise, I accept his hand and ascend into the carriage after her. "You never told me that."

"You never asked."

When he shuts the door behind me with a definitive *snap*, I frown between him and Dimitri. "Are you two not joining us?"

"Not yet."

"But what are you—?"

At that moment, however, a disturbance sounds from the ship, and all four of us turn as a member of Michal's crew races forward. Eyes wide, he bows low and addresses Michal breathlessly. "My apologies, mon roi, but you must come see—"

"What is it?" Dimitri asks curiously.

"Stowaways!" The young man straightens hastily and points to the ship, his cheeks ruddy with excitement. "Two of them from Cesarine!"

To my surprise, Michal doesn't move; he doesn't even turn, instead sighing heavily as if—as if *resigned*. "Where are they?"

"Here, of course," Lou says with a grin.

She strolls into sight with the air of one promenading through their garden on a sunny afternoon, which is almost laughable considering the bedlam in her wake. Michal's crew sprints after her with shouts of alarm, while the nearest vampires draw back with soft hisses of disbelief. Of fury. They must recognize her from All Hallows' Eve, or perhaps they sense the power rolling off her in waves. Either way, they are not pleased, and nothing about Louise le Blanc's presence in Requiem bodes well for Michal.

"You look much better, Célie," she says to me. "Funny, that—who would've known food suits you?"

Her own skin remains pale, however—*too* pale—and those

purplish bruises still linger beneath her eyes. Fingers trembling slightly, she looks almost feral in Reid's nightshirt—which she hastily tucked into worn leather pants—while a three-eyed raven perches precariously on her shoulder. *Talon.* A treasured pet, while also a symbol of the le Blanc family and her personal spy. But how did they—?

My stomach plummets through the carriage floor at who steps out behind them.

Quite suddenly, my confusion over the row between Michal and Odessa vanishes, as does all concern for Lou. Indeed, every thought in my head departs at the sight of the austere woman marching toward me. With each sharp click of her heels, she seems to *snip, snip, snip* all the strings tethering me to reality.

"Oh no," I whisper, half rising.

Oh no oh no oh no—

Leaning over to peer out the carriage window, Odessa says, "A relation of yours, I presume?"

I cannot bring my lips to move again, however. They've gone quite numb.

Because Satine Tremblay is the last woman in the world who should be on Requiem. Chin held high—back straight and stiff as an iron poker—she follows Lou with a look of utmost contempt on her beautiful face. Not a hair of her intricate chignon out of place, not a crease in her iris-blue gown. Though she holds a parasol high overhead, even the sleet seems to fear her. Not a drop dares to land upon her person.

Hastily, I refasten Michal's cloak over my nightgown and attempt to smooth my tangled mass of hair. A ridiculous impulse, of course, because—because—

Because this cannot be happening. The silver strands of hair at her temples wink in the torchlight, but my mind rejects them just as violently as the rest of her. It isn't possible. I would've smelled her *and* Lou if they hid on the ship, but beyond that, she just—she cannot be here.

For one wild, irrational second, I think to hide, to *flee*, as her emerald eyes lock with mine.

They pin me in place, narrowing infinitesimally as she inspects my new face. Only a lifetime of etiquette training prevents me from slumping in my seat. *I never told her I became a vampire.* I never told her *anything*, yet here she is now—surrounded by them. Does she know? Does she care?

The Chasseurs haven't exactly been discreet since we returned. Rumors of vampires have swept the city—probably the entire kingdom by now.

Though Jean Luc kept my secret, she must know about Michal by now. She must know about Requiem. And if she does, surely she must also know about *me.* And I hope she does. Just as swiftly as the thought descends, I realize I don't want to tell her anything.

Michal—the traitorous swine—steps neatly from the carriage as she bears down on us.

"Célie Fleur Tremblay," she says in the sharp, cutting voice she reserves for prepared diatribes. "Where on *earth* have you been? Why have you not written? What is this I hear about a scarlet dress and a *brothel*?"

I lift a weak hand, cringing. "Maman, it wasn't like—"

"Of course it was. Do you think I'm a fool?" Turning swiftly before I can explain, she points a finger at Michal like a judge with her gavel. Two bright spots of color appear high on her cheeks, and her nostrils flare with righteous indignation. "And *you*—what do you have to say for yourself? Did you care at all for my daughter's reputation when you whisked her away to this island of corruption and filth? Did you care at all for her mother's nerves?"

She does not wait for an answer. She never does. Someone should stop her now, however, before she finds her stride, otherwise we'll never hear the end of this. I gaze pleadingly at Odessa, at Michal, at Lou, but no one is foolish enough to interrupt. Lou, at least, has the decency to look apologetic. *Sorry*, she mouths with a grimace.

Dimitri simply grins—a wide, enormously entertained grin that makes me want to throttle him.

"You did not," my mother seethes. "Of course you did not. Even immortal, Michal Vasiliev"—I wince at the confirmation—"you still think like a man, but I will not tolerate such slapdash courtship from *anyone*—not you or the Devil or the king of Belterra. Do you understand me? There are conventions for such things. There are *rules*. They exist to protect young ladies from harm, and you have willfully disregarded each one in this desperate and, frankly, *unattractive* bid to procure my daughter's companionship. You've compromised not only her reputation, but also her engagement and her career—"

Even my mother must eventually inhale, however, and when she does, the sound carries across the entire harbor, which has fallen silent. As if it too has drawn a breath and held it, waiting for Michal to react. He is king here, after all, on this isle that values cruelty and calls it strength, and every eye fixes upon him in eager anticipation. My mother is not Odessa. My mother is an outsider, an interloper, and she just insulted him. He must react.

My limbs begin to tremble as he tilts his head.

This is bad. The useless thought plays on a loop, over and over again, yet I cannot think how to stop it. If I intervene, I could make things worse for both of them—his subjects cannot perceive him as weak, or tensions on the isle will escalate again. Neither, however, can I stand by and watch if he threatens my mother. Though my mind instantly rejects the thought of him doing such a thing, it also remembers Priscille and Juliet, even Christo, who lost his tongue for a simple question.

Please.

Like he senses the direction of my thoughts, Michal flicks his gaze to Odessa. She stares back at him in unspoken challenge. A current of understanding seems to crackle between them—a fissure of disapproval—before Odessa shakes her head and sits back in her seat, glaring out the opposite window as if unable to watch the proceedings. Lou frowns at her.

Michal, however, seems to make a decision.

When he inclines his head to my mother in a graceful bow, my limbs go hot and loose at the same time. "I apologize, madame," he says. "I have been careless with your daughter, but rest assured, she is in no danger from me. Indeed—" His voice softens further, and he addresses those shadows darker than the rest. "—if anyone should attempt to harm her or her companions whilst on Requiem, they shall swiftly regret it." Though he remains the portrait of civility, his black eyes glitter with malevolence as he adds, "Or perhaps not so swiftly."

Even my mother blinks at that. She deflates slightly as if just realizing the implications of trespassing on an island of vampires. Her sharp eyes dart around us. "Well, yes, that would be quite—er, I mean—"

She cannot seem to decide whether such a threat would be welcome or inappropriate.

I empathize completely.

"Get in the carriage, Maman." Lips still numb, I open the door before she can insult anyone else, and Lou seizes her elbow and frog-marches her inside. They settle on the bench opposite Odessa and me. "We should finish this discussion somewhere private."

As if desperately attempting to bring the situation back under her thumb, my mother glares out the window at Dimitri. "And what are *you* smiling about, young man?"

"This isle has needed a lady's touch for a very long time, madame—and how privileged we are that it should be yours." He flashes his dimples, bowing low and ignoring Odessa's scowl. "Célie has told me such wonderful things."

Though my mother harrumphs, a pretty wash of color spreads through her cheeks, and I watch his reaction closely. Once more, however, he *doesn't* react; instead he winks at me before rapping his knuckles against the door and walking away. My mother watches him go with a slightly mollified expression. "Well now, that—*that* is a gentleman, Célie."

Shaking her head, Lou leans closer and says in a low voice, "My mother once cursed an unfaithful consort to never speak my name without experiencing the agony of childbirth."

"Why are you telling me this?"

She leans back as if pained, her movements slow and stiff. "Just offering a little perspective."

"I'll return for you at dawn, Célie," Michal says before I can question her. "Your room and trousseau are exactly as you left them. If you wish it, Louise and your mother may stay with you, or they may reside elsewhere. Any room in the castle can be cleaned within the hour." Giving my mother another curt bow, he turns to leave, but my hand snakes out unexpectedly. It catches his wrist.

"Michal."

He tenses slightly at the catch in my voice, and the hair on my neck lifts as I *feel* the vampires focus on where I touch him. Swallowing hard, I struggle to withdraw my hand, to ignore the ache of dread in my chest. But I can't do either. I *can't* because Odessa is right, and everything has gone so irrevocably wrong. Because Lou is sick, Filippa is a revenant, and Frederic is dead; Death himself has stepped through the veil, and Odessa is fighting with Michal for reasons I don't understand. Requiem has descended into disarray. And my mother—she sits in the middle of it all, her familiar eyes burning with disapproval as she watches me touch a man who is not my betrothed.

"Is everything going to be all right?" I ask him.

He doesn't answer for a long moment. He simply stares at my hand around his wrist. Slowly, he turns his arm, sliding his own hand down my palm until our fingers touch. "I don't know," he says honestly.

And then he is gone, stalking after Dimitri until the rain swallows him whole. It feels oddly sinister to watch him go this time, and I flex my fingers as the shadows follow, wishing I'd asked a different question.

CHAPTER FIFTEEN

Like Mother, Like Daughter

"If I ask you to stay in your room tonight," Odessa asks when we reach the east wing, "would you do it?"

She stands silhouetted in my bedroom door, flanked on either side by the half-transformed demons of black marble. Their tortured expressions and batlike wings bring back memories of a simpler, happier time—when I remained blissfully human, blissfully naive, blissfully alone after my abduction.

Now Pasha and Ivan stand guard in the corridor, and Lou leads my mother down the sweeping stairs to the chamber below. With a deafening *caw!*, Talon returns to his preferred perch upon the mezzanine and hunkers down to watch us with his beady eyes.

"Why?" I ask Odessa.

She rubs her temples with the beleaguered air of someone desperate to leave. "Just this once, can we skip the deluge of questions? The castle is not safe tonight—"

"You said the castle is never safe." I study her with increasing suspicion. "What aren't you telling me? Are you and Michal planning something?"

"No," she says sharply—too sharply—before her voice softens again with what looks like supreme effort. "Please, Célie, as a personal favor, just stay here until Michal collects you at dawn. Do not leave your room."

"Odessa, what is going on? You and Michal have been acting—*strange* since we came ashore. If you want my cooperation with this mysterious plan of yours, you could at least include me in the details."

Her expression hardens, and her hands jerk as if she forcibly restrains herself from clapping them over my mouth. "There is no plan," she hisses. "There are no details. As a friend, I am simply asking you to stay in your room."

My eyes narrow. "Well then, as a *friend*, shall I remind you that revenants are still crawling across the isle? That the veil is in pieces?" I gesture to the tapestry behind her, where a golden-haired maiden once slept upon a crimson settee. She isn't sleeping any longer. With a knife in her chest and ashen skin, the maiden has clearly died; a black moth lands in the pool of blood beneath her. As in the market, the corridor beyond the tapestry appears drained of all life. Softened, somehow. Faint. Like an echo. "Something is causing this slow *rot*, and I intend to find out what it is—starting with the grotto. As Frederic performed the ritual there, I assume that is where the door formed too."

I remember Michal's hard, sidelong look. If the grimoire holds answers, they are lost to us for now, which means we must find our own. "Perhaps I can heal it," I say. "Perhaps I can send the revenants back to their graves."

Odessa sighs impatiently. "I hardly think it'll be that simple—"

"How can we know unless I try?"

"That rip will still be there in the morning," she says, her voice firm. "I'll even accompany you to see it. For now, though, just—take a bath. Rest. And no matter what you hear tonight, stay in your room." She levels me with a dark look. "I mean it, Célie."

Before I can refuse—because I *absolutely* refuse—Lou appears at my shoulder. "Of course, Odessa. We promise to be good little girls and stay hidden away all night long. Will that suffice?" She doesn't wait for Odessa to answer; with a cheery smile, she shuts the door in her face, murmuring, "*That* wasn't suspicious at all," over Odessa's vicious curse.

I lift a finger to my lips, silencing whatever else Lou might say, and wait for Odessa to pivot on her heel, for the sounds of her footsteps to fade up the corridor. Then—

"Why did you promise that?" I round upon Lou with a heated whisper. "Now we have to sit here and twiddle our thumbs—"

"Says who?"

"Says *you*—"

"I lied." Lou shrugs, thoroughly unbothered despite leaning on the balustrade for support. "She wasn't going to leave until we told her what she wanted to hear, and you weren't going to do it. That isn't a judgment," she adds hastily when I scowl. "Just a statement of fact—and now you won't be breaking your word when we slip off to the grotto. You'll be breaking mine."

I eye her warily. "Listen, Lou, maybe you should—"

"If whatever you're about to say is anything other than *come with me*, I don't want to hear it." Setting her jaw, she pushes herself from the balustrade—swaying only a little—before raking her hair into a bun. "I'm *fine*."

"You don't *look* fine."

"Well, we can't all look like vampire goddesses, can we? Some of us just look like *regular* goddesses—"

"That isn't what I meant, and you know it." I grip her elbow when she forces a laugh and starts down the stairs. "The veil is clearly affecting you more than the rest of us—which makes sense," I say as her eyes narrow. "As La Dame des Sorcières, you draw your magic from the land, and clearly, Frederic's ritual poisoned it. You almost collapsed when I tore through the veil for the séance, and here—well, this doorway seems much worse. I don't think you should come with me to see it."

Her nose wrinkles delicately. "And I think *you* should bathe before we go. Satine might swoon if she sees your nightgown in proper light."

We both look to where my mother stands beside the hearth, glaring down at the kittens scampering over her feet. They somehow reached the castle before we did. Likewise, every candle in the room has been lit. For some inexplicable reason, my chest warms at the sight of them.

All of them.

As before, they spill across every surface: the grand staircase, the marble floors, the vanity table and cluttered mantel, even the cracked silver tea tray upon the floor-to-ceiling bookshelves. The entire room sparkles in effusive candlelight. Except now I have no need of it. Now I can see in the dark. Michal would've known that, but I still appreciate the gesture.

My mother sneezes.

"Why did you bring her with you?" Tearing my gaze from the glow on my mother's hair, I drag Lou down the stairs and behind the silk dressing screen to the right. As with the kittens and candles, hot water and thick, jasmine-scented foam already fill the tub to the brim; steam curls from its surface in intoxicating tendrils. "How did you get here in the first place? I would've scented you on the ship."

"Are you sure? You sounded a little preoccupied."

"Were you *eavesdropping—?*" Oh God. If Lou heard me discussing *blood sharing* with Michal and Dimitri, my mother must've heard too, which means . . .

My eyes dart toward the dressing screen in panic. *She knows.*

Smirking at my horrified look, Lou lowers her voice and drops onto the stool by the tub. "She isn't an idiot, Célie. She would've figured it out eventually."

"Did she . . . say anything about it?" *About me?* I can't bring myself to voice that particular question, however. Sometimes it's better not to know.

"I think she's trying to pretend it never happened." Lou glances up at Talon, who has grudgingly flown from the mezzanine floor to the top of the screen in order to better eavesdrop. "Makes it easier for you, I suppose. You can decide when and where to broach the subject. And to answer your other questions—Talon followed you this morning. He saw someone murdering Frederic, and he flew to Chasseur Tower to warn me. By the time I reached the garden, you'd already left for the harbor. I couldn't catch you." Her lips purse abruptly. "*Thank* you for that, by the way—leaving without saying goodbye."

I glare at Talon, unfastening Michal's cloak before stripping my nightgown overhead. It crumples in a stiff pile at my feet. Once, I might've shuddered at my nakedness in another's presence, but it feels rather less important now. *I think she's trying to pretend it never happened.*

Of course she is, and that—that really is for the best. It's what I want too. My mother refused to support me as a Chasseur; why would she ever accept me as a vampire? Still, the thought weighs like a pit in my stomach, heavier than I expected. I probably disgust her now. Perhaps she even fears me. Perhaps that's why she refuses to acknowledge that I'm no longer human.

The injustice of it rears its head like a snake, striking at me without warning.

All at once, it matters very little that I didn't want her to bring it up—she still should have. She is still my *mother.*

"I wrote you a note," I tell Lou stiffly, "but I'm sure you already know that since you were having me followed."

"As if I could ever tell Talon what to do. He *likes* you, Célie, and he could tell you were upset when you fled the house. Anyway, we both felt *very* betrayed upon learning you'd run off to Requiem again—"

"Again?" Stepping into the tub, I hiss at the blistering temperature of the water. "I was *abducted* the first time—"

"—and we went to your room to have a nice long cry about it. That's when your mother arrived."

I dip my hair beneath the water, scrubbing the strands with lavender soap on the side table. "And you let her in the house because—?"

"We didn't," Lou grumbles. "A certain vampire of yours *broke down our door*, in case you've forgotten. It wasn't like we could pretend not to be at home. She saw the blood on our table straightaway, and she nearly went into hysterics—she said she knew you'd been there because she'd just visited Jean Luc, and she wasn't leaving until we produced you."

My stomach pitches like I've missed a step, followed by a swift, sickening spurt of shame. *Jean.* How could I have forgotten him? "How is he?" I ask quickly.

With the cup and pitcher on the table, Lou rinses the soap from my hair. "Coco was able to heal his wounds, but . . . he lost a lot of blood, Célie. A full recovery is going to take time."

I lower my gaze, unable to speak around the sudden knot in my throat—unable to defend myself at all. He nearly died, and it would've been entirely my fault. "Is he the one who sent the Chasseurs?" When Lou says nothing, I wrap my arms around my waist, feeling sick. "He wanted to kill us? To kill *me*?"

"He doesn't know *what* he wants to do with you." Sighing, Lou shakes her head, and tendrils of her long chestnut hair slip free from the knot at her nape. The freckles across her nose stand out in sharp relief. "But I think it'd be best if you stay here until he figures it out. Jean Luc has never been particularly even-tempered, and when Reid tells him about the revenants, he might conflate his approaches to the undead."

"He might kill us all, you mean."

To her credit, Lou doesn't lie this time. "He might."

In true Lou fashion, however, she refuses to dwell, plunking the pitcher down and saying, "Anyway, I was gently shooing your mother from the wreckage of my kitchen when she threatened to storm the shores of Requiem alone. She said she knew the harbormaster, and he would tell her exactly which ship to board."

"And you couldn't have prevented her? You trapped a revenant in a hatbox, for goodness' sake!"

"Well, I wasn't going to do that to your *mother*, Célie," she hisses, "and I couldn't let her come alone either. She has no idea about the dangers here. Even if this island wasn't *crawling* with vampires, magic has broken, hasn't it?" Grudgingly, she lifts a hand, and we stare at her trembling fingers together. "It's like you said—that idiot Frederic tampered with the natural order, and without the natural order, magic cannot exist as it should, including the enchantments on this isle. They'll be volatile. Erratic." Her gaze flicks to the screen, to the paper-thin silk with its once vivid violets and golden geese. The flowers have withered.

The geese are skeletons.

"I have to mend the veil," I say softly.

"Do you know *how* to mend it?"

"No." I cast a fleeting look around the screen as a bone-deep chill settles inside me. "After what Coco said about her aunt's grimoire, I thought maybe it might hold the answer, but . . ."

"We don't have it," Lou finishes. "I hope Frederic is rotting, wherever he is."

Part of me agrees, but . . . *one problem at a time.*

I need to deal with my mother.

With a sigh, I look back to Lou—determined yet unsure how to return Satine Tremblay to Cesarine—and find her staring up at the mezzanine. After a long moment, she flicks a finger to where a dozen painted portraits leer down at us between the shuttered windows. During my last stay on Requiem, those portraits became as familiar as old friends: three beautiful women draped in scarlet, the hook-nosed boy with his hounds, the lecherous old man with bulbous eyes. All of them appear dead now, except for—

The crone with a wart on her nose.

"Mathilde," Lou says simply, and my brow furrows as I remember. "My great-great-grandmother."

"Is she . . . still alive?"

"God, I hope not. She left the Chateau before I was born, but she'd be over two hundred years old."

My mother's footsteps click toward the screen, and another angry sneeze precedes her as she steps pointedly around it. The kittens bob along in her wake, swatting at the hem of the violet gown in her hands. She lays it carefully upon the table. "No woman can live to be two hundred years old, Louise le Blanc, and if she can, I am *sure* she laments it. Now, as the two of you seem to have lost all social graces, I must insist on inviting myself to this conversation."

She sneezes again.

"Are you . . . allergic to cats?" Lou asks tentatively.

"Yes." She snatches the thick towel from Lou's hands. "And *I* will do that, thank you, as Célie is *my* daughter."

We both blink at her, startled.

"Er—right." Lou shoots a contrite glance in my direction before hastily skirting around the screen. "I think I'll just have a quick word with Pasha and Ivan about procuring some food." She hesitates. "I assume there *is* food in this castle, right? Of the human variety?"

I nod mutely, but of course she cannot see me. In another moment, she closes the door to the bedroom, and silence reigns. I cannot stand it any longer than a few seconds, however. Not even with my mother. "I didn't know you were allergic to cats."

"Since I was a little girl." She sniffs and holds out the towel. "Are you finished? Your skin is starting to wrinkle."

It isn't, of course. My skin cannot wrinkle ever again, even in water, yet I step from the tub without a word, allowing her to wrap the towel around me. She doesn't speak either as she hands me silk underthings. I slide into them obediently, and she forces me upon the stool next, sweeping a gilt-backed brush through my hair. I sit very still beneath her ministrations, my throat unexpectedly thick.

My mother has never brushed my hair before.

She has never . . . tended to me this way. That duty always fell to my nursemaids and sister, while Satine Tremblay watched and censured from afar. Her hands are far gentler than I anticipated. Indeed, as she separates the hair at my crown, braiding it into a coronet, a shiver of pleasure lifts gooseflesh at my neck. "Your hair has grown too long," she says tartly. "We must arrange for a cut when we return home."

Home.

Just like that, the moment ruptures, and I close my eyes in defeat.

She does not want to have this conversation—not truly—but as she extends my gown, jerking her pointed chin for me to step into it, it seems we have little choice. For all her faults, my mother traveled a very long way, and perhaps she deserves some answers before she leaves again without me. Because—whether she chooses to acknowledge my new circumstances—I can never go home again. Requiem is my home now.

Requiem is for vampires.

Unsure how to begin, I swallow hard and glance down at the gown. Sewn of deep violet silk, it features voluminous sleeves that fall from my shoulders and taper to cuffs at my wrists. Ribbon laces up the front of the corset bodice, which angles to a V between my hips before flowing into a lavish skirt. The entire ensemble is lovely.

But of course it is lovely. My mother chose it.

Resisting a sigh, I fold back the screen and gesture to the squashy armchairs by the fire. "Shall—shall we sit down?"

"I thought you had plans at the grotto."

With another great sneeze, she nudges aside a pair of kittens that've just realized I'm in the room. They tumble over themselves to reach me until I crouch, taking pity on them, and stroke each of their heads. "I shall see to moving them elsewhere."

"You will?" Her eyebrows pinch together. "But do you not—like them?"

"Of course I do, but if you're uncomfortable—"

"Why do they paw at you like this?" she asks abruptly. "Why do they mewl?"

For someone determined to ignore the heart of an issue, my mother has the uncanny ability to get straight to it. And I suppose the beginning is as good a place as any.

"Because cats are guardians of the dead," I say heavily, "and I'm a Bride of Death."

Her sharp inhale echoes between us.

Perhaps a better daughter would lie. Perhaps she would reassure her mother, would fall into her arms and weep at the reunion, but I cannot bring myself to do any of it. I can only seem to scratch this fat orange tabby's chin. He needs a name—all of them do—and I focus intently upon the white heart on his breast while my mother waits for me to continue. *Toulouse.* Yes. This one shall be called Toulouse.

After another moment of silence, her mouth thins with impatience. "Well? Are you going to explain this unseemly moniker or not?"

Not.

"Maman," I say quietly, and the word is a plea. "I do not think you want to know."

"Do not presume to know what I want," she snaps.

A spark of anger ignites in my chest at that, but I tell myself she's grieving. I tell myself she's hurt.

"As you wish." With a slow exhale, I lift my chin to meet her gaze and instantly regret it. Filippa and I inherited our faces from our mother; if the two of us are black-and-white nesting dolls, this woman is the toymaker, and she carved us from her image. "When Morgane trapped me in Filippa's casket, Death touched me. He marked me separate, and he saved my life. Because of him, I can walk through the veil between realms and speak to spirits."

Her lips twist in dismay at that, but she does not speak. *Of course she doesn't.* We've never spoken about that nightmarish fortnight I spent with Filippa's corpse either. Not once. After La Mascarade de Crânes, Jean Luc returned me to my parents; he explained what had happened as my mother wept and my father stared, white-faced, out the parlor window. Neither inquired beyond the necessities—*is her mind intact? How quickly will she recover?*

Did anyone see?

Does anyone know?

At last, she opens her mouth to speak, but after hearing her question, I desperately wish she hadn't. "What do you mean Death *touched* you? Are you quite—quite unharmed?"

A bizarre impulse to laugh bubbles up my throat, and I almost give in to it. I almost slump forward—right there on the wet marble floor—and shake with laughter at my mother's feet. Because even *she* must sense how ridiculous, how utterly absurd, such a question is while we're surrounded by vampires and speaking of Death incarnate. Even she must know the answer.

Of course, the question she asked and the question she meant are two entirely different things.

Just as quickly as it arrived, the urge to laugh vanishes, and I rise slowly to my feet. "I don't know, Maman—would you consider dying in a sacrificial ritual before reawakening as an undead creature who craves blood *unharmed*, or are you simply asking if Death stole my virtue? Do you fear he ravished me in Pip's coffin?"

Her eyes widen that I would dare voice such sensitive matters aloud, and she splutters incoherently.

She never talked to me about sex either. She never talked to me about Filippa's murder.

I stare at her now, flames licking my insides as I remember Father Algernon's first visit after the catacombs. *Corruption of the soul*, he whispered to my parents. *Rotten fruit.* He thought I'd been possessed by demons because of my nightmares. He thought I'd been tainted with sin. Though my mother dismissed him instantly when he suggested an exorcism, I often wondered why she ever allowed him in the house. If she'd approached me first, she might've realized holy water was never the cure.

And now—now perhaps it's too late to have this conversation at all. "You should sleep," I say tersely, gesturing to the enormous bed in the center of the room. "You have a long journey ahead of you."

"But we haven't finished our—"

"We have." Stepping over the kittens, I stalk up the stairs to the door. Lou antagonizes Pasha and Ivan in the corridor beyond, and never in my life have I wanted so badly to join them. When my hand touches the doorknob, however, I hesitate, glancing down at her one last time. She still stands beside the silk dressing screen, her mouth parted slightly as she stares up at me, looking inexplicably bereft. "I'll speak to Michal about arranging your passage back to Cesarine in the morning. You never should've come here, Maman."

To my surprise, she doesn't argue, and in the yawning silence that stretches between us, I turn the doorknob and leave.

CHAPTER SIXTEEN

The Tear in the Veil

To my relief, Pasha and Ivan do nothing to stop me when I seize Lou's hand and pull her toward Michal's study. They seem to care very little about Odessa's warning. Indeed, they even share a dark look when I inform them where we're going. "Well then," Ivan says, bowing low and gesturing for me to precede them down the corridor, "far be it from us to stand in your way, mademoiselle. Of course you must flout Odessa and roam the castle."

In the same politely mocking tone, Pasha says, "You know better than us, after all."

I return their cold smiles with one of my own.

Their attitudes suit me just fine. All the more reason to leave them here. "Actually"—I bat my lashes sweetly, looping my elbow through Lou's—"I need you to stay with my mother. She'll be remaining in my room until morning."

The smiles slip from their faces, and a muscle feathers in Ivan's jaw. "We do not answer to you, humaine."

I ignore the supposed slight.

"But you *do* answer to Michal, and Michal said you're at my disposal, which means you're now at my mother's disposal too." Turning on my heel, I tow Lou forward, and she cackles with undisguised glee at the incredulous looks on their faces. "She takes lemon in her tea," I call over my shoulder as we round the corner. To Pasha, I add, "And I suggest you tie back your hair—she won't like it that way at all."

Lou is still laughing when we reach the obsidian doors of Michal's study. "Last chance to return to our room," I say to her, studying her face anxiously.

"Not a chance I'm missing this."

After a brief hesitation, I nod and push the doors open, but wherever Michal went upon leaving us in the harbor, it clearly wasn't here. Frowning at that, I cross to the curio cabinet, and the scent of candle smoke and roses nearly bowls me over as I click open the trapdoor in its floor. Lou lifts the back of her hand to her mouth, coughing, as she too smells it. *Death.*

Yes, the grotto is definitely where he stepped through—probably upon the very islet where Frederic took my life. With a lingering shadow of apprehension at the memory, I peer into the steep stairwell while Lou turns back to Michal's desk and snatches a candlestick, struggling to light the taper with a flick of her finger. It takes three attempts. "This place is still eerie as shit," she whispers, shaking her head in exasperation. "Fucking vampires."

"Are you ready?"

She nods, and as one of said vampires, I exhale slowly and descend the stairs first. Cobwebs coat my fingertips as I trail them along the stone walls, and really—Lou has a point. Why on *earth* wouldn't Michal clean these? It can serve no purpose to live in such inhospitable conditions. And perhaps it's just the silence, the shadows, the damp and ancient air as we slink belowground, but a chill skitters down my spine all the same. In a low voice, I ask, "Why do you think Odessa told us to stay put tonight?"

The sound of rushing water soon joins the soft cadence of

Lou's breathing, the thump of her heart. Though hunger twists my stomach at our close proximity, my mind flashes instantly and intolerably to Michal—to the potent taste of his blood—and I grit my teeth to maintain focus. "I don't know," Lou says after hesitating a moment. "She seemed nervous, but if something *is* lurking in the castle tonight, it doesn't seem interested in us."

This castle is very old, and it has many bad memories.

"Not yet, anyway," I say.

She exhales a soft laugh. "Not yet." Then, quieter still, "Your eyes are glowing."

And so they are. With each step, the strange silver light of my eyes—the light that marks me a Bride of Death in the spirit realm—shines brighter and brighter, illuminating the path to Michal's bedroom. The temperature creeps down with us. The air thins. Behind me, Lou's breathing grows labored, each exhale condensing into mist, and the first flakes of snow drift through the gloom to settle upon our hair. "Will I be able to see it?" Lou asks. "The tear in the—?"

The stairwell opens to Michal's cavernous room in the next second, however, and her voice breaks off at the sight before us. Any answer I might've given withers on my own lips—because nature, it seems, has answered the question instead.

Across the grotto, precisely where the islet once rose from the sea, swirls a colossal maelstrom.

"Oh my god," Lou breathes.

She catches my arm to steady herself—as if ensuring the scene is real—and for several moments, the two of us can do nothing but stand at the bottom of the stairwell and stare out at the price of Frederic's magic. Distinctly ominous with its hypnotic, slow-moving water, the whirlpool fills the width of the entire grotto. Bands of dark water eddy against the mica-flecked walls, and at its epicenter, the sea swirls down, down, *down* into a great chasm, a black abyss. It looks like the pupil of an evil and all-seeing eye.

Awareness prickles my neck.

"This goes deeper than the spirit realm." As I speak the words, I feel strange—keen—every hair on my body standing up as if crackling with energy. My eyes pulse brighter. If I focus, I can almost hear faint laughter, can almost *feel* gentle warmth emanating from the maelstrom's depths. Indeed, though snowflakes fall everywhere else in the grotto, they melt several feet above the water. And the sensation coursing through me—I recognize it. I've felt it once before.

Lou says nothing, simply stares at me with round eyes.

"After Frederic slit my throat, I sort of . . . hovered over everyone, and this golden light appeared. It called to me." Though I hear myself speaking, my voice sounds very far away, as if from deep underwater, while I stare into the maelstrom's eye. "Mila was there too. She told me not every soul chooses to remain in the spirit realm like ghosts do. She said some souls choose to go on."

Lou looks even paler now—almost bloodless. "Where do they go?" she whispers.

"Through there, I suppose." I gesture to the maelstrom, watching my arm move as if it belongs to someone else. "To whatever lies beyond it. Frederic tore the veil wide open."

That sense of strangeness intensifies the longer I stand here—as does a strong impulse to touch the water—and soon my knees bend without my permission. When I extend a hand toward the nearest ripple, however, Lou seizes my wrist in alarm. "I don't think you should do that."

A sharp, metallic scent punctuates her words. Like the strike of flint on kindling, my thoughts sharpen instantly, and my gaze snaps to where her nose has started to bleed again. "Lou?" Ignoring the sudden punch of hunger, I push to my feet to steady her. "We need to leave. You shouldn't be this close to the—"

"This is nothing." Voice faint, she sways again, wiping the blood from her face and staring at it in bemusement. "Getting a bit embarrassing, though. I can't keep—bleeding in front of vampires." Her fingers tighten around my arm when I move to drag her away. "No, Célie. You came to mend the veil. We aren't leaving until you do."

"I don't even know if I *can* mend it, and you look—"

"I hope you aren't about to say *fine*." Dimitri ambles toward us from the stairs, his hands in the pockets of a midnight velvet suit. A lock of his damp hair—freshly washed with citrus soap—falls across his forehead as he frowns down at us. "Because that would be the greatest lie ever told." He jerks his chin toward the maelstrom. "That thing is making her sick—making the entire *isle* sick, really, if all the blood and dead things are any indication. I stepped on a *maggot* in the hall upstairs—"

"So"—Lou shudders—"more blood and dead things than usual, then."

Dimitri grins at her. "You're a cheeky thing. I like it."

Though a dozen questions spring to my tongue, I push them all aside, instead looping my arms beneath Lou's shoulders and dragging her away from the water's edge. To my relief, she doesn't fight me, and distance from the maelstrom seems to stem the blood flow from her nose. Luckier still, the sight and scent of it seems to have little effect on Dimitri—and from experience, I know the sight and scent of La Dame des Sorcières' blood is among the most seductive in the world. My eyes still narrow with suspicion as I help Lou onto Michal's bed. "What happened to you, Dimitri? Where did you go after All Hallows' Eve?"

He sighs heavily before gesturing to the maelstrom—to the dark water dripping down the cavern walls that isn't really water at all. "Is this really the conversation we should be having right now?"

"It is."

"Then I suppose we must have it—though truthfully, there isn't much to tell." He strolls forward to lean against Michal's bedpost, tipping his head toward a recess in the cavern wall. I never noticed it as a human, probably because the swathe of black velvet covering the door blends perfectly into shadow. "Michal keeps his linens in there. They shouldn't be too hard to find. He's very *cleanly*, my cousin."

"I'm fine," Lou murmurs again, her eyes fluttering shut as she falls against the pillows. "Just a little light-headed."

"Are you sure?" When she nods, I perch beside her on the edge of Michal's bed before turning back to Dimitri. "And to be fair, everyone must seem cleanly to you. You've been living in a hoarder's den for the last five hundred years."

He rests his head against the carved mahogany wood and considers me for a moment. Then— "I threw it all out."

"*What?*"

With a solemn nod, he says, "I caught up with Frederic and your sister after leaving the grotto"—my chest freezes to ice—"and he promised to cure my bloodlust if I cured Filippa. Obviously I didn't realize the plan he had in mind, and I refused as soon as he revealed it."

"He wanted you to kill me," I guess.

He nods again, this time terse. "I should've ended his miserable existence right then, but I needed his grimoire first. The sick bastard guarded it jealously—kept it hidden at all times, wouldn't even let Filippa touch it." He shakes his head in disgust. "I'm not proud of myself for staying with them. I cannot condone my actions, but I've been trying to find my way back to you all since the day I left."

"Which is why you helped Michal," I say shrewdly, "when the huntsmen attacked him."

"I deserve that." When he sighs again, the sound is softer than before. Defeated. "Of course I deserve that, but . . . no, Célie. As hard as it might be for you to believe, Michal and I were like brothers once. No matter what we are now, I don't want to see an axe in his neck. *That* is why I helped him."

He moves to sit beside me on the bed, leaning forward to brace his forearms on his knees. Rubbing a thumb against his palm. When he looks up again, his eyes are sorrowful. Sincere. And I almost believe him—I *want* to believe him—as he says, "Words can never express how sorry I am about my role in your death. I know you didn't want to become a vampire, didn't *deserve* to become a vampire, and I will carry that regret with me for the rest of my eternal life."

I want to believe him so badly.

"It wasn't—" I swallow hard around the words, my voice a whisper. "It wasn't all your fault, I suppose."

The shadows in his eyes deepen as he realizes what the admission costs me. With the ghost of a bitter smile, he wraps an arm around my shoulders and pulls me to his side. "You're the best of us all, Célie, and I've always said it—much too sweet for Requiem."

They'd been among the first words he ever spoke to me. *Sweet creatures never last long in Requiem.*

And he'd been right.

My chest constricts with emotion, and suddenly, I cannot look at him anymore. It takes another moment to clear the lump from my throat. "Were you able to steal the grimoire?" I ask at last, already knowing the answer.

"I was not."

"Then how—?"

"Your sister found a cure."

"She did?" My attention sharpens to a knifepoint, and I look up hastily, searching his face. "How? What cure?"

"Ah." He releases me, his smile still a touch bitter as he reclines back on his palms to gaze at the ceiling. "I thought we might reach this little sticking point eventually, but I made a promise never to tell. I intend to honor it."

Beside me, Lou's eyes snap open, and she skewers him with a glare. "That isn't an answer."

His grin sharpens. "And that's rather the point."

"How can we ever trust you if—"

"You can't," he says simply. "But let's be realistic, shall we? There is nothing I can say—no evidence I can provide—that will garner your complete trust after what I did on All Hallows' Eve. Regrettably, I know this. I accept this. And all I can do is promise"—he sits up, makes careful eye contact with both of us—"that no harm came to anyone during my recovery. You may choose to believe me or not, and there is nothing I can do to alter your decision. However . . ."

He spreads his arms wide, gesturing to his chest, his teeth, and his eyes, which blaze with fervent light. "Just *look* at me, Célie. I haven't felt this way—I haven't felt this—this at *ease* since my own transition. Do you understand the miracle of that? Do you understand the *relief*?" He whirls to Lou next. "That I can sit beside you now—a human, the most powerful witch in the world—and hold a conversation without dreaming of a dozen different ways to kill you is unprecedented. I've never experienced it before. In over a thousand years of vampirism, I've never had this kind of *freedom.* I am healed. I am whole. And I will never return to the man I was before." He seizes my hand then. Squeezes it tight. "If you choose to believe *anything*, please, Célie, let it be that."

Over his shoulder, Lou meets my eyes, hers giving away nothing.

Leaving me to make my own decision.

His words are pretty, to be sure, and they *sound* genuine . . . but I've always wanted to believe Dimitri. That's always been the problem.

Returning my attention to the maelstrom, I ask, "How do we fix this?"

Lou struggles to sit up before Dimitri seizes her hand, hauling her upright with gusto. Her lips twitch. "I think the better question is how are *you* going to fix it, Célie. The maelstrom is a symptom, just like everything else. The real sickness is the veil."

As if sensing our conversation, the maelstrom shifts malevolently in response—the faint laughter vanishing abruptly, the gentle warmth freezing to ice—and several distended limbs thrust through the water's surface, desperate to break free of its current. I gape at them in horror.

An arm.

An elbow.

A foot.

"Revenants," Lou whispers.

Dimitri grimaces in distaste, and I nearly retch at the sight of them—all the sailors who perished around the isle when its magic wrecked their ships. Their corpses bob in the current once, twice, before the maelstrom surges viciously, swallowing them once more. And despite my hideous relief, it seems too cruel a torment to fathom: to drown, to die, to be dragged from death by an invisible hand only to drown all over again. This is their fate until we mend the veil—a task that has *perilously* fallen to me.

"Just try, Célie." Lou touches my hand with trembling fingers. "That's all any of us can do."

Nodding mutely—determined not to let her see my fear, my doubt—I attempt to look beyond the maelstrom. I focus on my hurt, my anger, my *hope* for Dimitri until the entire grotto shimmers, rippling like a mirage. And only then do I realize the full extent of the damage we caused. Because the veil—I no longer see it. I *feel* it, yes. I sense it. The shorn edges should be right *here* for me to guide back together, yet they aren't, which must mean . . .

I take a slow step backward, eyes widening as they search the cavernous ceiling, the walls, even the ocean beyond.

Nothing.

The realization impales my chest like a shard of ice thrown from Death's own hand: *He tore a hole through the veil when he stole*

Filippa from me—a permanent one this time. Not like the little cuts you leave behind.

The little cuts.

Why did I think it would be simple? After such catastrophic evidence to the contrary, why did I think Death would've simply wedged himself through a crack, perhaps twisted and contorted and hunched his broad shoulders to fit? No, this tear—Frederic's tear, *my* tear—must span the entire grotto, perhaps the entire castle, and how do I mend what I cannot see or touch? "I—I don't think I can," I breathe in dawning horror. In dread.

"Of course you can," Lou says fiercely. "You just need to try again."

Dimitri and I pull her up the stairs as she tries and fails to surge to her feet, and behind us, the maelstrom swells. A dozen more revenants resurface with it. They flounder in its swirling depths, and I feel myself nod, hear myself speak without believing any of it. "Perhaps—perhaps we should talk to Michal before we do anything else. He said he had ideas . . ."

My voice trails away, however, as the distant chords of a violin and the gentle clink of crystal drift down the stairwell toward us. I tilt my head and listen curiously. Soft voices soon join the revelry. A crooning laugh. A peculiar jangle, a metallic dissonance that could be another instrument. Though I cannot discern more through the rush of water behind us, the earth and stone above, it sounds almost like a party.

Then someone screams.

CHAPTER SEVENTEEN

A Black Soirée

With an arm around Lou, I rush up the stairs and through the curio cabinet, but Dimitri catches us at the door to Michal's study. "Whatever you're planning, I'd reconsider. Never is it a good idea to go chasing after screams in Requiem."

"But someone could be hurt—"

"And what of *you*? Are you not supposed to be tucked safely in your room?"

Tugging my elbow out of his grip, I stare up at him suspiciously. "How do you know that?"

Lou interrupts before he can answer. "Maybe Odessa was right, Célie. Maybe we should return to your room."

But *that* doesn't sound like Lou at all. She never hides from a fight, not even while pale and weak from our time in the grotto. Concerned, I lift a quick hand to her forehead, but the difference in our temperatures is too great for such a method to prove effective now. She swats my ministrations away and rolls her eyes. "I just think in light of—well, *everything*, perhaps we shouldn't charge off after the bloodcurdling shriek in a vampire-infested castle. If things go poorly, I don't think I'll be much help at the moment."

"Nor I," Dimitri agrees quickly, and for no reason at all.

I frown between them, dropping my hand. "Is there something I should know?"

Dimitri scoffs. "Isn't said bloodcurdling shriek enough?"

"No, it isn't—and once again, that isn't an answer." All the more determined now, I stride past him, grasping Lou's hand and pulling her toward the east wing. "But you're right—you should probably go back to our room. I'll escort you back before investigating—"

"Oh, no," Lou protests, digging in her heels. "You aren't leaving me with your mother."

"But if you're frightened—"

"I never said *frightened*, but even if I did, I'll never be frightened enough for that." Wiping the last of the blood from her nose, she squares her shoulders and marches in front of me unassisted. Now *I* hesitate, tearing my gaze from that smear of scarlet and swallowing against the dull ache in my throat. I'll need to eat soon, but I still have no idea how to do it—or rather, from *who.* Perhaps Odessa can help me until Michal returns.

My stomach lurches unpleasantly at the thought of her.

The lilting chords of the violin are louder up here, the murmuring voices too. Clearly, someone *is* hosting a soirée tonight, and as lady of the castle, I cannot help but feel Odessa would've known about it. Likewise, as neither Lou nor I received an invitation to said soirée, I can only assume she did not want us there. The thought stings more than it should. Though the vampires of Requiem have made it clear they detest me—and the feeling is quite mutual—I am one of them now. I have nowhere else to go.

Abruptly, Pasha's and Ivan's smirks rise in my mind's eye, their sneering and satisfied expressions. *They knew*, I realize with a sick twist in my gut. *They knew I wasn't invited to—whatever this is.*

Is this soirée the real reason Odessa warned me to stay in my room? Why Dimitri insists I return there?

Are they . . . embarrassed by me?

"Is there anything I can say to dissuade you?" Dimitri asks quietly.

I lift my chin in defiance. "No."

"I didn't think so." He sighs as if resigned, watching Lou disappear around the corner as that peculiar jangling sound grows louder, along with the laughter. "Fine, Célie. Just—promise no matter what you might see tonight, you will not intervene."

I scoff at him, already squaring my shoulders and turning to stalk after Lou. "I could never promise such a thing, and I most certainly *will* intervene if necessary." Because in the end, it matters very little that the vampires dislike me, that Odessa might've excluded me.

If they're hurting someone in this castle, I am going to stop them.

We follow the noise to the north wing of the castle, creeping to a halt outside the door of a much smaller and darker hall than the gilded ballroom of the masquerade. Sure enough, a dozen or more vampires mingle inside. Candlelight flickers upon their lovely faces, the crystal-cut stemware in their elegant hands, from a single chandelier hung high upon the arched ceiling, and instead of marble, ebony wood comprises everything from the parquet floors to the paneled walls to the minstrels' gallery. The quartet of violinists cannot mask the guests' soft hisses and jeers.

Because in the center of the hall—trapped in an iron cage—a revenant shrieks and claws at its captors.

Lou inhales sharply, seizing my elbow as she too spots the poor creature.

Someone has thrown a goblet of blood in its face; the liquid drips down its skeletal cheeks in macabre scarlet tears while a trio of vampires laugh, baiting it with a spear. No. Tendrils of rage lick up my throat. *Torturing* it with a spear.

They're torturing it.

As if realizing the same thing, Lou tightens her grip on my arm, or perhaps she recognizes the full significance of the situation before I do. Perhaps she recognizes the green ribbon tied around the revenant's wrist, the shredded butterfly wings pinned upon its back, because she thrusts me into a shadowed alcove near the door in the next second. She dare not speak, however. None of us do—not even Dimitri, who darts after us with a vaguely sick expression. *Do something!* I mouth at him, and Lou nods intently.

Grimacing, he pushes us to our knees behind an urn. *Like what?*

A dozen eyes flick in our direction as he crouches too, but curiously enough, the other vampires remain equally silent. Instead they smile.

Long, sharp smiles that lift the hair on my neck.

They dressed the revenant as me.

The thought should surely incite horror. It should spark fear. Vampires are vicious by nature, yes, but such cruelty transcends the bounds of usual violence—that they would ensnare and torment a helpless creature just to send a message is sadistic. It is *evil.* When another vampire seizes the revenant's wings, however, jerking its body against the bars for his friend to stab it, my vision clouds not with dread, but with rage. Because this—*this* is the truth of a vampire.

They are not beautiful, and they are not civilized.

And I want to hurt them. My entire body shudders with the

impulse. I want to smash their crystal flutes and claw at their cold smiles, their colder eyes. With a vitriol stronger than any I've ever felt, I want to bring them the pain they've brought this revenant. If not for Lou holding tightly to my arm, I'd stalk straight to the cage and unleash it upon everyone. I'd *relish* the bloodbath to follow, and—

And that heinous thought is enough to keep my feet rooted, to send my eyes darting around the hall in search of Michal. Because if anyone can bring a swift end to this soirée, he can.

No telltale sign of silver hair reveals itself, however, and as my gaze slides back to the revenant, I realize Michal cannot possibly be here. Even if the attendees *hadn't* dressed the poor creature as me, he never would've approved of something like this. No. I cast one last sweeping look across the room before switching tack to Odessa, but she too seems to be absent.

My brow furrows in confusion, and I glance at Dimitri, who resolutely avoids my gaze.

For someone determined to exclude Lou and me from the guest list, shouldn't his sister be here? Unless she didn't know about this gruesome soirée either. Perhaps she simply suspected the vampires would resent my return after All Hallows' Eve, and she warned me to hide as a kindness. And who *are* these vampires, anyway? Do they live in the castle too? Perhaps they're distant relations, or—

Lou nudges my ribs, gesturing toward the ceiling, and every excuse I might've given vanishes in a wisp of smoke. Because—it's them.

Odessa and Michal.

They're here.

Half-hidden behind the balustrade of the gallery, they stand locked in a heated argument, wholly oblivious to the scene below—wholly apathetic—as the revenant attempts to tear the bars from its cage. I stare at them in abject disbelief, my mind struggling to reconcile how two people for whom I've come to care could ignore such cruelty in their presence.

It is not my job to rein in Yannick, Michal once told me, but I thought—

My heart plummets.

Foolishly, I thought he might be—well, *changing* somehow, because the Michal who stroked my hair in that coffin, the Michal who risked his life in the grotto, cannot be this Michal too. His eyes narrow to glittering slits as he looms over Odessa. "If you do not reveal their identities, cousin, the blood of this entire room will be on your hands. Is that what you want? A massacre?"

Odessa throws back her head and laughs in response, but the sound lacks all mirth. "How rich to pretend you care about these people. Now let this *go.* No one brought a revenant into the castle. According to my sources, it found its way inside all on its own, and where one goes, others will follow. This is a real threat. If we do not address it, we'll have much greater problems than ribbon and fairy wings—"

"Butterfly wings," he snarls.

My eyes widen as I realize about what, or rather *who*, they are talking.

Lou's nails bite into my forearm now. Lifting a finger to her lips, she shakes her head when I move to rise, her turquoise eyes huge and her freckles stark. Even Dimitri places a restraining hand upon my shoulder. My mouth goes strangely dry at their reactions.

Because we have nothing to fear from Michal and Odessa, which means we have nothing to fear from anyone in this room. They just need to—to stop this, whatever it is, and release the revenant. Or perhaps not *release* it, but—

It snaps its teeth at a vampire who gets too close, and the rest of them jeer, shifting, pacing in a way that reminds me inexplicably of the cage they formed on All Hallows' Eve. A cage in which they trapped not a revenant, but other vampires, before tearing them to shreds. Juliet's screams ring in my ears at the memory.

And more than one pair of eyes flit to the gallery now, tracking every minute move of their king.

"Michal." Hissing his name through her teeth, Odessa does not cower from their audience, or the vicious light in his eyes. Instead she steps ever closer. "I do not think you realize how precarious our situation has become, so allow me to phrase it plainly: if you do not protect this isle, someone else will."

Her threat only seems to amuse him.

"Oh?" he asks silkily, arching a brow, and I crane my neck to look at Dimitri, silently beseeching him to intervene. Why *hasn't* he intervened? This is his cousin, after all, his sister, his *family*. "Is that someone you?"

Though Michal's voice remains light, his bearing seems to darken with the words, to pulse with a heavy and indefinable sense of power. Of presence. When he steps closer to Odessa, she winces slightly as if she too feels his weight. "As you have spoken plainly, Odessa, allow me to speak plainer still: *I* am king of Requiem, and I will defend this isle until darkness claims us both. If you do not agree with my methods, you may leave—*all* of you may leave—but know this—" His black eyes flick to the revenant below, to the vampires around it, who have fallen preternaturally still as they watch. As they wait. "When I discover who did this, I will find you, and I will make you carve a stake from your loved ones' bones before driving it through your heart."

Bile rises in my throat.

He shouldn't be saying these things. The mood of this room—it feels different from the mood on All Hallows' Eve. It feels poised on a knife tip, and my unease deepens when Odessa moves in front of Michal, stepping right onto the balustrade to block his view of the room below.

From my vantage point, however, I can still see him.

I can still see her too.

Dimitri. I entreat him silently, desperately, but he turns his face away from me. His fingers tighten on my shoulder.

"We cannot act in the interest of one at the expense of many, and we cannot—we *cannot*—lose our heads." Odessa lifts her chin in defiance, and emotion much darker than anger fissures behind her eyes when she speaks again. Emotion much deadlier. "Otherwise, one might question why you sent me to a witch's house in Cesarine rather than to find your own family. My own *brother*." A bitter pause. "If Dimitri hadn't found us in Cesarine, would you have ever looked for him?"

Dimitri's grip turns painful now. He still does not interrupt, however, not even as Odessa and Michal lock eyes.

In that single look, something unspoken passes between them—a dark understanding—but it vanishes too swiftly to follow. "I assumed he was dead," Michal says, lifting a careless shoulder. "Alas, we couldn't be so lucky."

Odessa recoils as if he struck her.

Beside me, Lou suppresses a groan while several vampires hiss in outrage. Worse still, one tosses the blood from his goblet high, and it soars toward the gallery in a magnificent arc, missing Odessa and splattering Michal's polished boots. The room draws a sharp, startled breath as Michal glances down at the blood.

Michal, no.

He cannot hear my silent plea, however, and when he strikes, no one can move fast enough to stop him. He simply steps from the gallery and appears with his hand at the offending vampire's throat, squeezing until the latter's eyes bulge. Every hair on my body stands up, and my intuition screams at Michal's reaction—not only the violence, but also something else, something critical that I cannot see or explain. I can only *feel* it. This entire situation—it does not make sense. It does not belong, does not *fit*, and didn't Michal defend his cousin only hours ago? Didn't he urge Odessa to speak with him, to listen to his explanation? *He seems different now*, he told her. *He seems better.*

Yet even as this bizarre sense of wrongness spreads, the atmosphere in the room shifts again. It coils like a serpent in the grass, and Michal has not yet realized the danger.

He still squeezes the man's throat slowly. Too slowly. "You forget yourself, Léandre."

"Stop this at once." When Odessa materializes behind him, I do not recognize the blazing light in her eyes. *Wrong!* My mind screams the word, and this—this has gone far enough. Someone must act. When I move to rise this time, however, the acrid scent of magic creeps around me, trapping me. I cannot speak. I cannot move. What is *happening*? Though I glare at Lou in furious accusation, she merely shakes her head, clinging to consciousness as she slides down the wall. Her eyelids flutter as Odessa snaps, "Stop this *now.* You are the one who has forgotten yourself, Michal, not him."

The vampire chokes and claws at Michal's hand. "Is that so?" he asks quietly.

"Can you truly not see it?" Odessa spreads her arms wide to encompass both the spluttering vampire and shifting crowd. "Your priorities have clearly changed—"

He snarls at that. "Do not blame Célie for this."

"Oh, this started long before you fell in love with a *human.*" She spits the last as an insult, and I momentarily cease struggling against Lou's enchantment, stricken. "This started with Mila's murder. For centuries, this isle has been our most jealously guarded secret, but because of you—because of your *obsession* with these women—the world has found us. The huntsmen *will* come. Perhaps not today, perhaps not tomorrow, but they will gather their courage eventually. They will bring their silver and their hatred, and they will come." In the tense silence that follows, the revenant lashes out, catching the nearest vampire by surprise and sinking its skeletal fingers into her wrist. She hisses in pain before breaking its arm. Odessa's lip curls. "And the revenants are already here."

Michal tips his head, considering her. Considering them all.

I resume my desperate struggling, begging Lou with my eyes to release me. Begging Dimitri. Because what Odessa said—it isn't all true. I *told* her it wasn't true. Revenants have risen, yes, but Les Éternels have nothing to fear if they act with discretion; if they remain on their isle and feed with consent, Jean Luc will never lead the Chasseurs here. He'll have no reason to do so, except for—well—

The truth of it dawns slowly, gently, as if even my subconscious had been waiting for me to realize.

Except for me.

I am the one who attacked him. I am the one who provoked a response. I am the one who revealed the secret of Les Éternels, of Requiem, of silver, and I am the one who forced Michal to make his debut to the world last month. The tension in this room—the violence—belongs solely to me, but . . . what else should I have done? What should Michal have done? We were trying to catch a killer, trying to protect the innocent and avenge his sister and—

My gaze slides back to Odessa's beautiful, lethal face. *If Dimitri hadn't found us in Cesarine, would you have ever looked for him?*

Odessa set aside her personal convictions to follow Michal's leadership. She set aside her despair at her brother's bloodlust and betrayal for the sake of Requiem—because Dimitri was dangerous, because he allied himself with Frederic.

At last, Michal releases the vampire, who crumples to a heap at their feet. "What are you saying, cousin?" Though soft, his voice cuts clearly through the hush of the room. Shadows gutter across half his face. "Do you challenge me?"

Odessa stares at him. Her eyes glint like knives, and her hands tremble. "I do not want this."

"Are you sure?" Michal steps closer, still tilting his head. "Clearly, you are not alone in your displeasure. Did you not plan for this exact stage, this exact moment when you invited me here?" She says nothing, and when he smiles, a physical chill sweeps through the hall; it lifts the hair on my neck, and I thrash harder against the enchantment. *Please, Lou.* Not even a finger twitches from my struggle. *Please let go—*

"And yet I ask you," Michal continues, "who has protected you all these years? Who has provided?" Though his gaze does not stray from Odessa, he clasps his hands behind his back and addresses the room. "Huntsmen, revenants—they are but a fleeting moment, and we are eternal. Let them come. We will eliminate this threat as we have eliminated all others."

Odessa, however, does not yield. "Célie will not stand with us when the huntsmen come. Are you truly willing to eliminate *every* threat?"

"As I see it," Michal says coldly, "the greatest threat before us now is *you*."

Everything stills at the words. Everyone quiets.

Though I still strain to move—strain to speak, strain to scream and throw myself between them—I remain motionless, trapped in this hideous moment as if floating in a dream. It feels surreal. It *cannot* be happening. I refuse to acknowledge the hatred in Odessa's gaze as she looks upon her cousin, the disgust in his own as Michal shakes his head, scoffing, and turns away.

"As I thought," he says in dismissal.

And she strikes.

Plunging her hand into his chest cavity, she seizes his heart, and he half turns—bemused—as his mouth parts on a shocking spurt of scarlet. *No.* Disbelief floods my system in a staggering wave, but Odessa does not stop. She does not falter. With a swift twist of her wrist, she thrusts outward with her free hand, and the vampires scatter in blind panic as Michal's body crashes through them. And perhaps I am screaming now, screaming and screaming as the world tilts beneath me, as he smashes against the wall in the far corner of the room, collapses, and moves no more. *This cannot be real.* I cling to the words, cling harder to Lou, whose entire body quakes as she whispers frantically in my ear. *This cannot be happening. Get up, Michal. GET UP—*

"He will not get up again, Célie," Odessa says quietly, and to my horror, I realize I've spoken the words aloud; Lou's enchantment has finally broken. Still I do not move, however, paralyzed with fear as Odessa looks directly at me. "Longue vie à la reine."

CHAPTER EIGHTEEN

Le Roi Est Mort

Long live the queen.

The words hover in the silence of the hall for a single moment—or perhaps all eternity—as time seems to stop, and I stare into the corner where Michal lies alone and slightly slumped, concealing the hole in his chest as if still refusing to show any sign of weakness. No one moves to inspect his body. No one celebrates his abrupt and tragic downfall, or even speaks at all. The vampires who hissed and jeered only seconds ago have frozen around the perimeter of the room, half-crouched and hidden in shadow, blood dripping from the shattered flutes in their hands. Stunned. Terrified. Dimitri's grip now bruises my shoulder, and Lou struggles to breathe, tensing as if preparing to flee.

Waiting.

We're all waiting, even me—*especially* me, waiting and waiting for something to happen, for Michal to sweep to his feet and regard us with that cold and penetrating gaze, to mock us for accepting his death so easily. Any second now, he'll wrench his heart from Odessa and slide it back in his chest before snapping her neck neatly in two. He'll toss her into the revenant's cage with Léandre, and he'll force us to watch as the creature rips them both to pieces. Because he is Michal Vasiliev.

Hundreds have challenged him in his thousand-year reign, yet he alone remains—didn't Odessa herself speak those words before All Hallows' Eve? *Here there is only darkness, and darkness is eternal.*

Creeping numbness spreads though my limbs as I watch him now, willing his body to rise.

Any second.

When Odessa drops his heart, however, it hits the parquet floor with a sickening, mundane thud.

And something ruptures inside me.

Lurching to my feet, I fling aside Dimitri's hand and bolt across the room, skirting around the revenant's cage and skidding to a halt when Léandre rises up to meet me. All at once—like another spell shattering—everyone else moves too. Vampires dart from the shadows like cockroaches, some vanishing through the door and others swarming to Odessa, while Lou appears at my shoulder. I pray she doesn't start bleeding again. "Célie—"

"He's DEAD!" Shouts echo through the corridors now—screeches and inhuman shrieks—ricocheting from the walls with a feral sort of glee, of rage, of disbelief until the entire castle seems to vibrate with the calamitous news, until the streets below teem with it too. "The king is dead!"

Dead! Dead!

The king is dead!

"LONGUE VIE À LA REINE!"

"Long live the queen!" A vampire near us screams the words, cackling wildly as she flings the revenant's cage open, and the winged creature lunges into the thick of the room, snapping and snarling—sinking its teeth deep into Léandre's foot—before sprinting through the door and out of sight.

Odessa stares after it with wide eyes. "Fuck."

Longue vie à la reine! LONGUE VIE À LA REINE!

"This is bad." Lou seizes my hand and backs around the now-empty cage, her eyes darting frantically in search of an escape. "This is really bad. This wasn't supposed to happen like—"

"Pasha! Ivan!" Odessa snaps her still-bloody fingers, and Pasha and Ivan attempt to detach themselves from the scores of guards pouring into the room, each adorned in their night-dark uniforms and golden crests—except it isn't the dragon and cross any longer. Now two foxes dance around a pillar of flame with words I cannot read, and the realization dawns swiftly, intolerably, sickening in every way. *This was planned.* Raising her voice over the tumult, Odessa thrusts her hands toward the door and contorts to see Pasha and Ivan through the crowd, but Dimitri appears at her elbow instead. "The revenant!" She thrusts him toward the door, panicked. "*Catch* it! Do not let it escape!"

With a quick nod, he darts after it, and—and he knew too. He *must* have known, which means everything he said in the grotto—

This was all planned.

"He's DEAD!"

"*Dead.*"

"The king is dead!"

Lou's hand grows slick in my own. "We need to get out of here. *Now.*"

Behind Odessa, a sallow-faced vampire tracks her movements with predatory intensity. She hasn't noticed him. Amidst the chaos, no one has noticed him, yet when he strikes—lunging for her throat—Odessa shrieks and whirls, decapitating him with a single swipe of her hand. Her eyes glow with indignation. "How *dare* you? It has been *thirty seconds* into this regime—"

Snarling across the room, Pasha and Ivan shove their way toward her, and I—

I dart to Michal's body.

Léandre's friends descend after two steps, however, forming an ominous circle around me and Lou. Desperate now, I strain to see through the gaps in their elegant bodies, searching for any opportunity to break through them. Because we must reach Michal before they do. We must—help him somehow, protect him, though my thoughts skitter wildly at how to do either of those things when he—when he looks so—

Dead! Dead!

The king is dead!

The floor starts to tilt, and blood roars in my ears as Lou presses her back against mine. We might be outnumbered, outmatched, but she will not leave me; I will not leave him either. Furious pressure builds behind my eyes as the shrieks outside escalate. Lou is right, this is not good, yet I *will* reach Michal. If it kills me, I will drag his body from this place, and I will—my chest shudders—I will bury him. No one deserves to die alone in the corner, but especially not Michal. *Not him.* I choke on another sob, darting forward, refusing to yield even as the vampires block my path, hissing and leering in anticipation. *Please not him.*

"Look how she trembles." Léandre's eyes glint with fervor as he steps down from the cage overhead. Deliberately gentle, he takes my chin in his hand, guiding my gaze away from Michal with the ease and entitlement of an aristocrat. Beneath us, the floor tilts again, and I grip his wrist to steady myself. He raises his golden eyebrows with a condescending smile. "Oh, how quaint you are, Célie Tremblay. How *lovely.* At last, we meet Michal's human pet—though not so human anymore, are you, my sweet? Still learning to be a vampire, yes?" He turns my face this way and that, examining it from every angle before exerting the barest pressure on my chin. I lift obediently to my toes, where I can see Michal's body over his shoulder. *I can see Michal.*

That sob climbs higher in my throat.

"Ahh, submissive too! Be still my cold, dead heart." Léandre's wistful sigh belies the evil gleam in his eyes. He reminds me of the vampires in the aviary—beautiful and elegant as they discussed how best to split my body between the four of them. I am no longer human, however, and my body no longer trembles with fear. Now it trembles with rage—a rage so potent, so vitriolic, that when Odessa glances in our direction, still surrounded by guards and revelers, I meet her gaze headlong. *Let her see me*, I think savagely. *Let her see what is to come.*

Her brow furrows slightly at my expression. A flicker of unease.

Good.

"Oh, sweetling." Pursing his lips in concern, Léandre wipes the tears from where they spill down my cheeks. "Oh, you poor wretched thing. You will need protection if you mean to stay in Requiem."

"She has it." Baring her teeth in a fierce grin, Lou lifts her hands, and the nearest of Léandre's friends wince and draw back from the light sparking at her fingertips. Though I see the tension in her shoulders—the great effort it takes to remain motionless, upright—the others do not. *Still no blood.* "I suggest you let her go now, Leopold, and we part ways as unlikely friends."

His head twitches in irritation. "Léandre."

"Not an improvement," Lou assures him.

Dead! Dead!

The king is dead!

The words still ring through the air like a war cry, and perhaps they are; this was a coup, after all—a triumphant one—and all over the isle, its citizens will be flooding the streets to fight or to feast or to mourn because their king is dead. *Michal is dead.*

I act without thinking. I act before Lou or Léandre even realizes I've moved, snapping his wrist and relishing the gruesome *crack* of his bones between my palms. Surprise flares briefly with it—because that was easy, too easy—and Léandre releases me with a howl of rage. As if I've left my body completely, I feel myself move around him, slipping between two of his friends—

One of them seizes my collar, my *neck*, and pain erupts down my spine as she wrenches me backward. Cursing viciously, Lou leaps to incinerate her arm, but Odessa materializes quicker than both, her expression blazing at the chaos unfolding in her court. "Let her go," she says sharply to my captor, a woman with flaming-red hair who glances to Léandre for permission instead. Odessa's eyes narrow.

Ignoring her, he flashes a savage smile in my direction. "You'll regret that, sweetling."

I lift my chin and glare back at him.

"Enough, all of you." Odessa pushes past us into the center of the circle. Though Pasha and Ivan both move to follow, bodily removing Léandre, she halts them with a curt hand. "You seem to have conflated my empathy for your plight with Michal as permission to do as you please. This could not be further from the truth."

"Couldn't it?" Though Léandre bares his fangs, he doesn't dare attack her with a horde of sentries at her back. Instead he glares at me with unconcealed rage and longing. "Are you not still protecting her, just as your cousin before you?"

"This has nothing to do with Célie," Odessa says in an impatient voice, "and everything to do with her master. Do try to *think*, Léandre, won't you? She is a Bride of Death. It would be foolish in the extreme to provoke him by attacking her." She seizes the flame-haired vampire by the shoulder, adding, "And if you continue to ignore me, Violette darling, I will pry this arm from its socket and use it to flay you in the street during my procession. Do we understand each other?" Her grip on Violette's arm tightens, and slowly, grudgingly, Violette releases my neck. "Good. Very good. Now—"

Throwing a disgusted look around the room, she walks *up* the cage in the next second, ascending over the mob to stand tall and proud before them on top of the iron bars. Somehow more vampires have joined the fray; they spill out into the corridor, wind through the guards, yet all of them—*all* of them, even the oldest, the foulest—avoid Michal's corner like it's diseased. Keeping one eye on Léandre, I creep toward it.

Odessa clasps her hands as she surveys the hall, and the gesture is so achingly familiar that I pitch forward, stumbling a little, and catch myself on Pasha's arm. He does not speak to me, does not stop me either, instead shunting me toward Michal as Odessa speaks in a clear, ringing voice: "The time has come, darlings, to get our house in order. We are not children"—she dips her head to the cage beneath her—"and we do not require playthings. We are *vampires*, and anyone who cannot comport themselves accordingly will lose the privilege of this isle."

Though crashes and shouts still echo from deep within the castle—and strange music unfurls from the Old City—all vampires within earshot fall still at her words. After so much commotion, such silence feels unnatural, even oppressive, as hundreds of predatory eyes gaze up at her without blinking.

Except mine.

They fix not on Odessa but on the fallen man in the corner of the room. Beautiful and terrible and alone.

Michal.

Falling to my knees beside him, I pull his body into my lap, and its heavy weight feels so real, so solid and stark amidst the dreamlike quality of this night; if not for the wash of scarlet on his chin and unnatural hole in his chest, I could imagine he is simply sleeping. My tears fall thicker now. Faster. They fleck his cheek before trickling down his jaw and disappearing into his leather surcoat.

I never asked him how to sleep. The thought is bizarre, unwelcome, yet it strikes like a bolt of lightning as I hold him, as I stare hungrily at the smooth planes of his face. Only once have I seen it like this, before the horrors of the grotto—relaxed and untroubled, completely at peace. I clutch his waist tighter, rocking him slightly, hating the words and the lie. *At peace.* As if anyone could find peace after such a violent and unexpected death. His cousin tore his heart from his chest. The hole is still there—leering at me—and—and I never asked him about philophobia either, or where he would most like to visit in the world. Why did he visit Les Abysses so many times and Paradise only once? Did his parents name him after someone? A loved one?

Had Michal ever been in love?

Though Odessa claimed he loved *me*, she also ripped out his heart a moment later, and I—I don't know what to do with any of it. Tracing his brows with my fingers, I memorize his face. I don't even know how vampires honor their dead—if they honor their dead at all. I do not know what Michal planned for himself, and the likeliest one who does is the vampire who killed him.

You never asked, he told me, and now I never can.

Somehow, we always seemed to talk about me—about my past and my sister and my parents. Are his parents still alive? Did he turn his father and stepmother like he turned Mila? But—no. Even as my eyes dart around the hall, searching for pieces of his face, I remember Odessa's supercilious voice: *In his entire existence, he has sired only his ungrateful little sister.* And she hated him for it.

How will I ever tell her?

I hear rather than see Lou move behind me, blocking us from anyone who might be watching. I hear Odessa too—her voice if not her words—and the procession gathering in the entrance hall several floors below. The strange music lilts higher from the Old City, growing wilder, less inhibited. Is the song to commemorate Odessa's rise or Michal's fall? I don't know—*I don't know*—and I wish someone would tell me what to *do*—

Unbidden, my gaze settles upon Pasha and Ivan, who both stand below Odessa in front of the cage. Wiping fresh tears from my cheeks, I study them with growing unease.

Then I sit bolt upright.

Instantly, Lou crouches beside me, her eyes wide as she searches mine. I seize her hand, terror-stricken and trapped beneath Michal, mouthing, *My mother.*

My mother is still in the castle.

The last of Lou's color drains from her face, and she too whips around—stumbling slightly—to stare at Pasha and Ivan, who should be standing guard outside our room. Pasha and Ivan, who left my human mother alone and defenseless amidst a vampire horde. *Oh God. Oh God oh God oh God*—

Squeezing my hand in reassurance, Lou lurches to her feet, and the lights at her fingertips flare as she shudders a breath. As she collects herself. As she slips through the crowd toward the door. Several watch her go, their heads turning slowly, their eyes glowing like animals' in the dark. They want to follow her. They scent her fear—they taste it on their tongues—and tonight, they want to abandon all ceremony and succumb to their primal instincts. Just as quickly as the urge flares, however, they seem to realize Lou is not frail or feeble; she is not prey. She has managed to trick them, and not a single vampire moves to follow La Dame des Sorcières as she vanishes into the corridor. Hideous relief surges as I listen to her sprint up the corridor, turn left, right, and hurtle down a flight of stairs without meeting a single soul.

Lou will protect my mother. She will hide her, and both of them will survive the night.

Still, a shiver of anticipation ripples through the room as Odessa finally descends from the iron cage, and sentries fall to either side of her to start the procession—and though I know nothing of Requiem and its rituals, I do know vampires. I know the true revelry is about to begin.

Many will die tonight.

I can only pray I won't be one of them.

I brush a loose strand of Michal's silver hair from his forehead, and I hold him closer as Odessa leads her courtiers and sentries from the hall. Perhaps she has forgotten me. Perhaps *all* of them have forgotten me, yet why would God answer a vampire's prayer? He won't even allow us to say His name. Sure enough, Léandre and the flame-haired vampire, Violette, hesitate by the iron cage to glance back at me. "Later," she croons at his soft hiss. "We shall find her later."

"You will not." Seizing her arm, Ivan tows her out the door. "You heard our queen."

"She still has use for the Bride." Pasha cuffs Léandre around the head when he snarls. "You will not interfere."

"What *use*?" Léandre snaps, but Pasha doesn't answer, instead thrusting him after the others and removing a key from his breast pocket. He turns pointedly to face me.

"Stay," he warns. "Her Majesty will return for you at dawn."

I'll return for you at dawn, Célie.

Face crumpling, I press my forehead against Michal's shoulder as his earlier words echo through the empty room. As Ivan closes the door with a definitive *click* and thrusts the key into the tumblers, locking me inside and leaving me alone with the corpse of my kidnapper, my protector.

My friend.

CHAPTER NINETEEN

Blooms of Heather

I do not know how long I sit in that corner with Michal, my eyes swollen and my face wet. Time loses all meaning. Distance too. Though I focus my senses on the east wing frequently, I cannot tell how many moments pass between each stretch. I know my mother remains safe, however.

Lou has bolted the door with magic and cast the entire room in strange silence, but I can still hear my mother demanding to leave—demanding to find me, demanding to summon Jean Luc and raze this entire isle. I close my eyes against the faint, echoing sound of her voice, inhaling deeply and committing Michal to memory: that rich, decadent scent of his blood, the woodsy leather of his surcoat. Both mingle with the lingering bite of Lou's magic.

Dull pain pulses down my throat, behind my eyes, and I wonder again—for the thousandth time—why she stopped me from intervening. Did Lou really hate him so much? Did she really want him to *die*, or did she not think Odessa capable of committing such a heinous act?

When the doorknob rattles, I tense, but whoever it is doesn't stop to investigate the locked door, instead following his companion to the entrance hall. Beyond it, the streets have succumbed to complete debauchery. Though eerie music continues from the Old City, the tone has shifted since Odessa and her retinue made their debut; the strings now shriek like saws, and the drums pound a violent and disconcerting rhythm. I struggle not to listen—not to examine the silence between drumbeats or the abrupt, blood-curdling screams.

At one point, I thought I heard Monsieur Marc's jubilant shout, but I quickly buried my ears in my hands.

If not for Lou and Dimitri, I could've prevented all of this. I sensed the shift in the air before Odessa killed Michal. I *knew*, somehow, that this time was different, that he was in real danger. I could've saved him.

She was just trying to protect you, says a small voice of reason. *They would've torn you apart too.*

But they didn't. My eyes snap open as another wave of fury washes over me. They *didn't* hurt us—they ignored Dimitri, and they feared Lou too much to attack when she fled the hall in search of my mother. And for all her posturing, Odessa refused to let Léandre touch me either. If only we had *acted* instead of crouching behind that urn, we might've been able to prevent such senseless violence. Now Michal's heart lies outside his body, gruesome and frightening upon the floor, half-hidden in the shadows of a cage.

His *heart*.

Though I sense it there, I cannot bring myself to look at it—to even acknowledge it—and I cannot touch it either. I cannot return it to his body. That fury crests higher with the admission, and I hate myself for having such weakness. Such fear. I am the worst sort of coward, and I have failed him in utterly every way. Michal, who has never failed me once. Michal, who climbed from the sea with a knife in his chest when I needed him. Michal, who raced toward me—*toward* me—when I confronted Death himself.

He deserved so much more than this. He deserved so much more than *me.*

I remember his dismissive wave in Les Abysses when I accused him of planning to maim my loved ones. *Every relationship has problems.*

Focusing on the memory, I part his leather surcoat and allow bitter regret to flow through me; I focus on his empty chest, and I slip through the veil to search for him, just in case. No silvery form awaits, however. Wherever his soul has gone, it isn't here, and snow falls gently upon the heather around his corpse. I frown at the sight of the small purple blooms. They grow straight from the black parquet floors, and Michal's chest—my frown deepens. The hole has vanished, the skin there nearly glowing with vitality. *Strange.*

The tears freeze upon my cheeks as I glance at the cage, where more heather creeps over his heart.

"Michal?" Voice a whisper, I shake him slightly, but his eyes remain closed. "Can you hear me?"

I wait another long moment for him to answer. When he doesn't, fresh tears trickle down my nose, and I return to the realm of the living, staring at the hole where his heart should be—dark and out of place against his broad alabaster chest. And I cannot fix it. I cannot fix *any* of this, yet I know I cannot remain sprawled upon this floor forever. Sooner or later, the sun will rise, and with it, Odessa will return with her nefarious plans.

She can choke on them, for all I care.

Unless the lock on the door has been reinforced by magic, it cannot hold me.

If Lou can still cloak an entire room, she can cloak us too. I can compel the necessary sailors at the harbor, and we can sail back to Cesarine—or to Chateau le Blanc. Odessa would not dare pursue us into the heart of witch territory. It would be the safe haven we need to plot our next steps, to regroup. We could research revenants in its great library. We could start our search for Death and my sister, could wait there for Mila's report. We could take Michal with us.

We could scatter his ashes someplace peaceful.

I clench his lapels until my fingers ache, envisioning the grove of pear trees in winter—the stark beauty of snow upon their spectral boughs. *He would like it there.* Still I cannot bring myself to move. The instant I do is the instant this nightmare becomes real, and—and *can* one burn a vampire to scatter their ashes? Each time I've seen a vampire meet true death, their body has turned to—to—

Realization crashes into me with the force of a battering ram. It makes me dizzy, light-headed, as I sit bolt upright and stare at the hole in Michal's chest.

His *perfect* alabaster chest.

Not an inch of it has desiccated, and according to veritably everyone, Michal became a vampire very long ago. In death, shouldn't his body have returned to its true age like Yannick's and Juliet's did? Shouldn't it be a withered husk? I spread my hands upon his shoulders with fervent energy, sliding them down his arms and *feeling* the contradiction. Though perhaps cool to the touch, his body remains hard and powerfully built, *alive*—and shouldn't the scent of Lou's magic have faded by now? My fingers curl almost brutally into his biceps. Perhaps a witch *did* enforce the lock on the door, or perhaps—perhaps death has changed since literal Death stepped through the veil. Perhaps Michal *is* dead, and this is just—this is what death looks like now. Perhaps flowers grow over all vampires in the spirit realm.

I brush a hand over his chest, and the scent of magic wafts with the movement.

It wafts *from* the wound.

Without making the conscious decision, I slide out from beneath him and dart toward his heart. Insidious laughter creeps up my throat, but I dare not release it. *Not yet.* Because if I'm wrong—

No.

I cannot think it, cannot even consider the possibility. Because Lou never would've controlled me with her magic otherwise. Pasha never would've left me alone under a simple lock and key, and Odessa—*Odessa.* I nearly choke on her name, remembering that blazing light in her eyes and her insistence—no, her desperation—that I remain in my room. She and Dimitri didn't want me to see. For whatever reason, they didn't want me to know she'd be plucking the heart from Michal's chest like the strings of the violins outside.

I scoop it up from the shadows without hesitation now; whatever fear I might've felt has transformed into something else altogether, and I cradle it carefully between my palms as I dash back to his side. "Michal, you *idiot*," I say breathlessly.

Before the entire theory can collapse, I plunge his heart back into his chest.

For a moment, nothing happens.

Nothing happens, and I can hear each of my own ragged breaths in the silence. The scent of magic remains thick and sharp in the air—sharper now than before—as I force his chest back together and close the wound. *Please.* To whom I pray, I do not know, for God surely does not sully his hands with dead vampires and witches' magic, yet I still do. I pray. "Wake up," I whisper fiercely. "Wake up, Michal, or I'll follow you through that maelstrom and find you. I'll drag your soul back into this foul room or—or worse, I'll *stay.* You'll never know a moment of peace because I'll be wherever you are too, pestering you and *pestering* you and never answering any of your questions. How many do I owe you now? Six?"

I suck in a breath, fingers shaking, as the edges of his skin try to knit themselves together.

"And those are just from a ten-minute conversation." I press the edges tighter, holding them, but this wound seems too great for his body to heal on its own. "Imagine how many I'll accumulate during an eternity of—"

"I don't—need to imagine."

Michal coughs, gasps, and I beam down at him through a haze of tears as his entire body shudders. I nearly lie on his chest now in an effort to close the wound, as if the strength of my will alone might make the difference, but he doesn't seem to care. "Célie." Chuckling low, he circles my wrists with his fingers, gently stilling my efforts. I cannot help it—fresh tears sting my nose as we stare at each other. His brow furrows. "What are you doing here?"

"You insufferable *ass.*" I cuff his arm lightly as one of those tears spills down my cheek. "How could you do something like this? How could you be so *stupid*?"

"I said I'd collect you at dawn."

Bemused, he watches the tear's progress before frowning and lifting a hand to wipe it away. He grimaces at the movement, and together, we look down at the hole in his chest, which Lou's magic still has not healed.

"What do we do?" I ask in a hushed voice.

He still lies flat upon his back, and I still lean over him, pressed entirely too close and probably covered in blood all over again. His head falls upon the parquet floor with a hollow thunk. "I need blood," he says simply.

"Oh." I nod hastily. *Oh God.* "Oh, right—"

"No need to look so frightened, pet." He grimaces again, fingers exploring the mangled mess of his chest, before struggling to sit up on his elbows. "Arielle is waiting for me in Odessa's room."

"What?" I resist the urge to scowl, helping him rise and ignoring the sharp pinch in my stomach. "But—you're meant to be dead. *Odessa* is meant to have killed you. Isn't it rather dangerous to bring Arielle into the subterfuge too—for all three of you? Er, that is—" My eyes widen at the sudden possibility. "Odessa *is* part of the subterfuge, isn't she? And Lou and Dimitri? This"—I gesture helplessly down his body—"was all part of some brilliant and hitherto secret plan no one included me in for reasons you're about to explain? And it'll preferably return the revenants to the grave and mend the veil too?"

I add the last part hopefully.

Michal falls back again, closing his eyes with a strangled laugh. It ends in a cough. "No. I mean—yes, Odessa assisted with the planning and coerced Lou into participating. I assume Dimitri stepped in when you refused to remain out of sight. But no to everything else." He cracks open an eye to look at me as high, unearthly voices rise in harmony with the music outside. "Melusines," he says at my unspoken question. "It seems not all the villagers will mourn my passing." He looks disgruntled at the thought. "Odessa will be intolerable."

I help him up again, and this time he drapes an arm across my shoulders; I wrap both of mine around his waist. "And just how," I whisper with a glance at the door, "are you planning on reaching Odessa's room without being seen? This place is crawling with vampires—"

His chin jerks toward the gallery overhead. "There's a passage."

"A secret passage?"

He flashes a grin, and at the sight of it—so natural and unguarded, so *unexpected*—my stomach swoops to somewhere around my knees. "Actually, we chose this room because the passage upstairs leads to a stage in the Old City, where a dozen minstrels wait to herald my miraculous return from the dead."

"Sarcasm is the lowest form of wit, Michal."

"But it *is* still wit, Célie."

At my scowl, he winks—he actually *winks*—before bending his knees in preparation to—what? I follow his gaze to the balustrade and realize his intent. Michal is going to *jump* with a great gaping hole in his chest, and—I hasten to bend my knees too, to support him as we leap from the floor below to the railing above. Though I nearly stumble, startled at the speed with which I just moved, Michal seizes my shoulder to prevent me from falling.

"This passage connects to a dozen others in the castle to form transportation channels and escape routes for the royal family. As the last members of that family, Odessa, Dimitri, and I are the only ones who know of them." His jaw clenches tight with pain. "And now you."

"Are you all right?" I ask in concern. "We shouldn't have—"

"I'll be fine, Célie."

I allow him to lead me to the center panel behind the musicians' chairs, where he slides his fingers beneath the trim on its edge and swings the entire thing open. With some trepidation, I peer into yet another dark and dank passage. "Don't think this absolves you from excluding me tonight."

"I require absolution?"

My face snaps toward his in disbelief. "I just held your heart in my hand, Michal. Your *heart.* Worse still, I spent most of the evening thinking you were—"

His eyes search mine as if seeking an answer for something. "Dead?"

"Yes," I hiss indignantly. "*Murdered* by one of my only friends in this wretched place."

Again, I glance toward the door. If any vampires wander too near or turn their attention too close to this room, the entire charade will come tumbling down on their heads. Shaking my own, I push him into the passage as gently as possible before swinging the panel shut behind us. We plunge into total darkness. Though I can still see well enough, I instantly regret the loss of light—or rather, the way my other senses heighten in its absence. The scent of Michal is enough to scramble my thoughts on a good day, let alone while clutching each other in the dark.

When he eventually speaks, his voice rumbles from beside my ear. "I'm sorry. I wanted to tell you about tonight, but Odessa . . . she preferred we didn't involve you."

"Why?"

To his credit, he does not lie. "No one judges you for it, Célie, but you've made your distaste for Requiem known. This isle is Odessa's home." A pause. "*My* home. Quite simply, Odessa didn't involve you because you didn't need to be involved, and I deferred to her judgment because I spent most of the night dead upon the floor. For the plan to succeed, she needed to feel confident in it—and in her ability to make these decisions without me."

"So she'll just—what? Pretend to be queen until the two of you decide otherwise?" Then, before he can respond: "Why *did* you decide to do this? Does it have something to do with the revenants?"

With slight pressure on my shoulders, he tries to start up the passage, but I dig in my heels, forcing him to stay here until he answers the questions. With a sigh, he says, "Odessa doesn't need to pretend. She *is* queen. Our performance tonight might not have been real, but the transfer of power was. I ceded the throne when I arranged for my public execution. For all intents and purposes, I *am* dead."

I wait for him to continue. To explain. When he doesn't, I glower up at him, but glowering isn't effective as leverage. "You still should've told me," I say at last.

"Like you've told me everything?" I recoil at that, and he seems to instantly regret the question, shaking his head and disentangling himself from my arms. Staggering slightly on his feet. After casting an apologetic look in my direction, he says, "We should go. The sooner I feed, the sooner we can leave—I've arranged a meeting with a witch on the far side of the isle shortly after dawn. She is very old, very private, but she might know how to kill a revenant."

"A witch on the far side of the isle?" I repeat faintly. "You can't even *walk*, Michal. And even if Arielle *does* help, how do you intend to traipse across the isle without anyone seeing you? You're supposed to be dead—"

"No one will see me."

"You don't know that!"

"I know this isle better than anyone, Célie. I knows its tricks, its traps, its secrets, and I know my own senses too—they're sharper than those of other vampires because my body is older and stronger. Odessa is the only creature on Requiem who could track me, and fortunately for all of us, she has better things to do." His jaw pulls taut enough to snap. "Are you satisfied now? Shall we go?"

I rush to support his elbow when he starts forward again, changing tack in an instant. "Yes, all right, *fine*, you're very powerful—I shall find you a medal—but are you sure Arielle will be able to help you?"

"You needn't join us if you'll be uncomfortable, Célie. You can wait in the passage."

My head is shaking before he even finishes the sentence. Because of course I cannot simply leave him to Arielle with such a serious injury. He almost died—I thought he did—and—and—"Is her blood potent enough to heal you?"

He keeps his eyes trained carefully upon the path ahead. "She *is* a werewolf."

"Yes," I snap, "but this isn't a simple wound, is it? I can still see your heart through your ribs. Given the circumstances, wouldn't it be more appropriate to drink something stronger? You—"

Michal halts abruptly. Sensing the change in him, I release his arm without another word, and violent flutters erupt in my stomach as the full weight of his gaze lands upon me. "Speak plainly, Célie. What are you suggesting?"

Shit.

"I, ah—" Panicked, I glance around us in search of an answer, but nothing in this dismal passage seems likely to rescue me. "I am merely *suggesting* you might heal faster—better—if you drink from someone more powerful."

"You mean a vampire."

"P-Possibly—"

"Which one?" When I do not answer, he sways again, planting a hand against the low wall beside him. His entire body bows with strain. "Which vampire, Célie? Name them, and it is done."

For one belligerent second, I almost rattle off a name—any name—to spite the provocation in his eyes. Just as quickly, however, I imagine him actually *feeding* from the unknown person, and anger scorches through my chest, incinerating the possibility. And just like that, there is nothing else for it. Michal cannot feed from Arielle, and he cannot feed from anyone else either. "Me," I say a bit forcefully, lifting my chin before I do the sensible thing and flee. "You're going to drink from me. Now take off your shirt."

CHAPTER TWENTY

Blood Sharing

Michal eyes me warily for several seconds, as if I'm a strange and dangerous animal that could turn at any second.

I quite like it.

"Shall we?" I gesture to the hard ground, relishing the twinge of pain on his face as he finally nods and eases down the wall. That vindictiveness fades, of course, when I move to step over him and catch sight of his chest again. My breath hitches. "Why did you do it?" I ask him again. "You never answered me."

He tugs the cravat loose at his throat. "My priorities have shifted."

"And that means—?"

"Célie," he pleads.

"Right," I say hastily. *Later.* "Should I just—?" I motion toward his lap, refusing to feel awkward, even as Dimitri's laughter echoes in my ears. *Vampires don't share blood with other vampires outside of* very *intimate situations. Sex, Célie. I mean sex.*

But none of that matters now. Michal is *hurt*, and besides, nothing fundamental changed between us after I drank from him in Cesarine. Now I can return the favor. Now I can help him too. "Should I sit with you?"

He nods again, resting heavily against the wall and closing his eyes. Whatever triumph he might've felt at provoking me seems to have yielded to exhaustion. "Your shirt," I remind him. "We should take a better look at your chest."

"I can't get it over my head."

"I can do it."

Trying not to disturb him, I sink onto his legs as gently as possible, careful not to brush my shoulder against his chest. With slow, painstaking movements, I first ease the leather surcoat from his shoulders, down his arms, before sliding his shirt up his body and over his head to reveal the wound beneath. It looks all the more shocking without clothing to shield it. All the more gruesome. "Is there a particular place the blood tastes best?"

With a ragged breath, he eases his knees farther apart, and my backside settles in the cradle of his thighs. I swallow hard as the billowing train of my gown floats around us. "Anywhere," he says faintly. Though he does not open his eyes, he drapes one arm across my legs, while his other hand settles lightly upon the small of my back.

Anywhere.

It becomes impossible to swallow now. My throat constricts to the size of a needle, and—as if sensing my irrational nerves—he begins to draw slow, soothing circles upon my back. "This dress is beautiful," he murmurs. "You should wear it always."

"I—" I gape at him, momentarily distracted, and wonder if his heart transplant has also transplanted his personality. Then I remember my manners, glancing down at the voluminous violet skirt. "Thank you. I believe Romi created this one under Monsieur Marc's guidance. Would it be all right if we use my, ah—" I shake my head quickly to clear it. "What I mean to say is—do you find my wrist—?" *Acceptable*, my mind screams. *Do you find my wrist* acceptable? But the distance between my brain and mouth proves too far to travel, and I stumble over the words.

His eyes open to slits. "I find your wrists perfect."

Oh God. We're sitting entirely too close for him to look at me this way, but I cannot think how to move without making the situation worse. Indeed, his body seems to fill the entire passage—all long legs and broad shoulders and *blood*—until the scent of him overwhelms everything. Until my head spins with it. *I should hold my breath.* Yes, I should hold my breath and look away, should offer my wrist without further conversation, yet *now* my mouth decides to speak. "O-Or you could drink from my throat if you prefer."

His hand pauses on my back. "Is that what you would prefer?"

"I just meant—if it would help—"

"Célie." He speaks my name softly—so softly I must lean closer to hear it—and brushes the hair from my neck with aching tenderness. "While I appreciate the offer, there are . . . things you should know before we do this."

The way his voice lowers on the word *things* feels strangely significant. "Is this more nonsense about blood sharing?"

"It isn't nonsense."

"Of course it is." I blink at him anxiously, searching the planes of his beautiful, ashen face; his color has grown worse, and his mouth tightens with pain. He needs to feed, and he needs to do it quickly. When I move to twist in his lap, however, to straddle his waist and ease his access to my throat, his hands slide to my hips, stilling the movement. "I understand the implication of intimacy, but it isn't like we're *actually* having—" My throat closes around the rest of the sentence, and I pivot hastily at his strained expression. "I thought you said vampires share blood all the time—"

"Not all the time, but they can, yes. They *do.*"

"Why is there a problem, then?"

"There isn't a problem. It's just—when two vampires share blood, they—they change. They change, Célie," he says softly.

"Michal—" Though I wriggle to free myself, panic mounting at the glassiness of his eyes, his hands remain like manacles around me. "Let me go." Voice firm, I clap my hands upon his jaw and force him to look at me. "If you don't feed soon, you're going to die—*really* die this time—"

"I won't die."

"You don't know that! No, *listen* to me." Careful not to jostle him, I seize his wrists and pry them from my hips, trapping his hands against my chest as I manage to turn at last. Nose to nose now, I ask, "Will it hurt me if we share blood?"

His voice is a whisper. "No."

"Will it hurt *you*?" The barest shake of his head, and at last, his body surrenders, falling back against the wall once more. "Then we're doing this. Now shut up and take my blood." And without another word, I release his hands, thrusting my own behind his head and lifting it to the crook of my shoulder, forcing his mouth to my skin.

He exhales once—a cool, delicious breath that sends a shiver down my spine.

Then he parts his lips, and his teeth pierce my skin.

Instantly, I suppress the urge to moan. A languid sort of pleasure ripples outward from the sharp, aching pressure of his mouth, and when he adjusts his grip, biting deeper, harder—his tongue cool against my skin—I tip my head back. I relish the sensation. I forget that I am Célie and he is Michal, and I breathe his name.

His hands curl into fists at the sound.

He keeps them pressed to his sides, however. He takes care not to touch me at all, holding his body completely still—tightly leashed—but I've never possessed his strength of will. My mouth parts on a harsh breath at the inexorable pull of his teeth, his *tongue*, and I cannot help it—I want to touch him now. I want to do *more* than touch him. Worse still, I want him to touch me too—really touch me—and all at once, I might die if he doesn't.

My gown.

The thought rises swiftly, imperatively, because the swaths of violet silk are in the way. Wresting my skirt upward, I free my legs before settling against him, skin on skin, my bare knees clamped around his hips. "Michal," I say again, and he shudders slightly at the plea in my voice. My entire body tightens with him. Because I've never felt Michal shudder before. With the realization comes a heady sense of power, and I seize his hands, bringing them to my hips and dragging them up my waist. Gasping at the strength in those fingers. "Touch me. Please, Michal, you have to touch me."

Beyond the roar of my blood, a distant part of me skitters wildly at the words, at the near frantic roll of my hips. *Too much. Too soon.* But I want it. Oh, I *want* it, and when I push closer, our hands slide up my waist, the tips of his fingers brushing the swell of my breast. Every thought empties from my head.

"Célie—" He tears his mouth from my throat with a pained sound, his gaze instantly falling to our hands on my body. Though the wound at his chest has closed, he doesn't seem to notice. He remains focused upon his fingers as if entranced, and he spreads them slowly, exploring the curve of my waist, before his thumb just brushes the tip of that breast. I gasp. My legs jerk. An almost violent longing rises in his eyes, which shine too brightly in the darkness. "We shouldn't do this."

"Why not?" I ask breathlessly.

"Because you thought I died." He speaks the words quietly, as if trying to convince himself instead of me. Though I pull at his hands, desperate to move them up—or perhaps to move them down, down, *down* and ease this building tension between my legs—they remain resolute upon my waist. They hold me away from him, even as I strain to press closer. He grits his teeth. "Because you hate me, remember? Because I never intended to ravish you in this filthy passageway."

I nearly sob in frustration now. "What if *I* intended to ravish *you?*"

He presses a light kiss to my throat before wiping the last of my blood away. His bite has already closed, and for some intolerable reason, confusion flushes through me at the realization—that this moment has finally come, and now it is going, going, almost *gone*, slipping like water between my fingertips. And I can do nothing to hold it. "Tomorrow," he promises in a low voice. "We'll talk tomorrow."

That confusion flares inexplicably hot in response because why not *now?* I don't understand that strange look in his eyes, this deep and unending ache between us. This is no simple flirtation. Sometimes, like now, he even seems to—to *want* me.

Men never see me that way. They covet me—oh yes—in a different way from how they covet women like Lou and Coco. Reid and Jean Luc both placed me high upon a pedestal to admire, and to an extent, so did those in Les Abysses. Léandre too. His tastes might trend darker, more depraved—he wants to break my porcelain skin instead of polish it—but it often feels like two sides of the same coin when men look at me.

No one has ever looked at me the way Michal does.

I push the thought away, agitated, before rising stiffly to my feet. Because clearly he doesn't want me now either. Clearly this has all been a terrible mistake, and I've crossed some invisible line again. I—I should've just healed him without complicating everything—he was grievously injured, after all—but I always seem to say the wrong things around Michal. I always seem to *do* the wrong things. And it *hurts.*

"Have you ever considered," I say, "that I might not want to ravish you tomorrow?"

He pauses halfway through tugging on his shirt, his chest whole and unblemished again. Each line of his body long and hard and perfect, from his broad shoulders to his tapered waist. I expect him to placate, or perhaps argue. I expect him to fight back. Instead he gives a soft laugh at whatever he sees in my expression, and the sound of it freezes the heat in my belly to ice. "No," he says simply. "You probably won't."

I lift a hand, instantly regretting the words. "Michal—"

"It's fine." He steps away from me, slipping the shirt back over his head, before nodding up the passage. "Someone is coming."

Though I tense, alarmed, he doesn't seem concerned at our imminent discovery, and in the next second, it becomes clear why. The dulcet scents of cinnamon and vanilla swirl through the dank passage just before Lou herself rounds the corner, holding five sputtering lights at her fingertips. They cast a faint glow upon her distinctly disgruntled expression. "What are you two doing?" she asks suspiciously.

"Nothing," Michal says curtly.

She seems to realize she interrupted something, glancing pointedly from Michal's untucked shirt to his rumpled coat on the ground. "It doesn't *look* like nothing—"

"Where is my mother?" Clutching her free hand and dragging her closer—hideously relieved—I inspect every inch of her apparently unscathed person. She still leans against me for support, however, practically sagging in my arms. "Is she all right? Are *you* all right?" Then, before she can answer, "You look even paler than before. How did you find us? What time is it?"

"Almost dawn." She flicks the tiny lights above our heads, where they continue to flicker weakly and cast strange shadows upon our faces. "And we're both fine—though by fine, I mean hysterical, at least in your mother's case. She allowed me to ward our room, but it took another hour to coax her into drinking that same draught I gave you in Cesarine. Thankfully it knocked her out cold." She glances at Michal. "You should know, however, Madame Tremblay is not at all pleased with Requiem at the moment, and I cannot say I'm particularly thrilled either."

He shrugs into his leather surcoat. "Imagine our disappointment."

My brow contracts at that. "You could thank her, you know. Her magic did save your life."

"My life was never the one in danger."

"What does *that* mean?"

"Nothing." He bows curtly, and with supreme effort, some of the ice seems to melt from his expression. "You're right. Of course you're right. Thank you, Louise, for aiding us in the coup tonight. Odessa and I could not have accomplished it without you."

If possible, Lou looks more suspicious now than she did before. Her gaze cuts between us. "You're welcome—not that Odessa gave much of a choice. It wasn't meant to shake out like this," she adds to me before grudgingly disentangling herself and approaching Michal to inspect his chest. He stiffens but suffers her ministrations in stoic silence. "Pasha and Ivan were supposed to sneak us into the hall during Odessa's procession to heal Michal—there's another secret passage near the east wing—but obviously that didn't go to plan." She cuts a rueful look in my direction. "As soon as we heard the revenant's scream, I knew everything was about to go to complete and utter shit. Another rather unexpected and unwelcome addition to the plan."

"You aren't wrong," Michal says.

"Anyway," Lou continues, ignoring him, "Odessa thought if we told you about"—she waves her hand at his chest—"all of this, you never would've agreed to it."

"And she would've been right," I say indignantly. "Everything spiraled *completely* out of control. Even without the revenant, how could anyone think this plan was a good one? When does faking one's death *ever* work out in the end?"

Michal reties his cravat with deft fingers. "Is that a rhetorical question, or would you like an answer?"

My eyes narrow at him. "Now that you mention it, I think I *would* like an answer."

"All right." He lifts a shoulder, thoroughly unbothered. "It works out this time. The whole of Requiem thinks Odessa overthrew a corrupt and inconstant king. The isle is renewed, united under her leadership, which enables her to do what is necessary to protect it. The vampires trust her. They believe in her. They also believe I am dead, which enables *me* to do what is necessary as well."

"Which is?" I ask swiftly.

He merely smiles in answer. Sleek and knife sharp.

Lou shakes her head as if thoroughly exasperated by both of us—or perhaps the entire species. Then she sighs and spreads her fingertips against Michal's chest to inspect something we cannot see. "Tonight was indeed a clusterfuck, but it looks like you figured out how to heal Michal on your own."

"His body didn't desiccate"—I ignore his probing look—"and flowers bloomed around his body in the spirit realm. Heather, I think."

Lou purses her lips. "Dames Rouges often use sprigs of heather in protective enchantments. They allegedly bring luck." She removes her hand with a nod of approval. Then she flicks his torn shirt, which mends itself instantly in a small burst of magic. The blood vanishes from our clothing, but a fresh trickle appears down her nose instead. She wipes it away hastily. Fresh guilt seeps into my stomach at the sight. *She cannot be near the maelstrom.* "I'm not a healer by any means, but everything feels right to me. Does it feel right to you?" she asks him.

Michal nods.

"Excellent." Lou claps her hands in grim satisfaction. "Then I'll be going. I sent Talon along first to explain everything to Reid, and Odessa has arranged passage for Satine and me to return to Cesarine at daybreak—less chance of meeting any unsavory characters that way." She grimaces at Michal, who once more looks the perfect aristocrat after buttoning his coat. "Vampires *do* prefer to sleep during the day, right?"

When he nods, I stare at her, inexplicably stricken, but—but of course she must leave. The more distance she puts between herself and the grotto—between herself and this door, this unnatural entrance to whatever lies *beyond* the spirit realm—the better.

With a bleak smile, Lou squeezes my hands, and Michal tactfully turns away to give us the illusion of privacy. "I spoke to Father Achille before I left," she says quietly. "After we deal with the revenants, he might be open to a reconciliation with Requiem, but until then, Reid will keep Jean Luc from doing anything stupid. Coco has already summoned a council of trusted Dames Blanches and Dames Rouges to Chateau le Blanc. If all goes to plan, they'll ally with the Chasseurs to oversee graveyards throughout the kingdom, and together—hopefully—we'll be able to contain any new revenants. Beau is also establishing a curfew to keep the streets as empty as possible for patrols."

I glance at Michal, who still pretends to ignore us. "We'll investigate the revenants as well. *Someone* on this isle must know more about them—specifically, how to lay them to rest."

Lou nods swiftly. "We'll scour the libraries at Chateau le Blanc as well, but, Célie—" She wrings my hands, her expression solemn. "None of this will matter if we don't close the veil, and *you* are the only one who can do it. You know that, right?"

Swallowing hard, I squeeze her hands harder still. "Yes."

"Of course you do. Good." She nods again, and again, inhaling deeply, her fingers still refusing to relax around mine. "Good. That leaves just one more itty-bitty, teensy tiny problem before we go." If possible, my heart sinks lower at the apprehension in her voice. Anything that makes *Lou* feel apprehensive must be very unpleasant. "It's, er—your mother," she says, and my worst fears are confirmed. "She refuses to leave without you, and nothing I've said has changed her mind."

CHAPTER TWENTY-ONE

Farewell

Color rises high on my mother's prominent cheeks as she glares between us, her lips pursing in a severe line. "Absolutely not," she snaps. "I will not leave without her."

Michal, Pasha, Ivan, Lou, and I all gaze helplessly back at her. Or rather, Lou and I do. Michal stands behind us with a mask of calm, while Pasha and Ivan have adopted slightly more menacing expressions—not that my mother cares. She refuses to acknowledge either of them, instead standing tall and proud and *furious* at the foot of the grand staircase in my room. They hover behind her like two enormous shadows.

As it turns out, Odessa bade them to remain with my mother through the *festivities* tonight, and she was none too pleased when they rushed to her aid instead. They returned—tails between their legs—shortly before Lou came to find us. She recounted the whole story as we trekked through tunnels to the east wing. "I think they're half in love with Odessa—a fact your mother hasn't missed," she added with a sly grin. "You should've heard her before I coaxed her into the sleeping draught." She imitated Satine Tremblay's sharp, no-nonsense voice then: "Monsieur Sokolov, you understand she will *never* regard you as a suitable match with hair longer than hers? And stop *scowling* at me, Monsieur Volkov, or I shall be forced to reveal your unseemly temperament to the young lady—"

My mother is the one with the unseemly temperament now, however. She refused to allow Michal, Lou, and me to even clear the stairs before charging toward us, hell-bent on making her opinion known. "I will not stand for it," she says again. "Requiem is no place for anyone of gentle repute, and—though I can only command my daughter—I highly encourage *all* of you to join us on that ship and leave this wretched isle."

I resist the urge to groan. "I *told* you, Maman. I cannot leave until we've dealt with the revenants." *And the veil*, I add silently. *And Filippa. And potentially Death himself.*

She thrusts her hands upon her hips, somehow managing to look down her nose at me while standing three steps below. "Then neither can I."

"But it isn't *safe* for you here—"

"I fail to see how you are any safer. You are my daughter, and I will not abandon you to this place."

Cursing inwardly at her newfound maternal instinct, I descend another step and nearly trip on Toulouse, who has managed to climb the steps at last. I bend to snatch up the tabby kitten, petting his head furiously for something to do with my hands. Under different circumstances, I might've been, well, *touched* by my mother's reluctance to leave. Perhaps I still am, just a little. "Clearly, you don't understand what happened here tonight—"

"Oh, I understand perfectly. This one"—she points an accusing finger at Michal—"feigned his death to cede all responsibility to his cousin, leaving the two of you free to frolic across the island and do *God* knows what while the rest of us pretend you're being held under lock and key. I will admit," she says loudly when I open my mouth to argue, "I do not understand the purpose of the latter.

As I highly doubt you are going to *reveal* said purpose, I must assume the vampires still require you for some reason, but I must emphasize—most emphatically—this is not a reason to stay. You owe these foul creatures nothing, Célie."

These foul creatures. My chest tightens at that. She still speaks like I am not one of them, but what does she *expect* if I come back to Cesarine? That I'll simply return to the nursery until a nice young man—rich and titled, of course—takes pity on me? That we'll court for a month or two before he proposes, that we'll marry in the spring, that we'll raise our lovely, dark-haired babies right down the street from the town house? The idea is absurd, laughable, and if my incident with Jean Luc is any indication, I'll end up eating all of them—my faceless husband, my children, *and* my parents.

So I draw myself up to my full height, just like she taught me, and I tell the truth. "I have no reason to go back."

Her eyes narrow.

"Then allow me to repeat myself—neither do I." Voice crisp, she emphasizes each word before turning her resolute gaze to Lou. "If you wish for me to return to Cesarine without my daughter, I hope you brought an entire stock of that ghastly sleeping draught. Even with it, you shall need to knock me unconscious and pour it down my throat to keep my person upon that ship. I shall simply leap into the sea and swim back to this hateful rock if you do not—"

"There are always ropes," Pasha suggests with relish.

My mother twists around to look at him, grimacing at the sight of his rather gloriously windswept hair. His lip curls back at her because he knows. "Young man, it took weeks of investigation for me to find my daughter—and before that, weeks more to hear even a word of her whereabouts. It shall take a very strong rope to keep me from finding her again." She glares between Toulouse and me as if we've also offended her somehow, bringing a hand to her mouth to muffle a cough instead of a sneeze. "And if magic has indeed broken, I assume the protective enchantments around the isle aren't quite up to scratch either. It shouldn't take long for me to return. The harbormaster owes me a favor—I made quite a smart match for his son last season, and the newlyweds are expecting their firstborn any day now. Louis cannot wait to become a grandfather."

I stiffen inexplicably at that. I remember Louis's son, of course, but now he is married. *Now he is expecting a baby.* Instead of examining my reaction, however, I press a kiss to Toulouse's tiny nose.

"Please extend our felicitations," Michal says smoothly into the nasty silence that follows, but before my mother can respond—or rather, snarl at him—Dimitri strides through the door with a beleaguered expression.

"What's this I hear about you leaving?" Marching straight past Michal, he pulls me into a fierce embrace, careful not to squash Toulouse. Michal sighs heavily. "I *told* Odessa we should've included you in our little farce, but really, Célie, we have the whole thing worked out. You needn't leave unless you absolutely—"

I push him away, still a little miffed at being excluded. "I'm not going anywhere, Dimitri. Lou and my mother are the ones leaving."

My mother swells indignantly while Lou cringes at the oncoming explosion. "I most certainly am *not*—"

"Well, of course she isn't." Dimitri frowns as if I've suggested something preposterous, sweeping down the last of the stairs and seizing my mother's hands. Sweeping his lips across her knuckles. Her eyes bulge in shock, and she hastily draws away, her cheeks flushing at the impropriety, before coughing again. *Her throat must tickle.* "I told you, Odessa has it all arranged. She regrets not being here to explain in person, but she thought it best to get started on our little revenant problem instead—she and a council of witches are discussing solutions as we speak." He claps his hands. "Anyway, a sentry is waiting to escort Lou to the harbor, and Pasha and Ivan will remain here to guard this room—with you in it, of course," he says to me, winking. Then he turns back to my mother. "If you'd like to stay, Madame Tremblay, your presence will only lend credence to the ruse. We *are* supposed to be imprisoning your daughter, and our courtiers might grow suspicious if this room falls too still." Arching a brow at Lou, he adds, "I assume the shield you cast upon it will cease with your departure?"

Lou nods wearily, bending to scratch the head of another kitten. "I can barely maintain it now. At least my nose isn't bleeding any longer." Our eyes meet, and fear shines bright and clear in hers for the first time since the séance.

She doesn't know what will happen if the veil remains open. To her. To the other witches.

"A dangerous habit, that," Dimitri says sagely, "and especially on an island of vampires, but what do you think, Célie? Shall your mother stay with us a little while longer?"

Unbidden, I glance around to Michal, who gives no indication one way or another of his opinion. Indeed, he keeps his black eyes carefully neutral as if determined not to make the decision for me. I scowl at him. *Right.* Turning back around, I speak through my teeth. "I *suppose* it'll be fine if Pasha and Ivan guard the door—*really* guard the door this time," I add with narrowed looks in their direction—"and you remain inside the room, Maman."

"I am not remaining inside this room."

Exasperated, I nearly fling my hands in the air. "Fine, then! Can someone please fetch some rope?"

My mother scoffs and looks away, crossing her arms tightly against her chest. "So *crass* you are now, daughter. I cannot fault you, I suppose, with the dreadful company you keep—"

"Have we finished?" Voice quiet, Michal addresses the room with thinly veiled impatience. "If so, Célie and I must go. The sun will be rising soon, and we have business across the isle."

"I shall fetch my coat," my mother says stiffly.

"Maman!" Preparing to *wring* her obstinate neck, I return Toulouse to the floor with his siblings, where they scamper over Ivan's boots and ignore his ferocious scowl. "How many times must I say it? You are *not coming*—"

"Madame," Dimitri interrupts, clasping her hands once more and bowing low, "I completely understand your reticence to part with your daughter. You are her mother, after all, and a beacon of virtue at that. Of course you wish to remain with her, to protect her where my cousin has failed." A warning rumbles from Michal's chest, indiscernible to the humans in the room. Dimitri's lips twitch. "Allow me to assure you, however, that she will be in no real danger. The witch they seek is a friend of our family, and moreover, she might possess the knowledge we require to debilitate the revenants. She will not harm Célie, and if she tries"—he straightens with that devilish gleam in his gaze, struggling to maintain a straight face—"I swear both the witch *and* my cousin will deal with me. I shall protect your daughter, madame. Have no fear."

Frowning, my mother studies Dimitri closely for several seconds before sniffing in approval. "That is because *you* are a gentleman." Her lips purse as she turns to me. "You will report to this young man the instant you return. Do you understand? If anything or *anyone* runs afoul"—here she skewers Michal with a pointed look—"he must know."

"Yes." Dimitri nods gravely. "You must both report to me."

Chortling despite herself, Lou glances back at Michal, and I follow her gaze, keenly aware of his presence on the step above mine. My hair brushes his chest when I turn, and gooseflesh erupts down my back as he lifts a hand—hidden to my mother—and winds a lock around his fingers. He gives a gentle tug, and I respond instantly, instinctively, shifting backward until I press flush against him. Heat suffuses my belly at the contact.

Have you ever considered that I might not want to ravish you tomorrow?

I am such a liar.

"Of course we will," Michal says smoothly.

Though his black eyes glitter with the promise of retribution, he smirks back at Dimitri, who looks enormously satisfied for some reason. My gaze narrows on him.

A knock sounds on the door in the next second, however—extinguishing the heat in my belly—and after another quick tug of my hair, Michal vanishes down the stairs in a whisper of movement. I just catch his heel behind the silk dressing screen as the door swings open to reveal another sentry—this one hard-faced and unfamiliar, cloaked in the same dark attire as Pasha and Ivan with gold foxes on the chest. "I am here to escort the witch," he growls.

Staring up at him in distaste, Lou sighs. "That's my cue."

Then she pulls me into a fierce hug—as fierce as she is able—and my arms wrap around her in a state of mild disbelief. Because I don't know when I'll see her again. Because I don't want her to leave. Because all of this is happening too fast, and—and because I don't think I can do any of it without her. Unable to find my voice, however, I can only nod helplessly as she says, "I'll send Talon with any news, but in the meantime, do *try* to be careful, won't you?" She pulls back to search my face. "And remember what I said about the veil," she adds in a rush. "You *can* fix it. I know you can, but if you need help just—just send word. One or all of us can be here in a matter of hours." I will never ask them to come back, however. I will never ask them to harm themselves for my sake, and perhaps she knows it. Perhaps I imagine her eyes flicking toward the silk screen instead. "You aren't alone here, Célie. You'll never be alone."

I swallow hard.

Forcing myself to release her, I speak emphatically enough for her to *hear* me when I say, "And the same to you. No, I'm serious, Lou. If the revenants grow to be too much—"

But she shakes her head with a playful scoff, already turning away. "Nonsense. I *am* still La Dame des Sorcières. It'll be a cold day in hell when my dear dead mother gets the better of me." And—before either of us can succumb to tears—she winks over her shoulder and climbs up the stairs, preceding the guard into the corridor and out of sight.

Part Three

Qui n'avance pas, recule.

He who does not move forward, recedes.

CHAPTER TWENTY-TWO

Mila Returns

The forest Michal leads me through whispers of an age before even Les Éternels.

Great cragged rocks jut forth from the misty ground, interspersed with ancient and moss-covered trees: beech, I think, and firs and maples. A freshwater stream cuts through the undergrowth to our left. Raindrops still glitter upon the ferns, but for the first time since my arrival, the clouds have calmed over Requiem. No rumble of thunder punctuates the early morning air. No flash of lightning.

As if sensing our presence, the wildlife around us cease their chatter. Only the gentle burble of water meets our ears. Indeed, the eerie presence in the harbor and castle doesn't yet seem to have reached this part of the island. It feels peaceful. Calm. Still—

I frown at the ferns nearest us, where water continues to trickle steadily from their fronds as if rain still falls from the sky. Instinctively, I swipe at one of the droplets and bring it to my nose.

Salt.

The water smells of salt.

"Step lightly," Michal says into the silence. "Stick to the rocks along the bank if possible and try not to disturb the vegetation. This forest is rife with magic," he explains at my questioning look, tucking his hands into his pockets and strolling forward. "We don't want to disturb it."

"Really?" Curious despite myself, I hasten after him, picking up my skirts and cursing myself for not changing my shoes—thin satin slippers with delicate ribbons up the ankles. They'll be ruined within a mile. "More so than other parts of the isle? Why?"

"Because the witch in residence doesn't like visitors. Those are tears, by the way." He nods toward the foliage, toward the trees, which all continue to gently drip, drip, *drip*. "The entire forest started to weep after All Hallows' Eve."

"Oh." I glance around at the jewel-bright droplets, and I wonder at how something can be so beautiful yet so unnerving at the same time. "How . . . comforting."

Michal grins, and at the sight of it, I stumble upon the pebbled bank. Though the forest is strange, this new Michal is stranger still. Since staging his death, he seems . . . lighter, somehow, almost *relaxed*, which makes no sense at all; he might've shirked his crown, but the stakes have never been higher for any of us. His devastating grin widens at my reaction—because he notices the stumble, of course—and I nearly choke at the dimple in his cheek. Just the one, so different yet so similar to Dimitri's. How have I never *noticed* it before?

Slowing to walk alongside me, he says, "You needn't worry about a witch, Célie. You're a vampire now. Your strength equals any threat she might leverage against us."

I snort indelicately, my cheeks flushing for no apparent reason. "Strength has never exactly been my forte, Michal."

He arches a brow. "And you're against trying new things?"

"Of course not—"

"Have you, then?" he asks steadily. "Tried them?"

"Tried *what*?"

"Your newfound skills as a vampire."

If possible, my flush deepens as I look away, and Michal makes a low noise in his throat. "Not yet," I say stiffly. "There hasn't been . . . time." At the last, I cast him a quick, furtive look from the corner of my eye, but such subtlety proves unnecessary. Between one blink and the next, he steps directly in front of me, blocking my path and forcing me to look at him.

His own eyes have narrowed. "We have time now."

"But you said—"

"This is important too."

My hands fist in my skirts—because it isn't, not really, and there are a hundred things more important than exploring vampirism. We've abandoned Lou and the others to battle the undead in Cesarine, my mother insists on cohabitating with bloodthirsty monsters, and I still haven't told Michal about Death and Filippa. The last twists like a knife in my chest. No. In Michal's *back*. I need to tell him. I *know* I need to tell him, but he just died; he sacrificed everything without hesitation, yet I've done nothing but hesitate when it comes to him.

I don't think he'll hurt my sister, but—but what if he *does*?

What if he has no choice?

The isle—the entire *world*—is breaking, and at the center of it all stands Death and his revenants. That much is clear. This forest would not be weeping without them. The harbor would not be bleeding, the paintings dying. Worse still—Death seems to be scheming something more, and he seems to be scheming it with my sister.

I made a promise, my sweet, to exhaust every option.

Every option to *what*?

If only I knew; if only I could reveal Death without endangering Filippa, who clearly isn't herself.

"Aren't you curious, pet?" Michal tilts his head and watches me patiently. "To test your limits? To discover all this eternal life might offer if you give it the chance?"

"*No*," I say sharply—too sharp. I cringe internally at the vehemence in my voice.

A flicker of emotion crosses Michal's features at the word, there and gone again in the blink of an eye. Disappointment? Remorse? *It doesn't matter*, I tell myself firmly, but even I almost laugh at the lie. Nothing has ever mattered more.

"Are you sure?" he asks in that dangerously soft voice. "The Célie I know relishes knowledge. She craves the thrill of new experiences, of adventure, and she never allows fear to keep her from chasing it."

I scoff on impulse. This Célie of whom he speaks is much greater than I, but he needn't know that. He needn't know *anything* of this battle raging in my chest. "Don't be ridiculous, Michal. Of course I'm not afraid—"

"Prove it."

His black eyes glitter with challenge now. With burgeoning excitement. And though it makes me the worst sort of coward, I *am* afraid—of indulging my own treacherous curiosity, yes, but also of indulging *him*.

With a valiant attempt at indifference, I sweep past him. "We'll disturb the forest if we race across the isle."

He appears in front of me again, refusing to be deterred. "Not if we run on the water."

"But my gown—"

"I said *on* the water, Célie, not in it."

His hand snakes out to catch mine when I skirt around him again, and his eyes—they flick to our left for the briefest of seconds as if detecting movement. Instinctively, I follow his gaze to find a small tear in the veil between two saplings. The shorn edges ripple slightly in a nonexistent breeze, and snowflakes drift upon the earth below it. I frown as Michal turns my chin back toward him. Did he just *see*—?

"You needn't fear for your gown, pet," he says as if nothing happened. "All vampires can move with exceptional speed, but the fastest among us can outrun nature itself. You will not sink."

"I appreciate the sentiment, Michal, but I am not you. I very much doubt I'll be able to—to walk on water—"

"*Run* on water," he corrects me. "And you might be surprised. Will you at least try?" When I still look wary, he grins anew, and from his pocket he withdraws a very frayed, very filthy, very *familiar* emerald ribbon. My heart leaps at the sight of it.

"Is that—?" I lunge for it instinctively. After the events of All Hallows' Eve, I thought my ribbon lost, gone forever, and no small part of me regretted exchanging it with the silver ribbon of my costume that night. Frederic's knife irrevocably ruined *that* ribbon, of course, so perhaps it'd been for the best. "How did you find it?"

"It was never lost." He jerks the ribbon overhead when I swipe at it, and the tail dangles just out of reach. "I suppose you'd like it back now, wouldn't you?"

I glare up at him. "Yes."

"Fantastic." Quick as a flash, he tucks the ribbon back into his pocket. "Indulge this little whim of mine, and I'll give it to you. It could be useful, you know," he adds in a lower voice, and my belly clenches like a fist at the sound. "To learn the limits of your new body."

"Why is this so important to you?"

And it *is* important, I realize with a start. Despite his casual demeanor, his gaze blisters with an intensity that burns. "You need to know your advantages in order to press them. The revenants certainly will." An idea sparks in his eyes before I can argue. "If the revenants and ribbon aren't incentive enough, I suppose I could simply . . . flee."

My brow furrows. "What?"

He doesn't explain; instead that idea solidifies into a knowing, mischievous gleam, and—the split second before he turns on his heel—I remember his warning outside L'ange de la Mort: *Never run from a vampire.* My frown deepens. Because he can't possibly think—

In a streak of black and silver, he bolts up the stream, and my body reacts without conscious thought.

It bolts after him.

If a small, distant part of my mind—the human part—realizes what I'm doing, it remains wholly silent in wake of the instinctive, all-consuming rush of power down my spine. As before with Brigitte, my vision sharpens. It bleeds red as blood pounds through my ears. Each stone on the bank, each frond of bracken, each teardrop and each fiber of moss and grass and earth—it all rises before me with crystalline clarity before my eyes lock on Michal.

I can hear his laughter. Swift as I am—my hair blowing, gown billowing, feet weightless upon the water—I can still see each tremor of his shoulders, each stride of his legs, as he pushes farther away from me, faster and faster still. A snarl tears from my throat. I forget the emerald ribbon. I forget everything but the sight of his retreating back. Because I will have it. I will have *him*, and my own strides grow longer in response. I lean forward, and I lift my chest, practically flying across the water until Michal grows larger in my sight—until he glances back at me in surprise, in *delight*, and I brace without breaking speed, bending my knees and catapulting myself at him.

We collide in a crash of limbs, and he twists, wrapping his arms around my waist before we hit the ground. His back takes the brunt of the impact. Skidding through the rocks, he holds me tightly—laughing—as we finally slow to a halt. "I can't believe you caught me," he says, breathless, before dropping his head on the bank. "No one has ever caught me before."

I stare up at him, my chest tightening to the point of pain. "Do you often flee unsuspecting women?"

"Only the ones I steal from." He releases my waist, bringing one hand between our faces. My emerald ribbon winds through his long fingers, and when I touch it this time, he allows the silk to slip from his grasp. As it dangles down my wrist and tickles his cheek, he grins and blows it against my nose. "I knew you wouldn't sink."

Of course he did. All this man has ever done is believe me, help me, *save* me. Perhaps I don't need to hide things in order to protect my sister. Perhaps if I tell him, Michal will help her too, and together, we can extricate Filippa from Death's clutches.

Slowly, he brushes a strand of hair away from my cheek, his thumb lingering on my jaw. And with that single, unguarded movement, the last of my hesitation falls away.

"The man you saw with me in Cesarine was Death," I blurt out, wincing at the tactless delivery. Instant heat sears my cheeks as Michal blinks, startled, and the moment between us shatters. "I should've told you earlier, but my sister made some sort of deal with him, I think, because he promised her—well, *something*—"

"Death promised her something?" Michal's hands seize my shoulders, and he wrenches me upward, the warmth in his eyes freezing to black ice. "As in *Death*, the incarnation of a life-destroying power? Death, the entity that claimed you as its Bride?"

"Well, that isn't *precisely* how he introduced himself, but . . . yes," I finish in a small voice, and with a savage curse, Michal hauls me to my feet.

"What happened?"

Quickly, I recount all that occurred after we separated in Cesarine: how Frederic and Filippa found me in the rose garden, how Frederic threatened to kill me, how Filippa watched as Death tore out his heart. When I tell him about Death taking Frederic's blood and the grimoire, he turns away. When I tell him of the mysterious deal between Death and Filippa, he lets loose another stream of curses, and I hasten to reassure him. "But he honored their bargain! He left me alone."

"For now, Célie. Death has left you alone for *now*."

I wrap my arms around myself, unease prickling my neck. "You sound like you're acquainted with him."

"We've met," Michal says shortly.

He still faces away from me, so I can only see the hard line of his cheek, the corner of his jaw; it clenches as he glares down at the stream in an effort to master himself. "But how can that be?" I ask. "He just manifested a body on All Hallows' Eve."

"I met him before he acquired a body. He—did me a favor once, probably similar to the one he promised your sister." Though I burn with curiosity, I keep my mouth shut, and he surprises me by adding, "I've regretted it every day since. He is not someone you want to know, Célie, and not someone Filippa should trust. It'll only end badly for both of you." At last, he turns, and my astonishment soars at the subtle silver glow emanating from his usually black eyes. He blinks at whatever he sees in mine, equally startled. "Your eyes are glowing," he tells me.

I gasp and step closer, lifting a hand as if to touch the combined light of our eyes. "*Your* eyes are glowing."

We stare at each other for a beat, mystified, before I force myself to lower my hand. To glance around for any sign of the spirit realm. No ghosts have joined us, however—none that I can see—so I take a deep breath and whisper, "I really am sorry I didn't tell you sooner."

He studies me with an inscrutable expression. "Why didn't you?"

"Because I'm a coward."

His jaw clenches at that, and I'd give anything to read his thoughts as he recaptures my hand, staring down at my knuckles without truly seeing them. At last, he brushes a kiss against my fingers, though shadows remain in his expression. "You've forgiven me for much worse."

I stare up at him, willing those shadows to dissipate. "Michal—"

"Sorry to bother," Mila says wryly, poking her head out between two weeping trees, "but this seems as good a moment as any to interrupt what I am sure would've been a tender interlude."

Michal and I break apart, whirling, yet his eyes continue to glow as he focuses on his sister. I shake my head in an effort to clear it. "Can you *see*—?" But he nods before I finish the question, so I nod too, disoriented and confused. "Oh. Right. Of course you can. That's perfectly—perfectly—"

"Expected." Mila grins at us in a deprecating sort of way that reminds me of Dimitri. "Blood sharing is never something to be taken lightly—not that we have time to discuss such a delicate situation now. I just slipped away from your sister, who has holed up with literal Death in your old town house, Célie. Kind of you to mention *him*, by the way—"

"Agreed," Michal murmurs.

"Oh, I heard." Gesturing purposefully, Mila motions for us to continue toward the witch's cottage, and I try not to look offended by her eavesdropping. "They've built quite the luxurious laboratory for themselves. Even Odessa would be envious."

"A laboratory?" Michal asks in a sharp voice, and it's almost as if his dimple never existed. I slide the emerald ribbon into my pocket. "What sort of experiments are they conducting?"

"The sort with Frederic's blood. I couldn't discern their exact purpose, but they've also been running—tests, I think, on Filippa. Strange tests too," she adds with a grimace, "on everything from her blood to her brain to her womb. Death even collected a sample from the stitches on her cheek."

I hardly hear the last, however, my attention snagging on the two words before it.

Her womb.

They're running tests on her *womb.*

"From what I can tell, Death has also collected his own blood." When we stare at her, bewildered, she stares back unapologetically. "What? He might *look* human now, but he doesn't seem to be wholly one thing or the other anymore. That rip in the veil must've twisted him too." She gestures to the weeping ferns, and as she does, a dead butterfly flutters through her chest.

"Are they alone?" Michal asks, ignoring it. "Just the two of them?"

Mila laughs without mirth. "Just the two of them, yes—and a veritable army of revenants. Filippa tore a hole through the veil in your childhood bedroom, Célie, and led them all inside." Nausea churns at the thought, at the idea of corpses like the Archbishop trudging across my nursery carpet. "It appears you passed your abilities to her through your blood, just as you did with Michal."

My thoughts scatter wildly at that, like pins dropped upon the floor.

It's just—when two vampires share blood, they—they change.

I smooth the bodice of my gown for something to do with my hands. A knot of emotion obstructs my throat, but I cannot untangle the threads—not as those silver eyes touch my face, assessing my reaction, and Michal says, "I abdicated the throne."

Mila tears her gaze away. "I heard as much. The spirits have been unable to talk of anything else—and many realized your subterfuge when you did not pass through our realm. We never accounted for that in our contingency plan." Her eyes narrow. "Where did you go while you feigned death if not our realm?"

A furrow appears between Michal's brows. "I don't know," he says after a moment. "When my heart left my chest, I simply . . .

fell asleep." His frown deepens. "I *dreamed*."

"Your soul remained trapped," Mila says shrewdly. "It never left your body."

"Some might argue vampires no longer have souls."

She gestures down her own shimmering, translucent form. "Surely I am proof otherwise. Either way, it was strange magic, and I fear it will not be without repercussions."

"La Dame des Sorcières herself cast the spell."

"La Dame des Sorcières is not infallible. Her magic is just as broken as the rest."

Michal lifts a careless shoulder. "If there are repercussions, they'll be mine to bear."

"You really are a fool, brother, if you think that." With a scoff, Mila rises several inches above Michal, peering down her nose at him. "Whatever Death is planning, it will affect all of us—and he *is* planning something. I can feel it." Voice growing frustrated, she adds, "He and Filippa are being very secretive about what they say aloud, however, which leads me to believe they know someone is listening."

Any irritation Michal felt toward his sister seems to vanish with the words. "You need to be careful, Mila. Death is not someone whose attention you want to attract. Perhaps you shouldn't—"

"I've died twice now, Michal. I've already attracted his attention." Her jaw sets with determination, and her eyes—they burn with intensity now, with new and unfamiliar purpose. "I can only hope he soon regrets attracting *mine*."

Though Michal opens his mouth to argue, she whirls—hair flicking in his face—toward the witch's cottage, which grows between the roots of two enormous oak trees in front of us. Black shingles covered in lichen peek between their twisted branches, and diamond-paned windows glitter like jeweled eyes between weathered black woodwork—arched, ornate, yet slightly gone to seed from the elements and age.

Under different circumstances, I'd feel a rush of excitement at such an obviously magical dwelling, but now dread curdles my stomach.

"I'll report back if anything changes, but in the meantime . . ." Mila tips her head toward the cottage before turning away with a smirk, ignoring her brother's scowl. "Good luck with Mathilde, Célie, and a word of warning—she bites."

CHAPTER TWENTY-THREE

The Cottage

"Mathilde?" I blink at the name, startled, but—surely it's just a coincidence. Michal would've said if the witch we're asking about revenants is actually Lou's long-lost relative—her great-great-grandmother, to be precise—and moreover, why would such a prestigious and powerful witch have left her people to live as a recluse among vampires? "She doesn't mean—?"

"She does, in fact." Michal leads me toward the cottage as Mila leaves us, her laughter echoing behind. "Mathilde le Blanc is a very acquired taste on the isle, and I don't mean her blood."

"What did Mila mean," I ask slowly, "when she said Mathilde *bites*?"

In answer, Michal gestures to an enormous cast-iron pot on the top step, and I cannot help it—I peer into its depths apprehensively, expecting some sort of potion, perhaps poison, only to recoil in the next second.

Bones.

Mathilde has filled the pot with bones—animal mandibles and human femurs, ribs, vertebrae, and what appear to be the phalanges of an entire left hand. Flowering vines tangle between the latter's fingers before spilling down the sides of the cauldron. Vividly blue and eerily beautiful, the blooms seem to quiver as I bend to examine them with macabre fascination; I recognize the rows of needlelike teeth around their centers the instant before they lunge at me, snapping violently.

I back away hastily. *Bluebeard blossoms.* The same beastly little flowers grow outside Monsieur Marc's shop; Michal once told me they eat butterflies.

I suppose I should be grateful Mathilde isn't a cannibal. "And Mathilde knows about revenants?" *Will she know about Filippa?*

Michal watches me carefully now, as if sensing the desperate thought. My sister seems to live and breathe between us. "Mathilde knows about many things."

Carefully avoiding his gaze, I skirt around the cauldron. Though I've always been skittish beneath Michal's undivided attention, I feel as if my skin has grown two sizes too small after our unfinished conversation in the forest. *It'll only end badly for both of you.* "She *is* expecting us, right?"

He nods before joining me at the door, his cool presence spreading gooseflesh down my arms. "A mistake on my part, I think." Despite the rather unusual silence inside the cottage, he speaks in a low voice. I listen closer, wondering if she could be hiding from us—then realize the sounds of her breathing, even her heartbeat, are conspicuously absent. "I sent a letter requesting a meeting after we docked on Requiem. She never wrote back."

"Perhaps she never received it?"

"Oh, I think she did."

Michal moves to push open the door, but my hand snakes out to seize his wrist. "Don't you think we should at least knock first? This *is* her home, after all, even if she . . . well, isn't home?" My voice trails into a hopeful question at the end. Perhaps it was the Bluebeard blossoms and their picked-clean bones—or perhaps it's the silver doorknob—but suddenly, the thought of imposing on a witch who clearly doesn't want us here feels foolish.

"By all means"—Michal's gaze flicks to my hand on his wrist—"go ahead."

Blowing out a tremulous breath, I release him and knock three times. When no one answers, I knock three more. Nothing inside the cottage moves. When at last I turn—determined to persuade Michal to try again later—he quells my argument with a curt shake of his head. "You heard Mila's warning. We don't have time to play polite, Célie, and even if we did, Mathilde won't return the favor. We aren't leaving until we speak with her."

"How do you know she's even *here*?"

"She's here," he says simply.

Fine. *Fine.* Truthfully, no one on this wretched isle cares much for civility anyway. Mathilde feeds *flesh* to her flowers, for goodness' sake. Odessa ripped out Michal's heart, and Dimitri collected souvenirs from all the creatures he slaughtered in bloodlust. Perhaps the time has come for me to throw all good sense out the window too.

Feeling strangely defiant, I lift a piece of my skirt to grasp the doorknob, but Michal stops me again with light fingers upon my arm. "I think I should do that." Before I can do more than scowl back at him, he tugs the fabric from my hand and wraps it around his own instead.

To my surprise, the knob turns easily. Except—

"Fuck," Michal mutters.

He clenches his hand in my skirt, and instantly, I realize why: the doorknob has *bitten* him, and blood wells from two tiny puncture wounds in his palm. Two tiny fang marks. "She definitely knows we're here," he says with a bitter laugh.

I scowl down at the doorknob as its silver teeth melt back into smooth metal. "I thought Mathilde didn't care for vampires? Why all the *biting* paraphernalia?"

"Mathilde thinks she is enormously funny."

"Is she?"

"You tell me."

With a grudging smile, I lift my hem and tear away a piece of my silky underskirt. Though Michal's eyes track the line of my leg as I let the fabric drop, I try to ignore him. I try to ignore the heady scent of his blood too. "That still doesn't explain why she settled on an island of vampires."

"That was Mila's doing," he says quietly, watching me wrap the silk scrap around his hand. "She convinced Mathilde to retire here after passing down the title of La Dame des Sorcières to her daughter. They met when Mathilde was a much younger woman, and the two of them became thick as thieves."

My fingers go still around Michal's hand, and unbidden, my thoughts drift back to Filippa. My heart twists.

"How does Mathilde know about revenants? It didn't seem like—well, you and Odessa didn't seem to know what they even were before Coco named them, and she only knew because of her aunt's grimoire. Unless Mathilde knew La Voisin?"

"I'll let her tell you that. Now"—he pushes open the door after I finish wrapping his hand—"by all means, please come inside."

The two of us walk into the cottage on silent feet, entering a homely kitchen with an enormous stone hearth. Bundles of dried herbs hang from the rafters, and a copper kettle heats on the grate; the rest of the Bluebeard blossoms' repast appears to line the mantel in a strange assortment of skulls. "I take it you've . . . met Mathilde, then?"

Michal's eyes sweep the room for any sign of activity. "Yes. Twice. The first when she arrived on Requiem, and the second shortly after you did."

"What? Why?"

"Nosy little thing, aren't you?"

I glower at him before moving deeper into the cottage, poking my head into a small washroom and eyeing the tin bathtub, the nook of threadbare linens. "Try not to touch anything," Michal says as he passes behind, and it might be the most unnecessary advice ever given. After the doorknob, I've never desired to touch anything less than I do in this cottage.

I still crane my neck to look after him, however, as he bends to fit through the bedroom door. "What am I looking for, exactly?"

"Anything out of place—a sound, a sight, a scent. The last will be difficult, but not impossible. Wherever the witch is hiding, it'll reek of magic."

"The entire *cottage* reeks of magic."

I glance around warily, waiting for the floorboards to open up and swallow me whole. Part of me wishes they would—anything to cut this wretched tension between Michal and me, to dispel the lingering presence of my sister. He hasn't mentioned her since our conversation, and now—in this eerie stillness—it feels like he's waiting for me to mention her instead.

I open my mouth to speak, unsure what to say, just as he turns to do the same.

"I think we should—"

"We don't need to—" I say at the same time.

Michal's eyes narrow at whatever he sees in my expression. "What were you going to say?"

"What were *you* going to say?"

We stare at each other for a long moment, neither wanting to speak again, until the floorboards indeed begin to rumble beneath our feet. The vibration shatters the tension—as does the startled cry that escapes me as I leap forward, colliding with Michal's broad chest. His arms wrap around me reflexively, and he exhales a soft laugh. I shake my head. "This house is going to kill us."

"Come now, pet." He pushes the hair from my face with a burgeoning smirk—a temporary truce, I realize, until after we speak to Mathilde. Relief floods my system. "Don't tell me you're afraid of a little magic."

My shoulders relax at the feel of him against me, and my jaw unclenches. Because if Mathilde knows what to do about revenants, she might know what to do about Filippa too. "Shall we make a game of it?" Michal asks. *A distraction.*

I lift my chin, forcing myself to step away from him. "What do you have in mind?"

He leans against the doorframe, entirely too large for the space. "First to find the witch owes the other a favor."

Oh God. "What kind of favor?"

"Any kind of favor."

Flutters erupt in my belly. If imposing ourselves on a witch feels foolish, agreeing to give Michal a favor without any other qualifiers feels downright demented. *Only if you lose*, that defiant voice in my head argues, and with a little thrill of anticipation, I stand straighter in response. "Fine. Agreed. I hope you're ready to scrub the bloodstains from all my dresses."

"Starting with this one?" He gestures to the scarlet droplets on my skirt—*his* blood, I realize, my cheeks flaming. Always his blood. "I could take it now if you'd like."

My face burns hotter at the rush of images his words evoke—Michal kneeling before me, his hands sliding up my legs, my hips, as he peels the silky fabric from my body.

His grin turns positively wicked because he knows.

Because his distraction is already working.

Because when he looks at me like that, I can hardly remember my own name.

Clenching my thighs, I duck into a parlor down the hall before I can humiliate myself, and I take several deep breaths just inside the door. *Focus, Célie.*

Another fireplace dominates the center of the room; it allows for shelves upon shelves of books to line the walls on all sides. Mathilde appears to have hung them at random, filling every nook and cranny with little forethought or design. Indeed, the shelves look a bit like broken teeth. They jut this way and that, uneven, varied in shape and size, and when she ran out of wall space, Mathilde seems to have started stacking her books in teetering piles on the floor—beneath the desk, beside the settee, atop the tattered carpet.

The only semblance of order comes from a narrow bookcase in the corner. Unlike the other shelves, which float, this bookcase stretches from floor to ceiling, and the tomes within it appear in pristine condition. The embossed letters on their spines sparkle in the firelight. Their leather covers gleam. Indeed, I can still smell the mink oil with which she conditioned them. These books—whatever they are—must be her most treasured in the collection.

They also look jarringly out of place in the chaos of the room.

Curious, I approach the bookshelf to inspect the titles there. *One Night with the Bear King. The Wizard of Waterdeep's Staff. The Demon: Endowed and Enflamed.* Choking on laughter, I recoil, the tension further loosening in my chest. It seems Mathilde's most treasured books are erotica, and that—that is perfectly acceptable. Healthy, even. It is not, however, any of my business.

Moving to search the rest of the room, I stop short at a title on the center of the shelf.

The Secret Door.

I hesitate, feeling incredibly sheepish, but secret passages *do* exist on this isle. I've walked them myself, and they seem like the sort of thing a witch like Mathilde might utilize too—and that isn't even considering her relation to Lou, who would think the innuendo quite clever indeed.

Could it be that simple?

I stare harder at the book. Is Mathilde standing behind the bookshelf even now, snickering at me? True, I do not scent anyone—nor does the magic here smell particularly stronger than anywhere else in the cottage—yet I didn't scent Babette or Frederic either. Witches have always been able to disguise themselves from vampires.

In the end, the sound of Michal's footsteps in the garret overhead is all the motivation I need.

Squaring my shoulders, I grasp the book and pull.

A mechanism triggers deep in the wall.

Something—or *someone*—indeed cackles.

And every book on the shelf hurtles at me in rapid succession. With a shriek, I fling my hands over my head and scramble backward, but the books follow, flapping their pages like wings and pummeling every inch of me they can reach. And it *hurts.* Michal appears in the next second—his expression dangerous—and snatches one, two, three in midair before hurling them into the desk drawer, where they rattle and shake and threaten to collapse the entire piece of furniture.

The house rumbles again. The floorboards quake beneath our feet.

Cursing under my breath, I catch the next book, and in my haste, I nearly fling it through the wall. Its metal corner embeds in the plaster instead, and—trapped—it continues to flap angrily, shredding its pages against the wall. "What did you *do*?" Michal asks in exasperation, swatting aside a particularly fat volume as it launches at my head. "I told you not to touch anything—"

"The book said something about a door!" Seized by panic and another bizarre urge to laugh, I duck toward the settee for cover. "I just thought—maybe—Mathilde could've been hiding—"

The silver corner of another book nicks my cheek, however, and Michal's eyes dilate at the scent of my blood. He takes a deep breath to collect himself before seizing *The Secret Door* from behind my head. "This one?"

"Yes! *Look*—"

With a sigh, Michal opens the book, his eyes flicking down the page before he flips it toward me. "Is this the content for which you were hoping?"

The book depicts a pair of fairies locked in embrace, their winged bodies heaving and their expressions contorting in ecstasy. With an abrupt squeak, I squeeze my eyes shut, slamming the book shut too. "Put it back! Oh my goodness, Michal, put it back *now*!"

He chuckles darkly but obliges. The instant he returns the book, the rest of the books—now flapping around the room almost halfheartedly—fall still and crash to the floor. I exhale a quick breath, too relieved to feel embarrassed—or at least, *too* embarrassed—and lift a hand to the blood on my cheek. Michal watches with glittering amusement. "Shall we continue our search, or would you like to peruse the rest of Mathilde's extensive collection? I can be swayed to either pursuit."

Still that ridiculous urge to laugh. "We don't need to search anymore."

A devious smile spreads across his face. "Option two, then—unless you're forfeiting our game? There is no shame in defeat, you know. I'll be a very gracious winner."

"Michal." I speak his name through clenched teeth, refusing to give him the satisfaction of breaking right now. "What I *mean* is that I think I found her."

"Hmm. Not as much fun, that."

"I heard someone *cackling*." Forcing a scowl at his expression—because honestly, what is *wrong* with me?—I stalk past him to a sconce across the room, leaning close to inspect the brass sculpture at the base. It resembles a human face. Quite a wrinkled face, her eyes narrowed, her jowls sagging on either side of an aquiline nose with a wart on the tip. When a thin line of blood trickles from said nose, Michal's smile vanishes.

"Célie," he warns, but it's too late.

CHAPTER TWENTY-FOUR

Mathilde

The face lunges from the wall, snapping its teeth in this cottage's *third* attempt to bite me.

This time, however, I react too slowly, and the teeth catch my nose between them. Pain erupts across my face as those teeth clamp down, down, *down*, shaking slightly like a dog with a bone. Shrieking, I punch at it blindly, and Michal wrenches the hideous thing from the wall until its ears appear, followed by its neck. Its shoulders. Its chest and its waist and its—

Oh.

I gasp, still clutching my nose, as a decrepit old woman lands upon the carpet, rolling over to glower up at us. Without a word of explanation, she brushes the metallic tint from her ample bosom, the sleeves of her simple linen shift. Brass dust flies in all directions, but most of it—somehow—settles upon Michal's face. He blinks it from his eyes in distaste. "Hello, Mathilde," he says dryly.

"You'll be paying for the destruction of my property, leech," she snaps back at him, wiping the blood from her nose.

"Ah, how I've missed you."

"Don't you dare lay that disgusting charm on *me* like we're old chums. I told you not to come back, yet here you are, bold as brass." She stands on unsteady feet and rubs her backside with an irritable *harrumph*, surveying the two of us with beady blue eyes as the house gradually stops its rumbling. "Vampires. Always sticking their noses in my business—"

"I'm not certain I still *have* a nose," I say indignantly.

"And it serves you right, doesn't it? Teach you not to go poking it where it doesn't belong. How did you even get in here?"

Rolling his eyes, Michal shrugs out of his leather surcoat in an attempt to shake out the brass dust. "I own this house, Mathilde."

"Bah! Blackmail, pure and simple." She shuffles to the settee, collapsing upon it and lifting her stout feet onto the footstool, which wasn't there a moment ago. I blink suspiciously, peering around the rest of the room through my fingers. Unwilling to release my nose for fear of revealing a mangled heap of flesh and nostril to Michal. "And what is ownership, anyway, but the superficial right of possession? No, no, this property shall not be seized by any government while *I* live herein—"

Though Mathilde continues on—and on and on—I stop listening the instant Michal's eyes find mine. They narrow slightly, and I tense as he strides toward me, ignoring my protests and prying my hands from my face. He peers between them to inspect my nose—looking utterly ridiculous with brass powder across his cheeks—before shaking his head and murmuring, "Ruined, I'm afraid."

"Shut up, Michal." Pushing him away, I feel it tentatively for any sign of damage. There doesn't seem to be any, and a warm glow suffuses my chest at the sight of his treacherous little half smirk. Dangerous is what that is. What *he* is.

Very dangerous.

Belatedly, I realize I won the bet, and the possibilities both thrill and terrify me.

"Are the two of you even *listening* to me?" Mathilde makes an angry sound from the settee. "Of course you aren't. It smells like a gods-damned whorehouse in here—"

Michal arches a brow at the books scattered across the floor. "Are you sure that isn't eau de *Milking the Minotaur*?"

Mathilde squawks in outrage. "The audacity! You charge into *my* home, obliterate *my* parlor, and dare to insult my creature comforts? One would think the nosebleeds and tremors are enough. *Beastly* things, they are, most inconvenient—"

"—and also why we're here." Though Michal turns to face her, he halts abruptly when I reach up to wipe the powder from his face. Then—incredibly—he bends slightly to make it easier. I watch my fingers on his skin as if they belong to someone else, unable to withdraw them if I tried. Michal swallows.

In the next second, however, something sharp pokes between us. It spears him in the stomach as we spring apart, and he glares down at the fireplace poker Mathilde somehow wields from the settee. "Am I interrupting again?" she asks sharply. "I thought you were here to proposition *me*."

His disgruntled gaze flicks to her, and he jerks the poker from her hand.

In an instant, a wide smile splits her face, and she waggles her brows in an extremely Lou-ish gesture. "Shall I direct you to the guest bedroom instead?"

If God could choose *this* single moment to smite me, I might thank him. As he does not, however, I am forced to step in front of Michal and pretend this is a perfectly normal situation I've created. Fixing a bright smile on my face, I clench my hands in my skirt. "My apologies, madame. I do not know what came over me—"

Mathilde cackles. "I do."

With a heavy sigh, Michal says, "We need information, Mathilde, and if you give it to us, we'll make it worth your while."

"If you're talking of sexual favors, young man—"

"I am *talking*," he says, "of transferring ownership of this house in exchange for counsel about the revenants—specifically, how to kill them."

All humor I might've found in our situation shrivels to a knot in my chest.

Likewise, Mathilde's smile vanishes just as quickly as it appeared. "I'm not telling you a damn thing."

"Be reasonable, Mathilde. The revenants are becoming a problem, even for you. Those holes they've torn through the veil aren't just making the forest weep—they're making your house shake and your nose bleed. I assume they're affecting your magic too." He tosses the poker aside, and it lands atop her *creature comforts* with a muffled thud. She harrumphs again and crosses her arms. "If that isn't enough, they're also crawling through the streets of Cesarine in a blind rage. How long before they make their way to Chateau le Blanc? How long before they feast on your progeny?"

"My progeny are dumber than posts," she says shortly. "They deserve anything they get from the revenants, and I won't be lifting a finger to stop them."

I blink at her, horrified. "Lou is one of the cleverest people I've ever known."

Mathilde only sneers, turning to lean against the arm of the settee and staring irritably out the diamond-paned window. Her legs tremble only a little. "You can't have known many people, then, can you, petal?"

A different sort of heat licks up my spine now, and a noise of outrage tears from my throat. Civility be damned. "You will not insult Louise le Blanc in front of me."

"How convenient." She jerks her chin over my shoulder. "There's the door."

"You haven't even *met* her—"

"Don't need to. Don't want to." She lifts her beaklike nose obstinately, and there, right on the tip, is the familiar wart of which Lou is so fond. The comparison rankles. This crotchety old woman with her erotica and spite does not deserve a granddaughter like Lou. "Not interested in acts of matricide either."

"Says the woman who tried to drown Morgane in a toilet," I say heatedly.

"That was different!"

"*How*, madame?"

We glare at each other for a long moment, fierce green eyes pitted against beady blue ones. Then— "I wasn't supposed to get caught," Mathilde mutters.

"You filthy *hypocri*—"

"Consider it a favor to me." Michal hooks a finger under my bodice, shooting me a warning look as my teeth begin to lengthen without permission. I can still scent her blood, after all, and the smell of it is—I recoil abruptly with a spark of awareness. The smell of it is oddly . . . *familiar.* Even the sharp scent of the house and all its magic cannot quite disguise that underlying note of roses. Michal's fingers wind tighter around my bodice strings. "Come now, Mathilde. There are not many people to whom I owe favors in this world."

"No, it's just the one for you, isn't it?" Mathilde asks shrewdly, then cackles when Michal's eyes narrow. "Oh, don't look at me like that. Did you not expect me to overhear your repartee with this little tart? Perhaps you shouldn't shout it across the entire island, then, hmm? Word travels fast, mon roi"—her eyes glitter in triumph at his black expression—"or should I not call you that anymore? Imagine my shock at seeing such a very dead man strolling up to my cottage, arm in arm with the girl he died to protect. Seems to me that a quick note to the Old City would clear up any misunderstanding—"

I move instinctively, breaking away from Michal and debating how best to hurl Mathilde from the window. As if sensing the danger, Mathilde rises with unexpected agility, and something ancient stirs within her gaze. Something powerful. "Best check that temper, petal," she says in a low voice, "unless you want me to lose mine."

I touch my tongue to the tip of one fang. "Your nose is bleeding again."

Her gnarled fingers curl.

Before either of us can make good on our threats, however, Michal steps directly between us. "I would think very carefully about how you proceed, Mathilde," he says softly. "You make a powerful enemy, yes"—he tilts his head, eyes glittering as he studies her pale face—"but let us not pretend I'm the only one here who'd prefer their existence to remain secret."

Though we both frown, Mathilde doesn't seem confused by his cryptic warning. No, she glares at Michal with that same ancient power—shifting, assessing, tasting the truth in his words. It makes little sense, however; Mathilde lives on an island inhabited by creatures with preternatural senses. Surely she cannot hide from them completely, and especially not with broken magic. My teeth rescind as skepticism—and perhaps a touch of sheepishness—replaces that streak of protectiveness. I *did* think Michal died only hours ago. "Do the vampires not know about you, Mathilde?"

"Oh, they know a powerful witch lives on the far side of the isle," Michal says. "They know to avoid her if possible. They do not, however, know who she truly is. *What* she truly is," he adds significantly.

"*What* she is . . . meaning an ancestor of La Dame des Sorcières?"

"Among other things."

It isn't an answer, and everyone knows it. Before I can demand a real explanation, however, Mathilde harrumphs again, throwing herself upon the settee and settling into the pillows once more. "It seems we've reached an impasse, then, haven't we?" Still, all traces of that ancient power vanish, replaced by a rather curmudgeonly expression, as she crosses her arms and adds, "I'll keep your secret, but I'm still not interested in your *favors*."

She says the last like a dirty word, and Michal exhales slowly as if praying for patience. "Everyone has a price, Mathilde. What do you want if not my favor or my house?"

Her lips purse, and she folds her gnarled hands across her ample bosom. Then, after a moment of consideration, she says, "I want my hatbox."

If she expected a reaction to such a strange demand, she does not get it—not from Michal, anyway. *I*, however, blink at her in bewilderment, my brow furrowing as my confusion spirals higher. "Your *hatbox*? Do you mean the hatbox you gave Odessa?"

"*Gave?*" Leaping to her feet again—grimacing at the movement—Mathilde thrusts a crooked finger toward the ceiling. "I was *coerced*!

Tricked! She might as well have applied thumbscrews—"

"Deal." Without another word, Michal bites his palm and extends the fresh blood to Mathilde, who eyes it suspiciously. After another moment, however—in which still no one manages to explain—she sighs and extracts a silver knife from her pocket before slicing her own palm. My stomach contracts in macabre fascination as she slaps her palm against his. When she clicks her fingers irritably, the scent of magic blooms once more. Softer this time. Enduring. "A blood oath," Michal says, steadying her when she staggers slightly. "Your hatbox in exchange for everything you know about the revenants—and how to defeat them."

She seems unable to help herself. "And if I don't know how to defeat them?"

"As one of said revenants is trapped inside your hatbox," I say, "I certainly hope you do."

Mathilde curses, and her magic pulses in response—once, twice—before erupting into an acrid cloud of incense and earth. Of *rot.* Only then does she release Michal with a fierce scowl. "Have I mentioned how much I loathe vampires?"

Much like Mathilde's cluttered cottage, her garden bursts with foliage of every size, shape, and color. There are Bluebeard blossoms here, yes, but also rhododendrons, azaleas, and climbing roses. Tree peonies. Mauve wisteria. They all form a sort of natural barrier against the rest of the woods, boxing in the vegetable patch—cabbage, carrots, and cauliflower, leeks and mushrooms, and a dozen others I cannot name—along with a small patio of paver stones. A petal-strewn pond full of lilies and frogs completes the would-be idyllic scene.

Would-be because, tragically, everything is dead.

Everything except the bear.

I try not to stare as it plods around the water's edge, pointedly shuffling its back to us before dropping onto its belly and expelling a disgruntled sigh.

Above it all wafts the scent of rot and roses.

Michal and I sit with a grudging Mathilde at a rusted iron table beneath a willow tree. The fronds, brittle and black, rustle gently overhead as she calls for café. "Er—" I glance toward her cottage uncertainly. "Do you employ a cook, madame? I didn't see anyone when we—"

"—searched my home?" Mathilde drums her gnarled fingers against the tabletop. "Nosy chit. And I'm not your madame."

Right.

I clench my teeth in a smile, determined to get through this conversation without feeding myself to the bear. "Shall we get right to it, then? Can you tell us about the revenants?"

"I've just rung for café," she says irritably.

"Yes, I know that, but as we've established, there are no attendants in the house—"

"Who established that? Never put words in my mouth, you silly girl. Of *course* I have attendants—just because *you* couldn't see or hear them doesn't mean they don't exist." She exhales hard through her nose. "Who do you think I am?"

The back door opens before I can answer—and I *really* want to answer—but my mouth snaps shut at the sight of a tea cart clambering over the threshold of its own accord. Atop it, a carafe and four mismatched bowls bounce haphazardly with a pot of sugar and a pitcher of milk. The latter two slosh their contents with reckless abandon, leaving a trail of confectionary in the cart's wake. Mathilde harrumphs at them before clicking her fingers, and a mop lurches through the door next. It drops with a clatter halfway across the pavers. Though Mathilde snaps her fingers at it again—once, twice, three times—it refuses to move, and she scowls at the fresh trickle of blood from her nose.

"Don't get any ideas," she snaps when my eyes instinctively follow its path. At her tone, I lift my hands in a placating gesture. Because Mathilde and her magic are none of my concern. We're here to learn about revenants—and somehow, she seems to be the sole authority—which means I should bite my tongue; I should not pry.

Unfortunately, I've never been adept at either one of those things.

"Doesn't it *hurt*?" Unable to help myself, I gesture incredulously from her nose to the mop to the cart of café that shudders to a feeble halt a foot away. The carafe seems to groan. "Magic has clearly broken—just listen to that *pot*—so why continue to use it when it affects you like this?"

Mathilde stares at me like I've lost my mind. "Because I'm a witch."

"Yes, but—"

"Stop complicating things, petal," she advises. "I am a witch. For better or worse, magic is part of me. I can no more ignore it than a loup garou can resist the pull of the moon." She snorts derisively before pulling the cart toward her. "But what am I saying? That answer won't mean much to the likes of *you*."

I blink at her, loath to admit she's right, and it means very little. "Because I'm not a witch?"

"Because you're a vampire who still thinks she's human." Her beady eyes flash to Michal as I stiffen, and her lips twist in swift disapproval. "And there's nothing more dangerous than pretending to be something you're not. Isn't that right, leech?"

Instead of answering, he surveys the garden with his signature indifference. I know her words still hit their mark, however, because something shifts behind his gaze. Something hardens, his impenetrable mask sliding back into place. And I *hate* it. That difference in him—though subtle—touches my nape like a block of ice, and I resist the urge to shiver. When I press my foot upon his under the table, urging him to look at me, he flicks an arch glance in my direction and lifts a brow.

"Café would be lovely, wouldn't it?" I ask, pretending Mathilde is being a gracious host instead of goading us.

He makes no such effort. "We take blood in our café," he tells her coolly. "Are you offering?"

Mathilde's withered face splits into a smile, and she leans forward in a conspiratorial fashion. "Would you drink it if so? I've heard quite the vicious rumor to the contrary, but one never knows. It must be very thirsty business having your heart ripped out."

And she called *me* a nosy chit.

Michal leans back in his seat, his expression shrewd. "You've spoken to Mila."

"She might pop in occasionally."

Still cackling, Mathilde seizes a chipped plate piled high with buttery-soft croissants. If possible, my confusion deepens—at my body's memory of eating croissants, yes, and the bizarre pang of hunger that follows, but also at the abrupt turn in conversation. "How can *you* talk to Mila?" I ask her.

She narrows her eyes at my tone, before seizing a bowl and filling it to the brim with steaming black coffee. Hunching over it, she says, "Because I'm a Bride of Death."

"*What?*"

"Did you think you were the only one?" She takes a haughty sip. "Young people. So self-important."

"I—" My incredulous gaze shifts to Michal, who gives away nothing as Mathilde plucks a croissant from the cart. She pushes it into my elbow next, a bit harder than necessary, but I ignore her, pressing harder on Michal's foot. "Did you know about this?"

"Not until after your arrival."

Realization dawns. "That night you left the castle . . ." My voice trails off as I drift back to a different time, a different life, when Michal warned me—still human—not to roam the isle without him. "When you claimed you had business elsewhere, you came here, didn't you? To interrogate Mathilde about me."

Michal inclines his head.

"*Why?*"

"Your scent resembles hers." He lifts a shoulder, but the movement is too tense to be careless. "I recognized it almost instantly, though I didn't know what it meant at the time."

Mathilde hides a smirk behind her bowl of café. "You should've taken a leaf out of my book, petal, and stayed hidden. Death might fancy us, but no good ever comes from other people knowing it."

"Oh, not this again," Guinevere says in a bored voice, and together, we whirl toward the sound. "Death never *fancied* you, Mathilde, and for someone who claims to disparage company, your garden always seems occupied."

She drifts up through the pond in the next second—rolling

her eyes at the bear—and I startle at her unexpected presence, remembering the last I saw her. Or rather, the last I *dreamed* of her, alive, as she danced arm in arm with a human D'Artagnan. *Beware of your sister.* Unease shivers down my spine as I stare at her now, but at least Michal's eyes still glow silver too.

A strange comfort.

"What—what are you doing here, Guinevere?" I ask testily.

"The same as him." She sweeps a disgruntled hand toward the bear, which growls at her with its eyes closed. "Though I'd never choose a bear as my disguise. A swan, perhaps," she says thoughtfully, glancing at the pond, "but of course you would reserve your ire for me either way. Typical. May I ask where else I *should* be, Célie darling? Safe havens such as these are becoming few and far between."

"Safe havens?" Michal asks sharply.

Guinevere's eyes widen in shock and delight upon realizing he can see her. "Well, *hello* again, Michal. My, my, my, how fortuitous this invitation turned out to be." Guinevere settles into the fourth chair at the table and casts him a flirtatious look, batting her lashes and twining a ringlet around her finger. When he stares back at her, expressionless, her smile falters slightly. She blinks at him in confusion before flicking her silver eyes to me. They bulge in horror. "Why aren't you touching him? Why can he see me, Célie? What have you *done*?"

Now Michal does smile, sleek and knife sharp. "I think you know, Guinevere."

A beat of silence.

Then Guinevere swells, shooting from her chair in outrage, her mouth opening and closing like a fish, while Mathilde snorts and nearly falls out of her own. "This is—you cannot—Michal, how *could* you?" Guinevere wails, wringing her hands as Michal rolls his eyes. "I *waited.* I was—I was *saving* myself for when you—"

"*Saving* yourself?" Mathilde guffaws wildly now, pounding her fist upon the iron table. "Ha! You've been spreading your ether to every dangling participle from here to Amandine for the last five hundred years. It never would've worked between you. This one prefers an ingenue." She jerks her thumb at Michal before clicking her fingers again, and a book thuds inside the cottage. It ricochets off the doorjamb and flies into the garden, soaring straight through Guinevere's forehead. Michal catches it on instinct.

"*The Big and Little Deaths: A Ghost's Guide to Self-Gratification,*" he says dryly, arching a brow. "Niche read."

Mathilde bows her head, still cackling and enormously proud of herself. "For your pleasure, Guinevere."

Michal's blood creeps into my face, painting my cheeks scarlet with mortification. Because this has gotten ridiculous. Snatching the book from Michal, I fling it back into the cottage and snap, "We can discuss self-gratification at another time. You made a blood oath to tell us about the revenants, Mathilde."

She wags a gnarled finger. "Ah, petal, but I never said *when.*"

At Michal's black look, however, her crooked grin fades, and she gives another disgruntled harrumph. "Oh, all *right.* Wretched spoilsports."

Still, she takes her time fishing the blackened frond from her café before dumping the rest on her dead azaleas, which lap up the liquid greedily, shudder, and shoot up another inch. Then—"You're a Bride of Death," Mathilde says grudgingly, "so you know the requirements. I should've died at the ripe age of nine—slid right off a crag in La Fôret des Yeux and split open my head—but Death chose to spare me in the form of Josephine Monvoisin."

When I gasp, she nods in grim delight. Guinevere sighs, plucking an azalea from the vine and tucking it into her décolletage. She glances plaintively at Michal.

He closes his eyes as if pained.

"She found me at the bottom of the cliff, and she must've sensed his presence—was always a bit *too* interested in Death, if you ask me. Obsessed, even." Shrugging, Mathilde pauses dramatically to slurp the dregs of her bowl with relish. "My own mother didn't care whether I lived or died, so Josephine insisted I return to the blood camp with her and that wraith of hers." She clicks her fingers in agitation, trying to remember the name.

"Nicholina," Guinevere says by rote.

"Aha!" Mathilde snaps triumphantly. "Nicholina. Never liked her."

"You don't seem to like anyone," I point out.

"Too right you are, and for good reason—Josephine took me on as an apprentice of sorts, so she could poke and prod me every chance she got." Mathilde's lip curls. "I was just a child, so I let her do it. Couldn't wait to be rid of her, though, so I seized the chance to return to Chateau le Blanc when my dear old maman died. Never looked back."

She hesitates with surprising thoughtfulness, tapping her fuzzy chin. "Learned a lot from her. Evil woman, to be sure, but more powerful than anyone should be."

"And did you ever *read* Josephine's grimoire?"

Mathilde leers in evident pride. "Of course I did. She might've been powerful, but I was a plucky thing, even then. I snuck into her tent and flipped through it every chance I got. Tried to tear a page out of it once, but the damned thing refused to give it to me—so I copied it down instead." With a wince and a flick of her wrist, a single sheaf of parchment appears between her fingers. "She took my blood for it, after all."

Yellowed with age, the parchment carries childish handwriting in faded black ink, with a familiar title across the top:

A SPELL TO RESURREKT THE DEAD

Recognition flares, and I lean forward to tug the page from her grasp, skimming it eagerly. Frederic's scratch marks are absent in this version—Mathilde would've copied the spell before he was born—but the chilling *Blood of Death* remains the same. I turn the page over in search of something else, something new about the revenants, but find nothing. Michal bends to examine it over my shoulder, and even Guinevere pauses in curling a ringlet around her finger to listen.

"Is this it?" I look to Mathilde, crestfallen. "You—you really don't know how to defeat them?"

"More words in my mouth," she says irritably, snatching the page back. "You asked about her grimoire, and I answered you. What you've forgotten, silly girl, is that I lived with La Voisin. Do you think I let her steal my blood without learning how she put it to use? Do you think I didn't know her tricks? Of *course* I did. I followed her that night, and I watched her resurrect that corpse. I watched it nearly bludgeon her unconscious too, watched it take a bite out of her leg before she managed to kill it again—permanently this time."

"How did she do it?" Michal asks with an edge to his voice.

But—something niggles at the back of my mind, growing more insistent with each word she says. I'd never thought of it before, never questioned how any of the spells in La Voisin's grimoire came to be. In wake of Mathilde's explanation, however, it seems painfully obvious—of *course* La Voisin would've tested each one. She wouldn't have committed any of them to her precious grimoire if they hadn't proved successful, which means . . . "Did she tear a hole through the veil too?" I ask urgently.

Mathilde's eyes snap to mine. "*That*, petal, is the more interesting question."

The bear at the pond lifts its head.

"When Josephine resurrected that poor man, she tore a hole through the veil, all right, but a *small* one—it healed itself the instant she incinerated him. Turned him to powder," she adds in answer to Michal's question. "*Fire.* It'll kill any undead creature, won't it? Ashes to ashes, and all that. Vampire, revenant—doesn't matter in the end." She waves a dismissive hand, but nothing in her words feels trivial to me. Instead my skin crawls at the implication. Worse still is that niggle at the back of my mind. It insists I look at it—acknowledge it—but I refuse, recoiling from it instinctively.

When Josephine resurrected that poor man, she tore a hole through the veil, all right.

It healed itself the instant she incinerated him.

Though Michal's hard gaze settles upon my face, I refuse to look at him too. "Is there no way to help them?" he asks. "Only death?"

Mathilde skewers him with a pointed look. "They're already

dead, Michal. We can only outrun it for so long—outrun *him.* No one lives forever."

A heaviness settles over the garden with her words, and even the plants seem to wilt just a little more.

Mathilde doesn't seem to notice, instead continuing without missing a beat: "But the hole that night is nothing—*nothing*—compared to whatever opened on All Hallows' Eve. I've never sensed anything like it, which leads me to believe something went wrong with that spell of Frederic's." She pauses significantly, her eyes bright as they find mine. "Or something went very, very right."

Neither Michal nor I question how she knows about the grotto and Frederic. This is exactly the information we needed. Mathilde has given us a way to protect Requiem, Belterra too, and now we can start mending all those little rips of which Mila spoke. *Fire. It'll kill any undead creature, won't it?*

Why, then, do I feel so sick?

Swallowing the lump in my throat, I turn to look at Michal. "What do you think?"

Guinevere floats to the armrest of his chair, resting her chin on her fist and glaring at him in unabashed resentment. "Yes, Michal, what *do* you think about your dead lover and her dead sister?"

I flinch at that, but Michal ignores her, searching my face for a long moment—or perhaps a single second—before his gaze drifts past me to the pond. His jaw clenches. "I think it's time to leave."

It seems our truce is over.

That lump in my throat spreads, almost choking me now. I cannot bring myself to move. I cannot bring myself to leave. When I do, everything will change again; everything will break.

We can only outrun it for so long.

"The first agreeable thing you've said all morning." Heedless, Mathilde slaps her hands against the table and uses them to push to her feet. "D'Artagnan will escort you from my property."

"D'Artagnan?" Frowning, I glance toward the bear as it lumbers to its feet. Sure enough, its—*his*—eyes gleam familiar and amber from the thick black fur of his face. When he makes an odd chuffing noise that sounds like laughter, I recognize his voice. His sharp teeth. My heart pitches to my feet.

"I told you to beware of your sister."

CHAPTER TWENTY-FIVE

Le Lien Éternel

We take a different route back to the castle, avoiding the stream and instead picking our way through particularly heavy undergrowth. Nervousness pricks at my skin as I avoid Michal's gaze, but with each step, I can feel his resolve hardening as the teardrops have done in our absence.

The entire forest now sparkles with ice.

They glitter from the fronds like tiny crystals, slick and sharp, and I'd rather stab each of them into my eyes than have this conversation. Exhaling a slow, wintry breath, I search for something to say that doesn't involve my sister. Something to postpone this conversation just a little while longer. "So—er—why do you think all of *this*"—I gesture helplessly to the knee-high ferns around us—"happened?" When his black eyes cut to mine incredulously, I add, "The ice, I mean. The tears are all, well—frozen now, but of course you can already see that."

He shakes his head. "Célie—"

"The veil must be affecting the temperature. I saw a small hole earlier where a revenant must've torn through, and the spirit realm—it's much colder than ours. It always seems to be snowing there, or perhaps it's just ash—I've never been able to tell—but that would explain why the temperature is plummeting here too." The words fall from my lips faster than strictly necessary, then faster still, until I titter with nervous laughter. It burns all the way up my throat. "Still pretty, though, isn't it? All this ice. It makes me think of Yuletide gifts and snow-white scarves, of ice palaces and orange trees and—and—" I stumble a step at that, nearly slipping on a rock between ferns, but Michal's hand snakes out to catch my elbow.

It sears my skin through the violet silk of my sleeve.

"Célie." A muscle ticks in his jaw as he stares down at me, and for just a moment, something soft—almost vulnerable—shadows his features. I brace for the inevitable, my thoughts scattering wildly for something else, *anything* else, to postpone his next words. "Moje sunce. We need to discuss Filippa."

Filippa.

My eyes flutter shut as her name drifts between us, as fragile as the snowflakes beginning to fall. Though I cannot feel their cold, I still feel their damp, and each kisses my face as a memory. Filippa lacing her fingers through mine as we race toward the river with mud on our boots and leaves in our hair. Laughing. Dancing.

Filippa bowing her dark head over a storybook, tracing each word on the page.

Filippa peeling an orange for me. Filippa crying. Filippa throwing a knife at my back. Filippa standing over Frederic's broken body, clutching her stomach and turning away without a word.

My eyes snap open at the last, and the snowflakes catch in my lashes; they blur my vision until everything is white. That wretched lump rises in my throat again, but I swallow it back down.

Because my sister is a revenant now, and no amount of tears will change that. According to Mathilde, each revenant must die in order to mend the veil—to mend the natural order, the natural *world.* How can I condemn my own sister, however? How can I send her back to the grave she never deserved?

When Michal brushes the snow from my eyes—his touch gentle—inexplicable anger cracks open my chest. Because it isn't fair. *None* of this has been fair, and I haven't had a single choice in any of it. All at once, it becomes too much, too *painful,* and I recoil from his hand as if he slapped me. "No."

Though a muscle feathers in his jaw, his fingers cling to mine, refusing to let me go. "You heard Mathilde, Célie. The veil isn't going to heal itself."

"Perhaps I don't care." I lift my chin to ensure he hears every single word. "I am not discussing this with you."

"Why?" His voice hardens almost imperceptibly, but I still hear it. I still *feel* it. "I thought we were *friends.*"

"We *are* friends—"

"Do friends not communicate?" He shifts slightly closer as if unable to stop himself, and warmth suffuses my belly at that small movement. "Do friends not trust each other to help? To tell the truth?"

The truth. Even the words make me want to laugh, or perhaps scream. Because Michal and I have never told the truth—at least not all of it—and never to each other. Since we first met outside that graveyard, we've danced around whatever this is between us, ignoring it when possible and disguising it with games and questions when not. We have never been honest, yet *now* he wants to speak openly? How convenient when it involves my sister instead of him.

Instead of *us.*

"You want to communicate? You want to tell the truth? Fine." Gripping his shirt, I rise to my tiptoes to speak directly against his lips. I don't pause to examine the instinct, to question the ends or the means. "Tell me about blood sharing."

His eyes narrow. "That isn't what I meant."

"It's what you *should've* meant, though, right? I mean, everyone seems to have an opinion on the topic, but I still haven't heard much about it from *you*." Before he can speak, I plunge onward recklessly. Breathlessly. "Your eyes glowed like mine—you were able to see Mila and Guinevere without touching me—and I caught you during our race earlier, which you said has never happened. Is that what you meant by vampires changing when they feed from each other? They assume each other's abilities?"

His grip turns slightly possessive. "Among other things."

"What other things?"

When he hesitates, I step even closer, my chest grazing his stomach. I should care about this conversation. I should care about it very much, but all I can seem to think about is that small point of contact between us—the way his abdominal muscles clench at the brush of my breasts, the way his hands slide up my wrists to my elbows. "What other things, Michal?" I whisper.

At the sound of my voice, he curses under his breath, releasing me like I've burned him and stalking to the nearest tree; they grow farther apart here—vast and primeval—giving me plenty of time to chase after him. Which I do. Immediately. Snatching his arm, I say, "Just *tell* me—"

He whirls again at my touch, and any sane person would flee such a fierce gaze looming above them. I am not sane, apparently, as the sight of his intensity—such raw *emotion* from someone so controlled, so cold—only engulfs my body with fresh heat. "It's called Le Lien Éternel," he says tightly. "What we're doing—blood sharing—it forms the Eternal Bond, and we have to stop before it's too late." At my rapt expression, he exhales a harsh breath and says, "Please stop looking at me like that."

"And if we don't?"

And if I don't?

Cursing again, he drags a hand through his hair, and I cannot help but stare at the disheveled strands, transfixed. Have I ever seen Michal disheveled? I've seen him broken and bleeding, yes—and in various states of undress, his clothing stained and shredded—but no, I don't think I've ever seen him look so—so muddled, so *flustered* as he does now. The man has tied himself into veritable knots since leaving Mathilde's cottage, perhaps earlier than even that, and inexplicable emotion engulfs me at the sight of it. Of *him.*

The reaction must show on my face because his own darkens; glancing through the clearing, he wraps those cold fingers around my arms before walking us into the shelter of the nearest tree. The icy bark abrades my back as he says in a low voice, "The longer two vampires feed from each other, the stronger the bond grows, until . . ." He hesitates then, his black eyes burning into mine.

"Until?" I ask, pressing my body flush against his.

"Until it becomes irrevocable."

"Irrevocable?"

"You'll need my blood to survive, and I'll need yours."

"Oh." *Oh.* His words penetrate the haze of my thoughts too slowly, but when they do, they act as ice water on the heat in my belly—the flames hiss and twist, leaving me colder and slightly dimmer than before. I blink up at Michal as the stark reality he described settles over us. *The truth.*

An irrevocable bond. An eternal one.

For the first time since All Hallows' Eve, the chasm of eternity yawns open before me, wide and endless. *Eternal.* I should've realized what that word means before now. I should've realized what it would look like as a vampire. And perhaps I *did* realize, but not—not consciously. I never envisioned the actual years, the world and its people constantly in flux, ever changing, evolving, while I remain the same.

And Michal—

I stare up at him, momentarily lost for words in the face of this great, nameless future.

Michal has already lived it. For hundreds of years, he has walked this earth, experiencing things of which I could never dream, engaging in adventures, meeting every sort of person and creature and monster. *And loving them,* says the nasty little voice in my head. I flinch away from the realization instinctively; because of course Michal has engaged in intimate relationships before now, before *me*—dozens of them, probably, even scores. The thought of those beautiful, faceless people leaves me even colder than before.

I've loved two people in my entire life, and both of those relationships ended in the blink of Michal's eye.

Irrevocable.

The word still echoes between us in the stillness of the clearing. It takes on quite a different meaning when coupled with eternal life. Because who am *I* to make such a pivotal decision? I am not Michal, and instinctively, I know that I'm not one of his usual paramours either. I am still just Célie—only Célie—and I've been a vampire for less than a fortnight.

At my expression, he steps away stiffly. "You must regret ever meeting me."

"I never said that."

"It's what you *should've* said though, right?" Searching my gaze, he repeats my previous words. "It's what you should want?"

Though he phrases the last as a question, I cannot help but feel he doesn't mean it as one. *You shouldn't want me, Célie,* his eyes seem to say, and part of me still believes him. Part of me knows I should flee as far and as fast as I can from Michal Vasiliev, yet the other part steps closer.

"Are you going to tell me when this mystical bond forms?" I ask him. "Or has it happened already?" A sudden and unpleasant thought strikes. "Is that why I—?" *Oh God.* I gape at him as that heat claws higher, nearly strangling my words. "Is that why I'm *feeling* all these things about you? Because of this Eternal Bond?"

"We've fed from each other once," Michal says with thinly veiled impatience. "I hate to break it to you, pet, but whatever you're *feeling* about me is because of you, not the bond."

"*Me?*" Though I move to step around him—away from him—my hands catch his surcoat, and I pull him closer instead. His fingers lace through mine. "All of this is happening because of *you.* You and your—your eyes, and your loyalty, and your stupid dimple." His brows contract at that, but I plunge forward before he can speak. "When does it happen, Michal? When does this bond between us become permanent?"

"You don't want to know."

"*Tell* me—"

"The stronger the emotions involved, the faster it happens, but no one can predict the exact moment." He tears his gaze from mine with the air of someone trying to bring the situation back under his control. Apparently he cannot look at me to do that. Cannot touch me either. The thought fills me with a thrill of exhilaration, as does the realization that the bond hasn't happened yet. If we stop drinking from each other, it never will. Nothing needs to change between us—or at least, not *that.* As if echoing my thoughts, he says, "I will not feed from you again."

Instantly, the image of him feeding from Arielle—of him feeding from *anyone* else—rears in my mind like a snake preparing to strike, but I push it away. "Good. Agreed. Perhaps Arielle will let me feed from her too. She seemed to rather enjoy *your* attentions—"

"I intend to honor my word, Célie," he says softly, lethally. "Our bargain still stands. You can feed from me until you learn to control it."

"Oh no." I jab a finger at his chest, and that sense of exhilaration heightens as he glares down at it. "Oh no, no, no. I'll feed from whoever I wish, whenever I wish, and nothing you say can stop me."

Michal's eyes flash dangerously as he steps closer, his powerful body crowding mine against the tree once more. "Fine, Célie. As you wish." Then, with cutting honesty, "I meant what I said before, however. What happened in the tunnels—it cannot happen again. Whether you choose to feed from me or someone else, I will not take another drop of your blood"—those dark eyes flick to my throat—"no matter how tempting you might be."

I blink at him, startled. "Tempting?"

Though he does not clarify, heat still suffuses my body at the word, and we stare at each other beneath the limbs of the frozen yew tree, this moment between us stretching taut enough to snap. At last, I lift a shoulder as if indifferent, trying not to tremble beneath the weight of his gaze.

"Fine," I say simply. "You cannot feed from me again."

"Fine," he echoes. "Never again."

And then I kiss him.

CHAPTER TWENTY-SIX

Irrevocable

The instant our lips touch, his entire body tenses, and a low noise of surprise reverberates in his throat. I feel it all the way to my toes. I feel *him*. Pulling him closer, I practically climb up his chest in an effort to better reach his lips, to wind my hands beneath his arms and wrap myself around him. The rational part of my mind screams at me to stop, stop, *stop*—to release him now and back away slowly, to pretend this never happened—but for once in my life, I do not *want* to be rational. I do not want to stop. Just this once, I want to forget about undead creatures and esoteric bonds, and I want to kiss Michal as the entire world falls apart.

In the next second, however, his hands clamp around my wrists again, and he pulls back with painstaking restraint. "Célie, we can't—"

"Why can't we?" My voice is a whisper against his lips.

He groans in response. "Because if I kiss you now, I'll want to kiss you again, and again, and again, and it cannot go beyond that." His hands still slide from my wrists to my elbows, however, and up farther still. My shoulders. My neck. He lingers upon each as if trying to learn the feel of them, to commit each curve of my body to memory. At last, he cups my jaw and tilts my face, so I must look directly into his black eyes. They burn with indecision, with reluctance, with self-loathing and longing so stark that it takes my breath away.

I stretch upward on my toes, pressing another kiss to his lips—this one just a brush of my own. A shudder runs through his body at the contact. His hands slip into the hair at my nape. "Consider this my favor," I whisper. "Unless you don't *want* to kiss me?"

The indecision in his eyes sharpens instantly, and his fingers tighten, tipping my head back farther. Baring my throat to his predatory gaze. "I want to do more than kiss you."

"No biting," I warn him.

He nods and releases my hair with one hand. Sweeping a thumb across my cheek, he presses down slightly in the hollow and watches, transfixed, as my soft flesh yields to his touch. "Tell me what you want, Célie, and I'll do it."

"I want you to touch me. I've wanted you to touch me since Les Abysses, before even, but I've never known how to ask." The reckless words tumble from my lips without hesitation, but even I can no longer pretend they aren't true. Pressure burns behind my eyes. Because they've *always* been true—even when I thought Michal to be ruthless and cruel, I wanted him to touch me. Even when he abducted me, imprisoned me, threatened me with the people I love. It all should've mattered somehow, but it never did.

And *God*, I want him to touch me.

"You're sure?" he asks darkly.

My entire body tightens in preparation. Swallowing hard, I nod, and then—with a spark of daring—I tentatively wrap my lips around his thumb, pulling it into my mouth. He doesn't recoil this time, not like he did in Les Abysses. Instead he watches my lips upon him for several seconds, his expression hungry, before shaking his head and clicking his tongue in reprimand. "Who would've known that sharp tongue of yours could be so soft?" Withdrawing his thumb slowly, he drags the moisture across my bottom lip. Now it's my turn to shudder. Which I do. Violently. "But those aren't the rules of our game. You defined them quite clearly—you want *me* to touch *you*, not the other way around."

My brows dip in confusion. Because I want to touch him too. I want to touch him very badly. "But what do you—"

"Put your hands on the tree."

A thrill of shock—of unexpected pleasure—streaks through me at the pure authority in his voice, and gooseflesh erupts down my spine. Still, I've never done this before; I don't know how to move, how to respond to such a command, and though I refuse to acknowledge the creeping flush of my own insecurity, Michal still sees it. His voice gentles as he catches my hands, guiding them to the branch overhead. "Right here," he says. "Don't let go."

"And if I do?"

A sharp grin at the challenge. "I'll find another way to restrain you."

It takes every inch of my control not to release the branch after *that.* When I don't, however, Michal makes an almost feral sound of approval—and then he strikes.

Even with our shared abilities, he moves faster than I can react; between one blink and the next, he catches the back of my knee, hitching my leg around his hip, and pushes me into the trunk of the tree. I gasp at the harsh scrape of bark on my back, at the feel of his heavy body pressed into mine. *Enveloping* mine. Because Michal—he is *everywhere*, all hands and teeth and hard muscle, and when he kisses me, I realize he hasn't truly done so until this moment. In each of our brief interactions, he held me like glass, like something precious and fragile and irrevocably breakable, like something he could not bear to lose.

Now he has no such reservations. No such restraint. Now he kisses me like a man starved; he crushes his lips against mine, and when I gasp—overwhelmed by the intensity of it—he devours the sound as if determined to claim every part of me. And perhaps it should frighten me. Perhaps it *does* frighten me, but my thoughts have caught fire, disintegrated, and I can't stop hearing the words he spoke, seeing the slight tremble in his hand. *No one would be disappointed, Célie.*

If my heart could still beat, it would be palpitating. As it cannot, my stomach contracts instead—and someplace lower, hotter, a place I've always tried to ignore. It won't be ignored any longer, however. Not when I shudder in Michal's arms and he breaks away, dragging his mouth down my chin, my throat, my shoulder. *Tasting me*, I realize. Every inch of my skin. And I ache to touch him too.

Releasing the tree, I claw at his chest, but he nips my collarbone in warning. "Your hands, Célie," he murmurs against my skin, his free hand slipping to my leg around his waist. He catches the hem of my gown and inches it up my shin, over my knee, until the satin bunches above our waists. I nearly choke when he steps closer, fitting himself more snugly between my thighs. I still try, however—I *try* to lift my hands, to find purchase against the branch overhead.

Then he flexes his hips against me, and I nearly expire on the spot. Unable to help it, I reach for him again, half-crazed with this blistering *want.* "Michal—"

He chuckles and replaces my hands. "Perhaps I shall win next time, so you can touch me."

Next time. If possible, the flames in my body lick higher—because yes, there *will* be a next time, and my hips have started to roll against him now, seeking more of that delicious friction as my fingers bite into the wood. He trails his knuckles down my arms in response, not stopping until he reaches my ribs. Once there, he spreads his hands wide, watching hungrily as his fingers span below my breasts. He traces the underside of one with his thumb. "Do you remember," he asks softly, "the morning we met? You were wearing a nightgown, and it was raining."

"I remember," I gasp.

"*Do* you?"

Fresh heat suffuses my skin at his tone. It deepens the flush creeping up my chest. Abruptly, Michal bends to lave it with his tongue, and a low moan escapes me as he drags his teeth across the soft swell of my upper breasts. My grip on the branch slips. "You—you refused to help me—"

"I didn't want to help you."

"*Why?*" The branch begins to splinter, snow drifting between us, as he slowly unravels the front of my bodice—a corset built into the dress with violet ribbons. I forwent a regular corset because of it. Only a silk chemise protects my skin from the fabric, and as the gown falls open, Michal drags it aside, baring my chest to his gaze. His pupils dilate at the sight. His lips part on a rough inhale.

"Because," he says tightly, "even then, moje sunce, I knew that I could never know you—that I could never earn such a privilege. That I could never deserve it."

"But—you do know me." The words are breathless, spoken

hastily. "You know me, Michal. Better than anyone." The confession stretches between us like the tree sap at my back: sticky and difficult to remove.

When he takes my breasts in his hands—when he puts his *mouth* upon them—the sensation sends a bolt of heat straight to my core. With another gasp, I roll my hips, but my movements are growing wilder now, clumsier. In a mindless haze, I release the branch to grip his shoulders, to gain purchase against him, to relieve this sharply building *ache* inside me. His lips still against my breast. I feel them curve into a wicked grin.

Too late, I realize my mistake, but I cannot bring myself to care. My head tips back against the tree as I work myself against him. When I speak again, my voice quakes, and *God*, I need him to—to— "Michal, *please.* Touch me. I need you to touch me—"

"You broke the rules to our game."

"*Damn* the game—"

With a rumble of laughter and a quick, efficient tug, he rips the sleeve from my gown, and I realize what he plans to do the second before he does it. My eyes widen in shock. "You wouldn't *dare.*"

He pauses in winding the violet satin around both my wrists. "Shall I stop?"

The answer spills from me without hesitation. Without remorse.

"No," I whisper.

Never in my life have I felt more exposed than I do now, with Michal Vasiliev tying my wrists to the tree branch overhead. Never in my life have I felt more *alive.* Every inch of my skin burns with fire as he ties the satin into a neat bow, as he catches my chin and kisses me again. A feverish, *filthy* kiss that belies his tender touch. "Keep your hands still," he warns again, and his grin widens when my other leg clamps around his waist instead.

I wrench him closer, desperate to feel him again, and I revel in the sensation of his body moving with mine. If *this* is what sex feels like, I fear I'll never want to stop—until that ache, sharp and needy, quickly spirals higher. Almost too sharp now. Almost *too* needy. Though I thrash against him, I don't know what to do to ease it. I don't know what to *do*.

As if sensing my mounting panic, Michal snakes a hand between my thighs, and I nearly leap into the branches at the feel of him there. "Easy," he murmurs at my ear, and instantly, I relax into him once more. Gooseflesh erupts down my spine at the sweep of those strong, dexterous fingers. When I moan, he shudders and presses harder, drawing back to watch me with a hungry expression. "Do that again."

It isn't difficult to oblige. He works his fingers faster at the sound, slipping one inside me—*two*—and I think I might fly apart at the seams if he keeps touching me like this. Though the pressure builds higher and higher, relief lingers just out of reach; I nearly sob in frustration, my fingers curling around the silk restraints. "Michal, I *can't*. I—I don't know how to—"

"Everything you've done is perfect," he says, his voice strained.

At the last, he presses down on the most sensitive part of me, and my entire body shatters. A cry tears from my throat, and Michal's free arm wraps around me as my legs stiffen, as my hands tear through the violet silk like gossamer to clutch his face. Distantly, I realize I'm saying his name—that I'm saying it over and over again, that his eyes have closed at the sound of it, that he rests his forehead against mine as if he'd like to hear it for the rest of his life.

We stand there, clutching each other, for several long moments after my knees collapse. Neither of us speaking.

Le Lien Éternel, he called it. The Eternal Bond.

His voice seems to swirl around us now, equal parts comforting and confusing. *The longer two vampires feed from each other, the stronger the bond grows, until it becomes irrevocable.*

Irrevocable.

His arms tighten around me, and I return the pressure, burying my face in his shoulder and inhaling deeply. Because the truth is Michal Vasiliev hasn't fed from me again, yet this emotion unfurling in my chest . . .

It feels irrevocable to me.

CHAPTER TWENTY-SEVEN

Dust to Dust

After another moment, Michal tenses with the breeze, and I scent why almost immediately—

Decay.

It drifts toward us over the ferns like a harbinger, and I stiffen too. Because I recognize that stench; it smells slightly different here, laced with traces of lichen and earth and fur, but the putrefied base notes remain the same. *Revenant.* Sure enough, Michal pulls away from me with narrowed eyes. When he turns to search the clearing, I relace my bodice instinctively, my fingers blurring as I glance around him for anything unusual. Though the fronds ripple in the wind, I detect no other sign of movement. The overcast sky feels a bit brighter than before, perhaps—the forest around us remains unnaturally quiet—but other than that, nothing seems out of place.

My gaze catches on a slight disturbance to our left, where the undergrowth shifts again. My eyes narrow. It could be the wind, of course, but—

With a shriek, I tackle Michal aside the instant before the revenant bursts from the crystalline foliage, and it collides with the tree as we vanish beneath the fronds. Cold earth cushions our fall—snow flying in every direction—but Michal explodes to his feet before our bodies fully settle, thrusting mine behind his. He curses viciously at his first unimpeded sight of the beast before us.

And it *is* a beast, I realize, gaping at the misshapen creature as it shakes its head to clear the pain of collision. More than that, however, it's a— "Loup garou," I whisper in horror.

Michal nods tersely.

But this creature is unlike any loup garou I've ever seen. His maw—caught halfway through transformation, torn forever between man and wolf—curls over both jagged and blunt teeth, dripping fresh blood down his pelt. Though his torso remains humanoid and male in shape, his hind legs resemble that of a wolf; sharp claws jut from the paws where his feet should be, the tip of each elongated finger. Except—several of them have fallen out. Several of his teeth, too, and his flesh appears swollen in some places, sagging in others. I resist the urge to retch. He hasn't started to liquefy, at least, which means he must be recently dead. No more than a few weeks.

Swallowing hard against the stench, I clutch Michal's arm. "No sudden movements, Célie," he murmurs, his voice unexpectedly calm.

I almost scoff at that. Almost. He needn't warn me about the precariousness of this situation. Panic already lifts the hair at my nape. If not for Michal, the Archbishop would've *eaten* me in Cesarine, demonstrating a supernatural speed and strength to rival even vampires. And he started without a supernatural bone in his body. Not like this loup garou. For all we know, his abilities could surpass ours completely. If we flee now, we might not be able to outrun him, but even if we could, we cannot simply leave him here to terrorize the isle.

Ashes to ashes, Mathilde said. *Dust to dust.*

A heaviness settles over me as I gaze at his agonized body.

No one deserves such a fate.

The wind picks up again, catching our hair, my gown. Michal's cloak. The revenant's eyes—vicious and yellow—roll with torment as he straightens, turning toward us and sniffing the air as if catching a new scent. A bone-chilling growl issues from his chest. And in that moment, I realize the danger is greater than I feared—because the blood on his muzzle is fresh, yes, but it mingles with the slightly darker, crusted blood upon his chest, disguising the torn bits of flesh and teeth marks above it.

All at once, the cause of his death becomes painfully clear.

A vampire tore out his throat.

My fingers tighten on Michal's elbow as the loup garou's growls become louder, as he bares his teeth in unmistakable hatred. Though Michal's lip curls in response, I make a split-second decision before he can escalate the situation. "We need to help him," I say hastily, beseechingly, at Michal's ear. "If we can just reason with him—if we can encourage him to see sense—there might be another way to deal with the revenants, one that doesn't involve setting them on *fire*."

Michal shifts wholly in front of me, his eyes never leaving the revenant. "Mathilde said they cannot be helped—"

The loup garou steps closer then, with a garbled and guttural, "*Dimi—tri*," and my stomach plummets straight through the forest floor. If he knows Dimitri, this situation has just gone from bad to catastrophic, and his next ones only serve to underscore that point. "Where"—the revenant chokes, jerks, and I strain to understand him, leaning around Michal's arm—"Dimitri?"

My vision sharpens on those brutal wounds at his throat while

Coco's explanation of a revenant drifts back to me: *One who has died and risen again with the express purpose of terrorizing the living, particularly those the corpse in question once knew.*

Oh God.

With another vicious growl, the revenant lurches forward, lifting his nose again. Scenting the air around us before his malignant gaze settles upon Michal, who braces to strike. "He hasn't attacked us yet." I seize his surcoat swiftly, my nails piercing the leather, and Michal hesitates. "That counts for something."

At last, Michal tears his gaze from the revenant to search my face, and in his own expression—the tense line of his jaw, the bright unease in his eyes—I sense he understands exactly what I'm asking. *For my sister, we need to try. We need to succeed.* "Please, Michal," I repeat quietly. "There has to be another way."

To my shock, he doesn't brush me aside as the Chasseurs would've done; he doesn't tell me to flee or implore me to see reason. Instead he nods, and I nearly weep in relief at the momentousness of such a small gesture. Because it means he is with me. It means he won't kill my sister on sight.

Turning to the revenant, I ask, "Do you remember your name, monsieur?"

The revenant snarls in response, hunching to shake his head. Jerking and twitching as if unable to keep still. My heart twists at the sight of it—of his pain—and suddenly unwilling to stand it, I take a tentative step around Michal. "Stay close," he says in a low voice.

When the revenant hisses, shaking his head as if to ward off bees, I take a small step forward, speaking much slower and softer than before. "You didn't deserve what Dimitri did to you"—his snarl of agreement punctuates the words—"but hurting him now won't undo the pain. It'll only bring more upon yourself."

He paws at the ground again. He snorts and twitches as I wince, continuing gently, "Perhaps if you try to shift into one form or the other, the pain will lessen."

But he only snarls, his eyes rolling as he lumbers closer.

Michal materializes instantly at my side. To the revenant, he says, "Stop trying to control your adrenaline." If he sees my startled glance, he does not acknowledge it. "Allow it to flow freely through your body, and it might restart your transition. First your head," he coaxes as the revenant hesitates, stumbling slightly with a high-pitched whine. "Then down your neck and through your shoulders to your chest."

Even as he speaks, however, I realize any lingering scent of adrenaline upon the revenant is just that—lingering. His corpse can no longer produce it, which must be why he remains trapped between forms in the first place. Michal's eyes meet mine then, holding them, because he knows the same.

Helplessly, I plunge onward, wracking my mind for another solution. "Perhaps Odessa can concoct some sort of stimulant—"

But it's too late.

Roaring in anguish, the revenant rears up on his haunches in blind rage and splinters the branches overhead. When he hurls them at me, Michal spins us aside, and the full weight of reality crashes through the clearing like an avalanche. *This isn't going to work.*

The revenant charges.

Michal seizes my waist, and I scream in blind panic—I flounder, I *shriek*—as he launches me high over the revenant's head.

Though I land unexpectedly catlike in the boughs of the yew tree, I nearly lose my footing when I whirl on the ice, horrified, to watch him and the revenant collide below in a clash of teeth and limbs. *Oh God.*

Within seconds, my suspicions prove irrefutably true—this revenant *is* faster than the Archbishop. Stronger too. He sinks his teeth into Michal's shoulder with a bestial howl as I search frantically for a weapon. *Any* weapon. At the sound of Michal's groan, my grip on the nearest branch snaps it in two, and I fling the pieces aside impatiently. Because I have to do something. I cannot simply *watch* as the revenant tears Michal into—

My heart leaps into my throat as an idea strikes. Because—the branches, they're—

Wood.

With another crack, I tear a second branch from the tree, shredding the leaves and splitting it into two pieces, rubbing them together in a blur of brown and gray. *Fire.* Mathilde said we need fire, but this wood—it's still cold and damp from the teardrops, *too* damp, and a frustrated curse rises in my throat as Michal wrenches the revenant's arm from its socket, kicking the creature aside and clutching his bleeding neck. His chest rises and falls in fury; his muscles clench in pain.

"Come on, come *on*." Craning my neck to see below, I rub the wood faster as the revenant rises, as foul liquid leaks from the hole where his arm should be. Licking his lips, he stalks a circle around Michal with hackles raised. Michal turns with him, stepping lightly and blocking his path to the tree. To *me.* The revenant snarls.

Though the wood warms from the friction, no spark appears. Not yet. But when it does—

"Let him come to me, Michal." Hissing the words, hoping the revenant cannot hear, I add, "Bring him right to the roots of the tree."

Though I cannot see his face, Michal does not move, remaining staunchly between us, until—with a vicious curse—he nods once and takes a small step backward.

As if waiting for permission all along, the first flame sparks in my hand as the revenant mirrors his movement, but Michal spins in a blur, flashing to the point just below me. "Here!" He thrusts his hand upward for the kindled wood. The revenant moves faster, however; he leaps before Michal can seize the branch, trapping him against the tree. Horror curdles in the pit of my stomach. As if in slow motion, I watch as the revenant's claws sink deep into Michal's chest, as his teeth maul Michal's cheek, his *eye*—

Blood pours from the wound as Michal rears backward, temporarily blinded. He cannot see the branch as it plunges toward the ground. He cannot see anything.

I react without thinking.

With a strangled cry, I leap from the tree, snatching the branch midair and landing directly upon the revenant's shoulders, falling backward to bear us both to the forest floor. *Away from Michal.* And the fire—at last it erupts, licking down the wood and searing my hands. I scarcely feel its heat, however, instead plunging the impromptu torch straight into the revenant's chest. He arches with another howl of rage. He twists and jerks as first his ragged clothes catch fire, then his matted pelt. Still he claws at me, however—still he tries to bury his claws in my legs. I wrap them around his neck in a vise, hot tears burning my cheeks. And I hate them. I *hate* them because I do not deserve them—not as I seize each side of his face, twisting his head to sever his spine.

Michal.

More blood drips between his fingers as he clutches his eye. That scarlet liquid is all I can see. His name is all I can hear, pounding like the beat of a war drum in my ears—Michal, Michal, *Michal*—and I twist the revenant's head farther in answer. I wrench it from his shoulders completely.

He continues to fight, however; he continues to whimper and snarl for Dimitri.

I do not release him until Michal pushes from the tree to join us. Though he staggers a bit, he makes short work of the rest, rending the revenant's body into pieces and tossing each one into a hole between two roots, where they continue to smoke and burn. Except for the revenant's head. I still clutch it between my hands, and its eyes roll wildly in fear as I choke on the sob building in my throat. Because I want to close them. I *should* close them.

Instead I hand his head to Michal without a word, and I watch as he drops it atop the fire.

The snow stops falling at once.

CHAPTER TWENTY-EIGHT

Even the Sun Must Sleep

Michal crouches in front of me a moment later, his expression impenetrable.

I stare back at him through tears, determined not to look toward the yew tree. *Pull yourself together*, I tell myself vehemently. *Killing a revenant isn't the worst you've ever done.* Somehow, the admission only makes me feel worse. Perhaps because I've spent the last week imagining how my friends' blood would taste, or perhaps because I tried to slaughter Jean Luc. Though I didn't quite manage to rip out his heart, I did watch as both Frederic and Michal lost theirs. I reunited with my undead sister in the process, and met my fiendish husband, Death incarnate. Compared to *him*, this revenant should not matter.

My chin still begins to tremble as I look at Michal.

His eye, at least, has already healed. Though the blood remains, painting half his face bright scarlet, he suffered no lasting injury because of me. A tendril of relief unfurls at that.

And withers just as quickly, choked by the smell of smoke.

"Your hands," Michal murmurs, and slowly, I look down at my burnt and blistered palms as if they belong to someone else, my gaze lingering on his wrist when he offers it to me. Blood stains his skin there too, stains his fingers and his sleeves and every single part of him. Every single part of me. "Take it, Célie. Drink."

A terrible ringing starts in my ears.

Those hands—*my* hands—tremble as they accept his wrist, as they peel back the sleeve of his surcoat to reveal the veins beneath. I feel my head bow from outside my body. I watch my lips part, my teeth lengthen. And when I bite, piercing his skin, familiar panic claws up my throat. A maniacal laugh threatens to rise with it, but I swallow it down—I swallow it *all* because I must, because I died, because vampires feast on blood and gorge on violence, and because *I* am a vampire now. If I do not rip the heads from my enemies' shoulders, they will eat me, or stake me, or threaten me with a corpse dressed in my likeness.

With each pull of my mouth, my chest tightens. My head shakes.

And every reason why I left Requiem rushes back to the surface.

This revenant represents too much of what I cannot change, of my sister, of a situation spiraling further and further out of my control. And somehow I know—deep in my bones—the worst is yet to come. *We must all go to the clock room eventually.*

"I'm sorry," Michal says, his voice pained as he lifts my hair, as he holds it away from his blood and my tears. "I'm so sorry it happened this way."

Though he exerts gentle pressure on my nape, pulling my face from his wrist, I cannot meet his gaze. I just *can't.* Clenching my eyes shut, I turn away, but the darkness behind my eyelids rises swiftly to meet me. It smells of revenants and *rot,* like my oldest and most terrible of friends, but it—it shouldn't have been able to find me again as a vampire. Because I—I can see in the dark now. I do not need to breathe, so why does it feel like I'm suffocating, like pale fingers are caressing my throat in a loving embrace? *Are you frightened, sweeting?*

Cold fear grips my heart at that voice, and I recoil instantly, lunging to my feet.

No no *no*—

"Célie." Firm hands grip my own, and Michal's face swims into focus, his black eyes blazing with purpose. "Listen to me. Focus on my voice. Taking a life is never easy, and it shouldn't be. You did what was necessary to protect yourself, to protect me, and that creature—he was suffering. He was *suffering,* and you ended his misery as quickly and humanely as possible."

My body continues to tremble, however; I feel faint, disoriented, as I say, "I ripped off his head."

"You laid him to rest," Michal says firmly. "Do you think he would've preferred to spend eternity as he was? Anguished? Mindless? Your blood might've resurrected his body, but it left his soul behind. He no longer belonged to himself." He pushes the hair from my face before cradling my cheeks. "You set him free."

His words pierce my heart because they're true.

They make me feel even worse.

As if sensing the same, Michal moves behind me, his chest brushing my back and his hands lightly clasping my arms. "Pick something," he says, "and describe it to me."

"Wh-What?"

"I'll start." The air moves overhead as he gestures to the snow swirling around us, and too late, I realize I've accidentally fallen through the veil into the spirit realm. Another full-body shudder overwhelms me at the thought; I haven't lost control like this in weeks, but Michal—he followed me through. He came after me.

"The snowflakes look like falling stars," he says.

"Falling stars?"

He lifts his hand to catch one on the pad of his finger, lowering it to my eyeline. "Look closely—you can see the shape of them better now than you could as a human."

Because of his temperature—or perhaps because of the spirit realm itself—the snowflake doesn't melt, instead sparkling upon his alabaster skin, its shape delicate. Its lines flowing and flowering.

I catch another on my palm, and I stare down at its sharp, glittering edges before tossing it away. They looked like little spears. Like carving knives. "I—I don't think stars look like this, Michal."

"What do they look like, then?"

"I don't know," I admit after another moment, forcing myself to inhale the frigid air through my nose, to exhale through my mouth. I brush my fingertips across the frozen fronds and shiver again. "I've never seen a star up close."

"You should ask Odessa to show you sometime. She built a telescope last year—one of her more recent interests," he adds in quiet explanation. The moment feels almost ethereal, delicate, as if it might break at a noise too loud or a movement too sudden. "She even invited a couple of astronomers to come examine it."

"Did they survive?" I ask faintly.

"Yes." He lifts his hand again, and together, we watch as the snowflake flutters from his finger in a gust of wind. "Pick something else. Tell me what you see."

At his gentle command, my eyes skim around us, trying and failing to see anything but snow—and the yew tree, the corpse below it, which I do not ever want to see again. My breath hitches in response. The air freezes in my throat. "I can't—Michal, I can't do this—"

"Yes, you can."

Still positioned behind me, he takes my hands, guiding me backward one step at a time until the temperature increases and the snow ceases to fall, replaced by the thick and pungent smoke of damp wood. We turn away from the latter, however; instead we face a hollow in the distance where the ferns grow thinner and ice does not cover the landscape. Patches of heather ripple between the rocks and trees instead. *Dames Rouges often use sprigs of heather in protective enchantments. They allegedly bring luck.*

They're the same blooms that grew around his heart.

I blink away the memory, realizing Michal is waiting for me to speak. "I see . . . flowers," I say at last, glancing back at him as warmth blooms in my cheeks. I feel sheepish. Graceless. Michal inclines his head, however, now with a hint of challenge. Still waiting.

When I say nothing else, a small smile tugs at his lips. "Not as descriptive as I would've hoped. Try again."

I sigh heavily. "I see *purple* flowers—"

"What color purple?"

"Michal—"

"What *color*?"

"Mauve." That heat of embarrassment seeps into exasperation, and his grin widens triumphantly. "The blooms are mauve, cerise, *magenta*, and with the wind blowing across them like that, they look like waves."

And they do. They *do* look like waves, which of course remind me of the maelstrom, of my sister, of the revenants all over again. Just as my throat starts to constrict, however, I force my gaze back to Michal; I force myself to still, to calm, to stay present in this moment. I cannot control the future. I do not know what will happen, but here—now—I am standing with Michal in a beautiful place. With him, I am safe.

More than that, I am supported, and I turn in his arms as gratitude washes over me. "It's lovely," I tell him truthfully.

He presses a kiss to my forehead.

"It's where I first stepped foot on Requiem. The sea lies just beyond it"—he lifts his chin toward the horizon—"and my homeland much farther beyond that. I sought an escape," he says in answer to the question on my tongue. "A fresh start. Before she married my father, my mother worshipped the land much like witches do, and she taught me a little of what she knew—enough that I recognized those flowers as a sign of hope for my sister and cousins."

"But not for you?" Hungry for more information about his past, I tip my face to look up at him, to see him as he might've been in that faraway place, as a child clutching his mother's skirt and learning the language of flowers. I cannot picture such softness on him now, however. I cannot imagine Michal as anyone other than who he is: pale and enigmatic, a fortress unto himself.

He doesn't answer my question right away, still staring out at the field of heather as if seeing a different time, a different place. A different island. Indeed, he waits so long that I fear he might not answer at all. A wave of exhaustion sweeps through me at that, and with it, the last of the tightness leaves my chest unexpectedly. Somehow, I feel both brittle and incredibly heavy in its wake, as if a single frond might break me, or perhaps I've already grown roots in this dark and dismal place.

And I cannot help but wonder if it was ever the darkness I feared at all.

Michal's arms tighten around me before falling away. His voice softens with regret. "I never meant for us to turn out this way."

"Who?" I hesitate before turning fully, equal parts determined and frightened to hear his answer. It feels harder to look at him now than it did before—and not because I asked him to touch me. Not because I killed to protect him either. *No.* My chest aches at the sight of him because no one has ever followed me into the spirit realm before. No one has ever followed me into nightmares.

Distantly, I recognize he'll soon lose that ability. When my blood leaves his system, he'll never set foot there again.

As if sensing my uncertainty, he sweeps his thumb across my cheek with a wry smile. "So many questions." He leans down. For a split second, it looks like he might brush a kiss against my lips, but he pulls away just as quickly, leaving me strangely forlorn. "You look exhausted, pet. You should sleep for a while." With a heavy sigh, he adds, "It'll take several hours for the revenant to burn."

I recline within the roots of another tree—a different tree, this one across the clearing—and rest against its silver trunk, trying and failing to close my eyes with Michal standing beside me. Hands in his pockets, surcoat discarded, he leans against the tree and surveys the revenant's makeshift pyre. The yew tree hides much of the smoke, but a thin plume of it still escapes the naked branches to the sky overhead.

Someone could see it. Someone could come.

He doesn't seem concerned, however, his black eyes cutting to mine after several silent moments. They narrow slightly. "That doesn't look like sleep."

"I'm not tired."

"Right." He nods shortly. "And I can eat chocolate éclairs—just had one for breakfast, in fact."

Sighing at his cheek, I tip my head back, heedless of the ice on the bark. There will be no salvaging my hair, nor my gown. Even if Michal hadn't torn off an entire sleeve, all manner of gore stains the violet satin now. I try not to look at it.

"Was your mother a witch?" I ask after another moment.

He shakes his head with a mirthless laugh. "Oh, no. No, we aren't opening that door."

"You already opened it, Michal."

"Consider this me closing it again."

"Consider this me wedging my foot in the door. The only thing you've revealed about your rather extensive past is that your father was a cleric and remarried Odessa and Dimitri's aunt after your mother passed away. Why won't you tell me more about yourself?"

"Because the past is irrelevant, pet. We cannot live there anymore."

I study him, worrying a sprig of what smells like wild rosemary, but cannot bring myself to further argue the point. Not right now. Because Michal is right—I *am* exhausted, my limbs and eyelids heavy, and never before have I missed the oblivion of sleep as I do in this moment.

"Lou mentioned you took a sleeping draught in Cesarine," Michal says quietly. "Why?"

I scoff and toss the rosemary away, rubbing its astringent oil between my fingers. "I thought we weren't allowed to ask questions."

"If memory serves, you owe me several."

"You and your wretched *games*—"

"Not this time." He nudges my arm with his knee, coaxing me to look at him. And because it is Michal, I cannot resist the opportunity to do just that. I glance up at him over my shoulder, taking in his torn shirt, his rolled sleeves, the remnants of crimson on his striking face. He used the scrap of my sleeve to clean the blood as best he could, but—like my gown—the hideous truth of our encounter with the revenant cannot be so easily washed away. "Are you having trouble sleeping, Célie?" he asks.

Perhaps I am too tired for dishonesty, or perhaps I just want to keep telling the truth. To keep telling *him* the truth. "I haven't slept since All Hallows' Eve."

He stares at me like I've just spoken in tongues, his eyes widening slightly. "What?"

"I haven't slept," I repeat, heedless of his reaction. "It cannot be too unusual—vampires don't seem to need sleep, do they? I'm still alive, after all"—I grimace at the turn of phrase—"or rather, my body seems to be fine without it."

"Seems to be fine without it?" Incredulous now, he pushes from the tree, his hands sliding from his pockets as the full weight of his stare lands upon me. "Célie . . . are you telling me you haven't slept in over a week?"

I rise to my feet too, unsure what else to do. "It isn't like I haven't *tried*. It's just—when I close my eyes, my body refuses to—I don't know—*relax*. Before I took Lou's draught, I could never settle enough to sink into sleep, but even with it, the sleep felt more like paralysis than true rest."

"Fuck." Shaking his head, Michal drags a hand down his face

and asks, "Why didn't you tell Odessa?"

"Like I said, I didn't think it mattered."

"It matters," he says fervently, dropping his hand. "Vampires might not need sleep in the same way humans do, but we still need it—if not for our bodies, then for our minds. We consume vast quantities of sensory information per *second*, Célie, and you've maintained consciousness for *hundreds* of hours. Of course you're feeling on edge." With a sound of disgust, he turns away in an effort to collect himself, every line of his body hard and unyielding. Cursing again, he says, "This is my fault. I should've been the one teaching you these things, not Odessa. I should've—I should've *been* there—"

"Then why weren't you?"

It's perhaps the most frequent question I asked myself during those long and disturbing hours in Lou's guest bedroom—why? *Why* did Michal turn me after telling me he never would? Why did he let me go to Cesarine after asking me to stay?

As is often the case, the answer he gives is not the answer I imagined.

"I didn't think you wanted it," he says simply.

The words are too raw, however, and much too close to the truth to hide what he really means: *I didn't think you wanted* me. Instantly, I open my mouth to refute such a brutal claim, or perhaps to not, or perhaps to change the subject altogether, but he speaks again before I can decide. "No time like the present to correct my mistakes. Sit down, Célie. Please."

Still not looking at me, he jerks his head toward the roots and the rosemary. "Let me teach you how to turn off your senses."

Turn off your senses. The prospect sounds dangerous in a place like Requiem, but I return to the soft patch of earth regardless, trusting him, curling my arms around my knees. Michal crouches next to me again. Always crouching. Always tense. To see him sitting, lounging, sprawling like he did on the bank of the stream with me, seems as surreal and out of reach as sleep itself. "Lie back," he instructs, "and close your eyes."

I swallow hard. "I don't . . . necessarily *want* to close my eyes."

He levels me with a shrewd look. "Why not?"

"Are you really going to make me say it after what just happened?" When he nods, resolute, I grimace. "You know, Michal, you can be a real reprobate sometimes."

"And *you* know you aren't really afraid of the dark."

"Excuse me?" I blink at him, insulted and also terrified at his discernment. "You confirmed it yourself at L'ange de la Mort while I was still human—nyctophobia, you called it. You heard my pulse spike, saw my pupils dilate—"

"Oh, I have no doubt darkness elicits memories better left forgotten, but I think you've conflated fear of darkness with a fear of something else."

"Like what?" I ask warily.

"You tell me." He rests his forearms upon his knees as he studies me, his black eyes glittering. "What is it that hides in the darkness?" A suggestive pause. "Or rather, *who*?"

I narrow my gaze on him, not quite understanding his implication but not quite liking it either. Defensiveness pricks at my subconscious, and I tear up another sprig of rosemary for something to do with my hands. "No one can hide from me in the dark anymore."

"Then you shouldn't fear closing your eyes."

Reluctantly, I do as he says, and I hear the air shift as he nods in approval. "Good. Now silence that glorious mind of yours and listen."

I cannot help but crack one eye open suspiciously. "Do you really think my mind is glorious?"

He smirks down at me. "You know I do. And that is exactly the problem. Newborn vampires—all vampires, really—struggle with sensory overload until they learn to focus their attention. And you need to focus your attention in order to relax."

"That feels counterintuitive."

"Close your eye, Célie."

My lips twitch as I shut it again, but this time, I allow Michal's voice to wash over me like a balm.

"Imagine it like fire," he says. "A wildfire is much harder to douse than, say . . . candlelight. And sorting through the sheer quantity of information we perceive can feel like standing in a wildfire. It's too much. It's excessive. Such an onslaught triggers a physiological response even in vampires, making it impossible for us to relax. If we narrow our attention, however—focusing on just one sense, one detail—that fire narrows too."

My eyelids flutter. My grin gradually fades. "Into a candle."

"Into a candle," he repeats. "Sight is the easiest one to extinguish—you're doing it now by closing your eyes. Next is scent. You can extinguish that by—"

"—holding my breath," I finish, "which leaves . . . sound?"

His fingers brush my knee. "And touch."

They vanish a second later, leaving me adrift in the treacherous darkness of my eyelids. *You are not afraid of the dark*, I tell myself fiercely. *Not afraid, not afraid, not afraid.*

Michal's voice softens as he continues. "Focus on anything else you feel—the cool satin of your gown, its individual fibers, the moss and lichen underneath you. The damp earth. The tree roots. Even the air on your skin. Imagine each as a candle and simply . . . snuff them out."

Swallowing hard, I try to do as he says, and to my surprise, my focus sharpens on the individual sensations without difficulty. I feel them. I separate them from my body one by one, and I hold them apart in my mind's eye, blowing out each candle in turn. A thrill of satisfaction shoots through me—because I did it; for once in my life, *I actually did it*—yet now I am truly adrift without the mainstays of touch. Panic climbs up my throat once more, but Michal's voice still finds me in the darkness. He's still here.

After everything, he refuses to leave.

"Now do the same for sound. The wind through the trees, the ice melting, that rumble of thunder over the sea. If you listen closely," he adds, "you can even hear Mathilde bickering with Guinevere and D'Artagnan."

So I can.

Sitting with Michal, each noise seems to amplify as I shift my attention from one to the next, allowing them to build until they wash over me in a strange and soothing orchestra. My body grows heavier at the lilting chords, at even the faint voices of Mathilde and guests. My thrill of satisfaction quiets in their wake, and even the panic in my chest gradually eases.

Because I'm not alone anymore. Not truly. Not even in the dark.

Michal is here, and his voice wraps around me too—it cradles me as I take a last breath, as I hold it, as I blow out each candle and wait until the last possible moment to blow out his too.

Pressing a kiss to my forehead, he murmurs, “Čak i sunce mora spavati.”

But I’ve extinguished his candle before I can properly hear him, and I tumble headfirst into a dream.

CHAPTER TWENTY-NINE

An Audience with the Ice Queen

The dream starts out pleasantly, like a scene straight from a book of fairy stories: a castle of carved and gleaming ice rises around me, and snowflakes drift from the ceiling like falling stars. Some of them flowing and flowering, others sharp and crystalline. They glitter upon my fingertips, my cheeks, and I smile before catching one on my tongue.

At first, I do not notice when they still.

Nor do I notice the air as it thins, the frost as it creeps up my whisper-thin gown. Indeed, I do not notice anything until the castle itself steals over my feet, trapping them in solid ice. Startled, I glance down at my snow-white hands, at the shocking red of my fingernails. They match the winterberries growing in my hair.

The trail of blood glistening upon the ice behind me.

"Finally," my sister says in a bored voice. "I thought you'd never fall asleep."

"*Filippa?*"

I whirl in disbelief, nearly tumbling to the floor when my feet refuse to move, still frozen solid. And in a sickening swoop of intuition, I realize this isn't a dream at all—not with my sister standing feet away from me, cold and cruel and wrong, and not with that look of apathy in her unnerving eyes. One black and one green.

"What are you doing here?" Craning my neck to look around us, I gape at the glittering walls. The blood behind me, I realize, is not blood at all but a cloak of vivid crimson. I cannot place the fabric, however; it ripples in the strange silver light like liquid, like my hand might slip through it, *into* it, if I dared bend down to investigate. "Where *are* we?"

My gaze catches on the pedestal table in the middle of the room—snowflakes carved into the palest of wood—and the elegant bouquet of frozen snowdrops at its center. Behind it, the grand staircase sweeps upward to a sparkling landing before dividing and rising out of sight. I kneel to inspect the glasslike floors, where an evergreen forest has been sculpted beneath the ice. "Is this the spirit realm?" I ask in wonder.

She lifts a delicate shoulder before smoothing the near translucent fabric of her sparkling white gown. She does not wear a crimson cloak or berries in her hair. Instead, she appears almost wraithlike with her spill of black hair and bloodless skin, a dark gash in the fabric of this place. "Almost."

I glance down again, unable to help it. Shadows seem to drift through the evergreens beneath the ice, and—if I look closely—they could almost be . . . people. I repress a shiver when one moves too close, revealing muted yet undeniably chestnut-colored hair.

Frederic.

I jerk backward, away from him, stomach rolling.

"Why do you breathe?" Filippa asks abruptly, tearing me from my shock. My *confusion.* "You are a vampire, ma belle. You are dead, and the dead should not care of such mundane things."

My gaze flicks up to hers in growing horror. Because my sister has trapped the soul of her ex-lover in the floor. Because beside him, Evangeline gazes up at me too, her eyes desolate and empty. "B-Breath allows us to scent things."

"Oh?" Filippa arches a mocking eyebrow. "And what do I smell like?"

I inhale reluctantly, preparing for the worst, but instead my confusion deepens. My brow furrows. Because she—she doesn't smell like a revenant. I draw back slightly, inhaling her scent again. Again. But—no, there is no rot. The snowdrops on the table blacken and crack upon my realization, but Filippa pays them no heed. Instead she lifts her chin in a gesture so like our mother that the sight of it feels like a physical blow to my chest—or perhaps she has simply frozen the air inside me too. It makes no *sense.*

The loup garou—the privateers, even the Archbishop—smelled of decay and fetid things, of despair, but beyond that, none of them could communicate; they could hardly *think*, let alone speak. Not like Filippa.

Something went wrong with that spell of Frederic's—or something went very, very right.

Mathilde described the hole Frederic and Filippa tore through the veil as unique, unlike the rips the other revenants created. Anyone who has seen the maelstrom would agree, but . . . just how far do those differences go?

"Well?" Filippa slowly trails her fingers across the frozen snowdrops. "Do I smell like roses?"

A shiver runs down my spine at the suggestion. At that memory of roses and rot, of candle smoke and of true, suffocating darkness. I will not be frightened of my sister, however, or her newfound alliance. "You smell like you always do, Pip—like beeswax candles."

The lie rises of its own volition, or perhaps not—perhaps,

despite everything, I want to goad her, to gauge her reaction. Perhaps I want to *see* that flicker of irritation in her eyes, that subtle tightening of displeasure, and—

Hope sparks in my chest as her eyes indeed narrow. As her lips purse. *She doesn't want to smell like summer honey.* The awareness dawns slowly, though I don't yet understand it.

Instinctively, I push harder: "This palace looks exactly as I always imagined it—straight from the pages of *The Winter Queen*, isn't it?" I gesture to her gown, to the delicate silver hairpiece nestled at her crown, and a muscle starts to feather in her jaw—a slight movement, yes, but a damning one all the same. "You've certainly dressed the part. The cape is a nice touch. Did you sew the little diamonds yourself?"

With an ominous crack, the ice begins to splinter between our feet. "I know what you're doing, ma belle," she says coldly, "but you will not find what you seek in me. I suggest you stop looking."

That spark of hope kindles now, climbing higher, and I take another step forward, desperate to—to shake her, perhaps, to *embrace* her. To make her remember how much we once loved each other. Because the palace, the gown, the threats, even her alliance with Death—she seems to have donned each like armor, which means . . .

Perhaps there is still something inside her to protect.

"You've never been a monster, Filippa," I say fiercely.

"I do not expect you to understand." Filippa stands rigid, hands clasped at her waist in the perfect imitation of my mother, and watches our nursemaid drift aimlessly through the trees. "Nor do I require your approval. Though we once resembled each other, we have never been the same. Perhaps it is for the best I look like this now, and you look like that—our faces rather reflect the truth of it, don't you think? I am a monster who looks like a monster, and you are a monster who looks like God."

"How can you say that to me?"

"Because I know you." When I open my mouth to argue, to vehemently disagree with her scathing logic, she adds, "Why did you never follow me when I crept out to meet Frederic? I expected to find you behind me at least once, but you never ventured beyond the window. Were you not curious about him? Did you not wonder where we went?"

"Of *course* I wondered." Though I try to remain just as cool, calm, and collected as my older sister, my voice rings out sharp and indignant. "I asked you, Pippa. Every night, I asked, and I asked, and I *asked*, and you refused to tell me a word about him. Clearly, you didn't want me to know—of course now I know *why*—so I never ventured beyond the window because it would've been an invasion of your privacy. I wanted you to like me. I wanted you to *trust* me, but in the end, neither of us got what we wanted, did we?"

She says nothing in response—just continues her perusal of the shadows beneath the floor—and I wince, already regretting the bitter words. "Filippa—" I start ruefully, but she interrupts before I can apologize.

"He promised to return Frostine in exchange for my help."

The confession nearly cleaves my chest in two. "Oh, Pip."

She gives a mournful laugh, but of course, it isn't really a laugh at all. "I need your pity as much as I need your understanding and approval." Her gaze flicks to mine at the last, and in it, I see the lights of Frederic's and Evangeline's souls reflected. She kept them. Despite her quiet defiance, her sharp contempt—she kept them with her, and she is willing to sacrifice everything to keep her daughter too.

And there is my answer.

"I asked him not to involve you in this, Célie." Filippa glides past without looking at me, just as ethereal in this strange palace as a ghost in the spirit realm. Just as chilling. "I tried to keep you out of it, but Death is Death. In the end, what can either of us really do?" When I do not answer, she hesitates in the doorway, glancing back but revealing nothing. "The real reason I brought you here—it isn't because I wanted to see you. It's because he does."

Before I can say another word, Filippa flicks her hand, and I plunge straight through the ice, screaming and falling until my feet slam into hard earth. Disoriented, I brace my knees instinctively and drop into a crouch to absorb the impact. It takes several seconds to realize I am no longer in the ice palace—no longer with Filippa at all but staring up at a familiar face.

"Hello, my sweet," Death croons. "I've been waiting for you."

My body stills at the sound, every muscle tensing in preparation to run, every instinct screaming at me to *flee.* Because this—this isn't right. I shouldn't be here, wherever *here* is, and certainly not alone with Death. *Not again.* The last time I saw him, he ripped out Frederic's heart with a cheery grin—he drained all the blood from his body—and his revenants—his *revenants*—

Their putrid stench surrounds us, clinging to my hair, my skin, my very senses.

I need to leave.

Now.

As if sensing the thought, Death clicks his tongue softly and shakes his head in warning. "And here I thought you'd be pleased to see me," he says. "Truly, I thought you might even want to help me, given the circumstances."

He smirks at my incredulous stare—his silver eyes swirling in the dappled light of another forest—and leans against the trunk of a gnarled and ancient fir. As in Cesarine, tendrils of decay seem to unfurl from his being. They stretch outward into the foliage, blackening the boughs of the trees above him, turning their needles pale and brown.

"No?" He arches an amused brow. "You have no burning questions you'd like to ask? Nothing at all to say to me? That doesn't sound like the Célie I know."

The Célie I know. The words feel too intimate—almost intimidating—but instinct warns me not to argue; instead I straighten slowly, warily, my heart lodged in my throat. Because I recognize these trees—all pine and spruce and cypress. Evergreens. Their sharp scent permeates the air as awareness creeps through me. It prickles my nape, that indefinable feeling of being watched, as if these trees see us just as clearly as we see them—as if they're sentient, *alive*—their whispers carried on a curious breeze.

"La Fôret des Yeux," I whisper.

Death grins. "Very good. I assume you've been here before?"

I nod, gooseflesh erupting down my arms because—yes, I've been in the Forest of Eyes many times, and I'd like to remember approximately none of them. "Is this a—some kind of dream?"

Please let it be a dream.

"Just how often do you dream of me, Célie?" Still grinning, Death pushes from the tree, clad in only a thin white shirt—no coat or cravat—and fitted black pants tucked into knee-high boots. He extends an arm as if expecting me to take it, as if expecting the two of us to promenade through the rot and revenants. "Wait. Don't answer that. Best to keep a little mystery this early in our relationship."

My brows snap together. "We do not *have* a—"

An overhead branch crumbles before I can finish, and though I leap aside to avoid its path, a ray of light breaks through the treetops as the branch falls. It falls across my cheek, my throat, my chest with blistering heat. And for just an instant, I do not understand what's happening, what *hurts*—then I shriek, clutching my face and lunging into the shadows as smoke curls between my fingers. As it escapes toward the brilliant blue sky now peeking through holes in the canopy.

I blink up at those holes in horror. *Sunlight.*

It dapples the undergrowth all around Death, whose pestilence continues to spread, poisoning the trees and wilting their foliage. Needles flutter to the forest floor. Another branch splinters. From the angle of light, it must be midafternoon, which means—

Death tuts sympathetically as reality crashes through me in a sickening wave.

Which means I'm trapped.

Even if I miraculously *do* manage to escape both Death and his revenants—not to mention whatever else lives in this godforsaken forest—I'll have nowhere to go until sunset. Nowhere to hide.

Death knows it.

Strolling closer, he shakes his proffered arms at me. "Of course we have a relationship, Célie darling. You're my Bride." And something in his *voice* . . .

My heart plummets at the possibility that he could be—*controlling* all of this, somehow. The death and decay. The broken branches. Though he looks human now, we know next to nothing about his abilities in our realm. Perhaps he can—*and will*, my intuition warns—do much worse than burn me next time.

"This . . . isn't just a dream, is it?" I ask him.

Death shakes his head slowly. "They never are."

With that terrifying confirmation, the stench of the revenants finally overwhelms me, and I stumble back a step, nearly burning myself in another patch of sunlight. Though they keep out of sight, moving on unnaturally silent feet, I sense them just beyond the shadows, watching us. Waiting. *Scores* of them. The pines shudder at their presence as those tendrils creep farther from Death, withering everything in their path.

Except me, I realize with a brutal twist of my stomach.

Except the revenants.

"But—" I shake my head, still clutching my cheek and ignoring the sharp, needlelike pricks of pain as it heals. "The Forest of Eyes is *hundreds* of miles away from Requiem—"

"The spirit realm cares little for such mundane things as physical distance."

The spirit realm. My thoughts skitter wildly to falling through it outside Mathilde's cottage, but—but Michal and I returned to our realm before I succumbed to sleep. His watchful gaze is the last I remember beyond vague, muddled fragments of my mother's low voice, a warm cloth upon my face. It makes no *sense.* "How did Filippa—? Did she use the *veil* to bring me here?"

Death nods, heaving an impatient sigh when he realizes I'm not going to accept his arm. He seizes my elbow instead. "I've never heard anyone *think* as loudly as you do. Do you always scream your thoughts at unsuspecting onlookers?"

I open my mouth to answer—or to ask *how* Filippa used the veil to travel—but close it again just as quickly, dropping my hand from the freshly healed skin of my cheek. "Why am I here?" I ask instead, forcing myself to remain calm. "What do you *want* with me?"

"Ah. Now *that* I'm glad you asked." Death gestures to the hard-packed earth winding around our feet. My eyes narrow as I follow the path to what appears to be a . . . gate? Suspicion trickles half-formed through my thoughts. Because why would a *gate* be in the middle of the forest? "I'm afraid I need your help with a little experiment. Ignore them," he adds when my gaze darts to a pale hand on the tree up ahead. It slithers out of sight in the next second.

"Easier said than done."

"My revenants won't attack unless you flee—and you aren't going to do that, are you?" Death's eyes glitter almost impishly as he frog-marches me along the path, wrapping his free arm around my shoulders. "No, you're entirely too clever for such theatrics. This is an opportunity, after all, to uncover my diabolical plot, and anyway, you have no torch with which to incinerate anyone this time. *Such* an inconvenience, I know."

He punctuates the words with a squeeze, and I wince at his obvious strength. Worse still, if he's insinuating what I think he is, he knows about the revenant Michal and I burned, but—but how *can* he? We would've scented him if he'd been hiding, would've scented another revenant too.

Though my unease deepens at that, I dare not pull away from him. *Not yet.* Because loath as I am to admit it, Death is right—we have no idea what he wants, only that he wants *something*, and this could be my only opportunity to discover it. I would be a fool not to take advantage, not to wring even a single answer from him before he does—well, whatever it is we're about to do.

"How do you know about the loup garou?" To my surprise, my voice comes out even, and I thank every deity who might be listening for small mercies. "Did—did *you* send him after us?" I ask shrewdly.

Death scoffs as we pass through the gate. "Don't be ridiculous. Haven't I just said no revenant will harm you unless provoked?"

"Then how—?"

"You aren't the only one with spies, my sweet."

I blink at him, praying I misheard, but—no. He said spies. *Spies.* The word hums strangely in my ears—soft at first, a whisper of warning—before rising to an unintelligible din and stinging me. Stinging *hard.* Because a spy is so much worse than Death crouching among ferns to eavesdrop; it's worse than the revenants stalking our footsteps now. A spy is unknown. A spy is *dangerous*—especially if they know about Michal and his subterfuge. *And they would*, my subconscious hisses. *If they saw the revenant burning, they saw Michal too.*

My unease spikes to outright panic at the thought, but I force it down. This isn't the time to lose my head. As Death pulls me forward—so much stronger than me, too strong to overpower—I grit my teeth and stumble along in his wake, pretending I follow of my own volition. And in a way, I *do.* Death needs something from me—that much is clear—and if I can be clever, if I can manipulate that leverage, perhaps he'll tell me everything I need to know.

Still, I drag my feet just enough to seem convincing. "We

needn't be enemies, you know. I didn't particularly care for Frederic either, and my sister—well, I want her to be happy more than anyone. Have you ever considered simply *asking* for my help rather than threatening me with"—I wave my hand toward the dying trees, the shadows moving through them—"all of this?"

"Oh?" Death arches a brow and smirks down at me, as if he knows exactly what I'm trying to do and finds it enormously entertaining. His silver eyes, however, glitter with intrigue. With anticipation. He promised Filippa he would exhaust every option before involving me, so whatever he wants, he must want it very badly. "And just what information will you give for the name of my spy?"

I lift a delicate shoulder beneath his hand, bracing myself for what is to come. "I suppose that depends on the information you give me."

He barks a laugh at that, squeezing again in subtle warning as we round the bend and the first wooden cottage appears. With it, another scent joins those of the pine needles, the roses, the decay. Sharp, biting, and cruel, it nearly singes my nose when I inhale, but worse still is that I—I recognize it. My heart crashes to my feet.

Blood magic.

"I do love a good impasse," Death says, winking at my horrified expression. "Let's see which of us is the first to break, shall we?"

CHAPTER THIRTY

A Date with Death

After the Battle of Cesarine, Coco often spoke of her vision to build a permanent settlement for les Dames Rouges. It made sense; her people had been forced to wander the forest as nomads, never remaining in one place for fear of attracting unwanted attention. Though I never visited their camps myself, Coco described them as dark and dismal places under La Voisin's rule—hopeless, even, when temperatures plummeted and supplies became scarce.

Nothing like this charming village peeking out between evergreens.

Instead of felling the ancient trees, the blood witches simply built their cottages around them. Despite Death's presence beside me, a seed of wonder still cracks open in my chest as I gaze at their brightly painted roofs, their matching front doors—a motley assortment of blush, terra-cotta, and robin's-egg blue. Carved pumpkins from All Hallows' Eve still leer on the steps beside them. Plots of winter vegetables flourish in each garden, bursting with leeks and parsnips and squash as pine needles flutter down to blanket everything in gold. Including—

Firepits, I realize, eyeing the stone circles in every makeshift yard. The logs within them still smell slightly of smoke—of blood—and a chill skitters down my spine as I remember Coco mentioning such a ritual last March. We'd been planting seeds in

Lou's flower beds during their Ostara celebration when I'd asked about their autumnal rituals too.

"We light bonfires in November"—Coco patted the earth smooth while Lou sprawled in the grass beside us, twisting two blades around her finger to form a tiny crown—"to protect from evil spirits that might've crossed on Samhain."

I returned her ghoulish grin with a delighted one of my own—because Samhain and its spectral fingers seemed very far away then. Because they could never reach us while we basked in the sun on that brilliant spring afternoon, surrounded by dirt and flowers.

The irony of that conversation is not lost on me now.

And that wonder in my chest—it withers with everything else we pass, curling into itself like a dead spider until only Death remains.

I skirt another patch of sunlight as he lifts a hand to examine the string of pine cones draped along the wellhead in the village square. Scraps of parchment flutter from each cone, and on them, they've written— "Wishes," I say abruptly, inching closer to read the nearest one: *I wish to kiss someone I meet for the first time.* "This is a wishing well."

"*Was* a wishing well," Death says, perusing another piece of paper with idle interest. "Or have you not noticed this village isn't a village any longer?" At my blank expression, he sighs before plucking another bit of parchment from its pine cone. "*People*, Célie. Where are the *people*?"

"What do you—?"

"Listen."

Brows furrowing, I do just that, tilting my head and concentrating on the cottages around us, but . . . no sounds emanate from any of them. No rustle of curtains, no footfalls upon floorboards. My frown deepens as Death releases me to stalk around the well, jerking the scraps of parchment from each pine cone and skimming every wish.

I hear no breathing either. No heartbeats. *Odd.*

I glance behind us, to the left and right—unsure what, exactly, I'm hoping to find—when my gaze catches on the paddock beyond the wishing well, where the witches kept their livestock. The gate stands wide open between two enormous spruces, and the cows, sheep, and chickens living within have vanished with the rest of the village. There are no signs of struggle, however, or violence of any kind. No bodies, no blood other than that which has dried in the witches' bonfires. They appear to have simply . . . left.

My intuition prickles again.

Fled, the wind seems to whisper.

I glance at the cottage nearest us, taking in the drawn shutters before stepping tentatively toward the door. When none of the revenants stop me—simply watch from the shadows—I close the distance swiftly, ducking under a moldering branch and pulling at the handle. The door swings open without resistance. *Unlocked.* A single forgotten jar of elderberry jam rolls across the wooden floor, and a quick sweep of the pantry confirms it to be the only food left in the kitchen.

Twin waves of relief and dread crash through me as I close the door without a sound.

If I know Coco at all—and I think I do—she would've evacuated this place the instant Lou told her about Death and his revenants. It was her aunt's grimoire, after all, that helped them tear through the veil in the first place; the blood witches would be the first to whom Death turned if he had any questions. Coco would've made the connection. If she suspected Death might pay a visit, she wouldn't have hesitated to whisk her kin to safety. They kept their whereabouts—their sheer *existence*—secret for hundreds of years before this village, and they can likely hide for a hundred more.

Thank God.

Because if Death seeks blood witches, it cannot mean anything good.

I consider him warily now, holding my breath and awaiting his reaction, but he doesn't seem overly concerned with the empty village. He doesn't even seem surprised. Instead he dumps an armful of wishes into the well with a disgruntled expression before turning to find me. "*To inspire laughter,*" he says in answer to my unspoken question. "*To help others. To ask questions.*" Scoffing, he lifts his face to the wind and inhales deeply. "That one could learn a thing or two from you. Honestly, the only things to which I could even remotely relate were *visit a chocolate farm* and *do a handstand.* Humans are so incredibly tedious."

"There is nothing more human than chocolate and handstands." Then, before he can argue— "Did you know the village would be empty?"

"Yes." He inhales again, eyes narrowing on the tree line in search of something. "Do you know if the lovely Cosette burned her aunt's body?" he asks abruptly. "Did she ascend the ashes?"

I stare at him.

Whatever I expected him to say, that was not it, and any answer I might've given catches in my throat, which constricts to the size of a knifepoint. And it certainly *feels* like a knifepoint has lodged there—because the only thing worse than Death seeking blood witches is Death seeking *that* one. That very old, very evil, very *dead* one. I shake my head, mustering every ounce of my conviction. "There is nothing more personal than ascension to a Dame Rouge. *If* Cosette chose to ascend her aunt's ashes, it's really none of your—"

"Ah, well, that's just it, isn't it?" Death chuckles darkly, stowing his hands in his pockets and strolling into the trees without warning. He expects me to follow, and I do—oh, I do, chasing after him like a bat out of hell. *This is bad.* "It *is* my concern—and yours too, I might add. It'll be a damn difficult job to locate her body if Cosette didn't bring it here. The Chasseurs could've buried it anywhere . . ."

His previous words echo as if from a great distance, despite how I nearly clip his heel. *I'm afraid I need your help with a little experiment.*

Oh God. Oh *no.* I shake my head to clear it, convinced I've misunderstood, but—but why else would he need my help? *My* help, specifically? Why else would he break his deal with Filippa to bring me here? Though I desperately try to remain calm, my voice still climbs an octave too high as I say, "You want to resurrect La Voisin."

It isn't a question, but he answers it all the same, slipping the grimoire from his pocket and lifting it into the air without looking at me. Strolling through the trees without a care in the world. He even starts to *whistle.* "I knew you were clever."

My eyes widen on the hateful little book, and I wrack my thoughts for a way to—to distract Death somehow, to delay him as long as I can. "But Frederic—the ritual required his magic too. It required a blood witch. You'll need one in order to—"

"Alas, your blood is the only requirement."

"What about *yours?*" I ask without thinking—because truly, it doesn't matter whose blood he uses, only that he uses no blood at all. We cannot allow anyone else to rise from the grave, and *especially* not Josephine Monvoisin. "Or—or do you not have any? Blood, I mean."

"At the risk of encouraging that stupid idea in your head"—he glances back at me, arching a brow and returning the grimoire to his pocket—"yes, I have blood in this body, but it would be equally foolish to attack me. Death cannot die." Disappointment must flash across my face because he chuckles darkly, then extends his hands to the forest around us. "And I *have* used my blood, Célie darling, or did you think yours created all of our new friends?"

Though I refuse to acknowledge the revenants around us, I can still see them moving in my periphery, and they far outnumber my original estimation. Again, both relief and dread crest through me at the realization—because these revenants aren't my fault, and because—

I swallow hard.

Because who knows how many Death has created.

"*Please*—" I lengthen my strides to keep pace with him. "Whatever it is you're planning, I implore you to reconsider. The veil is already in pieces, and if you resurrect—"

I come to an abrupt halt, however, after bursting into a grove of birch trees and nearly colliding with Death's back. My mouth parts in shock. In awe. All around us, whitewashed pots sway gently upon ethereal branches, and I recognize both with a sickening bolt of clarity. "No," I whisper, retreating an instinctive step.

We shouldn't be here.

This grove—it is sacred to les Dames Rouges, forbidden to

outsiders except by explicit invitation. I should know. Cloaked in scarlet, I accompanied Coco here on the night after the Battle of Cesarine—along with Lou, Reid, Beau, even Jean Luc—and it was one of the most mournful and unsettling experiences of my life. *To honor her blood*, Coco told us, cutting open her chest and using her own to paint strange markings upon her mother's pot, *and its magic.*

Ascension.

It is the last rite of a Dame Rouge, in which loved ones lift the witch's ashes to their final resting place, freeing their spirit and granting them eternal peace. Typically, the entire camp would join the bereaved for the ritual—and a silent vigil beforehand at the deceased's pyre—but the circumstances surrounding this ascension had been different. Secret.

Coco ascended her mother, yes, but she was never meant to ascend her aunt too.

Unbidden, my eyes drift to the farthest corner of the grove, where two pots hang alone.

Death turns slowly to face me, his silver eyes almost glowing in the muted light. "Something the matter?"

I take a deep, calming breath and hold it, forcing myself to remain exactly where I am. I cannot flee. That much is clear. I also cannot help him, no matter the consequences. "Why do you want to talk to La Voisin?"

His eyes narrow as he considers me for a moment, as he tilts his head in contemplation. "All right, Célie," he says at last. "In another show of good faith—in an offer of *friendship*—I will confess that her grimoire has been . . . less useful than I'd hoped." His attention flits to the pots overhead. There are no names to distinguish them, no identifiers whatsoever as to whose remains could hide within. As if realizing the same, he adds irritably, "I might never have killed Frederic if I'd known how prosaic this would all become without him."

"And this"—I gesture to the pots, the grove—"has something to do with your experiments on my sister?"

"It has everything to do with my experiments on your sister." Death bends to examine a particularly low-hanging pot, this one adorned with dove feathers around the mouth. "Surely you've realized Filippa is different. She can think, even reason, beyond the base impulses of a revenant." He lifts a shoulder—the portrait of indifference—but his eyes shine a bit too brightly as he studies the painted markings. "I want to know why."

"And you think La Voisin can tell you that?"

"Among other things."

"*What* other things?"

"Perhaps she can tell us why the hole Frederic and Filippa tore through the veil is so . . . different than the others."

I frown at him, startled. *Different than the others.* It's true, of course, but I never attributed the difference to Frederic and Filippa specifically. My mind catches on the thought; it snags, but I cannot follow the thread with Death standing in front of me. Not when he curses at each pot bearing the exact same markings. "Fucking blood witches," he says.

Edging around him to avoid the sunlight, I say, "If their absence is any indication, I—I don't think they like you much either."

Death grins as he straightens to inspect another pot. "Oh, I'll find them eventually. Never fear *that*."

Dread congeals in my stomach. "Promise not to hurt them."

"I will promise no such thing." At my expression, his grin fades, and he turns away as if unwilling to look at me. Quartz beads hang from the lip of a third pot; they clink gently in the breeze as Death avoids my gaze. "I hear them, you know," he says after a long moment, and gooseflesh creeps down my neck at the unexpected confession. "The dying. They call to me—not with their words, but with their spirits. In those final seconds, they crave the peace of my embrace." Another long pause. "You did not."

"I didn't?" I stare at him, rapt, and try to remember, but my memories of Filippa's coffin swirl together in a sort of abyss now, like my own personal maelstrom. Time ceased to exist inside it. I ceased to exist too. There was only Filippa and Morgane, madness and magic, and the soul-deep surety that I was going to die. No one was coming to save me, and Morgane would never allow me to live. The hopelessness had been paralyzing. The desperation had been more so. Which is why it all sounds so unbelievable now—that Death spared me, that I somehow resisted him in that eternal darkness.

Now I look away swiftly, murmuring, "Do you speak back to them?" At his inquisitive glance, I gesture to the pots around us. "The dead and the dying?"

"These are not the dead, Célie. These are simply bodies—empty shells, if you will. Their spirits have already crossed over. But," he adds, speaking over me when I try to interrupt, "once upon a time . . . yes, I think I did speak back to them, in a way."

Though a thousand more questions erupt in response, I settle on the most useful. "But you hear them even in this form?" *Perhaps the most useful two or three.* "The dying are still able to—well, *die* while you're in our realm instead of yours? Their souls are still crossing over to—" I stop abruptly, pinning him with another wide-eyed stare. "Where *do* they go after they cross?"

"How should I know?"

"You *are* Death—"

"And you ask a lot of questions."

He pivots abruptly, his silver eyes narrowing, and—as the revenants shift, tense and restless—I know I shouldn't push him any further. Whatever just passed between us, Death did not like it. He did not like it at all. As if to distract himself, he reaches out to snatch the nearest pot before recoiling again just as quickly because—because the symbols *cut* him.

Black blood spills from his fingertips.

I recoil at the sight of it, at the peculiar *smell*, as he curses viciously in a language I don't recognize. Then, like a flip has switched inside him, he seizes the pot with a snarl and flings it across the grove, where it shatters against the trunk of a dying birch tree. Ash—the remains of a *person*—trickles to its roots, and I blink rapidly at the unexpected violation. At the sheer violence of it. More cuts open across his palm from the contact, but they heal almost instantly.

And that answers *one* of my questions, at least. I watch in horror as his fingers curl into his palm, hiding the fresh skin there.

"Apologies, my sweet." Smoothing his hair now, he exhales a harsh breath and closes his eyes as if regretting his loss of temper. As if trying to regain his control. Sure enough, when he turns to face me again, he speaks with frightening calm. "Show me where Cosette has hidden her urn, and we can be rid of this foul place."

I stare at him incredulously. *My sweet*, he calls me.

We, he says.

I don't like the sound of either one; I don't like them at *all*, and I liked his outburst even less. The sheer *danger* of my situation reasserts itself with those swirling silver eyes. It immobilizes me for several long, tense seconds. "I don't—" I shake my head and start again, swallowing the lump in my throat. "I don't know where they've hidden it. Ascension is sacred to Dames Rouges. Even Coco would never tell me—"

"Do not," Death says with that terrible, leering smile, "lie to me."

Shit.

The revenants shift closer in response—close enough now to see their rotting skin, their sunken eyes. The latter gleam in the shadows around the grove like those of nocturnal beasts. I resist the urge to shrink away from them. To shrink away from Death, whose eyes no longer gleam like his revenants' but actually start to *glow.*

"Be reasonable." I gesture around us with as much poise as possible, conscious of every single movement. "Why do you think there are no names on these pots? They don't *want* us to know who resides here, and those marks—the blood witches painted them to keep people like us from doing precisely this."

Us. We.

Death steps forward then. He stalks closer, sliding his hands into his pockets. "I make a much better friend than enemy, darling." Before I can speak, he bends his face to mine, articulating succinctly to ensure I hear every word. "You want to be friends, don't you? You want to play nicely?"

Holding my breath, I nod.

"Good," he breathes. "Now go get the pot."

And because I am alone—trapped—surrounded and outnumbered by Death and his undead creatures, I turn on my heel to do just that. I still lift my chin, however. I still keep it high as I pick my way across the grove to the farthest corner. There, two familiar pots hang without beads or glass or feathers as adornment; they hang separate from the rest, cloistered together on a birch tree partially hidden by the enormous fir beside it.

I eye the pots warily before bending to seize my nightgown. With a jerk of my wrist, I tear a strip of silk from the hem and wrap it around my hands, careful to cover all my skin. Then—with gentle movements—I slide the right pot from its branch, sending a silent apology to Coco and praying she might somehow hear it. *Forgive me.*

"Here." I thrust Josephine's ashes toward Death a moment later, feeling sick, but he clicks his tongue again, unwilling to touch it. And that—that brings me a savage sort of satisfaction. *Death can bleed. Death can feel pain.* I tuck the information away as I lower the pot to the ground instead.

When he instructs me to remove the lid next, to extend my hand over her ashes, I tell myself fiercely that it might not work this time. *This isn't All Hallows' Eve.* Still, my vision narrows, and my ears begin to ring as he jerks his chin toward a nearby revenant, who stalks forward to hand him a silver knife. Because it's all too familiar, too harrowing to experience again.

My blood is different now than it was then—my blood is part Michal *now—and—and even if it weren't, Josephine has no body.* I cling to the latter like a lifeline, repeating it over and over again, forcing my eyes to stay open, to watch as Death draws the blade across my palm. I wince at the sting of pain.

She cannot rise without a body. Filippa had a body.

Death tips my hand over Josephine's ashes, and together, we hold our breath as my blood trickles into the pot—less violent than on All Hallows' Eve, yet somehow even worse for it. Because I am still just as weak as I was then, still just as *trapped* as that frightened human girl in a glass coffin. *Please don't let it work*, I think desperately. *Please let my blood fail.*

We wait several long seconds for something to happen. Though the revenants keep their distance—hollow-eyed and silent—the birch trees seem to bend in the wind as if watching too. Death stands preternaturally still for another moment, his eyes fixed and his brows furrowed, before gently cracking open the pot and spreading the blood-soaked ashes upon the ground instead. As they congeal into misshapen lumps under Death's ministrations, my stomach twists.

And we wait.

CHAPTER THIRTY-ONE

Broken Butterflies

After five more minutes of staring down at the foul concoction, my breathing starts to ease, and the trees—they draw back as if satisfied. *It didn't work.* The realization feels surreal—unbelievable, even *impossible* after all the horrible things I've seen, yet even Death cannot claim his experiment has succeeded.

Josephine's ashes remain just as lifeless as ever.

Just as dead.

"It didn't work," Death echoes softly, and despite the relief coursing through my body, I still tense in response to that lethal note in his voice. He turns slowly to look at me, and I cannot read the emotion in his too-bright eyes. Then— "*You* didn't work."

Ah.

Swallowing hard, I choose my next words with great care. As powerful as Death might be, he also feels . . . fragile, somehow, just as porcelain as the fairies on my music box. Just as easily shattered too, and all the more dangerous for it. Unbidden, my eyes drift to the disintegrated pot across the grove. "The ritual required my blood, but my blood no longer exists—not as it did, not undiluted."

Death's face splits into a truly frightening smile. "I suppose I'll need to find another Bride, then, won't I?"

"There are no others." Speaking in a low and calming voice, I pull my hand away, and I edge backward as surreptitiously as possible. "I'm the last one."

"Oh, I don't think that's true." Though his eyes flash at the lie, he allows my fingers to slide from his, bending down to pick up a shard of Josephine's pot. Then—equally slowly, equally calmly—he grasps my wounded hand, drawing one jagged edge across the cut there. Deepening it. I bite my tongue to keep from crying out at the sting of Coco's enchantment. "*Most* of my Brides have crossed over, yes, but not all—not all, Célie."

You should've taken a leaf out of my book, petal, and stayed hidden.

His eyes never leave my face as he crushes the pottery shard and sprinkles the powder between us. His tendrils of rot creep over my bare feet. They feel like ice, like the darkness of my sister's coffin. Clenching my chin to keep it from trembling, I force myself to straighten, to meet his gaze directly. Because I am not Mathilde. It is too late for me to hide. "Perhaps you missed something in the grimoire. Perhaps there's another spell—"

He jerks the hateful black book from his pocket, snarling, "Do not patronize me, *darling.* As I said before"—he rips the first page from its spine—"this book"—he flings it at my face before tearing another—"is as useless"—*another, another, another*—"as *you.*"

True fear spikes in my chest as the pages cloud my vision, as that rot climbs higher, as I sense the revenants moving closer. Though I can *feel* their hunger, I cannot see them; I cannot see *anything*, and I strike out at the next page blindly, catching it between my fingers. "Stop! *Stop*—"

I stumble forward as Death wrenches the page away. "No, no," he says, laughing darkly and crumpling it with the others in his fist. "You don't *deserve* these, so you don't get them—and while we're at it, neither does your precious sister or your darling Dimitri."

Every other thought falls away with my hand, and I leap away with a hiss of pain as the wind lifts, as the branches shift, and as sunlight bathes my shoulder.

Dimitri.

There is only one reason Death would connect Dimitri to this grimoire. And with the realization comes a wave of resignation, an oppressive heaviness in my limbs as the pieces finally click into place: *Your sister found a cure*, Dimitri told me in the grotto.

Whatever that cure might be, it must involve Death.

"Dimitri is your spy," I say. "You made a deal with him too."

A rather sinister smile spreads across Death's face as I slide down the trunk of the nearest tree, settling among its roots. "Oh, Dimitri isn't so terribly bad. He painted part of the portrait for me, yes—and quite a vivid one too—but he must've missed something important on All Hallows' Eve. Filippa was not conscious for it, and regrettably, I killed Frederic before I could ask for details."

I refuse to cower as he drops into a crouch before me, the silver of his eyes still gleaming malevolently. "Perhaps I do not need La Voisin after all. *You* can fill in the gaps for me. We must start with you and your sister, of course, but the two of you weren't the only siblings involved, were you? Dimitri and Odessa played their roles too, and also Michal and Mila Vasiliev—the respective black sheep and golden goose of the family. Did you know their father was a drunkard?"

I know I shouldn't rise. I know a reaction is exactly what he wants—to unsettle me and to fluster me, to trick me into revealing something I shouldn't—but I also cannot help it. Not when

Michal and Mila aren't here to defend their family. "Their father was a cleric," I say tightly.

Death inclines his head. "Forgive me. I didn't realize the two were mutually exclusive. You won't want to hear, then, about how his father drank them into destitution."

My hands curl into my skirts, nearly tearing through the fabric at his politely mocking expression. I should tell him to stop. I should tell him to shut *up* because this has nothing to do with All Hallows' Eve. It has nothing to do with my sister or the revenants either, yet when I open my mouth, it isn't condemnation that spills forth. "How do you know all this? How do you know *him*? Michal said you did him a favor—"

"And I did." Death speaks the words with relish. "Dear Mila fell quite ill after the turn of her family's fortunes, and her dear brother grew quite desperate. They couldn't afford a healer, nor the medicine required to treat her. Michal tried to steal some, of course, but a soldier caught him in the act and beat him with hot rods in the town square—a luckier fate than most. At least he kept his hands."

Nausea threatens to rise at the images taking shape: Michal beaten, Michal broken, Michal young and frightened and *human* as he tried to save his little sister. And though I long to tear the insufferable smirk from Death's face, I need to hear the conclusion of this story. I need to hear it more than I've needed to hear anything else in my life. "And then?"

"He found me," Death says simply.

I blink at him in confusion. "What do you mean he *found* you? How?"

"The same way everyone does. I am not difficult to find."

His meaning doesn't penetrate at first, as if my mind refuses to even consider such a thing. When it does, however, all the air leaves my lungs in a painful rush, and I clench my eyes shut at the onslaught of fresh images. *Michal.*

"A reckless plan, to be sure," Death says idly, as if we're chatting about the weather and not the most horrific of tragedies. "He'd learned about me from his late mother, who worshipped the old gods in the old ways. And when I came for him, he did not embrace me like the others. No. He bargained for his sister's life instead—a new approach, even for me. I'll confess I was intrigued."

My eyes snap open in realization, and the sickness in my stomach turns to ice. "You turned him into a vampire," I whisper.

"I gave him the power to save his sister at the cost of everyone else—including that hapless soldier in the square, and the pretty family next door, and the lonely woman up the road, and his father's entire congregation. And *you*, Célie," he adds. His eyes swirl brighter and brighter still, alive with that *something* I cannot name. I also cannot look away. "When Michal made his choice all those years ago, he sacrificed *you* just as assuredly as he sacrificed all those other innocents. Infuriating how things turn out, isn't it? Your great-great-grandparents hadn't even been born when Michal Vasiliev sealed your fate."

I push to my feet, hands trembling with emotion. With fury, yes, but also with another I dare not look at, *cannot* look at, for fear of it ruining everything Michal and I have built. "He didn't mean to hurt anyone. He—he was just trying to save his sister—"

"He was selfish," Death says, and he too rises, looming over me like a pillar of smoke, of shadow. "He did not think of his sister. He did not think of *you*, and he will reap his just rewards until the end of time—that was part of our deal, after all. It's why you couldn't sustain yourself on animal blood. To possess immortal life, vampires must *take* it. Life," he clarifies darkly. "Just like me."

When I still don't speak, he steps closer for emphasis.

"Now," he breathes, and it sounds almost like a plea. "Tell me of All Hallows' Eve."

His appeal falls on deaf ears, however. Not since Morgane tortured me have I felt such animosity at the loss of my own free will—not when Michal kidnapped me, not when Odessa compelled me, not even when Frederic sacrificed me. Perhaps this corrosive hatred stems from Death laying the foundation for every *single* one of our catastrophic problems, or perhaps he is the breaking point. Perhaps instead he is simply the inevitable, and I've grown so *tired* of the inevitable that I want to scream. I want to scream, and I want to scream until my throat is raw, until someone explains *why* these horrible things keep happening to us. To *me.* Am I truly the one to blame? Or is it Frederic because he slit my throat; Filippa because she loved him?

Does it even matter?

Casting blame will not change the past. It will not right the wrongs. From all directions, every road seems to lead me exactly *here*, yet my life is just that—mine. It cannot be inevitable. It *is not* inevitable. And so a single word escapes through my tightly clenched teeth.

"*No.*"

Death blinks at me, clearly startled, but recovers just as quickly, his silver eyes narrowing as I struggle against our connection. "No?" He tilts his head in polite confusion. "Did you just— Célie, my sweet, did you just *refuse* me?"

"I do not belong to you. I do not belong to *anyone*."

"Is that so?" A dangerous smile touches Death's lips, and his eyes pulse brighter. "Shall we test this brave new theory of yours? An education is clearly in order, so what will it be, Célie? The sun or the revenants? *Wait*." His eyes pulse with excitement. "I know—let's take a little field trip, shall we?"

He seizes my nape, and I cannot stop him from forcing my head upright and making an odd grasping motion with his free hand. In response, the scene around us—the pots, the grove, the very *forest*—seems to ripple, bunching together like fabric. *And it is*, I realize in growing horror. Because Death is—he's gathering the veil in his palm. He's *pleating* it. Sure enough, in the next second, he releases me to punch through the folds, and a dark and familiar room appears on the other side. It smells of Requiem, of the castle. *Of my mother*.

All the air leaves my chest in a painful rush.

She sleeps fitfully in our bedroom, shivering despite the flames in the hearth. Though they bathe her face in golden light, she still appears pale and small against the stark black sheets. I count each of her breaths instinctively, anxiously, tracking the rise and fall of her chest for several seconds before tearing my gaze away to confront Death. "What do you think you're doing? Ivan and Pasha are just outside, and when they—"

"She looks a bit peaked, don't you think?" He doesn't spare her a single glance, instead watching me with something like hunger. "A bit . . . unwell. Listen to that rattle in her chest."

"If you *touch* her—"

"I won't need to touch her to stop her heart." When my eyes flash in shock—in *rage*—he shrugs and leans closer, his own eyes glowing brighter than ever. He lowers his voice. "I don't want to do it, Célie. I don't even want to suggest it, but if you insist on rebuffing my better nature, perhaps my worser one will persuade you. I need to know what happened on All Hallows' Eve, and I will do whatever is necessary to procure that information." A meaningful pause. "Do we understand each other?"

His grip returns to my neck when I refuse to answer, and he squeezes hard. Gasping, I snarl, "You will *not* hurt my mother."

"Good. Agreed. Then we have a bargain. You give me what I need, and your mother remains unharmed. Of course . . ." He hesitates with theatrical flair, tilting his head to consider us before bending low to murmur in my ear. I can feel his slow smile against my neck. "If my terms aren't acceptable, you *could* start feeding her your blood. She needn't ever know. Just a drop of it in her breakfast every morning, and even I could not part her from you."

"You're *sick*."

He chuckles darkly before releasing me at last, turning away to kick over La Voisin's ashes. "Just something to consider."

And I do consider it—as he strolls away, I consider my mother, and I consider him; I consider how free movement has returned to my limbs, how this might be my only chance. *It cannot be inevitable.* And—without considering anything else—I jump.

For a split second, my feet leave the ground, and hope dispels my despair, swelling like a bubble in my chest as I stretch a hand toward the veil and the bedroom beyond it. Toward my mother. Toward *Michal.* Death snatches my wrist before I can clear it, however, and he yanks me backward with that same cruel amusement, except now it doesn't look much like amusement at all.

It looks like fury.

"I find myself rapidly losing patience with this entire enterprise, so you will tell me about All Hallows' Eve." He mends the veil with a curt swipe of his hand. "You will tell me about your *sister*, and you will do it now."

It always comes back to my sister.

Like why the hole Frederic and Filippa tore through the veil is so . . . different from the others.

But I can't understand *why*—not entirely. Not enough to satisfy Death and his macabre fascination. And even if I did understand, I wouldn't tell him. I couldn't. "Look, I don't *know* what makes Filippa special, and I don't know why she created a door instead of a window. I wish I did, but the only person who might've been able to tell us is dead. You killed him. Frederic and my sister—they shared something, the two of them. And that sort of love is dangerous. It isn't for the likes of *you*."

Though he still scowls fiercely, Death tilts his head as if also intrigued. "I am going to bring it down."

Seven simple words, yet the ground seems to fall away as they land. Clutching another tree for balance, I pray that I misheard him. Misinterpreted him. "Bring what down?"

With a hard smile, he slowly steps over the shards of clay. "The veil, Célie. Imagine it—merging the realms of the living and the dead into one kingdom. You and your friends will no longer need to fear my embrace, will no longer need to grieve your departed loved ones after they rise again." Despite his smile, his entire body radiates intensity as he stalks toward me. "Evangeline will sing to you once more; Filippa will reclaim Frederic, and Michal will truly reunite with his sister, as will Lou with her mother, Reid with his patriarch, Cosette with her mother and aunt. Together, we will create a world without need of a reaper—"

"—but in need of a king instead," I say sharply, stepping behind my tree to halt his approach. "I assume you're willing to fill the role."

His smile turns sleek, and in lieu of an answer, he waves a hand toward the revenants again. "Burn it all to the ground."

"What? *No*—"

I whirl toward the village, horrified, but he folds the veil with another grasping movement, punching through it and seizing my arm at the same time. His grip only tightens when I struggle. "Do not fret at our parting, my sweet. I'm sure we'll see each other soon."

Though I scrabble at the veil for purchase, it tears beneath my fingers, and I pitch forward precariously, halfway between each realm but craning my neck to plead, "You cannot do this. Please, *think* about what you're trying to—"

Death laughs and pushes me through.

CHAPTER THIRTY-TWO

Romanticizing Nightmares

This time, I fall through the veil straight into Michal's bed.

More specifically, I fall straight on top of *Michal* in his bed, which might've been pleasant under different circumstances. Under these circumstances, however, I crash against him like a bag of bricks, and he wakes with a snarl, flipping me over and pinning me against the mattress in an instant. His teeth bared. His eyes bright.

His body taut and heavy and *very* naked.

A terrified squeak escapes as I gaze up at him, wide-eyed, unable to move with his hand clenched around my throat. At the sight of me, however, he relaxes almost involuntarily, his face close enough for me to see the precise second his mind catches up to his body. "Célie?" Instantly, his hand falls away, and he shifts backward with an incredulous expression that quickly sharpens to wariness. "What is it? What happened?"

He glances up before I can answer, and I follow his gaze to the torn veil near the grotto's ceiling, through which Death's laughter still echoes. Michal's black eyes narrow to shards of obsidian.

"Was that . . . Death?" he asks softly.

"Yes." I scramble upward to explain myself, to explain *everything* in an unintelligible rush of panic: "And he's—Michal, Death is trying to bring down the veil. All of it. The whole thing. He wants to bring it down, and he—he threatened my mother if I refused to help him. He threatened the blood witches too. And I think I might've told him too much, but I'm not sure because I don't *know* how Frederic and Filippa tore through the veil in the grotto. I don't know how to re-create it either, which means—"

"Célie." Jaw clenched, Michal pushes back to his knees and shakes his head. "Before we talk about anything, I need you to move across the room." He jerks his chin toward the staircase. "Over *there*."

I blink at him, startled. "What? Why?"

"Because," he says in a strained voice, "I am naked, and you quite literally just *fell* into my bed. If you want to have any sort of rational conversation, I need you to move out of it—quickly." His hand creeps to the hem of my nightgown. "Unless you'd prefer to use my mouth for something less civilized than talking."

My cheeks flame with instant heat—partly from embarrassment, but mostly from the visceral image of his tongue between my thighs. *Oh God.* Leaping from the bed, I dart across the room while tugging my nightgown back into place, and I don't risk another glance until I've reached the cold safety of the stairs. His lips have curved into a smirk.

"Start again," he says. "From the beginning this time."

From the beginning.

Right.

With a deep breath, I begin to pace, trying and failing to collect my thoughts. Panic creeps higher up my throat. This situation has spiraled wildly out of control, and every second we spend here is a second wasted. We need to *act.* "My mother—"

"—is safe at the moment." When I open my mouth to argue,

still flushed and disoriented, Michal says curtly, "Death needs to keep his leverage, and you cooperated tonight. What message would it send if he kills her now? How likely would you be to cooperate again?"

Another shiver sweeps through me, and I force myself to sit on the bottom step. To feel the stone beneath my hands. "He seemed so angry. Volatile."

"Let's hope he stays that way." At my confused look, he adds, "An angry Death means we still have the upper hand." Cursing under his breath, Michal stares at his headboard without truly seeing it, and the weight of my words seems to settle over him. "The *veil.* I should've known." Then, louder— "Tell me the rest. Tell me all of it."

With a deep breath, I nod and attempt to do as he says. To slow down. To start at the beginning. And as I concentrate on the chill of the steps, their timeworn smoothness, the words come a little easier as I recount everything that happened tonight. Michal's expression remains inscrutable through it all, except when my voice hitches at Death threatening my mother. Here, his lip curls slightly, but he doesn't interrupt; he doesn't speak at all until after I've stumbled through the rest, and a fresh bolt of anxiety shoots through me as I remember Death's parting words. "The village! Death said—Michal, he told the revenants to burn it to the ground." I vault to my feet. "I need to go back. We need to—to try to save their homes somehow. The blood witches—"

"—can rebuild," he says firmly. "There is nothing more we can do. Because of Coco, they managed to evade Death—an incredible feat, if he's as volatile as you say. And it makes sense. He isn't accustomed to experiencing human emotions. Anger, pride, greed—they'll be running rampant through his new body. I assume they'll have turned him into an arrogant bastard."

"They have," I confirm, though I still feel uneasy. "Death knows Mila has been spying on them too. She could be in danger. We need to warn her right away—"

"And we will." Across the room, his night-dark eyes glint with intensity, with *conviction.* "We'll send word to everyone—Louise, Cosette, Beauregard, even Jean Luc, who will in turn spread word to their people. Likewise, every creature in Requiem will know how to dispatch Death's revenants after tonight. Odessa will see to that."

Though my body remains tense, my mind recognizes the truth in his words. The revenants, at least, can be addressed; their deaths will mend the holes they've created. Still . . . *You will no longer need to fear my embrace, will no longer need to grieve your departed loved ones.* Death's voice drifts like a specter in my thoughts. We have a much greater problem than the revenants now, but—as we have no immediate solution—I ignore it for the moment, focusing instead on Michal. The tightness in my shoulders eases slightly.

"You aren't alone in this, Célie," he continues. "Death tried to frighten you tonight. He tried to isolate you, and he will continue to do so. No matter how he makes you feel, however, you must remember that you have the control. You have the advantage. You have—"

"You," I say without thinking.

He blinks as if startled, and for several seconds, his body goes completely still. I cannot read his face. Though his response is not unexpected, it still brings a lump to my throat. For once, I wish he'd simply let go, let live, let me *see* those emotions he tries to keep buried—for his own sake as well as my own. Because the vampire before me is only one fraction of the whole; before this, Michal was a young man who loved his family so deeply that he made a deal with Death, sacrificing everything for them. *He—did me a favor once. I've regretted it every day since.*

I cannot help but think, however—if push came to shove—he would damn the consequences and choose the same all over again. To save Mila.

To save me.

He inclines his head. "For as long as you want me, Célie." My breath catches at that, and I know he hears it because he closes his eyes—just for a second, as if the sound of it pains him somehow. And I want to ask why; I want to *know*, but his eyes have already snapped open. "Did he hurt you?"

Though I shake my head, my eyes flit unbidden to my hand, and he doesn't miss that either. His expression darkens.

"Come here," he says.

My feet respond instinctively; despite the quiet menace in his voice, I close the distance between us without hesitation, and I perch on the edge of the bed, turning to face him with a murmured, "I promise I'm fine—"

He takes my hand before I can finish, however, his touch exceedingly gentle as he turns my palm upward to examine the cut from Death's silver knife. I curl my fingers to hide it. "It really doesn't matter. It's nothing." Still I watch, transfixed, as his pupils dilate, as his fingers sweep up my forearm before hesitating on the soft, delicate skin of my inner elbow. I should be riddled with Death's fingerprints by now, but I'm not.

Because of Michal.

He still seems to sense exactly where the marks should be, however, because his eyes glint with cold and lethal promise when they finally meet mine. "I intend to be there next time Death pays a visit. He will never touch you again."

Gooseflesh erupts down my arms at the change in his tone, and with it, the more immediate situation reasserts itself—namely, his looming presence, his sinister expression, and his gloriously and inescapably naked body. Awareness returns with a wave of heat. It burns up my cheeks and ears, and I swallow hard, fixing my gaze upon his face and refusing to look below his neck. My stomach still tightens, however. It still flutters with anticipation. Because I am an *idiot*, and I should've—I don't know—demanded he dress himself at the onset of this discussion, or fled across the room and held it at a much safer distance. *Like across the kingdom*, I think with another inexplicable shiver.

If I had, perhaps I wouldn't now be realizing how Michal resembles an ancient pagan god, every inch of his body chiseled from stone. Perhaps I wouldn't be noticing how the candlelight reflects upon his chest, his arms, his torso, throwing each contour in sharp relief. Or how his presence here seems so much larger than anywhere else—potent, almost overpowering—despite him kneeling before me on silk sheets.

His eyes slowly heat as the silence stretches between us. As he gently—so gently—brushes a thumb across my knuckles. "Take my blood, Célie. Heal yourself."

Oh God.

Flustered, I clamber away from him with a stammered, "I—I really am terribly sorry about dropping in on you like this. R-Really sorry. *Terribly* sorry. This is—" I wave an agitated hand toward his body, staring resolutely across the cavern. At least the revenants within the maelstrom have gone—burned, probably, if the lingering scent of smoke in the air is any indication. "This isn't—I mean, my hand doesn't even hurt, and—and I should probably check back in on my mother. Yes." Nodding like a lunatic, I cringe at how horribly light my voice sounds in the cavernous room. How *hearty.* "Like you said, she's probably fine—and I'm fine too—but I did leave her alone in a castle full of vampires—"

Michal's arm snakes out to catch my waist before I can slide from the bed and melt through the floor.

"Nice try," he says in a low, even voice, "but Pasha and Ivan are stationed outside her door. Why are you running from me?"

"I am not *running.* I—I simply—" I cast about for the right words, finding none in the wake of the delicious weight of his arm around me. It feels . . . heavy. *Strong.* Almost sick with heat now, I close my eyes and clench my limbs to keep them from trembling. *This isn't the time. This isn't the place.* There are still so many—so many *things* we need to discuss, and my hand can wait. It *needs* to wait, or I fear I'll stay in this bed forever. "I didn't mean to intrude. That's all I meant. I never planned to come here—"

"Why not?" Michal asks dryly. "You can visit Death but not me?"

My eyes flick open as defensiveness sparks, and I cling to it like a life raft, even as my body inches back against his chest. "I didn't *visit* Death. He stole me from my bed, but—"

Michal's arm tightens near imperceptibly. "Your bed?"

"Not like *that.* He—I—" But the words tangle on my tongue as his blood roars through my ears, and I cannot think around this overwhelming need to press against him, *everywhere.* A thread of trepidation still holds me back, however. It knots in my belly, inexplicable and impossible to ignore—because this bed is not a tree in the forest.

There is no revenant poised to attack.

Michal and I are alone now, truly alone, and he is naked. If things progress much further, they might progress all the way, and—I shouldn't want that, should I? *Do not give him anything you cannot take back*, my mother once warned about Reid. At the ripe age of fifteen, I'd just told her I loved him, and for some reason, the confession had alarmed her. I understand her fear a little better now.

Michal is not Reid, however. Michal is so much . . . more.

For as long as you want me, Célie.

He seems to sense my rising panic. Without a word, his arm falls away from me, and he shifts back again, ignoring my small noise of protest. "You're frightened," he says simply.

When he moves to wrap the sheet around his waist, I seize his arm on instinct and admit the truth: "Not of *you*. I just—I've never seen a man naked before."

Our gazes catch and hold as the words evoke another time, another place, another Michal, and the memory of Les Abysses descends between us. *It isn't a dirty word, you know*, he told me that night.

What word?

Virgin.

To my relief, he doesn't look disappointed now either. Though he remains quiet for a long moment, something sharpens in his gaze as we study each other in the dim light of the grotto. It resembles longing and, strangely enough, feels just as vulnerable as my confession. "So look," he says at last.

His pupils dilate as fresh heat blooms in my cheeks, but still he does not move as my hand slides from his arm to his palm. Resolve hardens in my chest. Because I—I want to look at him. Even though I shouldn't, I want to look at him very badly, and now—now I can.

With a deep breath, I inch closer, taking in the hard lines of his shoulders, the sweeping slope of his chest. His abdomen. The taut muscles there contract slightly beneath my stare, and only with great difficulty do I tear my gaze away to study the V between his hips instead. An almost painful ache radiates from my belly at the sight. And I want to touch him. I *need* to touch him, yet lower still—

My mouth dries.

Though I haven't seen a naked man before, I never imagined one could look like this. "You're—" My voice comes out higher than usual, however—much too high—so I clear my throat and try again. "You look—you're beautiful, Michal," I finally manage. "One of the most beautiful people I've ever met."

The vulnerability in his eyes seems to splinter at the compliment, and he pulls his hand away with a sharp and self-deprecating laugh. It punctures the dreamlike quality of the moment. It brings us abruptly back to reality. "What did I tell you about romanticizing nightmares?" he asks.

Startled, I frown up at him, worried I've said the wrong thing, the *worst* thing. But—no. My frown deepens. I don't think I have. "Is that really how you think of yourself?"

"You should too."

"No, I shouldn't," I say a touch sharply, "and you shouldn't either."

Before I can press the issue further, however, a familiar meow erupts from the floor. An aggrieved one. Leaning over the bedside, I come face-to-face with a fat orange tabby, who cannot reach the edge of Michal's sheet despite his best attempts. We blink at each other for a beat of silence. Then—

"Toulouse?" Momentarily distracted, I bend to scoop him into my arms, and a saucer of milk near a small writing desk in the corner catches my eye. I recognize neither from my last time in the grotto. "What are you doing here?"

He meows again, and his brothers and sisters scramble from beneath the bed in answer, *all* of them, crying and attempting to claw their way up the bedcovers to reach us. I peer down at them, bewildered. "What—?"

Shaking his head, Michal exhales a harsh breath in answer before rising to his feet. Though I want to stop him—to finish our conversation—he vanishes behind the black curtain in the next second, and when he returns, he wears loose-fitting pants and a wooden expression. Tension still lingers in his shoulders, in his eyes, as he extends a linen bandage. *A peace offering.* When I reach out to take it, he catches my wrist instead, winding the fabric around my wounded hand with deft, gentle movements. "You cannot stay in your room anymore," he says in a low voice, knotting the fabric and brushing a kiss against my fingers. "Promise me. Not while Death thinks he can come and go as he pleases."

"But my mother—"

"—is safe from Death until the status quo changes, but if you're worried, Pasha and Ivan will remain with her at all times. She'll be safe with them." He bends to scratch Toulouse's head. The movement strikes me as oddly instinctive and—gentle. It also brings his face much closer to mine, and I study his fringe of dark lashes, the sweep of his silver hair. Such a striking combination. An unusual one. For the first time, I wonder whether his hair has always been this color, or if it somehow changed after becoming a vampire. I wonder if he ever owned a cat. Silly questions, perhaps, but there are so many things I don't know about him.

Did you know their father was a drunkard?

"Why are the kittens here?" I blurt out.

He doesn't hesitate in answering, now scratching Toulouse beneath his chin. "Because they make your mother uncomfortable."

And something in the ease of his answer undoes me.

Leaning forward without warning, I kiss him.

I kiss him because he is selfless and kind, and somewhere along the way, he learned to hide the best parts of himself. I kiss him because he cares about my mother, cares about kittens, cares about *me* despite the danger we pose, despite his world falling apart around him. It would've been so much easier to walk away. It would've been expected—celebrated, even—if he'd killed me and my friends on All Hallows' Eve. He would've retained his crown. He would've ruled forever.

Instead he sighs softer now—almost a groan—and responds in turn, kissing my jaw, my throat, before detaching Toulouse from my lap and setting him upon the floor. When he returns, his palms slide up my legs, and he parts my knees slowly, stepping into the space between them. I slide my hips to the edge of the bed in response, right against his, and wrap my feet around his calves.

"Don't go with him again," he says against my lips. "Not without telling someone. Promise me."

And I want to agree. I want to kiss him until neither of us can breathe, until I no longer blush scarlet every time I see him. I want to know what his skin feels like. I want to explore this overwhelming connection between us, and more than that, I want to understand it. I want to understand *him.*

Instead I say nothing, quietly hating myself because I can't promise it won't happen again—I can't promise anything when it comes to Death, who seems to hold everyone in the palm of his hand. My sister, my mother, even *me*, and also—

The truth I tried to forget crashes down on my head.

Dimitri.

I forgot to tell Michal about Dimitri.

If Death is to be believed, he owns Dimitri too—made some sort of deal with him—and I have a sneaking suspicion I know what it was. Worse still, we forgave him after his betrayal on All Hallows' Eve; we *believed* him, and that makes us the fools. Even his name curdles my stomach now. Indeed, I stiffen just as Michal's hands move to my hips, as his gaze descends to where our bodies touch.

"Michal."

At the sudden tension in my body, his eyes flick back to mine, the heat in them cooling slightly at whatever he sees. A furrow appears between his brows. "What is it? What's wrong?"

His voice is tight again, strained, and I don't want to tell him. *God*, I don't want to tell him—to ruin this moment—but as he lifts a hand to my cheek, searching my face, I realize this isn't about me. This is about him. Dimitri is his cousin, and he deserves to know what Death told me today.

Before I can say the words aloud, however, Michal speaks with such quiet intensity that I want to kiss him all over again. "We don't need to do anything you don't want to do, Célie. If you're uncomfortable—"

"I'm not," I say hastily, squeezing my legs tighter when he moves to step away. My arms snake around his neck for good measure, and I cling to him. "I'm not uncomfortable, and I—I don't want to stop"—he tilts his head at my jumbled explanation—"but I need to talk to you about—about Dimitri."

Michal blinks, clearly startled by mention of his cousin. "Dimitri," he repeats flatly. "You want to talk about . . . Dimitri."

I nod warily. "And Death."

"Ah." Comprehension flickers in the depths of Michal's eyes, and now *he* stiffens, his hands falling from my hips altogether. He pulls away with a curse, and reluctantly, I release him, feeling sick again as he stalks to the writing desk, pulls open the drawer, and withdraws a bottle of absinthe. He plunks it onto the desktop. "What has he done?" he finally asks.

Still I feel the need to—protect Michal, somehow, even when I know it isn't possible. "I don't know if it's true—"

"It probably is."

"Death said all sorts of horrible things—"

"Out with it, Célie."

"They made a deal," I say abruptly. "I don't know what Death agreed to give Dimitri in return, but Dimitri told him about All Hallows' Eve. He told him about the masquerade, about Frederic's ritual, about you and about me, even about Odessa and the fake insurrection." When Michal says nothing, I slide from the bed, careful to avoid Toulouse and his siblings as I approach him. "Like I said, Dimitri might not have been involved. Death could've been lying." A careful pause. "After all, he seemed to know . . . other things, as well. Things Dimitri couldn't have told him."

Michal withdraws two small glasses from his desk, pouring a small measure of absinthe into each. He doesn't look at me. His fingers clench white around the bottle. "Such as?" he asks calmly.

I resist the urge to place a hand upon his back. "He—he spoke of your parents."

"What of them?"

"Um, well—" My throat closes around the words.

"My father's addiction? My mother's heresy?" He slides a sidelong glance in my direction for confirmation, his eyes brittle and overly bright. "Dimitri knew of both."

"He also spoke of Mila." When I swallow hard, Michal tracks the movement reflexively before turning back to the absinthe. He stares down at it with palpable hatred, as if even the sight of it revolts him. And suddenly, I wonder at the presence of that bottle in his bedroom. I wonder why he keeps it here at all. "He spoke of how you turned her into a vampire. How *you* turned into a vampire."

Without a word, he extends one of the glasses to me, but I shake my head, remembering my last experience with the horrendous stuff—how I vomited all over his pristine boots. My vampiric body would likely reject it even faster. I have no idea how Michal can keep it down. "I'd rather die again than drink that," I say frankly.

"Fair enough." He downs each drink in one swallow—his face impassive despite the burn of alcohol—before returning the glasses to the desk and saying, "I'm sure you have questions."

"You don't owe me any answers, Michal." I draw to a halt at his side, turning to lean against the desktop. "I seem to remember owing *you* quite a few, though. I hope you'll be kind when the time comes."

A ghost of a smile touches his lips, and a deeper sort of warmth infuses my chest at the sight of it—because he hasn't shut me out yet. Because he isn't pushing me away. Instead he shakes his head and turns too, crossing his legs and mirroring my stance. "No more games, Célie. What do you want to know?"

We stare at each other for a long moment before I say tentatively, "Death said you found him, just like everyone else does." I hesitate. "How did you . . . do it?"

His expression hardens when he realizes my meaning. "Next question."

I nod quickly, somewhat relieved he refused to answer. *Someday, maybe, he'll want to tell me, and if that day comes, I will do my best to listen.* "How did you first transition?" I ask instead. "How did you *become* a vampire?"

"What color light did you see when you died?"

"It was sort of—golden."

He leans behind us to grab the bottle of absinthe, forgoing the glasses and drinking straight from the source before saying, "Mine was black. I walked into it, and when I woke, I slaughtered my neighbor's entire family. His daughter, Vesna, and I"—here he shakes his head bitterly, unable to keep the deprecation from his voice—"we were childhood sweethearts. I thought I would marry her someday. By the time I realized what was happening, she was dead in my arms with her parents and brother lying across the room."

"Oh, Michal."

He tips the bottle of absinthe in acknowledgment before taking another drink. "And I still turned my sister after that. I watched as she turned Odessa, as Odessa turned Dimitri, as the three of them slaughtered anyone who had ever spurned them, and when our parents disavowed us, I happily joined them in leaving a trail of bodies through the countryside. Whispers began to follow us, and villagers began to mark their doors with crosses—at the urging of my father, I think." He shakes his head and takes another drink. The gesture feels almost belligerent now, yet still Michal doesn't react to the alcohol. "Apparently, he cleaned himself up after we left, never touched the bottle again. I wouldn't know. He died before I ever came home."

"How—" I swallow hard and try again, staring at the bottle in his own hand. "How old *are* you?"

"I don't know," he says plainly. "People tracked time differently then—by month, by year, by the equinox each autumn and solstice each spring. Physically, I couldn't have been much older than you when I transitioned to vampire."

"Oh." Eyeing his bare chest incredulously, I privately disagree. "You must've, er . . . aged faster back then."

To my surprise, he grins—that sharp, mocking half grin I've come to love. "I've always been strong, Célie. Even as a human."

Noted. My own chest twists a little as his grin fades once more, and we gradually lapse into silence. I still have dozens of questions to ask, of course—possibly hundreds—but I sense Michal has reached his limit this evening. He grips the absinthe with both hands now, his knuckles clenching white around the label, and stares down at his fingers without truly seeing them. Though the silence stretches between us, I cannot bring myself to move, to leave him alone with his thoughts.

In my worst moments, my thoughts trapped me just as completely as any coffin.

Just as I reach for him, however, he asks in a devastatingly quiet voice, "Would you have hesitated with Filippa?"

It's the single most vulnerable thing I've heard him say, and in response, my hand shifts midair; slowly, it reaches to take the bottle from him instead. His fingers slip from the glass without resistance. Placing it behind us with a dull *thunk*, I step in front of him and wait for him to look at me. When he does, I step closer, wrapping my arms around his waist and resting my cheek against his chest. Right where his heart should beat. "You're a good man, Michal."

Though his body remains tense, he still brushes a strand of hair behind my ear. "I'm not a man anymore, Célie, and if you've listened to anything I've said tonight, you know I've never been good."

I lean back to study him through narrowed eyes. "Do you think *I* am good?"

"How can you even ask me that?" He sounds incredulous now, almost angry. "Célie, you're—" But his voice breaks off, and he looks away swiftly, clearing his throat. "Yes. I think you're good."

"Then listen to me. No, *listen*, Michal." Reaching up, I catch his face between my palms and force him to look at me. His eyes glint like shards of broken glass in the low light, bright and sharp and painful. "You accuse me of romanticizing nightmares, but I disagree. I've always been able to tell the difference." He exhales harshly, moving to turn his face away, but I stretch up on my toes to keep him still. "The world has never consisted of angels and demons. It consists of people, and people make choices. The Archbishop, Morgane, even my own father—almost every time, they make the wrong one. I know I do, and so do you."

When I release him this time, he doesn't turn away. He simply stares at me. He stares at me, and he waits to hear my condemnation. I can feel his body bracing for the impact, can *see* the self-disgust resolving in his gaze. And I empathize; for the longest time, I needed someone to tell me the truth—to just *tell* me that I'm weak, that I'm worthless, that I'll never be good enough, so I could accept it myself and move on.

I could never accept what wasn't true, however. And neither can Michal.

Still, Michal has hated himself in private for hundreds and hundreds of years; convincing him otherwise will be a difficult task. *Difficult, but not impossible.* Perhaps if he hears my words tonight, he'll listen to them later. Perhaps someday he'll even believe them.

"There was nothing wrong about trying to save your sister," I tell him fiercely. "You did your best for the people you love, and it was a brave and admirable decision—more than most of us ever choose to do. I can only hope to someday do the same." Rising to my toes once more, I press a kiss to his cheek. "Come on. Let's go talk to Dimitri."

CHAPTER THIRTY-THREE

The West Tower

We find him in the West Tower around dusk—a tower Odessa has claimed as her personal suite. Enormous and completely open, the room resembles a giant obelisk with stacked balconies running along its circumference, each overflowing with several lifetimes' worth of discarded hobbies: baskets of wool and knitting needles, a pipe organ, jars of propagated plants, paint pots and canvas frames, a palmistry hand, even two slowly revolving models of the solar system.

Abruptly, the scope of Odessa's life hits me like a fist to the face. Because she *has* lived several lifetimes, and buried each one in this room. The place is equal parts graveyard, classroom, and laboratory of a fickle scientist.

And it is *marvelous.*

After following Michal across the threshold, I peer up at a bizarre statue near the door, its face painted into an eternally chilling smile of white and gold. "What *is* that?" I ask in morbid fascination. "Some sort of guardian?"

Michal spares it an uninterested glance. "She calls it an automaton."

"And an automaton is . . . ?"

"A failed experiment." He steps over a spangled shoebox filled with brass cogs and gears. "Mila and Dimitri often snuck in here to rearrange Odessa's things. It drove her *mad.* Contrary to this general air of chaos, she claims a method to her madness, so she built Potvor to dissuade them from touching anything else. He exploded before she could finish him—"

"—and thus served his purpose," Dimitri says from across the room, "as we thought she'd rigged the place with explosives." He stands atop a giant chessboard painted onto the very floor, hands on his hips as he considers the life-sized pieces around him. "Des!" He raps his knuckles on the horse's saddle before craning his neck to shout behind him. "I think your queen can take this knight!"

Odessa pokes her head over the railing of the third-floor balcony. She holds a map in one hand and a protractor in the other; large spectacles sit on the bridge of her nose. "You will not move a single piece! I forbid it. This game is currently in play, and it is Panteleimon's turn, not mine."

Dimitri shakes his head in exasperation before moving the queen anyway. "Panteleimon is a peacock," he mutters.

When said peacock sweeps past him a moment later—wearing a collar of brilliant gold—we all watch, transfixed, as he nudges his rook forward to take the queen. Dimitri curses. Odessa sighs.

"You are an idiot," she says before vanishing once more.

"Yes, you are." Michal steps forward then, breaking the moment with his regal bearing and cold stare—so at odds with the man he allowed me to see below. The mask slipped back into place the instant we left the safety of the grotto. "We need to talk," he says to his cousin now.

Dimitri grimaces. "Sounds dull."

Michal's lip curls just as Odessa reappears on a stone staircase tucked into the back of the tower. "Whatever it is can wait." Sans spectacles now, she glides toward us in a sweeping robe of turquoise silk, pulling me into an uncharacteristically fierce embrace. "*There* you are, Célie. I was just about to come find you. It was all Michal's idea—as I'm sure you already know—but I need to make it perfectly clear I never wanted to make such a spectacle of tearing out his heart. I've always advocated for doing it in private," she adds sweetly.

"Though I didn't hear a complaint either," Michal says.

She ignores him, pulling back to look at me. Despite their repartee, her dark eyes shine with uncertainty as she waits for my reaction. She clearly expects me to be angry about the role she played in the insurrection, to be hurt by her part in the subterfuge. And perhaps I am. Instead of warning me to stay in my room, she could've explained what was going to happen; she could've included me. Instead she forced me to watch Michal die—forced me to watch *her* kill him, and feel every ounce of pain associated with that betrayal. And yet . . .

I cannot help but remember Michal's words.

No one judges you for it, Célie, but you've made your distaste for Requiem known.

Perhaps I'm not the only one who has been hurt.

This island might be strange and cruel at times—just like its inhabitants—but it isn't *only* strange and cruel. Clearly, Odessa has built a full and gratifying life here with her family; this very room is a testament to both.

Returning her embrace, I squeeze her tightly, and I try to convey the depth of my own relief that she did not murder her cousin. And perhaps an apology. "I understand," I say quietly. Then—"I'm also quite glad my friend isn't a power-hungry madwoman."

“Oh, she’s still that.” Hands in his pockets, Dimitri strolls forward with a grin as Odessa releases me hastily, turning away and blinking hard. My heart pangs at the unexpected display of emotion—or was it because I called her friend? *I should’ve sought her out sooner.* Though she’d never admit it, Odessa feels just as deeply as anyone, and the strain and uncertainty of the last few days must’ve weighed heavily on her.

Before I can join her on the plush settee across the chessboard, however, Dimitri steps in front of Michal, blocking my path. “I love that furrowed brow of yours as much as the next person, cousin, but shall we smooth it out before it becomes permanent? I assume you charged up here to reprimand me for something. By all means, let’s get down to—”

Michal seizes his collar abruptly, jerking him closer and leaning down to scent his throat. “I knew it,” he says over Dimitri’s protests, shoving him away again. With a curse, Dimitri careens backward into a mannequin riddled with pins.

“What are you—? Stop, *stop*!” Wide-eyed at the abrupt shift in atmosphere, Odessa moves in a blur to catch them both, but she releases her brother when he hisses and bares his teeth, whirling to face Michal incredulously.

“Have you gone *mad*?”

Michal steps in front of me, and Dimitri mirrors the movement, bringing the two entirely too close for a calm, well-reasoned conversation. Though I’d known this would happen, my stomach still plunges with regret as I remember Dimitri’s admission in the grotto: *As hard as it might be for you to believe, Michal and I were like brothers once.* Looking at them now, such a thing *does* feel quite hard to believe.

"I warned you what would happen," Michal says softly. "I warned you what I would do if you betrayed us again."

"What *is* happening?" Bewildered, Odessa straightens the mannequin while—against my better judgment—I force my way between Michal and Dimitri, determined to prevent any bloodshed. Though Dimitri has proven himself to be a snake, Michal might someday regret killing him. *I think.*

Neither one of them acknowledges me, however. Neither one of them steps back.

"Go ahead, cousin." Michal arches a coolly mocking brow, his chest tensing against my palm. "Tell your dear sister all about your deal with Death. He told Célie a little, but I'd like to hear more."

"Michal," I warn.

Because Odessa has gone completely still at his words—all except her eyes. They narrow, darting between the two of them as she clutches the mannequin. "What is he talking about, Dima? What deal with Death?"

Dimitri's expression hardens.

"I wanted to tell you," he says fervently. "I was *going* to tell you—" But he breaks off as Odessa's face twists, as she recoils from the confession like it's a slap. He seems to realize his mistake in the same instant. Lip curling, he takes another step toward Michal, his body bracing, pressing flush against my side. "You shouldn't have come here like this. It was badly done."

"As opposed to what *you've* done?" Michal asks.

"Oh, this is ridiculous—" Though I lift another hand to push them apart, Odessa beats me to it, seizing Dimitri's arm and wrenching him around with a truly terrifying snarl. Her dark eyes blaze like twin pillars of fire.

"Unless someone provides an explanation in the next *two* seconds, I will single-handedly disembowel each one of—"

"We found the source of his mystery cure," Michal says flatly. "I assume you noticed the subtle change in his scent?" When Odessa nods, he finally yields a step, and I let my hand fall from his chest before withdrawing to the settee on heavy feet. None of this feels like a victory. "I noticed it too, but I convinced myself the scent was mine—or rather, *hers*."

He tips his head to me, and I nudge Panteleimon aside to sit beside him, pretending the others aren't watching my every move. Pretending my presence—my *scent*—hasn't allowed Dimitri to mask his subterfuge. I still feel dirty, however. Tainted.

"And so I resolved to let Dima keep his privacy," Michal continues. "Whatever his method, it couldn't be worse than butchering the masses and collecting their trophies—"

"They were never trophies," Dimitri says through clenched teeth.

"—but I was wrong. It *is* worse, and it endangers more than the inhabitants of this island." Directly to Odessa now, Michal says, "Dimitri has been drinking Death's blood."

A beat of silence follows the ominous pronouncement, broken only by a splintering *crack* of wood.

Odessa has snapped the mannequin in two.

Instinctively, I rise again to help, but I stop short as Dimitri forces a bitter smile, rolling his eyes and stalking to the nearest chess piece. "Such *dramatics*." He leans against the enormous rook without looking at any of us, and I want to *shake* him for feigning indifference—for refusing to accept responsibility, for pushing us deeper into an already precarious situation. "Thank you for your concern, Michal, but I assure you, I have the situation well in hand. No one needs to treat me any differently, or scold me, or *fear* me—"

"No one fears you, Dimitri," I say quietly. "We fear *for* you."

"Funnily enough, I can't recall asking for that either."

"This isn't a game," Michal snaps. "You have placed yourself in Death's debt, and sooner or later, he *will* come to collect. Are you prepared to pay that price? Are you prepared for *us* to pay it? Already, he has threatened Célie—"

"He has?" Dimitri's eyes narrow, and his face snaps toward mine for an explanation. He almost looks concerned. "What happened? What did he say?"

"Does it matter?" I ask him.

"Of *course* it matters." Scoffing, he shakes his head in disbelief before meeting each of our gazes. "You're all acting like I've committed some unforgivable sin by obtaining this cure when in reality, the true sins came before it—and I'd still be committing them if not for Death. The grimoire proved useless. His blood *saved* me. You said it yourself, Michal: I am finally Dima again—finally *me*—and in return, Death asked for nothing except the occasional interview. And on *that* note, I've divulged no secrets, telling him only what he could've discovered on his own."

Odessa and Michal don't seem to believe him, however. At her skeptical expression, at his disgusted one, Dimitri heaves a harsh laugh, and his shoulders slump against the chess piece. "But it doesn't matter what I say, does it? It never will. Neither of you have ever understood my condition. After all these years, you *still* don't understand—Mila is the only one who even tried."

He glares between them, but the heat in his gaze feels more like despair than true anger. Like hopelessness.

"And why would you?" he snarls. "Odessa Petrov has never met a question she cannot answer. Michal Vasiliev has never once lost control." When he cranes his neck to look at me, I brace myself for the worst, yet it doesn't come. "Do you know what it is to be the bane of your loved ones' existence? The black mark? The stain? Do you know how it feels to consistently and irrevocably disappoint everyone around you?"

My heart gives a peculiar twist at that. Perhaps because the answer is *yes*, of course I do; of course *everyone* does, or perhaps because the truth of his words goes much deeper than that. Though none of us have suffered Dimitri's sickness, we *have* shared his desperation, and we've all turned to Death for a solution—me, Filippa, even Michal. Of course Dimitri would turn to him too. And of *course* Death would take advantage by using Dimitri to sow discord.

This is what he wants, I realize, staring back into Dimitri's catlike eyes. They look so much like his sister's—like Mila's too. A leaden sensation descends in my chest at the thought that this might be it; after all these years, this might be the moment their family fractures irreparably.

"Do not bring Célie into this," Michal says darkly. "You will not take advantage of her as you've done us."

"Take *advantage*?" Dimitri's eyes bulge. "You cannot be serious—"

"How have you even been *meeting* Death?" Odessa abandons the mannequin to stalk forward, her arms crossed tightly over her chest. Hopping from the settee, Panteleimon spreads his tail feathers and clicks his beak rather menacingly as he trails behind her. "I would've noticed—"

"You've been a bit busy, Des, and I can't say I blame you—" At the first vicious peck of Panteleimon's beak, however, Dimitri leaps backward with a curse, glaring down at the punctured leather of his boot. "Call off the cavalry, will you? Death *finds* me. All right? He finds me, and after I answer a couple of questions—nothing nefarious—I drink his blood. With it in my system, the bloodlust fades—vanishes, even. I haven't killed anyone since All Hallows' Eve." He seizes his sister's hands. "After what I did that night, I *never* would've returned without being sure I had it under complete control."

Michal's jaw looks likely to snap. "As if you've ever been in complete control—"

As surreptitiously as possible, I bend to adjust the hem of my nightgown, grasping the veil near the floor and tearing upward as I straighten. I don't know why I do it, except—well, if this *is* the moment, Mila should be here too. And I pray she is. I pray she's been here all along, watching this terrible scene unfold, perhaps searching for a hole to slip through—

"They're making a real mess of things, aren't they?"

Sitting next to me—or rather, drifting several inches above the settee cushion—Mila folds her legs beneath her and watches Michal and Dimitri with a strangely distant expression. After another moment, she says, "The revenants followed Death's word to the letter. The blood witches' village is gone—burned to ash—and half the forest with it. When the fire reached Domaine-les-Roses, the constabulary alerted a local contingent of Chasseurs, but I left before they arrived." *She was there*, I realize with a start, *watching the whole time.* The thought brings a sliver of comfort, of relief that she stayed out of sight.

“The flames burned me.” She holds out a hand without looking at me, revealing the opaque wound sprawling across her palm. “I . . . felt it,” she says simply. “It hurt.”

My brows flatten at that—at this incontrovertible proof that the veil between realms is in danger. Though I want to question her further, to warn her she cannot continue to spy, I keep quiet instead, unwilling to alert the others to her presence just yet—not while Michal and Dimitri continue their bitter argument, and not while she seems so very . . . far away. Is it the pain of the burn affecting her, or has something else happened since last we spoke? Perhaps in his rage, Death threatened her too.

I take her hand, squeezing it in silent question. *Are you all right?*

A small smile touches her lips, and when she speaks again, she sounds even farther away than before, uncanny and unfamiliar. “It’s strange . . . they’ve been angry for so many years that I can scarcely remember them otherwise, yet they didn’t start that way. It consumed their identities without them even noticing—until they could no longer see themselves, let alone the other person, through the hurt.” The words stick in her throat, as if even now, she cannot bear to loosen them. I suspect they aren’t about Dimitri anymore. Tearing her gaze away from her brother, she says quietly, “I just wish it could’ve been different. I wish I’d *known*. It feels so much sillier on this side of things—to have wasted so much time. Indulgent, even.”

She turns to me, and for the first time since meeting her—since watching her waltz past my bedroom door—she truly resembles a ghost. An imprint. A shadow of her former self. “Why do we always treat them the worst? The ones we love most?”

And I cannot remain silent any longer.

"Because we can," I murmur. "Because it's safe."

She shakes her head sadly. "No, it isn't."

Across the room, Michal and Dimitri stop arguing at the sound of my voice, and both turn toward us in unison. Odessa follows suit. Though a trace of silver light still flickers in Michal's narrowed gaze, he seems unable to see his sister now. Too little of my blood remains in his system, and I—I don't know how to feel about that. It hardly matters now, anyway, with Mila pulling her hand from mine. "You need to help them, Célie. Please."

"It isn't really my—"

"It *is* your place. It is. Michal isn't the only one who loves you." Squeezing my fingers, she nods to Odessa and Dimitri, who also seem to have put the pieces of our conversation together; they search the air around the settee for any sign of Mila. "You've been part of this family since the moment you stepped foot on Requiem. Do not waste it like I did."

I rise to my feet with her. "You wasted nothing, Mila. Your hurt mattered too."

"Perhaps"—she dips her chin in acknowledgment—"but he mattered more."

"Célie?" Michal approaches warily and extends a hand. "Is Mila here? Does she want to speak?"

I do not take it, however; at the slight shake of Mila's head, I sweep past his outstretched arm and wrap my own around his waist, folding him into a tight embrace. "This is from her," I murmur against his chest as she fades from view. He returns the pressure after several tense seconds, after which I pull back slightly. "And this is from me." Rising up to my toes, I press my lips against his, and I pour every ounce of my regret into that kiss.

Why do we always treat them the worst? The ones we love most?

Michal has come to expect the worst from people.

We all have.

CHAPTER THIRTY-FOUR

A Gesture of Friendship

The Chasseurs didn't find Filippa until three days after she disappeared. Her body washed up on the shores of L'Eau Melancolique—throat slashed and skin withered—and a fisherman alerted the local authorities, who sent word to the Archbishop in turn. I still remember the moment I heard the news; I'd been sitting in a dark corner of my mother's bedroom, flipping through the pages of *The Winter Queen and Her Palace* without truly seeing them. The curtains drawn. The candles doused.

When a knock sounded on the front door, I glanced up at the shadowed shape of my mother. She hadn't left her bed since waking to discover her eldest daughter had vanished in the night. She didn't move now either, even as the quiet knocking continued. With my father away on business and no servants left in the household, she should've been the one to rise, to dress, to invite the guests below into our home. She did none of those things, of course. Instead she stared at the ceiling with heavy eyes and matted hair, her nightgown rumpled and her sheets unkempt.

It hurt so much to look at her.

I loved her too much to leave.

Knock, knock, knock.

I closed my sister's book carefully, as if breaking the silence might somehow break our mother too. "Someone is at the door," I murmured, but she said nothing in return. I waited another moment, unsure how to manage the situation delicately. I'd never experienced an illness such as hers—never experienced such sickening apathy, such bone-deep exhaustion. For three days now, it had felt as if someone had hollowed out my mother and forgotten to fill her with something else. She simply . . . existed. "It could be news of Filippa," I added tentatively.

"And what news might that be?"

"That—that they found her."

"Oh? What do you think they'll have found?" When I frowned at her, confused, she closed her eyes as if unable to look at me, even in her periphery. "Your sister is dead."

She spoke the words with such flat acceptance that I pushed to my feet abruptly, trembling all over, and sent *The Winter Queen* tumbling to the floor. Hastening to retrieve it as the knocking continued, I said, "Or—or it could be Pére instead. He might've sent a letter, or a—a gift. He hasn't sent one in ages, and you've been asking for a token of his travels—the pearl necklace, remember? And I asked for a new book—"

Get up, I pleaded privately. *Please, Maman, just get out of bed—*

Her gaze found mine at last, and in her eyes, derision flickered. Disgust. The first emotions I'd seen in days. "He is not selling his wares, you foolish girl. He is purchasing those of another—a whore by the name of Helene."

Whore. Though I'd heard the word whispered in passing, I'd never encountered it like this—spat in my face like venom, startling and acidic. I recoiled from it, from *her*, blinking in shock and stammering, "But he wouldn't—he'd never—"

"Get out." Her voice emptied of all feeling again as she returned her gaze to the ceiling, as the *knock, knock, knock*ing continued downstairs. I remained rooted to the spot, however, desperate to somehow reach her, until she snapped, "Now."

So I did.

Still clutching that book of fairy tales, I walked down the stairs alone, and I pulled open the front door. When I saw Reid and Jean Luc standing on the steps in their freshly pressed uniforms, I knew—with a sick, swooping sensation in my stomach—that my mother had been right. That this was not good news. *Filippa.* Her name caught in my throat even as I saw it in their eyes. Though Jean Luc tried to hide it—averting his gaze, studying the parquet pattern of the dusty floor—Reid never hesitated to perform his duty. How many times had I held his hand after he delivered tragic news to unsuspecting relatives? How many times had he collapsed beneath our orange tree, pale and shaken, after consoling fresh widows and orphans? "They need someone to sit with them," he'd told me when I suggested one of his brethren do the job instead. "No one likes to sit in another person's pain—not when there isn't anything to be done about it." At my pursed lips and skeptical expression, he would pull me down in front of him, wrapping his arms around my chest and resting his chin atop my head. "And there is nothing to be done about grief."

I hadn't understood then, but I did now.

And when he stepped forward to hold *my* hand this time, a terrible ringing started in my ears. Without a word, he led me inside the foyer as Jean Luc hesitated behind us. "Célie—" he started, but I hardly heard him.

The entire scene had taken on a surreal, nightmarish quality, and I no longer felt part of my own body. *This isn't real. This cannot be happening.*

Too late, I realized the book had fallen again. I'd dropped it, left it there on the threshold, and now Reid was guiding me to the bottom step of the grand staircase. He was kneeling in front of me, waiting for me to meet his gaze, but I couldn't meet his gaze—because as soon as he spoke, everything would change, *everything*, yet also nothing at all. My sister would be gone, and I'd be alone; this cold and empty room would never belong in her book of fairy tales, and neither would we.

As if I'd ever let anything happen to you, Célie.

And suddenly, I couldn't stand to hear those last, damning words from anyone but me. I owed her that much. I owed her everything—should've followed her, should've dragged her back and bolted the window—but I refused to betray her now by cowering again. My sister never cowered.

Locking eyes with Reid, I said, "Filippa is dead, isn't she?"

Behind him, Jean Luc shifted uncomfortably. "Perhaps we should get your father—"

"My father isn't here." My voice sharpened to a knifepoint as I glared between them—abruptly angry, *so* angry—and dared either to dissent as the situation crashed back to reality with brutal and blistering clarity. *Whore*, my mother had said, and the word stuck with me in a way no other word did. Because my sister was dead, my mother was broken, and my father was gone, unaware, cavorting with another woman while our family splintered like a mirror, distorting our reflections. "He left over a week ago on another business venture, and my mother refuses to leave her bed. If you bring news of my sister, I am the only one to tell." Pushing to my feet, I strode past them to the threshold, seized the book, and clutched it fiercely to my chest. "So I'll ask again, and I implore you to answer *me* this time: Is my sister dead?"

A beat of silence met my outburst. Then—

"Yes." Reid shattered the illusion of our family with a single word. "I'm sorry, Célie. I'm so sorry."

I refused to cry until they left an hour later, until the door clicked shut and I slid against it, hurling *The Winter Queen* across the room and cursing Morgane, cursing witches, cursing Reid and Jean Luc, my father and his whore, my mother and this empty, godforsaken house. I even cursed my sister, who went where I couldn't follow and who I'd never see again.

Most of all, however, I cursed myself.

And when the tears came, they did not stop—not for a single moment, not even now.

I am so sick of crying.

"He wants us to fight," I say now to Michal and Dimitri, who both listen with rapt attention. "Death wants to distract us while he finds a way to destroy the veil. He wouldn't have mentioned your arrangement otherwise. He knew I would tell Michal, and he knew what would follow—a rift in your relationship, your family." Before anyone can speak, I pivot to appeal to Odessa, whose hand still trembles slightly upon Panteleimon's head. "I know I cannot ask you to trust your brother again, but can you trust me instead? Please? This isn't a fight we'll win while fighting among ourselves." At Michal's scowl, I add, "Dimitri needs to drink Death's blood, but perhaps we can use their deal to our advantage—"

"Or we could simply kill him," Michal says.

Dimitri scowls, crossing his arms. "Haven't we just established I need his blood to survive?"

"You assume I meant Death."

"I don't think we *can* kill him," I interrupt swiftly, stepping between them once more. "At the grove, his wounds healed instantly, and he also"—I shoot Michal an apologetic glance—"he felt much stronger than me. Faster too."

Michal's face hardens. Before he can speak, however, Odessa asks, "What other powers does he possess? What else did you learn?"

"Not much." Shaking my head, I wrack my thoughts for any detail I might've missed, any chink in Death's armor. "Obviously we know he can bleed, but his blood—it smelled ancient, yes, but also strangely like . . ." My gaze flicks to Dimitri, who looks resigned.

"Ours," he finishes in a grim voice. "I assume it has something to do with his hand in our origin all those years ago—probably where vampires' speed and strength comes from too."

Odessa frowns, clearly unimpressed with the conjecture. "Yes, well, that's all very good, but Death is not a vampire. Death is *death*. In his true form, he is all-powerful, infinite—he steals life with the touch of his finger, reaps souls with the slightest of breath."

"That's just it, though, isn't it?" Michal's eyes turn inward, narrowing slightly as he considers her words. "Death isn't *in* his true form. If he still possessed the ability to steal life and reap souls, wouldn't he have done it by now?" Though Odessa opens her mouth to argue, he shakes his head, interrupting her. "No. Think about it, Des. He attempted to resurrect La Voisin with Célie's blood tonight. In re-creating the events of All Hallows' Eve, he hoped to bring down the veil—"

Both Odessa and Dimitri gasp in unison. "*What?*"

"I'll fill in the gaps later," Michal says firmly, "but my point remains—Death told Célie that he'd find another Bride when her blood didn't work. Wouldn't it be easier to *create* another Bride instead? He could choose anyone."

Dimitri's brows furrow. "And if power is what Death wants, why not simply . . . kill everyone? You know, with all that touching and breathing business you mentioned." He shoots a furtive look at Odessa, who rolls her eyes, and shrugs unapologetically. "What? The veil wouldn't need to come down if he reaped all of us, and we would cross into his realm a lot faster that way."

"I don't think he can." The words fall from my lips as if they've been waiting all along—because the simplest explanation is usually the right one. If Death still possessed great and cosmic powers, he would be using them; instead he struck a deal with my sister and created an army of revenants. He murdered Frederic quite rudimentarily, slashed open my hand with a knife before burning down the blood witches' village in a fit of pique. "He seems to be caught somewhere in the middle—part human and part Death. I don't know if we can kill him, but I *do* know we'll regret it if we fail."

Michal's eyes fall to my injured hand. "Célie—"

"I'm fine, Michal." I hide it behind my back, fingers clenching over the bandage. "Either way, I think our greatest chance of defeating Death lies in tricking him somehow. Maneuvering him. If we can just lead him where he needs to go—"

Dimitri's brows furrow. "Which is where?"

"The grotto," Odessa says simply.

I should've known she'd already fit the pieces together. Indeed, she probably fit them together long before the rest of us.

Our eyes meet across the chessboard, and I nod, swallowing

hard at the palpable anguish—and anger—in hers. Perhaps I asked too much of her in regard to Dimitri. Him snapping her neck on All Hallows' Eve is probably the least of her hurts, and I wish we had time to sit together in that pain. I wish Dimitri had found a cure outside of Death. I wish my sister hadn't aligned with him, and I wish Frederic had never torn open that hole.

The time has come, however, to stop wishing and start *acting*.

"Death needs to go back to his realm," I say, "to the true land of the dead. Frederic created a door—which in turn created the maelstrom—when he resurrected Filippa. I don't know why their tear is so different than the other revenants', but it stands to reason we can reverse the damage they caused by sending Death back through it. We just need to decide the best way to lure him here. Any ideas?" When no one speaks, when the tension only thickens at Filippa's name, I plunge onward with determination. "All right—well—perhaps we can stage a meeting via Mila, or perhaps Dimitri can arrange *their* next meeting to take place—"

"—inside Michal's bedroom? That isn't suspicious at all." Rolling his eyes, Dimitri pretends to consider this before adding dryly, "Though if you really want to lure him to the bedroom, I'm sure we could find a way. You *are* his Bride—"

"Finish that sentence," Michal says in a cold voice, "and I will tear out your throat." His hands descend on my shoulders, and he gently turns my body toward him. His eyes remain tight, however—wary, almost apologetic—and I tense, knowing what he means to ask. "How do we close the door, Célie?"

As expected, the silence snaps taut, fraying with the pressure of everyone knowing this answer. No one wants to say it, however; no one wants to condemn my sister to another casket—no one except Odessa, who scowls and says, "We all know what must be done, Michal, and dancing around the subject will not make it any easier. This door might be different than the others, but in essence, it is still a tear in the veil. The only definitive information we have is that which you delivered yourself—when a revenant dies, they restore balance to our realm, and the hole they created repairs itself." She shunts her bishop diagonally to take Panteleimon's queen, and I hold my breath, praying for another solution. *Please, please, please.*

Neither God nor Odessa hears my prayer, however.

"The simplest way to check the king," Odessa says without looking at me, "is to eliminate the queen. If we want to close the door, Filippa must die."

Filippa must die.

Michal lightly kneads my shoulders in the silence that follows—bracing me, I think. Perhaps because my mouth tightens and my hands curl into fists. Perhaps because I've been seized with a sudden vision of throttling Odessa. *Filippa must die.* The words reverberate through my head; they pound through my blood with visceral heat. She spoke them as if stating the obvious, as if solving the simplest of equations, but there is nothing obvious or simple about executing my sister. Not to me. "We don't *know* that," I say evenly. "Filippa isn't like the other revenants—"

"—which isn't necessarily a good thing. I'm not at all sure fire will work on her." Odessa strides through the chess pieces with an inscrutable expression, pulling a piece of folded parchment from her robe. She thrusts it toward me, and—seeing little choice—I open it with stiff fingers. Slashes of black ink mark over a dozen locations on an intricate map of Requiem: the forest, the theater, the aviary. The largest X, however, crosses the castle. *The grotto.* Odessa taps it with a sharp nail. "If you require proof, Guinevere has been reporting holes closing all afternoon as my sentinels dispatch revenants."

Michal's hands slide down my arms. He does not shy away from me, however; instead, his dark eyes burn with regret. *They need someone to sit with them.* "The rip we saw in the forest," he confirms. "It was closed when I brought you back to the castle. Mathilde was right—killing the loup garou mended it."

Sharp, debilitating emotion weakens my knees. It hammers against the mental barrier I've constructed—that familiar and wretched *knock, knock, knock*ing—but I barricade the door with trembling fingers. I cannot open it again. I cannot succumb to grief, to despair, and I cannot—*will* not—bury my sister again.

Odessa shakes her head. "Once is an anomaly. Twice is a coincidence. Any more than that establishes a pattern." A pause. "I'm sorry, Célie."

I'm sorry, Célie. I'm so sorry.

Shrugging away from Michal's hands, I ignore Panteleimon's threatening stare and stalk across the chessboard, unable to look at any of them—even Dimitri, who has kept damnably silent beside his sister. Though I long to *shake* him, I meant what I said before; Death is trying to divide us, and we cannot let him.

Every person in this room found a loophole, which means I can find one too.

Breathing deep, I appeal to each of them through clenched teeth: "You kept your brother, Odessa, despite his affliction." Next I gesture to Michal, acutely aware of how he tracks each step, each turn of my heel, his eyes narrowed as if thinking hard. *No one likes to sit in another person's pain—not when there isn't anything to be done about it.* Michal is not the type to sit, however; he is the type to *do*, and until now, he has always held the cards. I can almost hear his brilliant mind whirring, scheming, grinding in frustration.

"You kept your sister," I tell him. "She has died *twice*, yet you can still see her, speak to her, as a spirit." To Dimitri, I say, "And you kept your *life*, to be quite frank. Each of you found a way to escape Death, but my sister didn't—until now. If there is a way to keep her alive, I am going to find it, even if that does make me a *foolish girl*." I exhale a harsh breath at my mother's insult, still pacing. "Did I mention my sister built an ice palace in the spirit realm? It looks just like the one we dreamed of as children, and she keeps Frederic's and Evangeline's souls trapped inside it. And *her* deal with Death? She asked for her child back. Her baby. Does that sound like a monster to you?"

"*Yes*." Odessa tugs the map from my clenched fingers, tucking it back into her robe with a valiant stab at patience. "Célie, she imprisoned her lover's *soul*—"

"Because she still loves him, Odessa," Dimitri says with a sigh. "Isn't it obvious?"

I whirl to face him at that, hardly daring to hope. Though he shrugs back at me in a noncommittal sort of way—hands still buried in his pockets—he also doesn't backtrack as his sister snaps, "Oh? And did she love him while she watched Death rip out his heart?"

Michal joins us at the center of the chessboard now, coming to stand directly behind me. "With the intent to bring him back. She knew she'd see him again when Death brought down the veil. It wasn't goodbye forever—just for now."

That glimmer of hope sparks.

Catches.

"Exactly—and *that* is the crux of the issue." Odessa throws up her hands and glares between us, clearly disliking the direction our conversation has taken. "She needs the veil to come down to reunite with both her daughter *and* lover. Our only avenue of preventing that is to remove her from the board. The door cannot close while she lives."

Throwing caution to the wind, I say, "Help me find another way, then. Please."

Though she hesitates—staring back at me with bright apprehension, and perhaps a touch of obstinance—Michal does not. His voice rumbles up my spine, and I shiver at the sheer weight of it. The finality. "Of course we'll help you." Turning slightly, I catch the ominous look he sends in Dimitri's direction. "Just as you've always helped us."

Dimitri rolls his eyes. "To be clear, that appalling display of dominance wasn't necessary. Obviously I agree; I was *always* going to agree. Célie is my friend." Though he turns to speak to me, I cannot help but feel he means the words for someone else. "If you'll still have me, that is," he adds quietly, ducking his chin.

Michal and Odessa share a tense look.

Instinctively, I unwind the bandage around my palm. Three pairs of eyes snap to the thin line of scarlet revealed in its wake, but I ignore everyone but Dimitri. "Are you *sure* you're in control?" I ask him, waving my hand below his face. "Inhale. Don't hold your breath."

He does just that, drawing in a slow and measured breath. Though his pupils dilate slightly at the scent of my blood, he remains at ease, leaning against the rook once more. A rueful grin twists his lips. "As delectable as I find you, mon papillon chérie"—Michal's low growl interrupts—"I am in complete control." Ignoring Michal, he leans closer with a wink, yet his eyes don't sparkle quite as brightly as before. "And I promise not to bite unless you ask me. *Are* you asking?"

My fingers close around my bloody palm as Michal appears at my side. "No," I tell them both sharply. Then— "What do you think, Michal? Can you work together again?"

A muscle feathers in Michal's jaw as he stares at his cousin, and his cousin stares right back. At last, Michal nods tersely, and as one, we all turn to Odessa. She sighs heavily before shaking her head in defeat, crouching before Panteleimon to stroke his brilliant head. "I suppose a broken clock is right twice a day—but there *is* a clock, and we don't know how much time is left. Even now, Death could be finding the answer he seeks."

Movement sounds from the corridor outside, and instantly, the four of us tense, each whirling to face the door and listening hard. *Footsteps.* Those are definitely footsteps. Too late, my stomach plummets with awareness. We'd forgotten to keep our voices down, forgotten the entire castle—the entire *kingdom*—believes Michal to be dead and me to be imprisoned. If anyone finds us here, it'll be anarchy—true anarchy this time. I doubt even Michal, Odessa, and Dimitri could defend themselves against an entire isle of murderous vampires. Dimitri curses bitterly in agreement, pulling me behind him as Michal and Odessa step forward. As they shift slightly, their stances widen and tension coils in their torsos.

Positioning themselves, I realize in belated panic, clutching Dimitri's sleeve.

Though my eyes dart for a place to hide, Michal shakes his

head as if sensing my flight response. "It's too late. Whoever it is will have already heard us. Stay with Dimitri," he adds sharply, "unless they overpower us. If that happens"—now he turns his head to meet my eyes, which widen at the malevolence in his expression—"I want you to run as fast and as far as you can. Go to Mathilde. She'll shelter you from the likes of Léandre and Violette until—"

The door bursts open before he can finish, however, and it is not Léandre and Violette who stand on the threshold.

"Pasha?" Odessa asks indignantly. "Ivan? What did I tell you? Célie's mother is not to be—"

She breaks off at the sight of their stiff and lumbering movements, and Dimitri curses again, dragging me behind an enormous bishop. With a trill of fear, Panteleimon vanishes up the staircase. It takes another second for me to understand why—for me to recognize the yawning pupils and clouded surfaces of Ivan's and Pasha's once-crystalline eyes, to detect the *rot* that wafts from their ashen skin. Dark blood has dried upon the slashes at their throats; it stains the golden foxes of their uniforms a gruesome black.

Revenants.

Inhaling reflexively, I fight the urge to retch. Their scent mingles with another, this one familiar and herbal and slightly bitter. I cannot place it, however—not as Michal and Odessa converge, blocking their path into the room. "Can you understand us?" Michal asks grimly. "Can you speak?"

Ivan lifts his hands with a rattling breath. When he speaks, his voice resonates much deeper than in life, harsh and guttural and terrifying. "A—gift."

Craning my neck, I peer around Dimitri and the bishop to see what he carries, but Dimitri thrusts me behind him again with a surreptitious shake of his head. It matters little, however, as Ivan raises his hand higher in the next second, revealing La Voisin's tattered grimoire between his fingers. The pages have been haphazardly sewn back together.

Ivan stares directly across the chessboard at me.

"*Shit*," Dimitri snarls, but I've already ducked out beneath his arm and darted toward Michal, toward Odessa, toward Pasha and Ivan and his gift from Death—because only Death could've done this to them. Only Death would've tried to make the grimoire whole again.

"What do you want?" I lurch to a halt between Odessa and Michal with Dimitri hot on my heels, his fingers fisting in the back of my nightgown. Though Michal looks likely to eviscerate both of us, I cannot bring myself to care; Ivan and Pasha have not come to attack, or they would've done it already. No, this reeks of something else—something altogether more sinister. I jerk my chin toward the evil black book. "Why are you giving this to me?"

"Gesture—of—friendship." Blood has congealed in Pasha's long black hair, but he doesn't seem to notice; he doesn't seem to recognize any of us either. From his pocket, he extracts a matchbox. My sense of foreboding deepens, and cold fingers of dread trail down my spine, raising gooseflesh in their wake.

"Don't take it, Célie." Dimitri's fingers tighten, contorting in the fabric at my back. "That book—nothing good can come of it."

"I don't think we have a choice."

Slowly, I reach for the grimoire as Michal and Odessa brace, as Dimitri inches so close I can scarcely move for the wall of vampires all around me. I am a vampire now too, however, and with a pointed step forward, I tug the grimoire from Ivan's rigid fingers. Extending my other hand to Pasha, I add, "The matchbox too, if you please. I—I think your master would want me to have it."

Pasha and Ivan both shake their heads in unison, and another wave of that peculiar scent washes over me with the movement. It burns my nose, my throat, and triggers memories of caskets in the belly of a ship, of Michal's silhouette in the grotto as he told me about his transition. And the split second before Pasha pulls out a match, striking it against the flint, I finally place it.

Absinthe.

Without a word, he sets himself and Ivan ablaze, and I can do nothing but watch—horrified—as they erupt, the fire licking up their clothes, their skin, before they collapse to the floor in twin pillars of flame. Michal seizes my elbows when I leap backward, spinning me away from them, while Odessa snatches wildly at her propagated cuttings. Though she dumps water from the half-filled jars over their bodies, it isn't enough. The fire only blazes hotter, *higher*, until Dimitri shouts and throws a blanket over the two, diving atop it to smother the flames. After another moment, he jumps away too—searching wildly for another means to save them—before sick realization descends, twining through the smoke and screams.

Ivan and Pasha are revenants now. If we douse this fire, we must light another; they cannot be allowed to live.

Do not fret at our parting, my sweet. I'm sure we'll see each other soon.

Death's message has been received.

"Fuck," Michal says.

Part Four

Le loup retourne toujours au bois.

One always goes back to one's roots.

CHAPTER THIRTY-FIVE

The Devil and the Sun

An hour later, Michal and I stare at each other atop his emerald duvet.

"We don't need to do this if you're uncomfortable," he says. "My blood will heal your hand, yes, but there is no reason for you to reciprocate. I can strengthen myself in other ways."

His low voice reverberates up my spine, leaving gooseflesh in its wake, but after Death's thinly veiled threat, I shouldn't be shivering at the sound of Michal's voice. After poring over the grimoire and finding nothing—not a single spell to help Filippa—I shouldn't be this keenly aware of his body either. We have other things, critical things, *apocalyptic* things, to focus on now. Indeed, Odessa and Dimitri are helping my mother pack at this very moment. Without Pasha and Ivan as protection, she can longer remain in my room. When Michal offered this grotto as an alternative, she accepted with a suspicious lack of protest, her eyes narrowed on the scant distance between us.

Even now—despite my throbbing palm—I cannot seem to think beyond the long lines of his thighs as they stretch out beside me; I cannot *see* beyond the sheer breadth of his shoulders as he leans against the headboard. Have I ever truly appreciated his shoulders until this moment? Surely I have, yet my mouth feels rather dry at the sight of them. Of *him*.

My mother has never spoken a kind word to Michal, yet he still opened his chambers to her. He removed the kittens from her presence, adopting all seven for both her and for me. I can still hear the ringing finality with which he defended my sister to Odessa, can still *feel* his staunch presence at my back.

Just as it always is.

"Célie?" he asks quietly.

We should've picked somewhere else to do this. Like a cold bathtub.

Shaking myself mentally, I drag myself back to the present and say, "You saw Pasha and Ivan. Death isn't going to stop, and until we've decided just how to lure him here, it would be . . . beneficial for you to feed too. To keep up your strength," I clarify, "and to—to see the veil as well. It might be useful. We have no idea what Death might do next."

"This is a risk too, Célie." Though Michal speaks in that cool, dispassionate way of his, I can sense the tension radiating beneath the facade. His entire body has clenched tighter than a bow, and instinctively, I know one stroke of my fingers will loose—*something* between us. "You've been lucky thus far, but if I drink from you again, the bond might form. Are you willing to risk eternity with someone like me?"

Irritation prickles my chest at that. *Someone like me.* He speaks as if such a fate would be reprehensible, the worst possible outcome in a situation filled with worst possible outcomes. But Michal has never been the worst thing to happen to me; in some lights—even the dim, flickering light of this grotto—he might even seem the best. By sharing his blood with me, he is not only healing the cut on my palm but also offering his physical strength, his speed, his protection in the fight to come. And I—

I want to protect him too.

My irritation contracts at the realization, squeezing until I'm almost breathless with it. I want to protect Michal. I do. Moreover, we'll need every advantage against Death, against Filippa, and that includes my sight. Still I hesitate, however, staring hard at the grimoire in my lap. Attempting to think around the deep, unending *ache* in my chest whenever I'm around Michal. Though an unbreakable bond with him no longer feels like the worst possible thing—perhaps never has—would I still pursue it if not under threat of Death? Would I still want it? Would I *choose* it?

Have I *ever* made a choice for myself?

Squaring my shoulders, I rise to my knees and level him with a look. "Emotions are the key, right?"

Michal nods warily. "Right."

"So . . . theoretically, if we feel nothing for each other, the bond cannot form?"

"Theoretically."

I sit up straighter, tossing the grimoire aside and clasping my hands. "Excellent. Seems simple enough."

He blinks like I've just spoken in tongues. His eyes harden. Then—just as I've opened my mouth to ask *why*, exactly, that slow smirk is spreading—he sits up too, leaning forward to drape his elbows on his knees. Bringing his face within a breath of mine. I hold very still, trying not to notice the rings of rich, molten brown around his pupils. The fringe of thick, dark lashes.

Was his hair always silver? The thought strikes again without permission as we study each other. *Or was it once dark? Has he always worn black?*

He tilts his head as if hearing my thoughts, lifting a hand to touch my own hair in a light caress. "You think it simple not to feel?" I force myself to nod. To *try.* Because the only way to strengthen ourselves without forming this—this *permanent* bond is to be painfully honest. And the painful truth is—no matter how much I *want* him—I cannot truly choose Michal while backed in a corner.

He deserves more than that.

My determination falters slightly, however, as his fingers tangle in my hair, his thumb sweeping slowly up my cheek. "Perhaps you're right, pet. Perhaps it is simple." A meaningful pause. "Show me."

My belly tightens almost painfully at the sobriquet. *Pet.* It drips with familiarity, intimacy, and something darker too. Something sinful and possessive. "Sh-Show you what?"

"That you feel nothing for me." His smirk spreads at my blank expression. "It should be easy, right?"

I reach up to seize his hand, to push it away with a scowl, but lace my fingers through his instead, tugging him to his knees. Pressing flush against him. "Right," I manage through a very tight, very dry throat. "This is—it's only to strengthen each other. Just to—to share abilities."

He takes my other hand too, guiding both behind my back and leaning low to brush a kiss against my throat. "You feel absolutely nothing?"

"Absolutely"—I resist the urge to tip my head back, to close my eyes and bare my throat to his lips—"nothing."

Nothing at all, except—my entire body shudders as he gently coaxes one of my sleeves down, down, down, revealing my shoulder, and *God*, I want him to bite me there; I want to *feel* the sharp sting of his teeth, the lave of his tongue, the weight of his arms around me. *Nothing*, I tell myself fiercely. *Nothing, nothing, nothing—*

He chuckles against the curve of my neck before drawing back once more, releasing my hands and pulling his shirt—loose and stark white—over his head. Revealing every inch of his perfect adamantine skin. His flat torso, his broad chest, his *shoulders*. "How about now?" At my stricken expression, he wipes his smirk away with a hand. "You made a real mess last time. Even an immortal only has so many shirts."

"*Me?*" My fingers react instinctively, fumbling to undo the midnight buttons down my front. *Pearls*. A ridiculous choice— "You're the one who shredded my gown to tie me to a *tree*."

"And I regret nothing." He nods toward the gown with a wicked gleam in his black eyes. *Brown eyes*, I correct myself reflexively. *Dark, sultry brown eyes—* "Do you need help with that?"

"No." With extreme strength of will, I force myself to look away from him, to slow down and unbutton each pearl one by one, to ignore how Michal tracks my every move with predatory focus. And that intensity in his gaze—that *hunger*—seems to sharpen each sensation; never before have I been more aware of my body, of the slick slide of pearl, the deliberate push of my fingers, the delicious friction against my skin. With a plunging neckline and billowing sleeves—and green silk so deep it looks black—this gown is striking on its own. On *me*, however—with my shoulder still bared—it looks . . . provocative. Powerful, even.

No. My fingers still as my gaze lifts to Michal. *I* feel powerful.

And when our eyes lock, a low sound of approval rumbles from his chest. He reaches for me, but I shake my head, undoing the last of the buttons slowly, *slowly*, while the gown parts down my body in the center. Jaw clenched—eyes burning with restraint—Michal stretches back against the headboard to watch as I shrug the gown from my shoulders and it slides down my hips to my knees, pooling against the duvet. Baring my silken undergarments to his gaze. No corset. The neckline wouldn't allow for one, but I cannot bring myself to regret the scant garment I wear instead. Not when Michal's lids have gone hooded and he stares at me like a feast to devour.

I hook a finger beneath the strap of my top, following it to the swell of my breast, until I reach the clasp at the front.

Without a word, I undo it, tossing it aside and crawling into his lap.

His eyes darken, and for several seconds, he simply stares at me, his entire body hard and still beneath me. When I lean forward to kiss his cheek, trailing my lips down his jaw to his throat, he swallows hard, and I *feel* the movement on my tongue. I want to taste it. I want to taste *him.* A soft sigh escapes me as I wrap my arms around his neck, and Michal seems to thaw at the sound; his fingers creep up my ribs as if ensuring that I'm real—that I'm here—before tightening when I nip his ear impatiently. Because I *am* real; I *am* here, and—

I draw back just far enough to meet his gaze, unwilling to relinquish my hold on him. Relishing the feel of his bare chest against mine. The cool slide of our skin as he shifts slightly, thrusting his hips upward. A bolt of heat spikes through my core at the movement, and I—I think I want to feel him elsewhere too. The realization leaves me overwrought, breathless. "You're the most beautiful man I've ever seen," I tell him, burying my face in his neck and bearing downward, rolling, rubbing, seeking that delicious friction down his leg.

His hands seize my hips when I find it, and he drags me along its length in a brutal grip. Gasping, I grind harder still, my hands scrabbling at his neck as the pressure builds. "I thought," he says through gritted teeth, "we're pretending not to like each other."

Now I do tip my head back, closing my eyes against the sight of his body as it flexes beneath me, as it coils. Tension has hardened his abdomen to steel, and his biceps clench; his shoulders strain. "In that case"—I can scarcely breathe at the feel of him—"you're the most insufferable man too."

His exhales a ragged breath of his own. "The least infatuated."

"I never think of you, *never*—"

"I never imagine you like this," he snarls. "Above me, below me, *around* me, your heels digging into my back." I gasp again at the imagery, and he releases my hip to grip my chin. "Look at me," he says, and I respond without hesitation, my eyes snapping open to find his blazing with heat. "I never dream about holding you, and I never lie awake until dusk, torturing myself over the way you say my name—like you revere me, like I'm a fallen angel and not the Devil himself."

I forget our game instantly, rearing back to glare at him. "You aren't the Devil—"

"And you aren't the sun."

He speaks the words furiously, as if I've torn them from his very chest, and in a wave of warmth, of longing, I realize what the confession cost him. And I realize what it means—to him, yes, but also to me. *You aren't the sun.* Perhaps I was once, and perhaps he wasn't an endless night; perhaps we've both become creatures darker than we were before, or perhaps we've always been this way. The sun and the night. The dark and the light. Two souls reaching for each other through time, twining together at last.

Holding his gaze deliberately, I draw aside my hair to reveal my neck in invitation.

His eyes ask the question his voice cannot. *Are you sure?*

When I nod, he strikes without hesitation, sinking his teeth into my throat and rolling our bodies, pinning mine beneath him like he did before. *Like he never imagined.* I've imagined it, though—in my darkest fantasies, I allowed myself to be with him like this. I allowed myself to arch, to moan his name, to pull at the laces of his pants until they fall free. When I touch him, he shudders, clutching my chin and pressing his thumb against my lower lip in invitation. With it, I remember another time—another *life*—and pierce the tip as I wanted to do in Les Abysses. I take his thumb in my mouth, and I suck. I *feed.* The grotto disappears with each pull of my mouth, and blinding white erupts behind my eyelids. A tendril of *something* cracks open in my chest as we hold each other. Tentative at first, then stronger.

Just as it swells with peculiar heat, however, stealing my thoughts—my very breath, suffocating in its intensity—footsteps echo down the stairs behind us. *Loud* footsteps. They crash through my consciousness in an explosion of awareness, and the heat snaps like a band, vanishing from existence between one step and the next. Leaving me gasping, oddly bereft, as Michal and I break apart, whirling toward the entrance of the grotto.

"If you're doing what it smells like you're doing," Dimitri calls, his voice preceding him into the room, "I suggest you finish quickly. Madame Tremblay is en route with my sister as I speak, and I doubt she wants to see her daughter dancing the Devil's waltz with anyone." He pokes his head around the corner as I scramble to cover myself in blind panic—my heart sinking like a stone—and Michal tugs my gown up and over my body in a blur of green silk. Dimitri winks at the two of us, grinning broadly. "Unless, of course, that someone is me."

CHAPTER THIRTY-SIX

Precious Daughters

Cheeks flushing, I hasten to refasten my buttons as Michal laces his pants, black eyes flicking to the floor in search of his shirt. He doesn't blush or duck his head in mortification like I do; he doesn't feel the frantic need to fill the silence with prattle as Dimitri strolls toward us, grinning like a cat with cream.

"D-Devil's waltz?" I ask a touch desperately.

"Sex, Célie," Dimitri says again. "I mean sex."

In one fluid motion, he bends to seize Michal's shirt and my discarded undergarment from the floor—the one for my breasts, oh God, my *breasts*—and flicks them at each of us in turn. And I cannot believe this is happening. It just *cannot* be happening—yet my face flames even hotter as I catch the scrap of fabric against my unsupported chest, using it as a shield against the room at large. Because I am not the sort of girl who can go without support—not without everyone noticing—especially not my *mother*—

Oh God. Her voice echoes down the stairs now, sharp and pointed, followed by an irritated response from Odessa. Panicked, my gaze darts from Dimitri to Michal, who tucks in his shirt before moving to stand beside me with a resigned expression, as if bracing himself for the fiasco to come. But I don't need him to stand *beside* me; I need him to stand in *front* of me, and I ignore his eye roll when I duck behind those broad shoulders. "Should I hide too?" he asks dryly. "Perhaps the kittens could make room under the bed—"

"I am not *hiding*. I am exhibiting good judgment—"

"Ah yes," Dimitri says, highly entertained. "This all looks extremely prudent. Your mother will never suspect a thing, what with the rumpled bedcovers and your various states of undress—"

"Shut up, Dima," I snap.

In a hasty attempt to unbutton my dress once more, I fumble with the pearls, but my fingers have grown thick and clumsy. Though Michal turns to help, my mother is practically upon us now. Any second, she'll burst into the grotto, and—

Michal shakes his head swiftly in defeat, wrenching the gown upward before pivoting to the stairs as Satine Tremblay appears with a sharp, "Célie! What in the world are you doing?" She strides forward, her dark brows furrowing as her canny eyes sweep over the scene. "Come away from there at once."

Fastening the last pearl behind Michal, I cringe and brace to meet my fate. I clutch the wretched undergarment behind my back and pray fervently that the deep green of my gown will hide—well, *everything*. Agitation pricks like needles beneath my flushed and oversensitive skin, and suddenly, I fight an overwhelming urge to laugh. What an absolutely ludicrous situation in which to have landed myself. It isn't as if I didn't know she'd be joining us soon. What was I *thinking*?

With little other choice, I peek my head out from behind him and greet her with a valiant attempt at nonchalance. "M-Mother! Hello! Were—were you able to pack without interruption? Did anyone detect you in the tunnels?"

Pointless questions with obvious answers. If anyone *had* observed her, they would've followed her here, and we'd now be battling for our lives instead of standing in this hideously awkward silence. And perhaps such a battle would've been preferable, as my mother's eyes are now narrowing between Michal and me—on my rigid posture, on his casually defensive position—and her nostrils are flaring with understanding.

Then her shrewd gaze lands on my throat.

Damn it. Too late, I clap a hand to the blood there—the *teeth* marks—and groan inwardly. Odessa suffers no such qualms. She echoes the sentiment with a loud and impatient sigh as she descends the stairs behind my mother, hefting an enormous trunk in her arms and angling it to fit down the narrow passage. She does not, however, look at all surprised when my mother closes the distance between us with the menace of a looming storm.

"Ah," she says darkly, eyes flashing. "*Ah.*"

"This isn't—" I start helplessly.

"Célie Fleur Tremblay, this is *exactly* what it looks like." She points a severe finger at my nose, quivering with righteous indignation and ignoring Michal completely. "Do not insult my intelligence by pretending otherwise. I *have* conceived two children, you know—in wedlock," she adds loudly at my grimace, "and the sordid requirements for such have not yet eluded my memory."

Please, I beg the heavens, or perhaps the hells, *let the ground open up and swallow me whole.*

It does no such thing, of course, allowing my mother to gain her stride. Indeed, she quite literally begins to pace in front of us, pale and agitated and clutching the collar of her worn burgundy gown. "Tell me, are *you* prepared to bring a child into this world? Are you prepared to birth it, to nurse it and to rear it, to dedicate it to the Lord? Such are the prizes of these wanton games, daughter!" I cringe again. "It matters not how *fetching* the libertine might be—" At last, she throws a disgusted glance at Michal, who glares at Dimitri, who coughs to disguise his snort of laughter. "In the end, the responsibility of such indiscretion falls upon the woman, not the man. Without a ring, you risk everything, *everything*, not to mention your immortal *soul*—"

"Vampires cannot conceive or spread disease," Odessa says flatly from behind us. "And vampiric philosophers have long debated whether immortals even possess souls to lose." To her brother, she adds with ominous sweetness, still holding the enormous trunk, "*Thank* you for helping with the luggage, by the way. Ever the gentleman, you are."

"Oh, come on, Des." Dimitri waves an errant hand toward Michal and me. "Someone needed to warn these two—"

But my mother hasn't finished, stabbing her finger at Dimitri now instead. "And *you*—" He has the good sense to act contrite, instantly adopting an expression appropriate for a close friend's sickbed. "I am disappointed in you too, young man. Though I expect the worst from *him*"—she doesn't deign to look at Michal again—"I expected more from someone of your impeccable moral fiber. I sincerely hope you do not *approve* of such—of such premarital fornication!"

Overwrought at the thought, she dissolves into a fit of great, wracking coughs, and I react without thinking, stepping around Michal to lay a hand upon her back. Even through the starched wool of her gown, her shoulder blade juts sharply against my palm. Likewise, the top of her spine—just visible beneath her chignon—seems to strain against her porcelain skin. "Have you lost weight?"

I ask with a frown, momentarily forgetting my humiliation.

She looks a bit peaked, don't you think?

"What are you talking about?" With one last irritated gasp, she brushes my hand aside and imitates the impeccable posture of a steel rod, as straight and unyielding as the ones in her corset. "Of course not. And surely I needn't remind you of the vulgarity of such questions, Célie. One *never* comments on the body of another." She looks scandalized at the very thought, and the response is so thoroughly my mother that I push Death's voice aside, banishing it to the farthest corner of my mind. *She's fine*, I tell it fiercely. *Of course she is.*

"My sincerest apology for enabling such impropriety, Madame Tremblay." Bowing, Dimitri presses a chaste kiss against my mother's hand. "From this moment onward, I shall endeavor to become the most diligent of chaperones. The two shall never again convene outside my presence, and if they do—"

My mother has lost interest in their hands, however; now she peers intently at mine, her gaze sharpening on the scrap of fabric clenched between my fingers. "Célie," she says suspiciously, "what is that in your—"

"I am glad to hear it, brother." Odessa drops the trunk at his feet, jerking her chin toward the black curtain that leads to the washroom. Beyond it, a second chamber awaits my mother—Mila's previous bedroom—furnished with simple yet sumptuous fixtures befitting a queen. "Can you also endeavor to unpack her *many* possessions in penance? You did enable impropriety, after all."

I could *kiss* Odessa.

When my mother bends—indignant—to check her trunk for damage, I hastily stuff the undergarment into Michal's pocket, scowling up at him when his lips twitch with suppressed laughter, daring him to utter a single word. Dimitri stifles another cackle, and I glare at him too. Because this *isn't funny*—not at all—and if ever a person could *perish* of humiliation, it would be me. Here. Now. So why am I biting my cheeks to keep from giggling alongside them? From *giggling.*

My mother will have a fit.

Before I can succumb, Michal steps forward smoothly, extending a hand toward the curtain. "You'll find your room through the passage, Madame Tremblay." A sharp smile. "*Dimitri* will escort you, as well as stow your belongings and tend to your mealtimes. It should be dinner soon."

"I have arranged for bread, cheese, and wine to be prepared," Odessa adds. "It is not much, and for that, I apologize. The castle must believe you are my prisoner, not my guest."

My mother sniffs in thinly veiled disapproval. "I quite understand."

"After you, madame." Still grinning broadly, Dimitri hauls her trunk to his shoulder and ushers her toward the curtain.

When the two disappear into the washroom, Michal withdraws my undergarment with a smirk, dangling it in front of my nose. "I assume you'll be needing this?" I snatch it away from him—choking on that same inexplicable laughter, my cheeks flushed and my stomach tangled in knots—and turn to don it as quickly as possible, acutely aware of his eyes on my back. Odessa rolls her eyes to the ceiling.

"Are the two of you quite finished?" she asks, but Michal shakes his head when I hasten to nod, instantly chagrined. He doesn't seem to mind his cousin's exasperation, instead stepping forward to button one of the pearls I missed. His fingers linger in the fabric, and a fresh chill sweeps down my spine at the slight brush of his skin against mine. Instinctively I tip my face toward his, staring at his lips.

"Not even close," he promises.

My breath catches.

"Oh, *enough*." Odessa slaps his hand away before snapping her fingers at us. "We need to *focus* to figure out our next move. Everything is difficult enough without distractions." She shoots a scathing look at Michal then, who spares her a fleeting glance. "As in *you*, cousin, so wipe that ridiculous grin off your face before it becomes permanent." Though she speaks sharply, her eyes seem to soften at whatever she sees in Michal's, and something unspoken passes between them. Something significant. She catches herself in the next second, however, shaking her head and planting her hands on her hips. "Guinevere never checked in this evening, which might work in our favor as it gives us more time to plan. We need to be very careful, very *clever*, as we think about this; we cannot simply lure Death here without proper channels in place to manage him when he arrives." She waves a hand toward the maelstrom. "This will likely be our only chance to push him through."

As one, we turn to look at the slowly churning waters, except—well, they don't churn so slowly anymore. Even the surface current now looks vicious enough to swallow a man whole. "I don't know that we'll be *able* to push him." Doubt creeps into my voice. "Not if he brings any revenants with him, let alone my sister. We'll need some sort of—I don't know—*distraction* to get him close to the water's edge."

"That," Michal says, "will need to be one hell of a distraction."

Odessa nods. "As will the lure. I doubt Death feels overly keen to return to his realm if the door is closing behind him." She clears her throat. "Speaking of which, I've been giving some thought as to how we might—"

Before she can finish said thought, however, a silver shape streaks through the floor, and I gasp at the sight of Guinevere, my eyes pulsing with cold light. Michal's follow suit. Immediately, I know something is wrong—Guinevere's cheeks have flushed opaque, and as her eyes meet mine, they bulge with panic.

No.

With fear.

"*There* you are!" With a little shriek of relief, she wrings my hand between us before attempting to drag me toward the staircase with all her strength. "Célie, you must hurry, *hurry*—"

"Guinevere? What is it?" Hastening behind her, I reach back to seize a bewildered Odessa's hand, but Guinevere has escalated past the point of coherency. Whatever has happened, she seems unable to articulate it—she simply pulls on my hand with increasing desperation, spluttering wildly between sobs, until Michal blocks her path halfway across the grotto.

"Slow down, Guinevere, and tell us what happened."

"It's—it's—*Mathilde*!" The name bursts from her on a wail, and I nearly stumble as a jolt of shock kindles straight to foreboding. Somehow, I know exactly what Guinevere is going to say before she says it, though I never expected Death to find her so soon. "Her cottage—oh, Michal! Her cottage is—it is *dying*, and the revenants—D-D-Death—" She wrings her hands again, dragging me and Odessa forward once more. "She told him no, and he—he—oh, you must come! Come *now*—"

"How many revenants, Guinevere?" Odessa asks sharply.

Though I do not know if ghosts can swoon, Guinevere looks in danger of doing just that. "D-Dozens and dozens, perhaps more!"

More? My eyes narrow on her pale face in disbelief—at the thin rivulets of water streaming down her cheeks. Are those—*tears*? Michal stares at them too, jaw clenched, before reaching out to touch one.

His finger comes away wet.

But—no. *No.* What is *happening*? Ghosts cannot cry; they do not have a body with which to produce fluid, yet there is no denying the moisture on Michal's fingertip. Behind us, the ocean thrashes as if laughing, and three more revenants emerge in the eye of the maelstrom. The current is much too strong for them to escape, however; it drags them back down again with brutal force.

"It'll take too long to reach the other side of the isle." With a deep, steadying breath, I pull my hand away from Guinevere, who seizes her neck and continues to weep. "Both Filippa and Death can—pleat the veil, somehow, to travel great distances." I screw up my face in concentration. I try to remember his exact movement, but the memory of Mathilde's withered face keeps intruding, her cackling laugh as she served us café. I shake my head hastily to clear it. "The depth of the pleats must correspond to the distance between locations, but he—he never explained it properly."

Odessa squeezes my hand, her dark eyes alight with apprehension. "You think you can do it too?"

"Only one way to find out." Though Michal speaks to me, his gaze flicks back to Guinevere, who still clutches her neck as if pained. "Mathilde's cottage is on the northeastern corner of the isle." Then, unable to help it, "Guinevere, are you—?"

"I am fine—*fine*!" She flaps her free hand hysterically. "M-Mathilde—"

Right. *Right.*

I've never been keen on arithmetic, however—geography, yes, but my interest always lay in the locations themselves rather than the science of cartography. Those details belonged with Filippa, who understood numbers in a way I never could. *Filippa.* Her name acts like a spark to kindling, burning through the panic in my chest. Did she help Death learn how to travel through the veil? Is she with him now, terrorizing Mathilde, or—or harvesting her *blood*?

You should've taken a leaf out of my book, petal, and stayed hidden.

"Célie?" Odessa crushes my fingers in hers, shaking them slightly in frustration. "Is anything happening—?"

Determined, I seize a fistful of the veil at random, ignoring Guinevere's strange behavior and focusing with every fiber of my being. The veil seems to ripple between my fingers in response, and—when I close my eyes to focus on *that* instead—a peculiar sensation travels up my wrist to my arms. A *tingling.* No. My brows furrow as I contemplate the sensation, which is more . . . awareness than anything else. Or perhaps pressure?

My eyelids flutter as I rotate the veil in my hand, considering the heft and *feel* of it like I've never done before. My concentration narrows to the individual filaments, each translucent thread, but instead of constricting to that point of focus, the veil seems to spread and diffuse under my attention—up my arm now, across my shoulders and down my chest, my stomach, my legs. It settles upon my body—no, *into* it—like a diaphanous second skin, light as air but tainted with an inexplicable sense of *wrongness.*

The veil feels sick. *Very* sick.

The holes in the fabric—they are wounds, weeping gently, spreading disease throughout the realms and poisoning all they touch. So many injuries, *too* many for us to ever heal. The veil hangs in tatters around me, yet still I attempt to fold the fabric as I watched Death do. I clamp the pleats tightly between my fingers. Perhaps each one holds ten miles of the spirit realm. *Or perhaps it holds fifty.* Like Michal said, we cannot know until we try, so I pierce the bundle with a single finger, imagining Mathilde's cottage and ignoring the slice of pain as I slash downward to open a window.

Dark water meets us on the other side.

I close the window quickly, murmuring, "We went too far."

Too late, I realize Michal has stepped in front of *me* now, his eyes rapt and anxious on my face. They blaze silver. "How do you know?"

"It didn't feel like Requiem."

Feelings have never been enough for Odessa, however, so when she opens her mouth to argue, I point to the sky beyond the grotto and say, "We're facing due west, which means I just opened a window somewhere in the waters between Requiem and Cesarine. I need to turn clockwise to reach Mathilde's cottage—northeast, remember?"

"Wait." Michal touches my cheek before I can turn. "Are you all right?"

And I cannot lie to him. "No," I whisper.

Then I adjust my angle, and I try again with less fabric—five pleats less, this time, and folded with more precision. Fresh pain sears my senses as I tear through the veil again, revealing the ruins of an ancient city. *Less sickness here.* I force myself to breathe. *Fewer holes.* Though I've never seen these crumbling structures on the island, they still *feel* like Requiem. Indeed, waves crest and crash in the distance, and faint traces of the breeze smell of brine, of algae, of—

Heather.

"We need to go farther south," Michal says.

With great difficulty, I close this window too, taking a step backward, then another. I cannot explain the decision, only the frustration gnawing at my chest. The growing weakness of my limbs. How does Death *do* this? How does Filippa? Already, I can feel my connection with the veil slipping. It is too sick, too broken to hold in my hands for long.

Still, an overwhelming sense of jamais vu washes through me as I turn for the fourth and final time, and even before I slide my hand through the pleats, I know this window is the right window. I just *know.* Even before I scent the Bluebeard blossoms, the bones, the rotten stench of revenants and ancient earth and Filippa, charred fur—

"Célie!" My mother's voice fills the grotto, and together, the four of us whirl to find her charging from the washroom—Dimitri trailing helplessly behind—her eyes wide and fixed upon the tear in the veil. "What are you doing? What is that? *Where* is that?" Then, incredibly—

"Filippa," my mother breathes.

Her face drains of all color, and my heart sinks too quickly for my mind to follow. When I follow her gaze, however, there she is: Filippa, just visible in the distance, standing with her back to us as her black hair billows in the evening breeze. She watches calmly as the ground beneath Mathilde's cottage convulses violently, as deep cracks appear in its foundation.

At the sight of her, my focus slips, and I blink rapidly, disoriented. Though the tear in the veil remains open, my *mother* should not be able to see it—not the tear, not the veil, and certainly not my treacherous sister beyond it. Because Satine Tremblay does not know Death. She is not a Bride, and I am not touching her in any way, which means—

Beyond the tear, a bear roars in unmistakable fury.

Everything happens in quick succession after that: Guinevere hurtles toward D'Artagnan with another shriek, Mathilde's silver hair flashes through the trees, and—with an almighty groan—half her cottage breaks away from the rest. It crumbles straight into the earth as the forest floor cracks open wide, exposed roots like teeth as they snap and swallow her bedroom whole.

And Filippa—

Filippa staggers on the edge of that abyss.

I do not stop to think. I simply *react*, diving recklessly toward my sister. Michal catches my hand at the last second, however, and a rush of movement sounds behind him. I hear rather than see Odessa seize his wrist; Dimitri lunge forward to catch her elbow. Though my mother cannot move fast enough to catch us, she needn't touch anyone to see the tear.

No.

Satine Tremblay simply leaps after four vampires, falling headlong through the veil.

CHAPTER THIRTY-SEVEN

Stardust

The next thirty seconds pass in a blur.

The instant our feet touch the forest floor, the revenants nearest us lunge—three of them—but Michal, Odessa, and Dimitri strike first. With brutal efficiency, they tear the revenants' heads from their bodies, their arms and legs too, before casting the pieces in all directions. There are too many, however, and my sister is right *there*—

D'Artagnan roars again, charging out of sight with Guinevere astride.

"Go," Michal snarls at his cousins, jerking his chin toward the other revenants. "Scatter them."

And I understand immediately. *Scatter the pieces.* We have no time to properly dispatch the revenants now, only to debilitate them, but all of this is secondary. It doesn't matter; all that matters is my sister, who still stands precariously close to the edge of the world—because it *is* the edge of the world. The ground in front of her continues to collapse, crumbling into the black abyss and leaving half of Mathilde's cottage teetering at its edge.

"Filippa," our mother breathes.

Too late, I realize my mistake, and a rush of understanding punctures my chest—I never told my mother about Filippa. I never *told* her that her eldest daughter survived the grave.

With wide eyes, she rushes forward to pull Filippa to safety, but I thrust out an arm to block her path just as the ground lurches to an abrupt standstill. Michal tenses beside us when an unmistakable curse rises from the cottage. And that *voice*—

My stomach clenches with dread.

Resolve hardens in Michal's gaze as he too recognizes Death, and—before I can say anything, *do* anything—he charges toward the cottage and vaults across the chasm, landing catlike upon the last remaining doorstep. He kicks the door open swiftly, and panic claws up my throat as he disappears through the debris. Because—*no.* No, no, *no.* There is only one reason Michal would confront Death on his own.

Or we could simply kill him.

But I *told* him—I told him it wouldn't work, and now—now he's going to—

My heart plummets to the forest floor.

Before I can move, however, my mother seizes my arm as Filippa turns at last, and a legion of revenants follow. They descend from the trees on silent feet, their faces eerie and empty—those who have faces at all. The flesh has rotted from at least a dozen, and their bones flash pale and bright in the moonlight. *Oh God.* It is my sister's cruel smile, however, that shoots a bolt of ice down my spine.

"Hello, Célie," she says, tilting her head curiously between us. "Maman."

Eyes round with horror, our mother stares at Filippa like she would a ghost, lingering on her no longer familiar features: the thick row of stitches, the mismatched brows and irises. The bloodless skin and the long black hair that shines so incongruously against the rest of her. Still smiling, Filippa extends her arms beneath my mother's gaze as if relishing her shock. Her fear. "How long has it been since the funeral? More than a year, yes?" If possible, her smile stretches wider. It pulls her stitches too tight. "Have you missed me?"

Death curses again, and the cottage—it shudders, the chimney caving in on itself. Though I strain for any sound of Michal's footsteps, I cannot hear him, and that silence echoes in my head as the toll of a funeral march. I twist out of my mother's grip, but Filippa blocks my path as smoothly as any vampire. "If you enter, little sister," she says simply, "you will not come back out again."

As if to prove her point, wood splinters deep within the cottage, and an entire wall disintegrates. Michal is still in there, however; Michal still needs help. Stepping toe to toe with my sister, I snarl, "*Move*, Filippa. I do not want to fight you."

Her smile hardens as the revenants shift with restless excitement. "My *darling* little sister, always in precisely the wrong place at the wrong time." She twirls her silver cross idly between her fingers as a sliver of moonlight pierces the clouds overhead. It plays strangely upon her face, casting her hewn features in sharp relief, deepening the hollows beneath her eyes and elongating the shadows of her cheeks. When our mother takes an involuntary step backward, satisfaction glows like hot coals in Filippa's gaze. "You are running out of chances, ma belle, and I am running out of patience."

I have little time for theatrics, however, and my sister hisses as I shove past her, catching my elbow and sinking her fingers deep into my flesh. "Do it again," she says. "I dare you."

Slowly, I look down at the blood trickling from my arm.

"Filippa, *Célie*." Our mother pushes between us as my teeth extend, but her hands still tremble as she lifts one to each of us in supplication. Her lips pale. Her heartbeat deafening. "Enough of this, both of you. Please, I—I forbid you to fight one another. Not after I just—not after *we* just . . ." Her fingers stretch outward to cup Filippa's cheek, and her wide eyes rove every inch of Filippa's new face. "You're here," she breathes.

Filippa's face twists in disgust—her stitches stretching, *pulling*—as she forces our mother's hand to her chest instead, forces to feel her icy skin, her dead heart. "Well? What do you think of my skin now, Maman? Do you rejoice, knowing your daughters will remain forever young? Or do you weep because they've been touched by the Devil?"

Our mother blinks at the pure venom in her voice, and at last, she seems to see beyond her daughter to the woman beneath—to the depravity, to the *rage*, to the wounds that cut so much deeper than we ever noticed.

Filippa doesn't stop there, however. No. She moves our mother's hand to her dead womb instead, saying, "I will succeed where you failed. My daughter will never question my love, my affection, and I will *never* force her to watch as I submit to my circumstances, as I succumb to them rather than teaching her how to think, how to speak, how to *stand*."

Our mother recoils in shock—in horror—staring at Filippa's belly.

"Tell me," Filippa says, her voice softening dangerously, "what did you do when you discovered Pére's infidelity? When he squandered your dowry to pay for his whore and to cover his debts—when he squandered *our* dowry next? Did you ever want to strike at him? Did you ever even *consider* it?"

Though our mother tries to pull her hand away, Filippa will not allow it. And Filippa is so much stronger than her now. "You—you ask the impossible, daughter," she says feebly. "You always have. If I had left your father, I never would've seen you again—"

"Do not pretend your cowardice had anything to do with us. Do not pretend you cared to see your children at all. You were *weak*, Maman, and I am *nothing* like you."

Maman rocks backward with an anguished sound, and I tear Filippa's hand away from her wrist. "You've crossed a line," I tell her, but truthfully, she crossed it ages ago. Though our mother has never been perfect, she doesn't deserve this cruelty. "Now get out of our way before I cross one too."

"No, Célie, no." Tears spilling freely down her cheeks, our mother shakes her head and clutches my arm as another wall of the cottage subsides. My stomach lurches. *Michal.* "This is not your sister's fault, and it is not yours either. It is mine, *all* mine, and I am so"—she wipes at her face, trying to square her shoulders, to straighten beneath Filippa's withering glare—"so terribly sorry for the pain I've caused you both. Your sister is right, darling," she says to me. "I have been a coward. *Worse* than a coward. I have been blessed with two extraordinary children, and I have never been the mother they needed. The mother they deserved. I have—failed them at each turn."

At that, Filippa blinks, and Maman seizes her advantage, lifting a tentative hand to her cheek once more. "But how could you think I would ever weep?" Her eyes sweep across her daughter's face, but no disgust stirs within them. With a start, I realize it never did. "How could this be the work of the Devil when I prayed for it? For *you*? God gave my daughters back to me, Filippa." She tears her gaze away to look at me now, and Filippa blinks again. She swallows hard, staring at our mother's profile with that same searing heat, this time as if committing it to memory. "He gave you both back to me, and I will not waste my second chance."

And though my sister does not acknowledge the declaration, perhaps cannot, she does look slightly—*affected* by it. As the words wash over her, her expression seems to shift, a subtle softening around the mouth and eyes. When she realizes I'm watching her, however, it hardens all over again, and I wonder if I imagined the whole thing.

"And neither will I." She steps backward, between two revenants—so similar to them, yet so different. "Whether you like it or not, Célie, the veil *is* coming down, and if you stand in my way again, I will drive this silver cross through your heart."

Though our mother gasps, I've had enough. I seize the necklace at her throat—wrap my hand directly around the cross—and wrench her closer as red-hot pain blisters my palm. "Wake up, Filippa. Your unborn daughter isn't the only person you've ever loved."

"And what of the man you love?" Another small, cruel smile plays across her lips. "Even if he survives Death, he'll never survive *you*."

I rip the necklace from her throat, dropping it at my feet.

"Get out of my way," I tell my sister quietly.

"No," she says.

And the stakes—they've become too high, too precious. Neither of us can stop. The lines have been drawn, and when Death laughs a moment later—a high, cruel laugh, followed by Michal's roar of pain—I know which side I am on. Reacting instinctively, I move too quickly for Filippa to follow, too quickly for the revenants too, and I dive across the abyss into the cottage.

Smoke smothers my senses as I crouch in the kitchen, holding my breath and lifting an arm to shield my face against the heat. My eyes burn. My hem catches on the edge of a broken floorboard, but I tear the fabric away and leap over a pit where the hearth has exploded. Mathilde's cauldron lies cracked on its side, her mantel half torn from the wall and her animal skulls crushed, scattered down the hall.

Burning. All of it burning.

Worse still, the planks underfoot seem to be—shifting, *folding*, the walls too. Deep cracks fracture the ceiling as it compresses inward like an accordion. *Magic*, I realize in horror. Mathilde's house *is* magic, and right now, it appears to be eating itself. Even as I think it, her cast-iron bathtub barrels toward me—I duck swiftly—crashing down the hall to the sitting room, which seems to be the mouth of the spell. It sucks everything inside, and I follow with a lethal sense of purpose, bursting across the threshold to find—

Michal.

My chest seizes as the bathtub collides with his back, and his grasp on Death's neck falters as the impact topples them both to the floor, which splinters beneath them.

Terror grips my heart.

Where half of the cottage fell away, the abyss yawns black, ancient, insidious, and the scents of roses and candle smoke—no, *brimstone*—rise from its infinite depths. They curl upward as

Michal falls through the floorboards, and the bathtub falls with him—on *top* of him, pinning his hips and legs and rendering him immobile. Trapped. Only his upper body remains visible through the smoke. His face, his chest, his *arms.* The latter strain toward the heavy leg of the settee for leverage as the house continues to collapse around us. To *burn.*

We need to get out of here.

Whatever Michal planned to do, he cannot do it with shattered legs. When I lunge toward him, however—desperate to help, to escape—Mathilde's carafe cracks against my skull. Boiling café spills over my hair; it scalds my skin, melts my *flesh*, but I whirl just in time to catch the cart before it barrels into me too, shuddering with righteous indignation.

Death heaves himself upright with a bitter curse. "This *fucking* house—"

He kicks aside Michal's hand as flaming sugar cubes pelt his head, and I want to charge at him too, to tear him limb from limb like one of his precious revenants. The situation has grown too volatile, however; the entire *cottage* threatens to plunge straight into whatever hell waits at the bottom of that chasm. It also seems to be—*fighting* us, somehow, if the carafe and cart and sugar cubes are any indication. *Protecting Mathilde.* Death's presence might've unleashed this chasm, but clearly, her house still obeys its master, and it does not want us here.

Swinging the cart with all my might, I hurl it at the back of Death's knees.

It collides with a sickening *crack*, and Death falls again. We have no time to celebrate, however, as Michal is still trapped. Though he twists to hoist the bathtub above him—his arms straining with effort—his legs lie too still beneath it. Broken. Shattered.

Useless.

What are we going to do?

The black abyss edges my vision, until the world around us feels the same. Dark. Everything is so dark, *too* dark, and—and we're trapped. The cottage quakes violently; it groans in an attempt to remain upright as I glance at Death, whose nose drips blood onto the settee. His hand curls slowly around its leg, and he snaps the wood with barely concealed rage. "Well, well, *well*, if it isn't my meddling little wife. That was quite the cheap shot, wasn't it? Not very submissive of you. Not very *nice*."

Panic threatens to suffocate me, sharp claws squeezing my lungs, puncturing my chest, but when Michal's gaze meets mine—fierce and hot—I rush forward, forcing myself to remain in the moment. Just like he taught me

Pick something, and describe it to me.

Ash stains Michal's cheek—*gray like a stormy night sky*—as I grip the side of the bathtub—*ivory clouds instead of gray*—and together, we pitch the cast iron into the chasm. He tries to rise, his jaw set and his face white, but those legs cannot hold him. He collapses almost instantly.

When I wrap my arms around his waist to lift him, he grimaces and shakes his head. "The cottage won't hold for much longer. We need to *run*—"

"I must confess"—Death stalks toward us with a hard smile—"I am growing rather tired of these antics." Lifting the settee leg in his hand, he examines its sharp tip with interest, and my blood runs cold at the sight.

A stake.

An ominous silence descends as he presses the tip against his finger, drawing blood, and an evil smile splits his face. *Oh God.* My arms tighten around Michal. This is not a fight I can win without him, and he can hardly stand. Instinctively, my eyes dart around for another means of escape, finding none. We really are trapped.

Death knows it.

He strikes with the speed of an adder, swooping low, but I anticipate the movement, lashing out to knock the stake aside before diving sideways, around him. *He will not kill me. I will not let him.* He catches my wrist with his free hand, however. He snaps the bone like a twig in his fingers. Though stars burst across my vision and sharp, debilitating pain radiates up my arm, I stifle my scream because that pain is nothing, *nothing,* to the fist of terror that seizes my heart as Death flings my hand aside, as he brings the stake hurtling down.

Down.

Not toward me, but toward—

Michal turns at the last second, and it plunges into his side instead of his heart.

And now I *am* screaming; I am screaming, and Michal is curling inward, his entire body shuddering, clenching, as Death bares his teeth in a furious smile. "*Right* there between the ribs. Uncomfortable, isn't it? Inconvenient." His eyes flash when Michal clamps his teeth, refusing to make a sound even as Death pushes the wood deeper, as he twists it with brutal force. "Though perhaps not uncomfortable enough. Let's see what we can do about that, shall we?"

The front door hurtles past us, the cauldron, the skulls, the *mantel.*

In the next second, the roof goes too—it tears from the cottage with a thunderous *boom*, and the rooms around us tumble with it, faster now. Even Mathilde's furniture cannot fight forever, vanishing into the abyss.

"Stop it! Please, we need to *leave*—" Tears stream down my face as I claw at Death's hand, but he doesn't seem to notice. He doesn't seem to *care*. Instead he rips another leg from the settee when it flies past, and my eyes widen in horror. No. No, no, *no*—

I throw myself over Michal's chest as Death stabs the second stake toward him, but Death shifts with the movement. Even in my periphery, the trajectory of his strike feels wrong, strange—and directed at me. At *me*, finally, and not Michal, but the realization comes too late; it paralyzes my senses, and I cannot react fast enough, cannot do anything but watch as the stake hurtles down—

Michal's hand appears from nowhere to block the strike. Death doesn't hesitate, however—grinning wildly now—driving the tip through Michal's palm instead. Forcing it straight through the other side. And I do not think; I simply lunge.

I tear at the tendons in Death's wrist, snarling and kicking and tackling him to the floor, but he seizes my hair with ease. He wrenches me off him—off my very *feet*—and my scalp nearly separates from my head as he snarls, "A couple of heroes. How touching." Then, still grinning maniacally: "Shall I show you what I *do* to heroes, my love? Shall I show you what awaits them in the end?"

Before I can answer, he seizes Michal's broken ankle, and he drags the two of us outside.

Though I cannot see my mother, I hear her startled cry as he hurls us across the chasm, and we land in a crumpled heap beside an unconscious Odessa and Dimitri. I stifle a groan. Filippa has bound them with silver chains, and the skin of their ankles and wrists smoke slightly, blistered and raw. A cross-shaped burn shines bright upon Dimitri's cheek. It matches the necklace in Filippa's clasped hands.

It also makes no *sense.* Dimitri served Death along with Filippa, unless—my eyes flit to Odessa, to the gash at her throat still bleeding freely—unless he fought to protect his sister. Unless he too drew his line in the sand. Dragging Michal into my lap, I wrench the stake from his ribs, his hand, fighting hysteria as he groans, his eyes fluttering. *We will not die here. Michal will heal. He* has *to heal—*

"It never needed to come to this." Death bites each word, pacing in agitation as the last of Mathilde's cottage slides into the abyss and the entire forest falls still. "We never needed to descend to such hostilities. Have I not been *perfectly* pleasant?" He gestures wildly to the revenants, to Filippa, as if expecting each one to nod in fierce agreement, but our audience remains eerily silent. They do not revere him. They simply watch him, hollow-eyed, and await his next command.

Except Filippa. She stands beside my trembling mother and watches *me.*

Death pays none of us any attention, however. He throws his arms wide, his strides lengthening as his agitation cracks open into full-blown rage. "Have I not asked nicely? Have I not painted a persuasive enough portrait? Everyone benefits when the veil comes down—*everyone*—yet somehow I am the villain in this wretched story. And how can I be otherwise when the heroes are so insufferable? When they refuse to see my *vision?*" Without warning, he seizes the nearest revenant, and it does not move as he rends its head from its shoulders. My mother screams, and I use the distraction to tear up my sleeve, to slice open my hand on the edge of Dimitri's chain. Though a phantom flash of silver appears near the chasm, I hastily duck my head, ignoring it, and bend low to whisper frantically in Michal's ear.

"Drink." I force my blood to his lips, and he groans, his eyes fluttering open. "Everything is going to be all right. Just drink, *heal*, and—"

"Oh, I don't know." Death kicks my hand aside with savage relish. "I'm not at all sure everything is going to be all right. I offered you a choice, after all, and you chose poorly. Now we must all suffer the consequences of your actions." Snatching his foot, I sink my nails through his boot and try to yank him off-balance, to wrest him to the ground. Instead I wince as he seizes my throat. I mustn't break, however; I need to *distract*—

"We will never—choose—you." I buck in his grip, gasping as his fingers tighten. As they threaten to crush my windpipe. "You said it—yourself. True death is—balance, perspective, and—peace." I scrabble at his wrist to draw his gaze, to draw *all* their gazes as that flash of silver solidifies, creeping closer. "The promise of life. Of meaning. It is not—our enemy. *You* are. We will never—serve you. We will never help you corrupt—this realm."

Instead of snarling as I expected, instead of baring his teeth and choking the life from me, Death nods solemnly. "I believe you," he says.

Then he throws me to the ground and snatches the abandoned stake from the grass. "This consequence is your own, mon mariée."

There is too much to comprehend in this moment, and it's as though seconds flicker and fall like stars across the night sky. Images flash before me. Death. The stake. *Michal.* But I cannot understand—will not understand—the implication of Death's white-knuckled grasp, of Michal's eyes widening, of the grass and mud beneath my nails as I clamber forward, faster, faster, as my throat burns and blood roars in my ears. No, no, no, no. *No.*

I need to reach them. Michal cannot die. Not *him.* Not ever—

"Enough." The silver phantom streaks across the lawn, seizes Death's wrist, and knocks the stake away. It lands beside me, rolling against my thigh as I finally reach Michal, and I pitch it as far as I can into the forest. It vanishes from view, and Mila smiles.

Mila.

She has not left us alone. She *saved* Michal, and now she—she—I frown, staring at the hand she holds surreptitiously behind her back. With the slightest movement, she rotates her index finger in a small circle before glancing back at me, and something in her eyes reminds me of another time. Another place.

Really, though, what do you expect when you repress your emotions? They have to go somewhere eventually, you know, and this realm is rather convenient.

She rotates her finger again, and suddenly, I understand. She wants me to tear through the veil. She wants us to escape through it, to give us a head start. A chance. I grab Michal's hand, squeezing it once in reassurance. Because perhaps this really will be okay. We can free Odessa and Dimitri, battle the revenants, save my mother, and . . . and . . .

My heart constricts painfully in my chest as the thought withers. As it dies. *With any luck at all.*

When have I ever been lucky?

"You will leave them alone." Mila speaks the words calmly, confidently, her hair billowing on the breeze as roses and brimstone thicken the air. She holds her head high, and she floats above Death, staring down at him like the monarch she would've been—like a queen, regal and unafraid. "Though you haven't yet asked our opinion, those of us who exist between the realms of the living and the dead find you to be horribly, terribly"—she moves closer with each word until Death's gaze narrows—"*inconceivably* awful. Have you truly considered what this realm will look like without you? What *any* realm will look like without you?"

"The realms *will* have me—"

"No, they won't." She brushes a lock of his hair aside with obvious familiarity, tucking it behind his ear and trailing her fingers down his chin. The movement is strangely . . . sensual, and his gaze darkens in response. "They're already losing you. Why else do you think everything is breaking—the veil, the witches, the *world*?"

He caresses her hand on his face, a slow smile spreading across his lips, and I feel the change like lightning in my belly, terror striking me into action. I hook a swift finger in the veil near his feet. Concentrating on that first memory of Mila—on the laughing ghost who waltzed down my corridor—I begin to tear, but a hard boot crushes my hand.

"And that," Death says, "was your final warning."

Michal bolts upright. "Mila, *run*—"

For just an instant, I think she might escape, but that instant passes when Death plunges his hand straight through her chest to the place where her heart should be. But . . . her heart isn't there; she is a ghost, *of course* she doesn't have one. She grins at him, raising her brows in victory—and then he clenches his fist. His grip tightens on something glowing, brighter than the rest of her, hotter too, and she gasps in surprise.

"That's interesting." Death tilts his head, intrigued, as he examines his hand in her chest. "That's very interesting."

Michal rears his head. "Let her *go*—"

Death ignores him. "Dearest little Mila, my eternal damsel," he purrs against her lips, and her life—or what remains of it—radiates between his fingers. "Will the third time be the charm? Surely you've realized by now that some memories, even imprints of memories, are best left forgotten." He twists his hand, and she falls to her knees before Michal, who desperately tries to reach her. I lurch to my feet, bracing to *rend* Death limb from limb, but Mila does not flinch or weep. Instead resolution burns in her eyes.

There is no fear there. Only acceptance.

She looks at Michal, her gaze as endless as the seas and the skies and the heavens themselves. She looks, and she looks, like she'll never stop looking. "I love you, brother. I've always loved you, and I'll still love you after I'm gone."

"*No*—"

"It's time."

Oh God. Not Mila. *Not Mila.* The girl who taught me to see the dark, the first one who dared me not to fear it. The ghost who held my hand and stayed. She always stayed.

She can't leave now.

I scramble for the veil, clutching at vapors, forcing my emotions to the surface as I tear and tear. Perhaps I can rip her backward, or . . . or push her through it. Perhaps I can save her as she has always saved us. "I never should have blamed you, brother," she whispers. Though tears stream down Michal's cheeks, he leans forward to press a furious kiss upon her forehead. "Do ponovnog susreta."

She smiles.

And Death fully clenches his fist before ripping the light from Mila's chest. "How touching," he says, and Mila's existence implodes into stardust around us.

CHAPTER THIRTY-EIGHT

The Sins of Another

I cannot think in the aftermath, in the great divide. I cannot *exist.* Because before there was Mila, and now there is not. Chest heaving, I clutch the grass in an attempt to orient myself, but Death treads on my fingers as he passes. "Come," he tells my sister. *My sister,* whose last words still ring in my head. "Mathilde clearly escaped. We're leaving."

He hesitates beside Dimitri before crouching to ruffle his hair. "And thanks for the tip, Dima. This trip has been most"—he flicks an arch glance to where Mila used to be—"productive."

As Death rises, Dimitri begins to stir.

No. *Dima.*

Thanks for the tip, Dima.

I close my eyes in defeat, letting the words wash over me. The betrayal.

Dimitri told Death about Mathilde.

All at once, the realization is too much. It's *all* too much—Dimitri, Mathilde, Filippa. *Filippa.* My head snaps up, and I stare at my sister in anguish, unable to touch her. Unable to *reach* her. Unable to let her go. The words tear from my throat, unbidden, and my voice breaks on a plea. "Don't go with him. Please."

Filippa glances back, hesitating for a second too long as our mother weeps beside me. "Pip," I breathe. And for just an instant—

one cruel, faltering beat of our mother's heart—I think she might listen. I think she might stay.

Then she turns and follows Death through the veil.

Maman falls to her knees as the revenants go with them, and I drop with her, cradling her in my arms and stroking her disheveled hair. She feels so feeble. So frail. As Michal struggles to free his cousins, she erupts into another fit of rattling coughs. *From the shock*, I tell myself. *Only from the shock.*

Dimitri crouches beside us in the next moment.

Despite his role in this, I allow him to pull my mother upright. Perhaps because his ankles and wrists still seep crimson, and in order to heal them, he must feed from someone who is not Death. Perhaps because without Death's blood, he will hurt them. He will kill them.

"I'm sorry," I whisper instead, unsure for what I'm apologizing.

He shakes his head. "I don't deserve your compassion, Célie."

"Dimitri—"

"Mila is gone because of me. I let slip about Mathilde, and now—now Mila is gone." His expression fills with revulsion. With complete and utter self-loathing. "I should have died instead."

Stricken, I reach out as he pulls away, but before I can catch his hand, my mother says, "He would have taken her anyway. You cannot blame yourself for the sins of another. We have enough of our own to bear."

"You should listen to her." Nodding to Dimitri, Michal brushes his fingers against my back as he and Odessa join us. Though his legs have healed, blood still oozes from the wound at his ribs; it stains his shirt, drips down his hand. It is his eyes, however, that draw my gaze—coal black and red rimmed, glinting with purpose.

"We need to leave," he says quietly, "before the blood draws others to this place."

"Can you take my mother back to the castle?" I ask Dimitri. "Please?"

Odessa wipes away tears before turning to Michal. They still carve tracks through the soot on her cheeks, sparkling in the dying embers of the fire. "You two shouldn't remain here either. It's too dangerous."

I lift his injured hand, examining the pieces of wood still in the wound. "We'll follow you in a moment."

When she still hesitates, Michal clasps her shoulder, and unspoken understanding passes between them. And I think I understand too; if tonight has proven anything, it's that the future is never guaranteed. Indeed, the weaker the veil becomes, the stronger Death seems to grow, and none of us know how much more this realm can take.

None of us know what will happen when it finally breaks.

Reluctantly, Odessa nods, sweeping forward to kiss both our cheeks. "Just—do not be seen. Please." To my mother, she says, not unkindly, "Can you stand, madame?"

My mother's attention has drifted, however, and she does not seem to hear her. Instead she stares at the place where Filippa disappeared with Death, and it feels as if she is disappearing now too. Her chin quivers. Her knees tremble.

"Maman?" I ask tentatively, dreading her answer.

"I let her leave," she whispers. "I let her leave again."

And for the first time since Filippa slipped out our nursery window, I realize—perhaps—I am not the only one who blamed myself. "We have enough of our own to bear, Maman," I repeat softly.

She doesn't answer, and Dimitri deliberates only a second before nodding purposefully and sweeping her into his arms. "Be safe," he says to us, and he trails after his sister.

Unlike Filippa, my mother does not look back.

A sharp impulse to follow fills me as I watch them go—not to care for my mother as I've done before, but to simply be together. *It feels so much sillier on this side of things—to have wasted so much time.* The words ache as I think of Mila, as I think of Michal, and with them, a bone-deep exhaustion descends. "It's never going to be all right, is it?"

"I don't know."

He pulls me against him, and wordlessly, I offer my wrist. Because he is hurt, and he is bleeding. Because we cannot return to the castle until he is healed. Even then, we cannot be seen, cannot be caught—not by the vampires, not by the revenants, not by Death himself, who still roams the island in search of Mathilde. And perhaps nothing will be all right ever again.

Shaking his head, Michal leads me deeper into the forest. "Come with me."

CHAPTER THIRTY-NINE

Please Stay

Steam caresses my face in the ruins of an ancient bathhouse. It curls my hair as I sit beside Michal at the edge of the water—a hot spring around which they built the entire village. And by they, I mean Michal.

Michal and his family.

Beyond Mathilde's cottage, beyond the surrounding forest and its fields of heather, lies the beach he once showed me at a distance. The ruins I glimpsed earlier while traveling through the veil. The site where Michal, Mila, Odessa, and Dimitri first stepped foot on Requiem, and—apparently—where they built their homes together. *I sought an escape*, Michal told me, lost in memories of that time so long ago. *A fresh start. I recognized those flowers as a sign of hope for my sister and cousins.*

Now he has brought me here too.

"This place . . . it's incredible," I tell him, swallowing hard and staring at the sculpted murals of the walls around us, the hand-carved whorls of the steps leading into the spring. My own hands clench and unclench in the bunched fabric of my skirt as I slip my feet into the water. This place is beautiful. Quiet. Peaceful. "I didn't realize you could—do things like this."

A shadow of a smile touches his lips. "My father taught me."

Then, nudging my knee with his own, "Not everyone grows up in the aristocracy, pet. Some of us needed to use our hands."

I fix him with a beady stare. "Not everyone grows up with a father to teach them things."

Instantly, I regret the barb, but Michal only laughs softly and says, "Touché."

And for some reason, his laughter eases the tension in my shoulders more than his pity ever would. It isn't funny, of course, but I fear I might suffocate beneath the weight of this night, and Michal seems to understand. "Why did you leave this place?" I ask him. "How did it come to be so"—I wave my hands at the crumbling stone, the creeping moss, the crusted salt upon the door—"abandoned?"

"The storms are worse on this side of the island." He takes my hand in an almost subconscious gesture, running his thumb along my fingers. Tracing the lines of my palm. "Courtesy of one Ysabeau le Blanc—another relation of your friend, and a spurned ex-lover of Dimitri's. We were forced to relocate when waves decimated half the village."

"He hasn't always loved Margot, then?"

"Margot is human, Célie. He has loved many a person before her, and he will love many after her too. Such is the curse of immortality." A heavy sigh. "To watch our loved ones leave us." Though my throat threatens to constrict again, Michal shakes his head ruefully and presses a kiss to my palm. "Not that Dimitri has ever been a paragon of faithfulness. He falls a little in love with everyone he meets."

"He didn't fall in love with me."

"Only because I would've parted his head from his shoulders. I still might," he adds with a disgruntled look, "if he keeps propositioning you."

I help him ease the bloody shirt over his head, tossing it aside to burn later. We don't want to attract anyone else to this place. "He only does it to get under your skin—a necessary evil, I think, as he seems to be the only one who can."

"Mila could too," he says wistfully, and to my surprise, he smiles again. "You should've heard them when they got together. They were absolutely ruthless. Odessa and I never stood a chance." And I wish I could've seen it; truly, I wish I could've walked the sandy streets of this village with Mila, could've sunbathed by the shore with Odessa and Dimitri. I wish I could've watched—no, helped—Michal create such a safe haven, far from the sickness of his childhood. More than anything, I wish I could've known them before, well—everything else.

Unclasping my cloak, I tear a strip away from the inner lining, bending to dip it in the water.

"What do you think happened to her? Mila?"

Michal closes his eyes as I lift my damp cloak, gently washing the soot from his cheeks. "I don't know," he says after a long moment. "I don't think we can know."

"Wherever she is, I hope she found peace." He gives a terse nod, and my gaze slips to his torso, to the angry wound still splintered with bits of wood, before sliding to his injured hand. I uncurl his fist tentatively, and he grimaces as I begin the painful process of cleaning it. "I'm so sorry this happened, Michal," I whisper into the silence.

His eyes snap open. "So am I."

My fingers still on his palm, and he meets my gaze with a hard, bitter glint in his own. "Not for the reason you're thinking. Though it may sound cruel, I am not sorry my sister has finally moved on. That was what she always wanted. I forced her to become eternal when I fed her my blood all those years ago, and *that* is why I am sorry. Because I took the choice away from her, just like I took it away from you."

"Michal." I press his palm to my cheek, breathing a sigh of relief as—free of the wood—his skin finally closes. As it heals. "I am the one who hesitated. I never told you, but in the grotto, I—I had the chance to move on. That golden light appeared—I know now it was Death—but I ignored him because I couldn't leave my friends. I couldn't leave you."

He shakes his head. "You deserved more than this life."

"Says who?" I ask wryly. "You?"

"Yes. Me." He slides his hand to my nape, pulling me closer to look directly into my eyes. No. Just to hold me. "I am the one who condemned you to an eternity of suffering. I am the one who must now watch, helpless, as you claim my mistakes as your own, as you slowly start to hate yourself instead of hating me. And I am still a coward"—he spits the word like a curse, unable to see the truth—"a selfish coward because you are not built for vampirism, Célie, and I knew it. I knew it would hurt you more than it hurts the rest of us—to hunt, to feed, to harm another living creature. Hell"—he releases me abruptly, dragging a hand through his ragged hair—"it hurts you to harm the dead ones too. But I didn't care. When I watched you die on All Hallows' Eve, I didn't stop to think; I couldn't let you go."

"That doesn't make you a coward, Michal," I say softly.

He exhales a harsh breath. "And I still wouldn't, if I had to do it all over again. I'd still turn you into a vampire to keep you forever. If that doesn't tell you the type of man I am, I don't know what will."

"Perhaps forever no longer seems so frightening."

"Petite menteuse." Though he scoffs and moves to stand—to escape, to hide—I catch his arm and rise with him, refusing to allow any distance between us. His entire body shudders at the touch, and he pivots hard—eyes blazing—before crushing his mouth against mine. "You are so beautiful," he says fiercely, pulling back at my gasp and clutching my face in his hands, "but you don't need to lie anymore. There is nothing you could ever say that would turn me away from you."

Breathless, I seize his wrists and glare up at him, willing him to kiss me again. "I am not lying, you insufferable cretin." My hands slide from his wrists to his waist, and I wrap my arms around him. I force myself to admit the truth—the whole truth this time, instead of just the convenient pieces. "When I woke up in Cesarine, you weren't there, and I thought you didn't—that you might not want—"

He swallows as if pained, and his touch softens, cradling my face like I am something precious. Something he still might lose. "Lou said you wanted to go. After what I did, I couldn't bear the thought of forcing you to stay."

"I thought you wanted to keep me forever."

"The benefit of forever is that perhaps someday you wouldn't hate me."

"I never hated you."

"Yes, you did."

"I feared you, Michal. Your control, your intensity, your

single-minded focus. I'd never before met anyone like you." I inhale an unsteady breath, focusing on the heady scent of him, of the water and stone and sea. I want to remember this moment. In a thousand years, I still want to see it in my dreams. "Most of all, however, I feared myself—feared the way I felt around you, feared the things I wanted." A pause. "I suppose you aren't the only one who has been a coward."

Though his lips curl in a small smile, it is the bleakest sight I've ever seen. The loneliest. Staring at his hands, he says, "I'd already taken your future. I didn't want to take everything else too. I couldn't stay away, though," he adds bitterly. "I told myself it was to warn you about the revenants, but really—I just wanted to see you. Needed to see you. Even if you didn't need to see me."

"I would've come back." I didn't know what I wanted. "I—missed you," I breathe. *I missed you so much.*

"Célie." He bows his head. "You'd still be alive if not for me—probably married, too, and dragging Chasseur Tower into its era of enlightenment. None of this darkness would've touched you."

"The darkness touched me long before you did." I lay my cheek against his chest, right where his heart should beat. "Why did you do it?"

His body tenses instantly against mine, and I know without asking that he understands my question. Why did you make me a vampire? Why couldn't you live without me? "Careful, pet," he says slowly. "Some answers cannot be unheard."

Perhaps he doesn't understand at all.

"There is nothing you could ever say that would turn me against you." Then, rising on tiptoe to whisper against his lips—"Why didn't you let me die?"

He doesn't kiss me, however. Not yet. Instead he stands very still, as if—as if somehow I frighten him too. *I do not fear pain*, he once told me.

No? What is your fear, then?

Staring at each other now, I think I know. I still do not say it, however, waiting for him to speak first, to trust me as I've always trusted him.

"You—" He falls silent then, shaking his head in self-disgust, and I rise even higher, pressing a kiss against first one cheek, then the other. His forehead. His nose. His chin. I kiss him, and I kiss him until his brows furrow in bemusement, until he forgets to look so angry and confused.

"Tell me."

And like a dam breaking, the words burst from him in a rush of heat. "You're the sun, Célie. I couldn't let you die because you are my sun; you are every good thing I've ever wanted and never deserved, and once I saw you, felt you, I could no longer live without you. When you aren't with me, I crave your presence, and when you are with me, I forget the darkness ever existed—you fill up every corner of my vision until I cannot see, cannot think beyond when you might next glance at me, what you might next say. You have blinded me to all others. I couldn't let you die because you are radiant, and everyone you look upon is brighter for it—better for it—and you don't even realize. You cannot see the effect you have upon us all." As if unable to resist, he kisses me this time, and I feel that kiss like a brand upon my skin, burning hotter than words ever could. He pours every ounce of his yearning into it, every ounce of his fear and his rage and his adoration, and the sheer intensity of it nearly knocks me back a step. Still I want more, however.

Still I want more.

Tearing his mouth away from mine, he says, "Does that answer your questions? Does that help you understand?"

He still hasn't said it, and—with a bolt of clarity—I realize he never will. He refuses to trap me with those final words, refuses to pressure me into saying the same, into feeling the same, when someday I might want to leave.

He really is the most insufferable man.

Flinging my arms around his neck, ignoring his slight wince, I tackle him back to the floor. "I love you too, Michal." A sharp intake of breath at that—of surprise, of disbelief—but I ignore it too, brushing my hair aside. "Now drink."

He eyes my throat warily. "But the bond—"

"I don't care about the bond. I love you, and I want to be with you." Hesitating at a sudden and terrible thought, I add, "That is . . . if you want to be with me."

Now Michal is the one scoffing, the one laughing, and it might be the most beautiful sound I've ever heard. He caresses my hair one last time—softly, reverently—before surging into a sitting position and taking me with him. He does not hesitate when he strikes.

And as his teeth pierce my skin—as that same intoxicating heat washes over me—something different happens.

Something changes.

It is not a slow and subtle thing; it does not build, and it does not come quietly. Instead bright, incandescent light bursts behind my eyelids as we click into place, and my entire being seizes at the sudden feel of him—not his physical body wrapped around mine, but a deeper and stronger presence. A darker one. And all those emotions he tries to hide—I can see them now, coiling like smoke through the lights. Becoming one with my own.

Flashes of memories come next, and I glimpse myself through his eyes as I burst from the graveyard, hysterical and dripping wet. His intrigue at the fanatical young woman twines through the darkness, pulling me into the next—to my wrists tied up on the ship, my scowl in his study, the way my hair spilled like ink down his chair. I see my own wide and terrified gaze glowing in the theater, feel his grudging concern, his fury when Yannick presses his mouth to my throat. I see my scarlet dress.

The bottle of absinthe.

The unexpected lash of jealousy as I drape my body across Bellamy, the bolt of lust as I fall against him instead, the panic at how he likes the feel of his arms around me.

More than likes it.

The smoke curls tighter in anticipation—the white lights spark and flare—and an emotion deeper than the rest unfurls as he stares up at me in the casket, paralyzing and impossible to ignore. Love. He fell in love with me in that moment. And he shudders as I realize it, as he shoulders the weight of my own emotions, my own memories. I see glimpses of them now too, flickering wildly like shooting stars in the night sky, until they too settle into darkness—into a single voice. His voice.

Please stay.

When we fall back into our bodies a moment later—shaken and breathless—I gasp in wonder at the newfound pressure in my chest, recognizing it as Michal's essence. His shadow. No longer frightening at all, but fierce and unyielding and cherished—so very cherished—as it twines together with mine, joining us irrevocably in Le Lien Éternel.

It somehow isn't enough.

Though the bond between us is staggering in its intensity, vital—though already I cannot live without it—I want to know this breathtaking man in every possible way; I want to touch him, taste him, give him every last part of myself.

He senses my decision the instant I make it. When my mouth crashes upon his, he groans, and I capture the sound hungrily, my hands sliding up his fully healed body. Over every glorious dip of his torso, across the hard swell of his chest and shoulders.

He lets me touch him this time. His breathing turns deep and ragged as I drag my mouth along his jaw, caressing every inch of his skin with my tongue. And perhaps it's the steam of the bathhouse or the heat of the spring—perhaps it's simply my blood—but a flush of color stains his cheeks as he seizes my shoulders and pulls me away from him, lifting us both to our feet.

Though I instantly protest, he shakes his head with a slow and seductive smile—a smile I feel, somehow, like a tug between my legs. Everything tightens in response. "You don't know how often I've thought of this moment, pet," he says darkly. "Now that it's finally here, you cannot expect me to let you have all the fun."

"Was that not"—my voice hitches as he kneels unexpectedly, his eyes fixed on mine, and slowly peels the damp gown up my body—"fun for you?"

"I can think of other fun things."

"Another game?" Clamping my knees together, I struggle to remain upright as he bares inch after torturous inch of my skin.

And I shouldn't feel this feverish beneath his gaze. I shouldn't feel this sensitive, yet the slightest brush of his fingers has me burning, writhing, and he knows it. "I thought you'd grown tired of playing with me."

"I seem to remember," he says, and his own eyes heat as he slowly reveals my calves, my thighs, my hips, "that you still owe me several questions."

"Ask anything you want." The words come out harsh, breathless.

"Oh no, pet. That would be too easy. Let's exchange those truths for dares, shall we?"

When he presses an open-mouthed kiss to my belly, I tear at the bodice of my gown to loosen the strings. I wrench it aside—wrench all of it aside—as his laughter rumbles through the bathhouse, and he straightens to stare at my naked body.

His grin fades then. His expression empties completely, but I can still feel him through the bond—the sharp clench of lust, yes, but also the deep and unending ache that blooms in his chest as he looks at me.

Taking his hand, I pull him flush against me, and his satisfaction envelops us through the bond. His joy and his relief. Mine. The word reverberates between us, and I cannot tell whether it came from him or me.

Still I kiss him in answer, however. Yours.

Without warning, he sweeps an arm behind my knees and tosses me into the pool.

Spluttering, I shoot to the surface indignantly—pushing sopping-wet hair from my eyes—to find Michal has already joined me. A wicked gleam shines in his eyes as he glides through the water, parting it with smooth and powerful strokes of his arms. His shoulders. Stalking me as a predator with prey.

Never run from a vampire.

I cannot help it. With a ludicrous grin, I dive beneath the surface and shoot toward the opposite end of the pool, but he catches my foot in an instant, dragging me back with laughable ease and pulling me against his body.

His naked body.

My legs wrap around his waist reflexively, and water sluices between us as he lifts me higher, pressing another kiss to my throat and walking us to the edge of the pool. Gooseflesh erupts when he presses me against it—because seeing Michal naked is so different from feeling his skin against mine, to realizing the full and immovable scope of him.

"First dare." He catches my earlobe between his teeth, tugging gently. "Try not to make a sound."

Before I can answer, he lifts me to sit at the edge of the pool, the water lapping at my calves as I brace my hands behind me. Then he spreads my legs. He bends his head. And he kisses me at the apex of my thighs.

At the first slide of his tongue, my hips jerk, and my back arches. At the second, my head tips backward of its own volition, and my eyes clamp shut lest I split apart at the very seams—something he seems intent on causing because with the third, he throws my legs over his shoulders. His arms snake around my backside, holding me to him, as he drags his tongue upward to that bundle of nerves before sucking deeply. And in that instant, I forget about his dare—I forget my own name—moaning loudly and seizing his hair to find more of that delicious friction. To press harder. To work my hips in time with his tongue until I—I—

My legs stiffen, clamping around his head, but his fingers bite into my own skin too; he refuses to stop licking, to stop feasting, until the bathhouse shatters around me completely. Even then—though I bow backward, unable to withstand the near violent pleasure—he follows until the last shudder leaves my body. Until I collapse upon the stone floor with loose and shaking limbs.

"That was—" I cannot find the right words, however, gulping great lungfuls of air as if they might somehow help me. "You—"

But Michal is heaving himself out of the pool now, kissing up my body as he comes. And another wave of impossible heat washes through me as he settles between my legs, as the length of him presses long and hard against my thigh. My vision swims at the intoxicating feel of it, and instantly, I reach down to take him in my hands. He shakes his head, however, his jaw clenched and his face strained as he kisses my jaw, my chin. "If you touch me now," he says in a strained voice, "the game will end too soon."

"But I want you to feel like this too," I say breathlessly. "I want you to—"

"I do." With a harsh exhale—perhaps a strangled laugh—he drops his forehead to my own, every muscle in his body tightly leashed. "You make it good without even trying." Then— "Next dare. If you don't want to do this, tell me now, and nothing will change between us. I can kiss you until you're ready, or forever if you'd like—"

My hands snake around his back, daring him to finish that sentence. "I want to do this, Michal, and I want to do it with you."

"It'll hurt, Célie."

"And then it won't," I say fiercely. "I've read the books. I know how this works."

"There are books about sleeping with soul-bonded immortal vampires?"

"More than you'd think. Mathilde owned three."

"Dare." His sardonic grin fades as he pushes back my hair to study my face. "Tell me if we do anything you don't like."

"I promise I will."

"Dare." He eases a hand between us, and if my heart could still beat, it would pound straight out of my chest—no, combust—as his fingers part my flesh, as he positions himself at my entrance. "And this one is important—when I tell you to bite, you bite."

I frown at him. "What—?"

The question disintegrates, however, as he inches inside me, and the sensation quite takes my breath away. It doesn't hurt, precisely, it just feels—full, almost too full. When I shift to ease the pressure, he slides in another inch. Another. His hips rock gently at first, but his fingers—they ease the sting, still working against me until I might lose my mind all over again. Until my heels press into the floor, and my back arches, and my body feels empty somehow. Bereft. I strain toward him, and my voice breaks around his name, part moan and part sob. "Michal—"

"Bite."

He thrusts harder with the word, and my body recoils like a band snapping, every muscle stiffening against the stab of pain. It still reacts instinctively to Michal's command, however, and I sink my teeth into his shoulder in the next second. I wrap my arms around his back, and I cling to him as he groans, as he stills, as he waits for his blood to sweep through me.

The instant it touches my tongue, the pain recedes—not wholly, but enough that my muscles begin to relax around him. Enough that his scent drives me mad. Enough that I—that I need him to—

I shift instinctively, tearing my mouth from his skin with a gasp. "Do it again."

Exhaling a harsh and satisfied breath—arms trembling with restraint—he pulls out completely before burying himself inside me once more. To the hilt this time. Pressure builds behind my eyes at the intrusion, and I claw at his back, jerking wildly and twining my legs around him. "Do it again," I repeat, hardly able to hear through the roaring in my ears. Through the heat.

So he does.

And that stinging pain gives way to a deeper sort of ache with each slow thrust of his body until my own begins to move in response. Until my breath quickens, and my nails bite into his back. "So fucking good," he grinds out, pumping harder now. Faster. And his words—they do something to me. Digging my heels into his back, I angle my hips to take him deeper, meeting him thrust for thrust as he increases the pace. And it's brutal now, hard and raw and primal, but I love it—I love it because his tightly leashed control is finally slipping, and it's slipping because of me. The sight nearly undoes me.

Instead I drag my tongue up the column of his throat, just like I did all those lifetimes ago in Les Abysses.

No one would be disappointed, Célie.

And Michal snaps.

He pulls out abruptly, flipping me onto my stomach before

wrenching up my hips and plunging into me once more. Overwhelming me. Consuming me. I'll never tire of it, of him. As he wraps a hand around my front—providing the friction I so desperately need—I feel more alive than I ever thought possible; more beautiful, more powerful.

Because of him.

He is the mirror I always needed, and at last—at last—I can see my own reflection. I can see it clearly. And when my release shatters through me—when he follows with a roar of pleasure—I hold him tightly afterward, waiting for the tremors to leave his body.

Refusing to ever let him go.

CHAPTER FORTY

Home

Michal finds a trunk of preserved clothes through a locked door in the corner of the bathhouse. He hid the key to these rooms years and years ago—*his* rooms, his first home on the isle—likely when he decided to leave them forever.

"This belonged to my mother," he says now, pulling out an ancient yet remarkably preserved gown. Though the cut is unfamiliar, the dress itself is beautiful in its simplicity: white on white-patterned silk—diasper, I think—with soft ermine lining and a thin silver belt. "Her favorite and her best. She only wore it on special occasions."

I trail my fingers down the delicate sleeves, swallowing the lump in my throat. It still smells slightly of sage and something citrus, perhaps lemon. "I couldn't possibly wear this, Michal. Look at what happened to all my other gowns." I cast a rueful glance toward the bathhouse, where I can still scent the bloody fabric of Monsieur Marc's creation. "I'd never forgive myself if I ruined this one."

He shrugs as if thoroughly unbothered, but he wouldn't have kept his mother's things all these years if they meant so little to him. "She would've wanted you to wear it."

"Would she have liked me?"

"She would've adored you." A rather wistful smile touches his lips as I nod, tentatively pulling the gown over my head and privately promising to kill anyone who touches it. Not a single *speck* of blood or smoke or viscera will damage the fabric. "My father and stepmother would've liked you too—probably better than me on most days."

I straighten indignantly. "That cannot be true."

To my surprise, his wistful smile becomes a smirk. A satisfied one. Pulling on his own strange outfit—a dark tunic with roughspun hose—he says, "I was a hellion in those days."

A hellion. Not a vampire or demon or devil, but an ornery little boy spreading mischief in his village. The thought leaves me strangely wistful too. "I wish I could've seen it."

He laughs outright at that. "And *I* am relieved you didn't. My father threatened to send me to a monastery when I was twelve—I locked our donkey in a stall with my stepmother's prized mare just to see what would happen."

My lips twitch. "And *did* something happen?"

"Oh, yes. Twelve months later—in the middle of a blizzard—he woke me up at two o'clock in the morning to help birth our new mule. I named her Snježana, and she lived until the ripe old age of fifty."

"*Fifty?*"

He nods, clearly still delighted with himself, and I cannot help it—I laugh too, glancing around hungrily for any signs of Snježana here. Sure enough, a mule figurine painted white stands on a shelf near the nightstand, along with a small portrait of a woman with Michal's silvery hair. *His mother.* She could be no one else, and my chest squeezes at the sight of her—the softness in her features, the way her eyes seem to sparkle even through the paint, so alike yet so different from her son's. Rounder. Cornflower blue instead of brown.

She is *lovely.*

"Adelina," Michal says softly, as if hesitant to interrupt the peaceful quiet of the room.

Adelina.

I recognize her. I've seen her portrait once before—a different portrait—stacked in the shadows of the grotto.

This oval frame, however, sits atop an ancient book on the language of flowers; beside it sits a bouquet of dried poppies and the wooden idol of a horned deity. Other odd trinkets fill the bedroom too: three golden rings—they look like wedding bands—and a knitted blanket, a rosary, a pair of worn leather boots. Did they belong to his father? An uncle? A long-dead cousin? A slow sort of awareness trickles through my fingers as I trail them along a hornbeam rocking chair, wondering at the history behind it. The story.

So many stories.

Michal left them all here, hidden and safe from the dangers of the castle, and abruptly, I wish we could stay here too. This place . . . it still feels like a home somehow, despite how time and the elements have ravaged it. It still feels loved in a way I've never known.

My hand falls away from the armchair. "Death isn't going to stop, is he?"

At the sound of Death's name, the magic in the room seems to darken a little. Michal's smile fades too, and I instantly regret its loss. *Just a little longer.* The thought aches in that deepest part of me, and—judging from his resigned expression—Michal senses it through the bond. *I want just a little longer with you.*

Coming up behind me, he wraps his arms around my waist and rests his cheek upon my head, as if we've always been like this. As if we always will be. "No," he says simply. "He won't stop."

"We'll need to lure him back, then," I manage. "To the grotto."

"Yes."

"We'll need to send him through the maelstrom before he finds Mathilde."

Michal hesitates this time. Then— "Yes," he says again.

I whirl in his arms at that, staring up at him as his wariness settles over me. His doubt. Though his dark eyes remain inscrutable as ever—hard, bright chips of obsidian—I can feel him now. He will never be an enigma again. "You don't think we can do it?" I ask accusingly, though it feels more like panic.

"I think"—he presses a firm kiss to my forehead—"there are very few things that we cannot do together, but with Death . . ." He trails off, his jaw clenching as he searches for the right words. I do not need the right words, however; I need the *true* ones, and thankfully, he seems to realize as much, his hands sliding down my arms to clasp my own. "There will be a cost, Célie. There is always a cost with Death, whether or not you realize you've paid it."

The words are too familiar, infuriatingly so at this point. "The witches say the same thing. All magic comes at a price."

Even Filippa used the expression to disavow our parents.

"For good reason," Michal says now. "Witches have lived long enough to understand the importance of nature in balance—a balance Death has upset by overstaying his welcome in our realm. Mila was right. Unless he miraculously discovers foresight, this will not end well for any of us, including him."

Mila was right.

Her name catches like a hook in my chest, painful and difficult to remove. And perhaps I never will. Perhaps that is how grief should be—perhaps, at the end of everything, grief is the cost of love. And I loved Mila like my own sister.

I love Filippa too.

"Perhaps we can force him to discover it." Swallowing hard, I straighten my shoulders and say, "I might have an idea."

CHAPTER FORTY-ONE

Two Huntsmen, Three Witches, and Four Vampires Walk into a Grotto

Raised voices echo through the grotto when we slip through the trapdoor an hour later—familiar voices, *angry* ones—and though I dart down the stairs toward them, Michal catches my hand, pulling me back for one last scorching kiss. When we break apart a moment later, he says, "It sounds like my bedroom will be occupied for the foreseeable future."

Sure enough, a veritable crowd of people have gathered at the foot of the stairs: Odessa and Dimitri, yes, but also Lou, Reid, and—*Mathilde.* My heart leaps at the sight of her. *She survived.*

They *all* survived.

Although, right now, Mathilde seems likely to roast her granddaughter on a spit.

"—without even an invitation." Looking harassed, Lou waves a crooked dagger in Mathilde's face. Blood drips from the blade—fresh, by the smell—and also spatters across her nightgown, which is just Reid's overlarge shirt. Wearing nothing else and with her hair in a braid, she clearly wasn't expecting an impromptu trip to Requiem. Moreover, it looks like Mathilde just pulled her from some sort of *attack.* "You can't just tear through my house and take us all hostage—"

Mathilde bats the dagger aside with a gnarled hand, flicking blood onto Dimitri's shoes. He looks down at it with a pained expression. "I saved your ungrateful skin," she snarls. "Those revenants would've *eaten* you if I hadn't showed up when I did, so you can repay the favor now by protecting *mine*."

Lou's mouth parts incredulously. "We didn't *ask* for you to help us. We don't even *know* you—"

"An intentional decision on my part, I can assure you." Mathilde crosses her arms with a beleaguered harrumph. "And one I instantly regret reversing. You are a *dreadful* grandchild."

Lou spots me on the stairs then, pushing past Mathilde with a fierce scowl. "*There* you are. Thank the gods you're finally here—this woman is a complete and total lunatic, and coming from me, that's really saying something. She just *waltzed* into my living room during a revenant attack—"

"A revenant attack?" I ask sharply. "In your *living room*?"

"More like an infestation." Lou waves a dismissive hand, striving to sound unconcerned and failing miserably. "They mostly attack at nightfall, but we dealt with them—"

"*I* dealt with them," Mathilde mutters.

Ignoring her, Lou speaks even louder now. "And then she started raving about Death and your sister and—"

"—and my precious collection of books! My *priceless* collection." Mathilde glares fiercely, though the effect is ruined somewhat by her own nightgown, a rather horrid floral creation with ruffles up to her chin. "I assume they've all gone now thanks to your lot. Tell me, what is the *point* of possessing all these"—she gestures between us in agitation—"these supernatural abilities if you can't even protect a helpless woman in her home?"

I halt mid-step, staring past them across the grotto to where my mother alone sits at Michal's desk. Though exhaustion lines her face—and tears still rim her glassy, hollow eyes—that isn't what captures my immediate attention. Because she isn't alone at all.

Jean Luc and Brigitte stand beside her in rigid silence, their expressions torn between wariness and open hostility.

Oh God. My entire body freezes as Jean Luc locks eyes with me. After I attacked outside Chasseur Tower—after I irreparably broke the love we once shared—I never expected to see him again, let alone to see him *here.* As quickly as the surprise strikes, however, it vanishes again, leaving only bone-deep sadness in its wake—sadness, and this yawning cavern between us. At least his wounds have healed; Coco's blood must've performed a miracle.

I swallow hard.

Jean Luc and I never would've worked, but we shouldn't have ended like this.

As if sensing my thoughts, Jean Luc breaks first, unable to look at me any longer. His eyes land on Michal instead—on our intwined hands—and harden. I cannot even blame Brigitte as she shifts in front of him, trying to block the view. To protect him.

Nor do I release Michal's hand.

"Hello," I say to them softly, tentatively, as Michal squeezes my fingers in encouragement.

Neither of them answer.

Clearing his throat to ease the sudden tension, Reid steps forward and says, "Jean Luc and Brigitte tracked the revenants to our house before Mathilde, er—"

"Kidnapped us," Lou snaps. "She tore through the veil straight on top of my kitchen table, and she snatched me up in the middle of decapitating Undead Grue. Reid grabbed my arm, and Jean Luc grabbed *his* arm, and"—she waves an agitated hand—"so on and so forth. I've never felt sicker in my *life* than I did in the spirit realm," she adds, shuddering. "Though this place is a close second."

"A dreadful grandchild!" Mathilde interjects, yet her hand quivers slightly as she points it at Lou. "And a helpless woman!"

Cursing, Lou stalks to Michal's bed before unceremoniously slumping onto it. Reid follows with an apologetic glance at Michal, who says dryly, "There is nothing helpless about you, Mathilde—and I notice *you* didn't stick around to chat with Death."

"Because I'm not an idiot. He is *Death*."

"And thank goodness you fled instead of fulfilling your marital duties." Though I carefully avoid Dimitri's gaze, his wrists and ankles still seep gently, filling the grotto with the delicate scent of his blood, and the angry red burn of my sister's cross remains on his cheek. "You're right about your books too, and also your cottage—the earth swallowed them, but they did put up quite a fight against Death."

"*Swallowed* them?" Brigitte frowns, bewildered despite herself, and glances from me to Mathilde. "Marital duties? *Her?*"

Though Mathilde skewers her with a glare, Dimitri interrupts before the witch can do something rash, like curse Brigitte into oblivion, or perhaps just bite off her nose. "Trust me," he says with a valiant attempt at a smirk, "it isn't what you think."

Mathilde's fingers twitch. "Watch yourself, boy. I am old, not dead."

"A pity," Lou mutters from the bed.

Impatience snaps through my bond with Michal as he descends the last of the stairs, parting the crowd and pulling me along with him. "Enough. The Chasseur has a point—we cannot proceed until everyone understands." Quickly, he explains all that happened at Mathilde's cottage, all that happened before it, until Brigitte's and Jean Luc's jaws have slackened—Lou's and Reid's too—and my mother closes her eyes and bows her head.

"Filippa?" Jean Luc takes a half step forward when Michal mentions her name, his own eyes widening before flicking to mine. Though he tries to mask his concern, I can still hear the spike of his pulse, his small intake of breath. I nod. "She—she's alive?"

"In a manner of speaking," Odessa says.

Jean Luc hesitates, his gaze softening slightly as he glances at my mother. "Can we help her?"

When she doesn't answer, I swallow hard. "We tried."

Michal squeezes my hand again, and though Jean Luc tracks the movement, he doesn't react otherwise. "Filippa is a symptom of the greater disease," Odessa says impatiently before rounding on Michal. "Why did Death leave us alive at Mathilde's cottage? His revenants outnumbered us—they'd even incapacitated Dimitri and me—and *you* were in no fit shape to defend anyone. Filippa held their mother as leverage against Célie, so why did he not kill us all? Why did he not end our little resistance then and there?"

"Isn't it obvious?" Mathilde—who sat herself on the bottom step, disgruntled, during Michal's explanation—taps her temple shrewdly. "He still hasn't found the missing piece—that special something that makes Filippa unique—and you lot are the only ones who might. If he kills you outright, the secret dies with you, and Death is a coward. He won't risk following you into his own realm. Not until the veil comes down." She harrumphs in disdain before speaking directly to me. "But mark my words, girlie—he'll soon tire of chasing Brides and creating revenants, and he'll punish you for thwarting him."

At that, every eye in the grotto swivels curiously in my direction. Skin prickling beneath their attention, I frown at Mathilde. "Thwarting him? I haven't thwarted him at all. I have no *idea* why my sister isn't like other revenants—"

"No?" Mathilde purses her lips, unconvinced. "No idea at all, hmm? Not a single thought in that witless head of yours?"

"Clearly *you* have one," Michal says in a terse voice. "I would encourage you to share it."

"At the risk of sounding obtuse," Brigitte interjects, "why does it matter if Filippa is different? I thought you said Death wants to bring down the veil, not create another"—those crystalline eyes flick to me—"shadow bride."

Though my own eyes narrow at the thinly concealed insult, I force myself to take a deep, steadying breath. "It matters because Filippa almost single-handedly brought down the veil when she came back on All Hallows' Eve. If Death manages to re-create those circumstances, the veil could collapse entirely. Life and death as we know them will cease to exist, and if our current situation is any indication"—I gesture to the maelstrom, to the castle overhead, to the market and forest and *world* beyond where walls seep blood and ferns weep tears, where everything fades into shades of gray—"that won't be a good thing for anyone."

"Including the Chasseurs," Lou says without lifting her head. She seems to sense rather than see Jean Luc's and Brigitte's reticence, or perhaps she just guessed. Burning revenants in Cesarine is one thing; it is tangible, *actionable*. Confronting literal Death while he rends the world apart is another.

Indeed, Jean Luc and Brigitte exchange a quick, furtive look. The former has never been able to disguise his emotions—in this case, wariness—and the latter doesn't care to hide her disgust.

"Regardless of what happened to Filippa," Michal says, ignoring them both and speaking directly to Mathilde, "Death will keep coming after you, and he is clearly growing desperate."

"Which is why you"—she pokes a crooked finger in his chest—"are going to hide me with the help of these fools." She jerks her chin toward Lou and Reid, then Odessa near the stairs. "Surely between the four of you, I'll be safe enough from anything."

"No one is safe while Death walks among the living," I say. "He'll find all of us eventually, even you, but if you *help* us, we have greater odds of defeating him. I have a plan—"

She starts shaking her head before I've even finished. "Not a chance."

"Mathilde, you are the oldest witch in living memory—"

Her eyes narrow. "That better be a compliment."

"—which means you're powerful," I continue determinedly. "More than that, you're clever—probably cleverer than the rest of us combined." Though Lou and Odessa both snort, I ignore them. "You've evaded detection for how many years now? Even your own kin didn't know you were alive. We could use that sort of cunning to our advantage."

"Careful, now." She peers down her nose at me, eyes glinting with that same uncanny awareness she displayed in the cottage. And for the first time since meeting Mathilde, I understand just how cunning she must've been to have lived this long as a human woman, not an immortal like Michal and Odessa. There is a difference between them, somehow. A vitality I cannot quite place.

Arching a silver brow, she says, "Flattery will get you everywhere."

"If the common good isn't enough," Michal says, "I shall rebuild your cottage by hand after we've banished Death."

"And my books?"

"All replaced, even the first editions."

"Deal." Mathilde cackles then, enormously satisfied with herself. "There are only three copies of *The Wizard of Waterdeep's Staff* in the world—two now—so good luck with that."

"You've read *The Wizard of Waterdeep's Staff*?" Lou asks incredulously, pushing up on her elbows to stare at Mathilde. Already, she looks much too pale, much too sick to do what must be done. We have no other choice, however; I can only hope her magic will be enough.

"This explains so much," Reid mutters.

"Yes, well"—Odessa waves an impatient hand before turning to me—"this is all very good, but what are we actually going to *do*? You said you have a plan."

"I had a *thought*," I say, glancing back at Michal, "at the ruins." When his eyes darken at the memory, I blush slightly, and—despite our less than cheerful circumstances—Lou's and Dimitri's faces split into identical smirks. I ignore them both. "What if we . . . pretend to bring Mila back?"

Michal understands immediately. "Another resurrection," he says at once, and through the bond, a tendril of his hope unfurls—small and tentative, but *there*. My own responds in kind, twining around his and holding it close, strengthening it.

"To bring down the veil—or at least to further damage it." I nod between him and Odessa, who looks skeptical. Truthfully, I cannot blame her. There are still so many variables, so many things that could go wrong. "If we can create a second maelstrom with magic—a *fake* maelstrom—we might be able to trick Death into believing Mila's resurrection caused it, just like Filippa's did on All Hallows' Eve. He'll think the veil is coming down, and he'll come to investigate."

"As if he'd ever believe it," Mathilde sniffs.

"That's where you come in. What if you create a *shock wave* through the veil? One powerful enough to bring Death snooping?"

"Even if I *could* do such a thing, I wouldn't be able to maintain such an illusion for long. A few minutes at most."

"Just to clarify," Jean Luc says incredulously, "your plan is to fake a resurrection and just—*hope* Death appears?" He glances between us as if waiting for the punch line to the world's most ridiculous joke. "To what end? So he can kill the spares?" He jerks his chin between himself and Brigitte, my mother. "I'm reasonably certain he doesn't need to keep the rest of us alive."

"It'll be a risk," Lou says. "All of it. Especially with magic behaving like it has been. Even now, I feel—weak, being this close to the maelstrom." She flicks Mathilde a probing glance. "I assume you do too, which is why you haven't agreed."

Mathilde swells indignantly. "Do you think I'm so easily manipulated? True power speaks for itself. The learned witch needn't exhibit her magic to prove herself—usually, that is." She plants her hands on her hips, an eager smile twisting her lips. "In this case, she must do both, apparently, in order to teach half-witted grandchildren their place." Turning back to me, she says, "*Fine*, I will create this shock wave, and then I will leave. Do you understand? I plan to be halfway to Zvezdya when this hell breaks loose—and it *will*. This is not Frederic you're dealing with. It isn't even your ghastly sister. This is *Death*, and he will not appreciate such buffoonery."

Odessa shakes her head. "And even if Death *does* fall for the shock wave, how are we going to incapacitate him? In case you've forgotten," she says to Michal, "he took *you* down within a matter of moments."

Jean Luc chuckles at that, but he stops abruptly at the sharp smile spreading across Michal's face. "A bathtub fell on me, Odessa."

"And that isn't quite the boast you think it is," Dimitri says. "Can we just . . . *push* Death into the real maelstrom, and send him back where he came from?" He blinks then before turning to me. "Is that where it goes, do you think? To the realm of the dead?"

"Of course it does. It *is* the door through which he came." Odessa heaves an exasperated sigh, turning on her heel to pace now. Nearly cracking the stone underfoot. "So—in this hypothetical dreamland in which we are all currently living—let's say we *do* manage to lure Death here. More improbable still, let us say we also manage to shove him into the maelstrom and through the veil. What then? The door still does not close without Filippa."

"We said we would find another way," Michal says curtly.

"There is no other way. It's always been her." To everyone's surprise, the words come not from Odessa but from me—and they're true. They've been true since the moment my heart ceased to beat, since Filippa used my blood and Frederic's magic to claw her way from the grave; they've been true since Death slipped through with her, since we tore the veil wide open—the four of us—and created that monstrosity in the sea. Even now, it beckons to me, but I resist, staring intently from one face to another before turning deliberately to my mother.

She rises from her chair slowly as our eyes catch and hold, and I close the distance between us, lowering my voice. "I wanted to save her, Maman. You must believe me. I wanted to—to change her back somehow, to love her enough that she'd *want* to change too, but Death has twisted her up inside. You saw her at the cottage. Filippa is not the same woman we knew, perhaps never *was* that woman, and Death . . . he made her worse. He slaughtered Frederic and preyed on her fears, her loneliness, and I"—pressure builds behind my eyes now, undeserved and *wretched*—"I think Filippa has felt alone for a very long time."

My mother says nothing when I take her hands. "Worse still, Death has convinced her that he is her only path to happiness, to her daughter. To her *future*." I swallow the lump of emotion in my throat; I have not earned it. I am sentencing my sister to death. "She will not forsake him, Maman."

When my mother simply stares, I bring her hands to my chest, willing her to forgive me. To feel that place where my heart used to beat—where sometimes, I think it still does. How else could it be bleeding like this? "Please say something," I whisper.

A shadow shifts in her eyes at that, and it terrifies me.

It reminds me of the woman trapped inside her bed, trapped inside her *head*, who could not escape even for her daughters. After another long moment, she draws her hands away. "I cannot give you my blessing," she says quietly, "no matter how badly you wish it. I cannot condemn either of you to such a fate."

Without another word, she turns away from me, vanishing through the curtain.

Leaving me to stare after her with this terrible ringing in my ears.

"I—" Choking down the word, I glance back at Michal, but it is Jean Luc who steps in front of me when I finally move to follow her. He touches my elbow with light fingers. I do not find pity in his gaze, however, or even the disgust so often present when he looks at me now. Instead it fills with understanding. With sadness.

And with it, I know we will never mend the rift between us. Not properly. Even with his forgiveness, we will never be like we were before he fell in love with me and I fell out of love with him. And—perhaps that is for the best.

Perhaps some hurts run too deeply to ever forget.

Still he squeezes my elbow and says, "I'll speak to her."

Then, as he turns away too—

"I'm sorry, Jean."

The words leave me in a breathless whisper, perhaps too soft for him to hear, but he still hesitates by the curtain, glancing back at me with an inscrutable expression. Perhaps he can disguise his emotions after all. With a sigh, he tips his head toward the desk, where a letter lies open upon its surface. *His* letter. "I know," he says quietly.

When he disappears after my mother, I return to the safety of Michal's arms, to his strong and steady presence, and rest my cheek against his chest. I still do not allow myself to cry, however; I still haven't earned it. Indeed, I even smile a little as Brigitte stands frozen by the curtain, staring between it and me as if unsure what to do. "Not to be rude or anything," she says at last, "but who the hell is Mila?"

CHAPTER FORTY-TWO

The Second Maelstrom

Within thirty minutes, Reid Diggory—previously renowned captain of the Chasseurs, decorated war hero, and husband of the most powerful witch alive—has become Mila Vasiliev.

Or at least, he looks a lot like her.

It took several failed attempts—several long, nerve-wracking moments as the maelstrom weakened his efforts—but slowly, piece by piece, Reid coaxed his magic into cooperating. The sharp scent of it still lingers on his skin as he presses the tip of a newly feminine finger to his nose. It breaks beneath his touch, and I wince as he groans, as the flesh of his face contorts and twists into Mila's features: her pert nose, her full lips, her flushed cheeks. A single freckle dusts the latter—a freckle I never noticed in all the time I knew Mila.

With a pang, I realize I never knew her at all.

I knew the imprint, yes, the illusion, but I never truly met *her*. Though this isn't technically her either—this is Reid breaking and re-forming his body to resemble her portrait—it still feels different, seeing her in full and glorious color. Those treacherous tears have not stopped burning since my mother's departure, and they threaten to spill over again as the final touch of Reid's transformation falls into place. My relief is a tangled, bittersweet thing.

Her eyes.

Warm and rich and brown, they gaze back at me from across the grotto. The exact shade of Odessa's and Dimitri's, yet spaced slightly farther apart and larger, rounder, with thick black lashes lined with kohl. I cannot look away. I cannot stop myself from studying her, memorizing her—the strong profile of her jaw, the delicate bones of her shoulders, the lush sable hair that cascades around her gown. Dove white. Michal described it to Reid with as much detail as possible, and the effect is . . . breathtaking.

She is breathtaking.

Michal, Odessa, and Dimitri have gone still as statues.

They stare at her like one stares at a shooting star or solar eclipse—like if they blink, they might miss her, and they'll miss her forever.

When she groans again, however—her voice too deep, too masculine—the illusion shatters, and I force myself to take a deep, steadying breath as Reid clenches her hands into fists. "I won't be able to hold this forever." Each word sounds labored, pained. "The maelstrom—it's too strong."

"Your voice," I whisper.

"I'm sorry." He shakes his head, clenches shut his eyes. *Her* eyes. "I can't—can't make it higher. My magic—"

Michal moves to stand beside me then. At the sound of Reid's voice, his jaw clenches, and his black eyes gleam too bright in the candlelight. Anyone else might've mistaken them for tears, but I can feel the anger licking up his ribs. No. The grief. Rather than making Michal look more vulnerable, however, it makes him look somehow fiercer, predatory even. Like a wild animal caught in a trap. "You look just like her," he tells Reid.

It does not sound like a compliment.

When Reid blinks, startled by his tone, Odessa rests a gentle hand against his arm. "Yes, you do."

Michal's lip curls.

Fortunately, Lou and Mathilde descend at that moment—one on either side—the former clutching his chin while the latter picks at his gown. "Her mouth is wider," Lou says, turning Reid's new face to examine it. Mila stands only a few inches taller than her, narrowing the height gap between them. "And her cupid's bow is less pronounced." She pats his cheek with a feeble hand, her freckles stark. "Yours has gone all pointy."

Mathilde slaps her hand away. "You saw the girl *twice.* You are hardly the authority—"

"Yes, well—" Rolling her eyes, Lou dangles a necklace from her fingers, the gilded edges of the pendant glowing slightly as the light catches them. Inside it, a portrait of Mila smiles back at us, serene and beautiful and alive. "I am the one holding the locket, and *clearly*, her cupid's bow looks different."

Michal stiffens beside me, and I run a hand along his arm before tracing circles into his palm. He calms slightly at the touch, though his jaw remains like adamantine.

"That portrait is the size of a thimble"—Mathilde snatches the locket away, though the movement leaves her swaying slightly—"and even if it weren't, the artist who painted it was a sham and blunderbuss to boot. In a desperate bid for glory, he eschewed civilization and forwent bathing for an entire *year*, claiming nature as his one true muse. You should've smelled him by the end of it—absolutely *fetid*—with only a handful of lousy landscapes to show for it." She lifts the portrait to examine it more closely. "All that aside, this might be his best work. Not hard to do with Mila." With an exaggerated harrumph, she tucks the locket tenderly into her cloak. "You're still wrong about her mouth, though."

She punctuates the last by leaning heavily against the bedpost, nudging aside the kittens that claw up her legs.

As with me, they've been swarming her feet since Michal freed them from the washroom to stretch their legs before our confrontation with Death. A thoughtful gesture, and not one Mathilde seems to appreciate. Scowling down at them, she mutters, "Mila was my dearest friend, and I undoubtedly knew her best."

I expect Michal to speak up now, or perhaps Odessa and Dimitri; I expect them to disagree and snap at the witches for claiming any part of Mila, but none of them speak. Indeed, Dimitri doesn't even turn from the water's edge, where he stands rigid, staring out at the maelstrom with his hands in his pockets.

Lou clears her throat into the silence, releasing Reid's face with a furtive glance at the vampires. At Mathilde herself. "You're probably right," she says at last. "Her cupid's bow is perfect."

With effort, Michal forces a small, cold smile—a man unaffected, a man in control, but those eyes still burn with black fire. Though his sister might've chosen to move on—might've even passed peacefully, like the moon over the sun—he still misses her, and he always will.

There will be time to grieve later, however, after we deal with Death. Perhaps we'll even give her a proper funeral; I'll learn how they lay their dead to rest in Michal and Mila's homeland, and it will be a beautiful tribute. But for now—

Mathilde snarls in pain, threatening to collapse as a kitten's claws catch in her knee. "Will someone do something about these *damned* cats?"

I jolt into motion—determined to save the poor thing before she accidentally punts it into the sea—but hesitate when Brigitte hurries forward with a basket instead. She plucks each kitten up by its nape, tucking them away without a word. I frown at her efficiency. At her *agility*. Indeed, when I bend to help, she snatches away the last kitten before turning sharply on her heel, her knuckles pale as she clutches the basket to her chest. Her eyes dart toward the curtain.

Toward my mother and Jean Luc.

Understanding sweeps through me immediately. Brigitte might hate us—might hate me most of all—but she hasn't acted on her feelings; she hasn't drawn her Balisarda and lodged it in my neck as she so clearly longs to do. No. Instead she has listened, has questioned, has even *helped* . . . and all because of Jean Luc.

Hoisting the basket higher, she brushes past me toward the curtain, but I reach out a tentative hand to stop her. "Thank you," I murmur when she turns, unsure what else to say.

She tosses her long braid over her shoulder, glaring at me as she scratches a kitten's chin. "I'm not doing any of this for you. I didn't ask to be here." Though her voice sizzles with venom—once, it would've filled me with it in response—I've been in her position, and it isn't one I'd wish on anyone. I've been stranded in the destruction of a lover's past too. Worse still, hers has marooned her in a grotto with his ex-fiancée.

Of course she wants to stick a sword in my neck. I cannot blame her for it, so instead I offer a small smile. An olive branch. "I'm appreciative regardless, Brigitte. Truly."

Instead of reciprocating, she flinches like I've slapped her. And that—that's fine too. *Expected.* Though I brace when she opens her mouth to speak, she seems to change her mind in the next second, scowling and shaking her head instead. Slipping through the curtain without another word. I can still hear as she joins Jean Luc and my mother, however, and places the basket upon the floor. The faint rustle of fabric as she sits down, the fainter whisper of greeting to Jean Luc. I can hear him take her hand.

I stop listening then and turn to Michal, who meets my gaze across the grotto.

I love you. I mouth the words without thinking, and he stalks forward to pull me into his arms. Without a word, he kisses me, and that bond pulses between us like a heartbeat. And it's enough. With him, it'll always be enough.

I still feel the torch he now carries, however. Though I try to ignore it, it presses into the hollow between my shoulder blades, and I swallow the lump in my throat before it chokes me. Because I—I cannot think about that torch now. I cannot think about it *ever*—cannot acknowledge its existence—until all of this is over, until I can do nothing else but regret it for the rest of my eternal life. *We don't have a choice. We never had a choice.*

Remorse pulses through the bond from Michal too—along with sickening dread at what he must do—but I don't acknowledge it either, and he remains mercifully silent.

Over his shoulder, Lou steps into the water, where she closes her eyes and lifts her hands with Reid as Mila standing sentry beside her. "Are you ready?" he asks in a low, strained voice.

Clenching her jaw, she nods. "No time like the present."

And we begin.

Mathilde rises from the bed as Lou flicks her wrists, and the water beyond the real maelstrom begins to churn too—slowly at first, so slowly—while Odessa and Dimitri assume their positions on opposite ends of the shore. They'll be responsible for pushing Death into the waters if I fail.

The thought should terrify me, and it *does*—that I might fail, that the veil might fall, that everyone here might surrender to Death in the end. Still, other than Reid, I'm the only one Death might allow to get close to him. I'm the only one with the element of surprise.

Leaving Michal to deal with Filippa, if she even comes at all.

She'll come, I tell myself fiercely. *Her future depends on this too.*

My stomach twists at that, threatens to empty all over this wretched grotto floor. *Her child.*

Still, our duplicity comes last, so together, Michal and I watch as the waters build momentum, the second maelstrom beginning to form. Blood trickles from Lou's ears at the effort, and Dimitri clamps his mouth shut with a groan while Odessa watches him like a hawk. "Stop breathing," she tells him, hardly moving her lips to prevent anyone from noticing. "Hold your breath."

He swallows hard and nods.

"And you?" Michal asks just as quietly. "Are you ready for this?"

No, I want to say, but of course I can't. Of course he senses it anyway.

"After Lou has finished, Mathilde will begin with the veil." Michal's arms tighten around me one last time. "If Death takes the bait, he could be here within moments."

"Within seconds," I whisper.

"And you'll have"—Lou's limbs tremble with strain now, her broken magic still moving an entire *ocean*—"about that long to push him."

Waves crash beyond the maelstroms at her words, a storm building—imploding—as the wind picks up too. It catches at our hair, our gowns, whisking the letters from Michal's desk and carrying them into the sea. Dimitri yields a single step as icy water sprays across his face, and Odessa plants her feet, bracing for the battle to come—because it *will* be a battle. Once Death realizes our deception, realizes we machinated the entire scene, his wrath will be endless. As Lou said, we'll have only seconds to push him, perhaps less; Michal will need to dispatch my sister only after Death has fallen through.

Say the word, Célie, her voice seems to whisper, except now I know that voice belongs to me. It always has. *To* kill *your sister. To burn her.*

Still the waters churn faster.

Faster.

As if reacting to Lou's magic, the real maelstrom seems to swell even larger, fiercer, seeking to consume her subterfuge. It spirals deeper until jagged rocks can be seen upon the seafloor. They look like teeth, and blood drips from Lou's nose now too. Reid holds her steady, anchoring her with Mila's small hands and gentle frame, as she begins to violently shake.

Whatever magic she is using to create the second maelstrom, she must be pulling it from her very bones. "Easy, girl," Mathilde mutters, and even she steps forward as if to help. As if concerned.

"I am—*fine.*" Lou spits the words through clenched teeth. Then, raising her voice over the roar of the waves: "We're almost"—she gives another great shudder—"there. Is everyone ready?"

"And what if we're not?" Dimitri nearly shouts to be heard, the wind whipping his hair across his face. "What then?"

"Too—bad."

Dimitri curses, and Michal releases me at last as Odessa snaps, "Death is the priority. We push him through no matter the cost!" When Lou's knees buckle in response, she points a finger toward the ceiling, adding wildly, "And I—I owe *you* a new broomstick, Louise la Blanc! I took yours apart and bathed it in an alchemical solution to make it fly, so don't you *dare* die on us—"

Lou forces a laugh despite herself, and lightning forks beyond the cave's mouth. Her blood trickles faster. "Broomsticks don't—fly."

"*Yours* might! When this is over, we shall all find out!" Then, fiercer than even the storm—"*Focus*, Louise. We are almost there!"

"No one will be flying anywhere until I get my hatbox!" Mathilde's eyes narrow at the force of the maelstroms, and she nods once to herself as if satisfied. My stomach plummets at the movement, and I watch—frozen—as she battles the wind to march to the center of the grotto. *It's time.* "A promise is a promise, you wretched creatures!"

Lou laughs louder, barely standing now, as Mathilde nods again to Reid, and he drags Lou beyond the curtain into the washroom. Hiding her. Death cannot see anyone he does not expect to see, and especially not a witch bleeding from her eyes and ears. *She'll be fine*, I tell myself anxiously. *She'll heal with distance from the maelstrom.*

Jean Luc and Brigitte will remain hidden too—sequestered with my mother—so as not to spook Death with their human faces and Balisardas. If he suspects our true motive too soon, all will be lost.

When Reid returns a moment later, the maelstroms still rage, and Mathilde fists her hand in the veil. "I hope you all live," she says, before spearing Michal with a glare. "And if you do, I'm quite serious about my hatbox—and my books! Every single one." Then she tears into the veil, her gaze flashing molten silver as the spirit realm ripples at her fingers and snow flutters into the grotto. "I'd hold on to something if I were you."

Swifter than I've ever managed, she vanishes through the gap, mending it in the same fluid motion.

The rest of us brace in anticipation as Reid steps into the water. His chest still heaves with pain, his face contorted with concentration. He'll need to ease his breathing if Death is to believe he is Mila, to believe she has risen from the—*wherever* ghosts go when they pass from the spirit realm. My own breath hitches at the thought. We didn't discuss any plausible stories for Reid. He won't know how to answer if Death asks any questions; I will need to answer for him, and—

And it'll take a miracle for this to work.

Still, I clasp my hands out of habit, or perhaps in prayer, and close my eyes as we wait for Mathilde's signal. For one second—for one single, glorious second—I allow myself to think of a better future. A future where we survive, where we banish Death, where Lou flies on a broomstick, and where I help Michal rebuild Mathilde's cottage before we flee to his home in the ruins. Never to be seen again.

When I open my eyes, however, I see none of those things.

Instead a fat orange tabby bounds out of the washroom, and—to my horror—my mother appears in his wake. "Come back here this *instant*—" She straightens at the roar of the wind, her pale face frozen in surprise, and I can do nothing but lift a panicked hand before Mathilde sends her shock wave through the veil.

The world implodes.

Seismic pressure shatters the ether, the very core of my being as the veil blasts outward, as it steals my vision, my breath, and I cannot find Michal to grab his hand—cannot find *anything* except the post of his bed, which I fling myself around to keep from falling. And it feels like Mathilde attacked *me* instead of the veil—swung a cudgel straight at my knees—as the grotto ripples, as it shudders with wave upon wave of aftershocks. Michal stumbles backward as if he feels them too, and my mother—

I gasp and release the bedpost, falling to my knees. *My mother.*

With a cry of shock—of pain—she collapses, hitting the ground with an indelicate thud and not moving again. Though the ether still trembles, though the ground still shakes and the sea still roars, I crawl toward her while Michal shouts a warning. I take her cold face in my hand.

Oh God.

"Maman." My voice comes out a croak as I shake her slightly, determined to rouse her before Death arrives. Through the rippling fabric of reality, Reid, Odessa, and Dimitri stare down at us in horror, completely unaffected by the shock. So why was *she*? "Maman, wake up. *Please* wake up. You must hide because—because Death will be here any moment, and if he—"

But Michal has joined us now; he kneels beside us with a grim expression, taking her wrist to check her pulse. "She's alive," he says swiftly. "Her heart is weak, but it's still beating."

She's alive. The words strike me like twin bolts of lightning, and I jolt upright, gaping at him even as I listen to her faint heartbeat. Because why wouldn't she be alive? What is *happening*? And where— "Where is Death?" I look around wildly for any sign of him. "Why hasn't he come? He must've felt—"

Before I've finished the sentence, however, an ominous slashing sound erupts behind Reid. The veil ripping, *tearing*, as Death and Filippa step through. "Well, well, well," he muses, his eyes widening as they pass from Mila to the maelstrom, to Michal and me on our knees. They skip over my mother completely. "What an interesting turn of events."

Rising on unsteady knees, I move in front of my mother as the last aftershock fades. I recall the lessons she taught us about maintaining composure while in the aristocracy, and I hold my chin high, fixing a hard smile upon my lips. Reid will not be the only performer in this charade. Sweeping into a perfect curtsy, I say, "Bonsoir, monsieur, and make yourself welcome."

"*Welcome*"—his brows rise incredulously as I straighten—"is not a word I've ever heard from you before."

I take a small step toward him, waving an errant hand. "Perhaps *welcome* is a stretch, yet I cannot say your presence here is entirely unexpected." Another step. "At least you've left your revenants at home this time."

Death's eyes narrow before flicking back to Reid—to *Mila*—as a moth drawn to a flame. "My revenants are never far away, darling," he says softly, and behind him, the veil flutters with their presence. How many wait beyond it, I do not know. Then— "How did you do it?"

Another small step. Another. As planned, Michal remains a safe distance behind me. I just need to get close enough without rousing suspicion; Death has never taken me seriously, and I intend to make him regret it. "As if I would tell you." Continuing my slow path toward him, I roll my eyes as if irritated. "You're the one who gave up after La Voisin's ashes." Step. Step. Step. "You never tried my blood on an actual *body*."

"Ah, my sweet, but Mila didn't *have* an actual body."

I arch a brow, flicking a sly glance at Michal, whose lip curls. "Says who?" he asks.

Even Death looks mildly impressed at that, if not a touch revolted. "You kept your sister's corpse after Frederic drained her? How terribly . . . disturbing. But why wait all this time? Why not revive her when you abducted our darling Célie?"

I lift my chin defiantly, and I pray our feeble explanation is enough. "We didn't yet know what my blood could do."

"Ah." Death lifts Mila's arm to examine it, running his fingers along the inner skin of her elbow. When Michal snarls softly, he laughs. "You figured it out, then. You—brought her back. Your blood has been the key all along."

It sounds like a question.

"Obviously."

"It didn't bring it down." Death stares out at the second maelstrom before reaching out as if to feel the veil, to test it, while I continue toward him. "How many more will it take? I wonder. Surely the veil cannot suffer much further abuse." When I do not answer, he tips his head, glancing back at me. Studying my reaction closely. "What changed your mind? Why did you do this?"

Thankful that my heart cannot pound in fear, I lift a shoulder. "You killed Mila. We wanted her back."

"Ah, yes. *Mila.* We haven't heard much from our beautiful friend, have we? I remember her being much more . . . talkative in life. And in death," he adds thoughtfully. "The two of us have been well-acquainted over the years."

Please, please, please, I think.

On either side of the shore, Dimitri and Odessa shadow my movements as surreptitiously as possible, but Death hasn't yet noticed them. He seems too absorbed in Mila, circling around her now. Drifting closer to the maelstrom as he trails a hand across her back. She trembles, closing her eyes, and his silver eyes flash with satisfaction—he thinks he's affecting her, when in reality, Reid is struggling to maintain his control. His limbs have locked. His jaw clamps tight. Bile still rises in my throat at Death's avid, hungry expression, but I swallow it back down. Because this was the plan. Dimitri, Odessa, Death himself—this is all going according to plan.

Except for Filippa.

She tracks the twins' footsteps too carefully—especially Dimitri's—her features sharpening with suspicion when I catch her eye instead. "Careful," she murmurs to Death, moving closer to him too. "This could be a trick."

Death scoffs.

"You felt the disturbance, did you not? You see her standing before us now?" Though Death speaks to Filippa, he still stares at Mila like his most prized possession, catching a strand of her hair as it billows in the wind. He tips his head toward the waters. "You see the maelstroms."

"I smell the magic," Filippa says sharply.

Death waves her anger aside. "You smell *me*—or perhaps your sister—as we cannot help but smell of the divine." His nostrils flare, and reluctantly, he shoots a disgusted look at Michal. "Though I notice you're rather tainting our scent these days. A pity, that."

Michal growls. "If you know what's good for you, you'll get the fuck out. Now."

"No, I don't think I will."

Michal's eyes flash as Death brings Mila's hand to his lips, and Reid shudders again, his breathing shallow. "Don't touch her," Michal snarls abruptly.

I hasten forward as Death ignores Michal, a slow and seductive grin spreading across his face. "Mila Vasiliev," he says, and thankfully, Reid gathers Mila's features into imperiousness rather than rage. "My eternal damsel. You are so much more beautiful *alive.* Tell me, darling, how does it feel to walk among us once more?"

Michal stiffens at the question. Odessa and Dimitri halt midstep. And I need to *act*, quickly, before Death senses any hesitation. "How do you think she feels?" I interject loudly. "She—"

"I was not talking to *you.*" His silver eyes remain fixed firmly upon Mila, and he arches a brow in question. Waiting. And I dare not look at anyone else either, lest Death realize something is wrong. *Just a few more steps.* A few more steps from me—or from Dimitri and Odessa—and we can do it. We can reach him, then Filippa. Energy surges through me, a rush of adrenaline that permeates the air, and the others seem to sense it too. Abandoning caution, they quicken their pace just as Death says, "Well?"

A trickle of blood drips from Mila's nose in response.

A thud sounds from the washroom.

Though I whirl toward the sound—perhaps my mother rose and she fell again—she remains crumpled on the ground, and that *sound—*

To my horror, the second maelstrom begins to slow, begins

to stop, and the winds die along with it, leaving us in hideous silence. No.

No, no, no.

My heart leaps into my throat as I glance helplessly at Mila, who appears much taller than before—her hair tinted red—with her nose melting into a pale, lumpen shape before re-forming into Reid's. Straighter. Larger—much too large for her heart-shaped face. *Oh God.* Realization begins to dawn across Death's features. Eyes narrowing, he reaches out slowly to wipe the blood away with his thumb. "What . . . ?"

And Reid strikes, unexpectedly punching him into the water.

Death falls as if in slow motion, arms pinwheeling through the air, before landing just short of the maelstrom with an enormous splash. Flicking his wrist at Michal's torch, Reid tears off toward Lou, and the torch indeed catches fire—as does Michal's hand, his wrist, his arm. The flames streak up his sleeve as if sentient, and he roars in pain, flinging the torch aside while Odessa, Dimitri, and I surge in unison toward Death. Though Filippa rises up to meet us, Dimitri doesn't hesitate. He knocks her aside, and she crashes into me, who crashes into Michal, who seizes her collar with a burning hand to hurl her into the maelstrom after Death.

Hair ablaze, she stabs him in the fist with a silver knife. He curses bitterly, but Filippa is already moving.

Wrenching her knife from Michal's fist, she flings it behind her with preternatural speed and precision, and I can do nothing—*nothing*—as Death surges from the water, as Dimitri lunges, the tips of his fingers just brushing Death's sleeve—

And Filippa's knife lodges deep within Dimitri's chest.

A scream shatters the grotto. I cannot tell if it belongs to

Odessa or me—not with blood rushing through my ears and Dimitri's eyes widening in shock. Not with his skin desiccating like he's—like he's—

He's dying.

My mind refuses to accept the words even as he staggers back a step, and Odessa tackles Filippa into the water, snarling and shrieking and sobbing. Extinguishing the only chance we might've had to kill her. And Michal charges Death, who laughs, but I miss that hideous silence of before. I miss it so much. Because no one else can hear Dimitri's last gasping breath.

And no one else can see him as he slips—his terrified eyes catching mine—and tumbles backward into the maelstrom.

CHAPTER FORTY-THREE

Don't Be Gentle

If Mila's death brought peace, Dimitri's death sparks war—violent, bloodthirsty war.

Michal releases Death to seize Odessa around the waist, preventing her from careening into the maelstrom after her brother. She kicks, screams, *thrashes* as though her body is alight with flames. "Dimitri! *Dimitri!*" Her pain—her fury—has a name, and she shrieks it as though appealing to the heavens themselves. When they do not answer, she shrieks at Michal instead—at *me*—spewing threats and curses, slashing at his arms and promising to make Death pay, to make us pay too. And my entire body trembles because she means it. She blames us for splitting her soul in two, and she should—she *should.* Tears stream down my own cheeks now. They blur my vision as I stare at the maelstrom, at the place where Dimitri once stood and now does not.

This is my fault. Dimitri is dead because I hesitated—because I—I tried to protect my own sister for too long, and now Odessa will never see him again. Michal will never recover.

"Dimitri! DIMITRI!"

She arches again, reaching for her twin—straining desperately toward the maelstrom—but Michal refuses to let her go; he holds her until her screams subside into broken sobs and she collapses in his arms. Stroking her hair with his bloody palm, he whispers fiercely in her ear, but I can no longer hear his words. Excruciating pressure builds in my head as Filippa kicks the torch into the maelstrom after him. I should move to catch it, to save it—but my legs refuse to hold me any longer. I sink to my knees in the waves.

Eyes wide, Filippa whirls toward me with a snarl of disbelief. "Were you really going to *kill* me, Célie? *Me?* Your own sister?"

I shake my head, unable to hear her, to hear anything but Michal's warning ringing in my ears: *There will be a cost, Célie. There is always a cost with Death, whether or not you realize you've paid it.*

Dimitri was our cost.

A sob wracks my body, but I stifle the sound with my fist. How could I be so *stupid*? How could I ever think this haphazard plan of mine would succeed? Time and time again, I have attempted to do right by my loved ones—to prevail over those who would harm them—and time and time again, I have failed. Not just *failed*, but hurt them worse than anyone else ever could.

My sister lost her future, her fiancé and unborn child, because I refused to follow her out the window. Now look at her—twisted with rage as she yanks the silver cross from her pocket and pitches it toward Death, who explodes from the water in fury. Across the grotto, our mother still lies unconscious. She would not be here if not for me—and neither would Reid, who anxiously attempts to revive Lou in the washroom while Jean Luc and Brigitte hasten to help. Odessa lost her brother. Michal lost his sister. Everywhere I go, pain and despair seem to follow, as if they feed on the shadows I cast. As if they *thrive* in my wake.

How much more will they be expected to pay? How can the

cost climb any higher? Already it feels as if I am drowning in their grief, absorbing its weight and sinking, suffocating, until there is only darkness.

Dimitri is dead.

Death has won.

As soon as I think it, a hand seizes my hair, wrenching me upward by the scalp. Though I twist, clawing at Death's wrist, he does not hesitate this time; he does not pause to listen, to look, to speak. Eyes blazing, he simply loops the silver chain around my throat and pulls.

White-hot fire erupts across my skin—a pain so consuming it obliterates all else—and my scream splinters the grotto.

"Yes," Death hisses through clenched teeth, and with a jerk of his chin, revenants spill through the veil into the grotto. *Dozens* of them, one after another after another. "It hurts, doesn't it?"

I can only claw at the chain in answer, heedless of the blisters ravaging my fingers, my palms—because I am going to die. He is going to *kill* me, and the last thing I'll ever see is Michal's panicked face—

No! I shout through the bond as Michal lunges, as revenants rise to meet him, as Death laughs again and pulls the chain tighter, splitting my skin and cutting off my scream. Hot blood pools around the metal, and Michal stills instantly. His face anguished. His eyes wide.

"*Finally*"—Death yanks me flush against his bare chest—"you're beginning to understand what's at stake here. Ah, ah, ah—" His face snaps toward Odessa, who circled to our right when Michal lunged, bending her knees to spring. A handful of revenants swarm around her too. "Don't get any ideas, or Célie's head will soon join your brother."

Though Odessa straightens slowly, her entire being burns with vitriolic hatred. "Stop this. Stop it *now.* You do not want a war with vampires."

"Do you know *what,* Odessa?" he asks loudly. "I don't think I *will* stop. Indeed, I don't think I've even gotten started, but I do like this little playacting of yours. What a brilliant performance." With long, furious strides, he drags me from the water by the silver chain. Though I dig my heels into the rock to slow us down, it does no good. Though I scrabble to slide my blood-soaked fingers between the silver and my skin, he holds it too tightly. I cannot find purchase, and the chain slices deeper into my skin. Blood spills down my chest in another sick parody of All Hallows' Eve. "What do you think, Célie? Shall we use the stage you've already set? I have a new theory I'd like to test."

"Let her go," Michal snarls.

"Oh, I plan to," Death says with a vicious, perverted sort of joy. "Your darling mate—such a *disgusting* word, by the way—will be the star of our second act. No need to look so grim, my love." Pulling me higher, he wrenches my cheek against his while I choke and splutter, my toes sliding upon the ground. "It'll be quite easy, in fact. You pretended to resurrect Mila—and I quite like the idea of re-creating that second maelstrom—so let's get to it, shall we? Who here do you love most? Is it your lover?" He tips our faces toward Michal, and the chain cuts a little deeper. "Is it your friend?" Next he forces me to look at Lou, who burst through the curtain with Reid, Jean Luc, and Brigitte at the sound of my scream. Blood drips from her eyes and ears, from Reid's nose. "Perhaps your fiancé? He *is* an unexpected surprise."

At that, Jean Luc sweeps his Balisarda from its sheath, but Death scoffs, jerking his chin toward Filippa; she strikes with lethal speed, twisting the sword from his grip and smashing its hilt against his skull. When he crumples instantly, Brigitte shrieks in rage—drawing her own weapon—but she cannot match Filippa's preternatural strength. Within seconds, she joins Jean Luc upon the ground. Spinning both weapons in unison, Filippa levels them at Lou's and Reid's hands. "Do not move," she warns, "or I will cut them off."

Neither of them dares disobey.

More revenants move to surround them.

"Or *perhaps*"—Death continues as if Filippa did not just single-handedly debilitate four people—"it is your darling mother you love most of all. Shall we take a closer look?" With a warning glance at Michal and Odessa, Death stalks across the grotto, still holding me against him by the chain at my throat. He forces me to my knees in front of her before leaning over me—thrusting my chest to the ground—and poking her brutally in the forehead. "Hello? Are you still in there?"

Her eyes flutter open at the assault, and it takes all my resolve not to snarl and rear backward, driving my head into his sneering face. "Don't"—I choke—"touch her."

"But why not?" Death asks softly. "I *own* her."

Her eyes flutter open as his words wash over me, and when she sees the silver chain around my throat—Death's hands as they slowly decapitate me—all the blood drains from her already ashen face. And her eyes themselves—how didn't I notice them before?

Once a deep emerald green, they appear almost gray now. Faded. Like part of her already exists in the spirit realm. She inhales a rattling breath. "Célie."

She looks a bit peaked, don't you think?

"Mother," I whisper.

Though I reach for her, Death gives a vicious tug, and I fall backward as she pushes herself into a sitting position. She presses a hand to her forehead. "What is—what is happening?" Her voice is weak, however. Too weak. Despite our proximity, I can hardly hear it, yet still her gaze drifts to Death's face above mine before sharpening slightly. "You—you will release my daughters this instant." *Daughters*, not daughter. My chest tightens at the word, but Filippa says nothing—*does* nothing—as I scrabble anew at the silver chain. "Do you hear me? Let them *go*."

Death crouches beside her, swiveling the chain around so it bites into my neck instead. It forces me to bow. Then he pinches her cheek as he would an errant child, hard enough to bruise. Then— "No," he says simply.

And he shoves her face away.

She pitches backward with a gasp, and now I *do* move—I lunge for her as Death rips my throat backward, jerking my body around just in time to see Filippa flinch in shock, in anger, before her expression abruptly empties once more. Her knuckles still clench white around her weapons, however. Tension radiates from her shoulders.

"Ah, ah, ah." Death points a finger at Filippa, triumphant. "See, that is *just* the thing! That look on your face. That look right there—I *keep* seeing it, Filippa darling, just like I saw it outside Mathilde's cottage."

Filippa remains completely still. "I don't know what you mean."

"You *liar.*" Laughing as if delighted, Death pulls the chain higher, and I rise with it, refusing to gasp. To react. Through the wall of revenants between us, Michal's gaze does not waver from me. And his rage—I can feel it building through the bond, dark and powerful and *sentient,* just waiting for the right moment. It dare not strike yet—*not yet*—but it tracks every drop of blood from my throat, every step of Death's behind mine. It wills Death to approach the shore once more. To approach *him.* He'll need only seconds to evade the revenants, to rend Death's arms from his shoulders, but I'll need to be free of Death first. I'll need to break the chain, perhaps snap his wrists, and flee before he can hurt me again.

He will never hurt you again.

The words belong to Michal, but they still pulse scarlet in my mind's eye, casting a bloody haze over my vision.

"In the blood witch camp," Death says, oblivious to our exchange, "Célie mentioned just how much Frederic loved you, and I couldn't help but wonder—has *that* been the missing piece on this chessboard of ours?" He tilts his head in rapt fascination. "It would fit, wouldn't it? La Voisin never loved anyone at all, so she wouldn't have understood its effects on her spell. But what if it *did* affect her spell? If simple blood can resurrect a body—if it can create a revenant—imagine what love could do."

He reaches over my shoulder to caress my face, watching Filippa's with keen interest. Then, without warning, he wrenches the chain upward, sweeping me off my feet. Blinding pain sears my throat—black edges my vision—and though Filippa strives to remain impassive, something flickers in her eyes again. They tighten infinitesimally.

"What if"—Death's voice takes on an almost feverish excitement now, as if she has given him exactly what he wants—"love brings back the soul as well as the body? A *true* resurrection." His free hand flicks to the maelstrom behind us. "And the ultimate affront to nature."

Filippa shakes her head. "Don't be ridiculous."

"What do you think, Célie?" He leans low to whisper in *my* ear now, and I turn to face him, to glare directly into those hateful silver eyes. "Do you agree? *Is* love ridiculous? Is it ridiculous for all these people to still love you after everything you've done? How many loved ones have they lost now because of you?"

I wriggle my pinky finger beneath the chain, ignoring the burn. "Because of *you*."

"You're my Bride, after all. Where you go, I will go. Where you stay, I will stay." He spins me in his arms with the words, pulling my head back with the chain. When Michal growls, Death grins. "He loves you too, doesn't he? They *all* do, and what a blessing that must be." The kind words directly belie the anticipation in his voice, however, the hungry gleam in his eyes. "Indeed, your dear old mother loves you *so* much she made a sacrifice upon arriving to Requiem—a most noble one. Would you believe she volunteered herself when a certain witch agreed to stop a certain vampire's heart?" He flicks a finger at first Lou, then Michal. "You can't get something for nothing, you know, and *this* something"—he extends his arm to include Odessa too—"required a second heart to stop beating for the spell to work. A *living* heart. Just temporarily, of course—or was it?"

The tip of my ring finger stills beneath the chain, and unbidden, my eyes dart to Michal and Odessa, who both look strangely—stricken instead of enraged. But that cannot be right. Death is lying, of course. A twinge of unease still reverberates through the bond, however, and I cannot tell if it belongs to me or to Michal. Even Lou lifts her head from Reid's shoulder, her eyes wide above the tracks of blood on her cheeks. Confused.

My stomach plummets.

"That—that cannot be true." I shake my head instinctively, swallowing hard against the fresh bite of pain. Of panic. Death is a manipulator, a *liar*, and he always has been—from the first swipe of his hand through the pentagram, he has tried to exploit our every move. "It never happened."

"Oh dear." Death tuts with relish. "Did no one tell you? Did you never wonder how they ripped out Michal's heart without killing him? How terribly . . . upsetting."

Forcing herself upright, Lou snarls, "Don't you dare do this, you condescending *prick*." She leans forward, heedless of the Balisarda at her chest—the blood on her face, the revenants' low growls—and speaks emphatically to me. Desperately. "Célie, we did not kill your mother. I needed to stop a beating heart to preserve Michal, but it was only for a few moments. She volunteered, and she just—she went to sleep for those moments. When I woke her up, she said that she felt"—she glances anxiously at my mother, who has closed her eyes in defeat—"that she felt fine."

Death laughs again, louder and crueler than before. As cold as the ice spreading through my body.

Lou cannot hear my mother's heartbeat like I can. She cannot hear how it has slowed, how her lungs now rattle in her chest. I attributed her declining health to stress, to sleeplessness and shock, to anything and everything except the obvious. Because how could she be dying? How could she be *dead*? The evil of my world was never supposed to touch her.

"Maman," I breathe. "What did you do?"

She does not open her eyes. "I do not regret it."

"She took one look at you and Michal and knew you loved him," Death says silkily. "I imagine the choice was rather easy after that—she could not risk her darling daughter's happiness, after all. And you *are* happy now, aren't you, Célie? So very, *very* happy with your decisions?"

Behind him, Filippa's hands tremble slightly around the daggers. She stares at our mother with a horrified expression—a horror reflected in Michal's face too. In Lou's and Odessa's and Reid's as Death finally releases the silver chain, murmuring, "I suppose we don't need this anymore." With aching tenderness, he kneels to take my mother's hand, pulling her to her feet and pressing a kiss to her fingers. And I'm going to be sick now; a wave of scarlet rises in my throat, but I force it back down.

How much more will they be expected to pay?

Everything.

Death has taken everything.

To me, he says, "Shall we *test* my new theory? You've lured me here under false pretenses, after all, and that was very foolish of you, Célie, very foolish indeed—though convenient, of course, as you also brought along anyone you've ever loved. Feels rather like kismet, doesn't it?" A sleek smile. "Shall we start with your mother?"

"To what *end*?" Fear sharpens my voice, and my entire body trembles as I throw my hands into the air. Michal and Odessa materialize through the revenants on either side of me, who do not react. None of us can fix this, however. *Nothing* can fix this, and I—I— "I cannot just *bring someone back from the dead*! I don't know *how*—"

He nods to the maelstrom, supremely unconcerned. "Only one way to learn, I'm afraid."

Unable to help it, I follow his gaze to the swirling waters—to their great and evil eye—before pushing to my feet in cold dread. Because if he kills my mother, I—I don't know if I'll be able to get her back. And—and what happens if I *do*? If Death is right, if love is the key, the entire veil might collapse when we return—*if* we return. My dread drops into terror at the realization. *I could die too. All* of us could die; because Death won't stop until he wins, until he destroys life itself.

This entire situation—this *nightmare*—is a brick sinking straight through the maelstrom, and Death has tied us all to it.

As if sensing the feverishness of my thoughts, Michal brushes a steadying hand against my back. And his rage is still there, but—tempered somehow by resignation, an idea hardening into resolve. I cannot concentrate on it, however, as Death continues without pause. "In theory, you should be able to go through the maelstrom to retrieve your mother intact—because you love her. Again, I assume it has something to do with her soul, or perhaps your soul; I have no way of knowing, as I do not possess one myself. Now"—he turns back to my mother—"no sense in delaying the unpleasantness."

Though Maman opens her mouth to speak, he shushes her with a finger before brushing it tenderly down her cheek. And her heart—it stutters at that touch. It *stops.*

No.

"*No!*"

"NO!"

Filippa and I cry out together, panicked, and Death glances back at us, a sinister smile touching his lips as he lifts his finger from her face. Her heart stutters once more. Twice, thrice, four times. Filippa—who has taken a hasty step toward us—freezes at the sound of it, as do I; as does the entire grotto, all of us listening and counting each beat. "Unless . . ." Death draws out the word in obvious glee. "Someone else would like to take her place? I am not unreasonable, after all. If there is another you'd prefer to use in her stead, I'd be happy to spare your mother. She'll become a Bride, just like you, but otherwise no worse for wear—perhaps even better. Certainly healthier." That evil smile grows, nearly splitting his face in two. "What say you, Célie? Who shall it be?"

Just like that, the situation goes from bad to impossibly worse.

Filippa's eyes lock on mine across the grotto, burning with fierce promise. I have known her too long and too well to misunderstand that expression—she wants me to pick someone else, *anyone* else, in order to save our mother. And there are plenty of loved ones here from whom to choose: Lou and Reid, Jean Luc, Odessa . . . and Michal. His fingers tighten in the damp fabric of his mother's gown—the most exceptional gown I've ever worn, yet ruined like all the others. Despite all my efforts, I could not save it.

And I cannot save my mother either. I cannot save anyone.

Savage anger flares inside my chest, blistering, consuming—burning away all fear and rationality as I force myself between her and Death, wrapping an arm around her waist. "Bring it down, then. Bring the veil down, so you can rule over a kingdom of people who *hate* you. You think they'll accept you? All those souls you've claimed? At best, you'll be dragging those at peace from their rest, and at worst, you'll be unleashing hell on earth. Either way, they will not revere you; they will not *love* you, and you will be exactly as you are now. Miserable and alone."

Death's smile vanishes instantly, leaving an ugly expression in its wake. "The clock is ticking, Célie. Make your choice."

I glare at him, refusing to answer. Refusing to *choose*, even as my mother's heart weakens, each beat punctuating her last seconds.

We all go to the clock room eventually.

Death clicks his tongue impatiently.

Tick.

But I cannot do it.

Tock.

I cannot kill my own mother.

Michal walks slowly to Death's side. "Célie," he says in a soft voice. "Take me instead."

And that idea I sensed earlier—his hardening resolve—unfurls fully formed down the bond. *Take me instead.* Instantly, my mind rejects the possibility, and I shake my head before he can suggest anything else. Because I can't—*he* can't— "Absolutely not." My head continues to shake even as he steps around Death, who grins anew and plucks my mother from my arms, spinning her toward Odessa. *Clearing the stage*, I realize with a distant sense of foreboding.

Tick tock tick tock tick tock—

"This is what he wanted," I hiss to Michal, treacherous tears pricking my eyes. "I will not do it. I cannot lose you."

Michal pulls me into his arms. "We'll see each other again."

"*No.*" I push him away again, vision blurring, but he refuses to let me go. "I don't know what I'm doing. I don't know where to *go.* Michal, it's just—it's too risky, and—and the bond." I seize on the excuse like a lifeline; I seize onto his shirt too. "If you die, I die, and I won't—I won't be able to bring *anyone* back."

Please stay.

His plea from so long ago reverberates back to me, and I repeat it now like a prayer. *Please stay, please stay, please stay.*

Death caresses both of our faces, entirely too close for comfort—so close I can see my reflection in the maniacal gleam of his eyes. "Oh, you needn't worry about that, darling. I *am* Death, after all. I can slow whatever effects breaking this wretched bond entails."

Michal shoves Death away before cradling my face in his hands. To my surprise, I feel no fear in the bond, only a steady warmth and—incredibly—a sense of gratitude. Of reverence. My chin quivers. "Do you trust me?" he asks.

And I want to say no. I want to say no *so* badly, but— "Yes," I breathe.

"You can do this." He brushes a kiss against my lips before stepping away, and I feel his absence like the loss of a limb, my hands reaching out for him still. "I'll wait until you find me. I will *always* wait for you."

He turns toward Death as the tears spill helplessly down my cheeks, and I cannot stop shaking my head. I cannot stop clinging to the bond—the closest I can get to Michal now. Despite his imminent demise, he sends wave after wave of reassurance through it, of comfort and *love.* And I love him. I love him so much. It should never have been like this. We only just found each other;

we should've had more time together—an eternity. And I finally wanted it. Despite the darkness of this life, I wanted to spend eternity with him—*with* him—and now I must let him go.

Odessa weeps quietly behind them.

"Get it over with," Michal says.

Death shakes his head, however, pulling a thin silver dagger from his cloak. "Now where would the fun be in that?" Leaning around Michal, he tips the dagger toward me. "I said I was reasonable, not benevolent. Though your paramour here has been a thorn in my side for centuries, I think *you* should do the honors."

My fingers wrap around the hilt.

Across the grotto, the clock on the desk strikes midnight. Its bells toll one after the other, twelve beats. Twelve breaths. Then—

"This isn't the end, moje sunce." Michal's hand joins mine around the dagger, positioning it at his chest. His eyes burn into mine, and his voice lowers, darkens, until it could just be the two of us in the grotto. No one else exists. "Truth or dare?"

Torn between a laugh and a sob, I cannot help but answer. "I thought you'd grown tired of playing with me."

"Never."

"Dare."

"Don't be gentle." His fingers tighten around mine, and he pulls me closer as if for a kiss. "Just make it quick."

So I do.

CHAPTER FORTY-FOUR

The Realm of the Dead

I slide the dagger between his ribs and straight through his heart. "I *will* find you," I whisper fiercely, but I do not know if he hears me. As the blade slides home, he closes his eyes, and his last breath sounds like my name. His hands fall from mine. And his body—it desiccates around the blade, aging years, decades, centuries in the span of seconds until—

Until he's gone.

Silent tears pour down my face.

His body fades into dust and then nothing at all, and I am left clutching a dagger where Michal used to be. My hands drop it instinctively—it clangs loudly, *cruelly* against the stone—and I stumble back a step, shoulders shaking now. Chest *aching.* Falling to my knees, I claw at the place where our bond resided—where *Michal* resided—yet find it empty. It's gone too.

He's gone.

And it feels like I'll never be whole again.

A small hand touches my shoulder as Death applauds, shattering the silence, and when I finally tear my gaze from the dagger, I find Odessa standing over me, her face pale and set. "This is not over," she says quietly.

In my periphery, Lou nods—just a single drop of her chin. To my surprise, Filippa doesn't lift her blades again; she simply stares between our mother and me, her expression vacillating between uncertainty and antagonism.

"A splendid performance!" Cackling, Death loops his arm around my shoulders and crushes my body against his like we're old friends. "Now, that wasn't so hard, was it? I *told* you that we'd make—"

"How do I enter the maelstrom?" I deadpan. "Do I jump?"

His wide grin slips for just a second before he affixes it back in place. "A fair enough question, I suppose, and one with an easy answer—yes." He shunts me toward the water's edge with more force than necessary, and I stumble again, nearly crashing to my knees. Numbness prickles along my arms, my legs, like needles sticking my flesh. Detached, I watch as Lou and Reid both move forward to help, yet Death blocks their path, glaring past them at Filippa, who still should've been restraining them.

"Filippa, darling?" He throws his hands in the air, exasperated. "Are those knives at your sides just props, or do you plan to wield them anytime soon?"

Filippa does not answer.

His eyes narrow, and any euphoria he felt at Michal's death seems to sharpen to a knifepoint as he stalks toward her, clicking his fingers in her face. "Hello?" he asks softly, dangerously. "Did you hear me? I asked you a question, my dear." When she merely looks up at him, thoroughly unaffected—her stitches taut and her mouth set—he cocks his head with dark amusement. "Oh, don't tell me you're having second thoughts. This is all part of the *plan*, or have you decided you'd rather waltz into the sunset with this lot than meet your precious daughter?" His lip curls. "What the hell was her name again? Frosty?"

At the mention of her lost child, Filippa's face twists. "Frostine," she says reflexively.

"Not an improvement." Death's brows rise in quiet disbelief. "And I must say, darling, I don't love your tone." His chin jerks between me and the maelstrom, but those silver eyes never leave hers. "However, if you insist on indulging this little fit of rebellion, by all means—join her. Keep your sister focused on the task at hand—ensure she returns to me—or you can kiss that little brat goodbye."

Filippa's fists clench almost imperceptibly around the knives. For just a second, I think she might attack, but instead she says, "Do it yourself."

Death stills. All humor vanishes from his expression, and the silence between them snaps tighter, deadlier. Still Filippa does not flinch—not until Death's hand darts out and captures her throat, squeezing until the tendons strain. And I should fear for my sister—for myself—but I cannot bring myself to care about anyone but Michal. My gaze flits back to the maelstrom. He is down there somewhere; he is *waiting* for me, and each second I remain here is a second wasted.

"And *why*," Death murmurs, tilting his head, "would I do that?"

A vein in Filippa's neck pulsates; the muscles in her jaw feather. When she swallows hard—her silence now an acquiescence—his grip loosens, and his thumb rubs tender circles against the bruises he left on her skin.

"Good," he murmurs. "Very good. You seem to have forgotten how this arrangement works, so allow me to remind you: If I tell you to join your sister, you will join your sister. If I tell you to bring her back, you will bring her back." He places his free hand tenderly on her stomach, and the dank scent of Filippa's fear spikes through the grotto. "If I *tell* you to slit your mother's throat, you will slit her throat, and what's more—you will be *grateful* for it because if you don't, you will never meet this stupid fucking baby. Do you understand?"

Filippa blinks, recoiling slightly at the threat, before her entire body morphs—before it hardens, and she shifts from prey to predator within Death's very hands. Leaning even closer, she bares her teeth at him in a chilling smile. "Yes."

"That's better." Nodding once—his own smile tight—he caresses her stomach one last time, his breath fanning across her face. If he is trying to break my sister, however, we'll be here all night, and already, the ache in my chest has deepened, throbbing now. It feels almost like a heartbeat, yet instead of pumping blood, it spreads . . . emptiness, a void, like a knife carving out my veins. The pain slows my thoughts, making it difficult to think, but—without Michal—I know that I am dying. The unbreakable bond has broken.

"Are you finished?" I ask flatly. "Should I jump now, or are you planning to ravish my sister in front of our dying mother?"

"Don't be so dramatic. She is hardly dying anymore." Death waves his hand, and my mother—who'd been gasping for breath in Odessa's arms—manages to stand, supporting her own weight. Her breathing eases, and her color returns. Reid immediately moves to examine her with Lou on his heels, while Death releases Filippa with a shove in my direction. "Ticktock, ladies," he says in a cool voice. "I shall care for your mother until your return."

Our mother swells indignantly between Lou and Reid, but before she can charge toward us, can intervene, Filippa offers her hand. When I stare at her, making no move to accept, she rolls her eyes and snaps, "Take it."

I have no desire to take my sister's hand, however; in this moment, I've never desired anything less. Understanding my refusal implicitly, she scoffs and wriggles her fingers. "I do not offer my hand out of *affection*, ma belle. We need to enter the maelstrom together, lest it separate us. This is not my first trip to the realm of the dead."

"I remember." The emptiness spreading inside me has started to seethe, and sweat drips from my fingers—down my spine—in a way that should not affect a vampire. Perhaps I will follow Michal in the natural way instead; perhaps his loss will burn me from the inside out. "I am the one who took care of your arrangements—*all* of your arrangements." Perhaps it is not the time or place to rehash the past, but my niceties vanished the instant I slid a knife through Michal's heart. If I'm honest with myself, they should've vanished much sooner; my sister never deserved them at all. And perhaps it makes me spiteful, makes me cruel, but another truth falls from my lips in a rush of resentment. "I was the one you left behind."

Filippa's eyes flash. "I *died*—"

"You were leaving either way."

With that, I seize her hand just as she moves to rescind it, sliding my fingers through hers just like we did as children. "Will it hurt?" I ask her.

She shakes her head, focusing hard on the maelstrom instead of my face. "Dying is not scary, Célie." We take one step together, then another, and I almost miss her next words as we leap into the heart of the waves. As we descend into the realm of the dead.

"Living is scarier."

Between one blink and the next, Filippa and I fall easily, painlessly, and land like feathers atop a pillow of soft grass.

I roll onto my back, holding a hand over my eyes to shield them from a brilliant sun; it hangs above us in a pristine sky of purest cerulean. A deep sense of serenity permeates the air, accompanied by a warm summer breeze that wraps around my limbs, and—just like the thick oaks lining the distance, like their sweeping branches and lush foliage—I lift my face to it. That hollow inside my chest has disappeared, replaced by an overwhelming and inexplicable desire to stroll through the flowers, or perhaps to lounge on a bank of the nearby river. *Strange.*

Blinking slowly, I look around, trying and failing to place our surroundings. Where *are* we? Though I don't know what I expected to find through the maelstrom, it certainly was not this. There are no revenants here, no creeping tendrils of decay; there is no eldritch haze to paint the flowers and trees in shades of gray. No snow and no ashes and no ghosts.

Instead the sound of rushing water, the scent of it, mingles with a faint hint of oranges.

This cannot be right.

I climb to my feet, turning in a slow circle to examine all sides of this—this place. *A garden,* I realize in a burst of awareness. And on the wings of that thought comes another, swifter still: I recognize it. I recognize death and its warm, golden light, though the gentle laughter from All Hallows' Eve has vanished. *This is where I would've gone.* The thought lifts the hair on my nape, and I feel strange, but not—not frightened.

Instead adrenaline courses through my body with each beat

of my heart until my lungs ache, and my vision blurs. I glance up at the sun again. It feels—hot. Uncomfortably so. My skin heats beneath its rays, but—no. I frown again.

No, that isn't right.

That isn't possible.

I rest a hand on my cheek to check my temperature, my forehead, my neck, and beneath my fingers—

"Oh God." My voice comes out a croak as I glance at my sister, at her perfect and unblemished face. "Oh God, oh God, oh *God*."

"What is it?" Standing slowly, Filippa takes her time stretching each of her limbs. She hasn't yet noticed that her skin, *my* skin, feels warm. And my heart—it's beating in my chest, frantic and stuttering and *alive.* And—and I just said *God.* I marvel at the word. I said it—I said it four times—and my throat didn't catch fire. I touch it again just to be sure, and my fingers come away free of blood. My injuries have healed too.

Gaping at my sister, I pray this isn't a dream—that I'm not hallucinating—but the thought withers when she blinks back at me with two emerald eyes.

Two. Emerald. Eyes.

Disbelief rises as I stare at her pale face, smooth from forehead to chin without a single stitch in sight. Her soft pink lips twist into a frown, but it is a *beautiful* frown. It is *her* frown. A sob builds in my throat, but on the way to my mouth, it erupts instead as a squeal. "*Filippa!*"

She balks at the sound, her brows snapping together in alarm. "What is it? What's wrong?" When I lunge toward her in reply, catching her hands and squeezing—*without* breaking her bones—she rears backward in surprise, snatching them away just as quickly. "What are you doing? Get ahold of yourself, Célie. You're acting like you've seen a—a—"

"A ghost?" Unable to resist my own excitement, I bounce a little on my toes. "Not quite. In fact, I'd say the opposite—feel your wrist, Pip."

Filippa scowls at the nickname. She never used to hate it. Still, she examines the porcelain skin of her arms before pressing two fingers against her wrist. Instead of her eyes widening in surprise, however, they narrow as she says, "How curious."

But this—this is far more than *curious.* This is a *miracle*, something I never even allowed myself to dream. This is the Filippa of my youth, the girl who fled our window fearlessly, who never looked back, with her long black hair cascading around her shoulders and her lashes batting against her cheeks. This is my *sister* again, which means I must also be—that I'm—

Pressing a hand to my chest, I search again for the ache I felt only moments ago, but only grief remains. Natural grief, memories, not the ravenous chasm of a broken bond. Swiftly, I run my tongue across my teeth to find them smooth. No fangs. No lust for blood or violence either.

Elation sweeps through me, stealing my breath, and as the last of the tension leaves my body, I feel weightless, light—so much lighter than I've felt in weeks, months, *years.* Because I am human again. I am *human.* Instantly, I whirl around in search of Michal, desperate to see him again, to show him, but find only my unsmiling sister.

She looks . . . contemplative.

"How is this possible?" I ask in an awestruck whisper.

Filippa exhales harshly before stalking through the garden,

away from me. Over the flourishing lawn and past a scattering of orange trees. The fruits hang impossibly heavy, tugging the branches so low that several kiss the grass, creating sanctuaries of sweet-smelling shade. Though she plucks an orange from the nearest tree, she does not eat it; instead she pitches it straight ahead, studying the fruit as it splashes into the river.

Before I can repeat the question, she says, "I suspected this place might . . . change us, but I couldn't be certain what those changes might be." She glances back, and a barrage of childhood memories overwhelms me at the sight of her: climbing up our orange tree, playing in the dirt, sneaking out to the banks of the Doleur each full moon. She doesn't seem to share them, however, instead adding, "Without Death, revenants cannot exist—no vampires either—and Death has fled this realm. He no longer exists here—not as he was, at least, not as he's *meant* to be—which must mean . . ."

"We've returned to who we would've been without him." I blink at her, torn from my juvenile reverie. "That sounds like a lot of speculation."

"Of course it is." She scoffs. "This is Death, the greatest mystery of all life, and to be frank, I don't know anyone else who has died, come back to life, and semi-died all over again. Do *you*? Perhaps we can invite them to tea and ask all the questions we want."

I scowl at her, and though Filippa's lips twitch in satisfaction, she still refuses to smile. Carving a path toward the river, she adds, "All we know for sure is, *that*"—she jerks her thumb behind us—"is our only way out of here."

I follow her thumb, glancing upward to where a single cloud hangs in the brilliant sky—a storm cloud, as jarring and out of place as a flower in the desert. Stranger still, it appears to be *raining*, yet no moisture dampens the air. My eyes narrow as I peer closer, and, with a start, realize the droplets aren't droplets at all, but shredded ribbons of veil. They ripple iridescent in the wind, beautiful even, until I remember who exists beyond it.

My breath catches at the thought, and I hasten after Filippa, who trails pale fingers along the vibrantly blooming flowers on her way to the river. Red roses grow in massive, spiraling topiaries without a single thorn; snowdrops glisten in dove whites and soft grays, smaller than the other species, and—I blink incredulously—even Bluebeard blossoms sway gently in the breeze. One of them even snaps at our heels as we pass, and Filippa's frown deepens. "What the hell are those?"

"You don't know?"

"The garden changes to suit the person journeying through it, Célie."

Curious. "Those are called Bluebeard blossoms." Thrilled to know something my older sister does not, I add with a touch of vanity, "They eat butterflies."

She casts me a disparaging look. "What happened to the little girl who loved butterflies?"

Her words loose like an arrow aimed straight for my chest, and with it, I realize I am not the only one who has taken a detour down memory lane. Instead of remembering me with affection, however—with longing—my sister seems to remember me with only disdain.

"She died," I say shortly.

And just like that, all desire to impress her vanishes too.

Scoffing under her breath, she tramps on an errant snowdrop in response, grinding it under her heel, but otherwise says nothing. I step over the fallen petals carefully, not speaking again until the silence lengthens between us. "What about the river?" Together, we glance toward the slow-moving water in the distance. It runs perpendicular to the garden, stretching left and right as far the eye can see—impossible to avoid—while peculiar mist obscures whatever lies beyond it. "It looks . . . significant," I add warily.

"Isn't it obvious?" When I say nothing, waiting with rapidly thinning patience for her to explain, she sighs in exasperation. "One must cross the river to reach their final resting place."

Ah.

"You've already crossed it," I say shrewdly, "when Morgane killed you."

"Frederic pulled me back." She casts a slanting glance in my direction, her lips pursing at my wide eyes and inquisitive expression. She rolls her eyes. "*Yes*, Célie, we can assume that created the maelstrom. This garden seems to be transient. If we linger long enough, the wind will increase speed, and the river will rise until it sweeps us away—and that is *true* death."

If we want to close the door, Filippa must die.

I swallow hard, tearing my gaze away to watch the slow-moving water instead. *Is that what happened to Michal?* And then—*did it happen to Filippa too?* The thought brings unexpected pain. Not for the Filippa walking beside me now, cold and unfeeling, but for the little girl who believed in fairy tales so very long ago. She never should've learned about this wind and this river; she never should've waited on this bank. "I thought this place would be . . . different," I confess. "Frightening, even."

"I told you, Célie." She stares out at the water too, though I suspect she no longer sees it. I suspect she sees what lies beyond every time she closes her eyes. "Death is nothing to fear . . . not in his true form, anyway. Our realm has twisted him." Though I want to ask how, *why*, I cannot bring myself to interrupt as she continues, her voice low and mournful: "When I returned on All Hallows' Eve, I felt a different sort of pull—more violent this time, more painful. It ripped me from beyond the river and back into our realm."

"Frederic's spell," I whisper.

"I couldn't have made the journey without it." She shakes her head, and wherever she just vanished inside her thoughts, she returns from it abruptly. Her mouth tightens into a grim line. "Michal said he would wait for you, but he never had a choice. The river will have already taken him, and it isn't meant to flow both ways. If we cannot pull him back out again—if we meet any resistance at all—"

"We don't have a choice either." I speak the words through stiff lips, refusing to acknowledge any other possibility. Filippa might know much about this place, but she does not know everything. Moreover, this time is not like last time. I am not Frederic, and I do not need a spell to find Michal. I am a Bride of Death, and even if I weren't, I would do anything to find him—*anything*, and no one can ever change that. Not Filippa, and certainly not Death.

Unbidden, my hand rises to my chest, and I rub the place where Michal remains. Part of me thinks I can still feel him there, waiting. "I *will* pull him out," I say fiercely—to Filippa or to myself, I do not know—"or I will cross that river myself. I cannot go back without him."

Filippa slows to a halt at the riverbank, her expression inscrutable, before inclining her head in acknowledgment and pivoting toward the river. I join her with renewed purpose, still rubbing that spot on my chest.

It's called Le Lien Éternel.

The longer two vampires feed from each other, the stronger the bond grows, until . . .

Until?

Until it becomes irrevocable.

What Michal and I share cannot be broken. Irrevocable means final. Eternal means forever. *Michal*, I think, and my human heart splinters.

Michal, I think, and a brilliant white cord appears in my hands.

I stare down in wide-eyed confusion, in *awe*, before curling my fingers around it. Though I feel its weight in my palm, I still close my eyes before opening them again, convinced it'll disappear. It doesn't. The cord remains, loose and unspooled between my fingers like—like a ribbon. I test it curiously, rolling it between my thumb and forefinger, and gasp when the cord tightens.

When it *tugs.*

It flashes brighter at the pressure, unraveling away from me and toward—my eyes widen even further, and my mouth parts in understanding. Toward the *river.* I take a tentative step forward before wrapping my wrist around it, pulling experimentally until the cord snaps taut. *Too* taut. Filippa turns to stare at me as I stagger forward, attempting to reel in the cord. It drags me closer to the river instead, and she tilts her head in confusion. In concern. *She cannot see it.*

"Michal," I breathe, and with one last, hard tug—my lungs seize.

Suddenly, I cannot breathe at all.

The cord strains in my grasp, immense weight from the other end propelling me forward. And I cannot stop it. Though I dig my heels into the grass, into the mud, I only slip faster. More than that, however—*I still cannot breathe.* Throat burning, I crash to my knees; I grip the tether with my free hand and lean backward with all my might, but still it pulls me onward. It carries me away from Filippa, who bends down to snatch at my forearm now. "This isn't funny, Célie. Whatever you're doing, stop it!" She squeezes harder, attempting to pull me upright. "*Stop* it, and get up—"

Though I open my mouth to answer her, no words pass my lips—no scream either. Instead river water rushes up my throat in a torrent, spilling onto my chest. Choking me, *drowning* me. My human lungs shriek in agony as I collapse forward onto the muddy bank of the river. The water keeps coming, however. It flows from my body like *I* am the river, yet my body burns like I've caught fire.

"Célie!" Panicked, Filippa drops beside me, still tugging on my arms, but the tether continues to yank too, to drag me closer and closer to Michal. *To Michal.* I can sense him now, so close to me. *So close, so close, so close—*

"No, *no*," Filippa pleads, her voice breaking, and only moments ago, I would've wept with relief at that brief glimpse of her humanity. It means my sister is still in there somewhere—hiding, perhaps, but *alive*—yet I cannot think beyond the darkness edging my vision. Distantly, I realize I am drowning.

Gasping and choking through the water, I manage, "*He—lp.*"

Another wave spews from my mouth.

"Célie! *Célie!*" Filippa slides her arms under my shoulders now, wrenching me back to my knees and holding me against her chest.

She doesn't know what to do, however. She cannot let me go, cannot even *see* the cord to sever it. "I am *trying*," she says despairingly, "but you—you have to show me how to—what to—"

But the garden is rapidly fading now, dimming to fathomless black around me. My last conscious thought flares indignantly. What a *stupid* way this is to die—to survive everything, *everything*, only to drown on dry land the moment I become human again. And everything has darkened now, growing darker and darker still—

A flash of silver sparks across the haze. Familiar, breathtaking silver. I focus on it until my vision sharpens, and Filippa's pleading voice fades in and out of range. "Come *on*, Célie—" Her arms tighten around my chest. "You will *not* die, you stupid, stupid girl—"

Though I should try to answer her, I cannot do anything but stare at Michal—Michal, who is rising from the river. Michal, whose hair breaks the surface first, then his onyx eyes. And—*oh God.* He is still more gorgeous, more devastating, than should ever be possible.

Spluttering now, I feel the last of the water leave my lungs as he throws a hand onto the bank and claws his way through the reeds, through the mud and the rocks and the lichen. Claws his way back to *me.*

I lean back into my sister's chest, bracing my heels in the ground. "Pull," I tell her desperately.

Filippa does as I say, even as she cranes her neck to see my face, to search it anxiously. "What is going *on*?"

"*Pull.*" I wrap the cord around my hand, again and again, to maintain the tension as Filippa drags us both to our feet, anchoring us against Michal's weight. *We're almost there. We're so close—*

The harder we pull, the faster he rises, until—gasping and soaking wet—he wraps the cord around his fist and his eyes lock with mine. With one last mighty tug, Filippa and I throw ourselves backward, and Michal heaves himself on the grass with a groan, gasping and coughing, his entire body shuddering.

Finally, Filippa loosens her hold, and my heart leaps because it's over. *It's over.* Without another cognizant thought, I sprint for him, but a second masculine voice stops me short: "Fuck," Dimitri says, pulling himself ashore by Michal's ankle before collapsing beside him. "Could that have hurt any *more?*"

Michal lifts his head. "You could've let go at any time," he growls. "I never asked you to tag along."

Dimitri scoffs and jerks his chin toward the river. "Right. Because I wanted to stay over *there* alone."

I stare at the two of them, speechless—then I stare some more, unable to believe what I'm seeing. Because Michal has not returned on his own. He—he somehow brought *Dimitri* with him, which explains the sheer weight of the cord. Filippa and I brought them back—both of them—and now they're pushing to their feet together; now they're making their way toward us, and they're grinning—grinning and *alive.*

And I think my heart might burst as Michal pulls me against him, as I fling my arms around his neck.

"I knew you'd find me," he whispers into my hair.

When I kiss him, I hold nothing back.

CHAPTER FORTY-FIVE

A Gentle Night

A moment later, I run my hands over Michal's face, tracing his flushed cheeks and his chiseled jawline. Learning him all over again. His skin looks different now—still pale, but fair instead of alabaster—and when my fingers reach his throat, a steady pulse greets me. He exhales sharply at the touch, as if pained, or perhaps simply relieved. His chest still rises and falls with great effort after almost drowning, and water sluices down the hard planes of his body.

His *human* body.

Michal has turned human too.

"You are so beautiful," I whisper, and now my fingers trail over his shoulders, down his arms, across his abdomen. So alike, yet so different from the Michal I've known. And I cannot stop touching him, near giddy with excitement—with a touch of fear, but mostly with anticipation. And questions. Dozens upon dozens of questions, all of which surge forward at once, tangling my tongue until I can say nothing at all, can do nothing except gape up at him. *So beautiful.*

As a vampire, he resembled a fallen angel, or perhaps an avenging god—dark and untouchable, born of Hell itself—but now, as a human, he exudes warmth and vitality. An energy I cannot quite pinpoint. *His hair is still silver*, I think in wonder.

Grinning wider, he pushes the wet strands from his face and says, "You aren't disappointed?"

And I thought I knew every version of him—the villain, the accomplice, the friend. I've seen him as a brother and a cousin, as well as a craftsman and a king. He has been my abductor. He has been my savior. I have even known him as my lover, yet I have never seen him like this—exhilarated, yes, but also hesitant and unsure as he waits for my response.

This Michal feels . . . newly vulnerable. Through the bond, I sensed only hints of that vulnerability before, but now I can *see* it in how he swallows and searches my gaze. I can *feel* it in how his hands slide down to grip mine, his fingers clinging as if terrified to let go.

I love it.

I love *him*.

"Disappointed?" I stretch to my toes, peppering his face with kisses. "You look like—like a dream, like a—"

He captures my mouth swiftly, swallowing the rest of my words until we're breathless once more, before whispering against my lips, "We aren't dreaming, Célie. This is real. I am Michal Vasiliev, son of Tomik and Adelina, and it is a pleasure to meet you in earnest."

I clutch him closer in response, and his body melts into mine, one hand splaying against my lower back while the other cradles my jaw in reverence. When he drags his nose along my throat, my core tightens, but my teeth—they do not lengthen. I do not crave him that way anymore, yet my body seems to wind that much tighter because of it. I love him, and I *want* him, and when I close my eyes—turning my cheek into his palm—the feeling could be heaven.

"God, I missed you." My voice is a ragged whisper between us.

"I missed you so much. Please tell me you aren't—that you aren't upset." Pulling back to look at him again, I hasten to explain myself. "I had no idea what would happen by coming here. If I *had*, I would've warned you, and you could've—I don't know—chosen differently." I inhale a sudden, anxious breath at the word, and my lungs expand painfully, still aching from the river water. "Your *choice*, Michal. Death and I took it away from you, and I—I am so sorry—"

He laughs at that, sweeping my hair aside and kissing me again. "This *was* my choice, pet. And how could I ever be upset when I'm holding you in my arms?" Another kiss, this one slower and more sensuous than the last. His voice lowers. "How could I be upset when I can taste you on my tongue?"

Behind us, my sister scoffs, but Dimitri only laughs in delight—whether at her or at us, I do not know. I do not *care*. My cheeks still heat like an open flame, however, as I say, "Yes, but you've—you've been a vampire for a thousand years, Michal, and now . . ."

"Célie." His thumb brushes my lower lip, and he presses down, just like he always did. A shiver sweeps my spine. "Please hear me now because I will not say it again: I have never cared whether you're a vampire, whether *I* am a vampire, and I do not care that we're human now either. Because you're right—I *have* lived a thousand years, and for every single one of them, I've been waiting to find you." He laces our fingers together, lifting mine to kiss them gently. "To be with you like this—it has meant everything to me. You are worth any cost."

And so is he. "I love you, Michal Vasiliev."

He smiles again, and the sight of it—wide and uninhibited—literally takes my breath away. "I love you too, Célie Tremblay. Moje sunce."

"If the two of you are finished," Filippa interrupts with a scowl, "perhaps we should *return.* I'm getting a toothache." And just like that, the sweetness of the moment vanishes, dissolving into the breeze.

Leaving us standing here—dripping wet and shivering—on the shore of a celestial river.

I whirl to face her, to demand she allow me a few moments with this man—my *soul mate*—who could've been lost forever, but the wind increases at that moment. Flower petals swirl between us in an eddy of snow whites, blood reds, and shadow blacks. Filippa catches one between her fingers, lifting it between us, and my stomach churns at her grim and determined expression.

Eventually the winds pick up, the river rises, and it sweeps you away.

Dimitri's hair ruffles in a boyish way as he glares daggers at my sister. "Who said *you* were coming with us?" He crosses his arms, his brown skin more vibrant without the pallor of vampirism. That isn't the only change, however. Whereas Michal and I are . . . livelier, Dimitri seems strangely steady. His gaze doesn't dart from person to person as it once did; it doesn't track the pulse in our throats and wrists. Even with Death's blood in his system, he hadn't been this—well, serene.

"*I* am here to ensure everyone follows Death's instructions," Filippa asks coolly. "We are *all* marching straight back through the veil, and there is nothing you can do to stop it. In case you haven't noticed, you lost those sharp teeth of yours. Unless you kept the knife I buried in your heart?"

Dimitri bares his teeth in a hard smile, taking a purposeful step forward, but when I reach out and touch his arm, he stills. He turns to look at me—to *really* look at me now. A smile cracks open his face at whatever he sees, his dimple flashing, and the sight fills me with immediate comfort, like the first sparks in the fireplace on a long winter night.

"Célie," he exhales in surprise. "You're—*you*."

He charges forward then, stealing me from Michal and pulling me into a bone-crushing hug. "I thought I'd never see you again. I thought I'd never be able to apologize and tell you what it means to have you as family—"

Filippa bristles instantly. "She is *not* your family."

As if innately sensing how best to rile her, he pretends not to hear—pretends she doesn't even exist—and spares her not a single glance. I laugh loudly before he says, "I know it was sometimes hard to do so, but you believed in me. You *trusted* me. I should have been more careful with that." Releasing me, he looks to Michal, and in his eyes shines true sincerity. "I should have been more careful with *all* of your trust."

"Dimitri," I say, squeezing his arm reassuringly, "I know."

He nods once, gratitude alight in his gaze, and picks a drifting snowdrop from his hair.

Then he flicks it directly at Filippa.

She swats it away with a fierce scowl before gesturing to the gust of wind. "This is all very *touching*, but if we don't leave soon, we won't be leaving at all. That cannot happen."

"Again with the *we*," Dimitri says incredulously. "What makes you think we're going to make this easy on you? What makes you think we're going to *help* Death's favorite little minion? Do we look like fools?"

"I don't think you want me to answer that—and Death isn't my *master*."

Michal silences them both with a wave of his hand. "Where *is* the way out?" he asks Filippa. "Point us to it, and we can . . . discuss this on our way."

A tendril of unease appears at how he says *discuss*, but before I can question it, Filippa stabs a finger behind us toward the storm cloud. "*We* go back the way we came." To Dimitri, she says, "I am not sure, however, where *you* are going. Death needs these two, but you aren't part of the plan—"

"What *is* the plan?" Dimitri spreads his arms wide, incredulous. "Is it here in the garden with us? I'd love to hear it if so—"

"Enough." I step between them while maintaining careful eye contact with Michal, who no longer seems to be listening to their argument. Indeed, the incandescent light in his gaze has dimmed slightly since spotting the storm cloud, and I don't like the implication. I don't like it at all. "We should go—"

A gust of wind sweeps past at that, much faster than before; it bends the topiaries and tears several flowers from their stems. Filippa gestures from them to the rising river, which creeps ever closer to our feet. Her voice turns derisive. "We must take care not to touch any water."

Cautiously, Dimitri eyes the slowly churning, almost hypnotic depths. "It pulled me under straightaway, yet I can't—" The longer he stares, the deeper his brows furrow in confusion. "I can't actually remember where it took me. Not the exact place, anyway. I suppose it was more a . . . feeling than anything else."

Filippa stalks past him, rolling her eyes. "No one can."

I hesitate before following her, glancing back at Michal, who still hasn't spoken. "What *was* it like?" I brush the damp hair from my face, kicking a stray orange from our path. "The other side?"

He smiles softly at that. "It felt like home."

"Oh."

Michal takes my hand before I can say anything else. "It felt like my home a long time ago—before all of this, before I became a vampire. And it felt"—he searches for the right word, his own eyes scouring the distant birch trees—"peaceful, yes, but also incomplete." When I glance up at him, he squeezes my hand, pouring every ounce of his regret into that touch. "*You* weren't there. I know I promised to wait for you, Célie, and I did. I *tried.* I waited in that garden until the wind picked up, until it forced me toward the river—until I heard *Dimitri* shouting in the distance, clinging to a branch by his fingertips." He shakes his head ruefully. "I never expected to see him again, so when I *did,* I—I just couldn't let him go. I tried to help—he slipped—and in the end, the wind took us both. The river swallowed us whole."

Michal opens his other palm, and the white cord sparkles between us. "And that is when this showed up in my hand."

"The bond," I whisper.

From up ahead, Dimitri cranes his neck to look back at us suspiciously. "What are you two whispering about?" Then, to Filippa, "Can you hear them?"

"Do me a favor," she says sweetly, "and take *ten* steps away from me now. You smell like river water."

Narrowing his eyes with a razor-sharp smile, Dimitri steps even closer, and my sister glowers before marching ahead without another word, her jaw set and her eyes determined. Dimitri watches her for a moment, head tilted in abject frustration, and stalks right after her.

Michal takes my hand when I move to follow, shaking his head subtly as his voice lowers. "Célie . . ."

I glance up at him, the hair on my nape lifting at the way he looks back at me—as if trying to memorize my eyes, my lips, the curve of my cheek. As if suspecting he won't see them again for a very long time. But . . . no.

No.

"Don't do this, Michal," I warn, tightening my fingers around his. Because I know what he plans to say. I know what he plans to *do*, and I will not let him. I will *not*—

"I cannot go back with you," he says quietly.

My stomach sinks, and my throat burns like I'm still choking. I scowl at him. "What are you talking about? Of *course* you must come back." I wave my hands to the garden around us, that hateful river, before stabbing a finger in his chest. "The entire *point* of all this was to resurrect you—"

"If you resurrect me"—he catches my finger and brings it to his lips—"the veil will come down. Death will win."

My scowl deepens at the truth of his words. His truth isn't the only one, however; mine exists too, and I refuse to live without him. "I cannot go back without you. The bond"—I tug on the cord, and it pulses brightly between us—"it'll bring me right back here, remember? We cannot be apart."

Frustration builds inside me as he sadly shakes his head. I was so focused on rescuing Michal, on reuniting with him, that I forgot everything that comes after: Death, namely, and his ticking clock. The fate of my mother, of all our loved ones. The fate of the entire world. We stare at each other as the bleak reality of our situation settles between us.

"Death—his magic—has kept the bond alive." He closes my hand around the cord, and perhaps it's my imagination, but it seems to dim slightly at his words. "If you return to the realm of the living, it'll vanish." A pause. "You'll be free."

Free.

Instantly, that frustration spikes to anger, and Michal flinches as I rip the cord closer. "Don't be stupid. If I return alone to the realm of the living, I will not be *free.* I will become Death's Bride in truth, and it'll be all your fault—your noble, *infuriating* fault." I glare up at him, seizing his shirtfront. "You once called me a martyr, but I've never met anyone as hypocritical as you. I will not let you sacrifice yourself again." Then, lifting my chin, "Twice was enough."

When Filippa snickers from up ahead, I turn to glare at her too. She stops walking, refusing to cower as she says, "Let me get this straight—when Frederic did this, it was wrong, but now that it's you—now that it's Saint Célie—the ends justify the means?"

"Don't talk about her like that," Dimitri snarls. "Frederic is *nothing* like Célie—nothing like my cousin either. Your dear old *Fred* never thought about anyone but himself. Case in point: he murdered your *sister* to bring you back, and he didn't think twice about the consequences. Not just all this"—he waves an agitated hand at the storm cloud—"but also how it would affect *you.* Can you honestly say you approved of that sacrifice? Can you honestly say you wouldn't have hated him if you'd lost Célie forever?"

Though Filippa opens her mouth angrily, she snaps it shut again as his words wash over her. And when her gaze flicks to mine, I look away swiftly, unable to meet it. *Do you think—if she stood here now—she would choose death in order to let you live?* "He said it should've been me," I whisper to my feet.

All three of them still at the words. Even the wind dies

momentarily, and I glance up to find Filippa looking stricken. After another moment, she swallows hard. "He was wrong."

Dimitri shakes his head, his expression darkening as we four hesitate—torn between the river and the veil. True death and life. "There is no happy ending for you and your daughter. Death does not care about you, Filippa. He does not care about anyone. If you do not obey his every whim, he will cast you aside, and if you *do*, he will never bring back your daughter. Without Frostine, he cannot control you. You have always been just a pawn to him—and so have I." His voice softens. "The two of us are alike in that way."

She blinks rapidly, her hands falling limp at her sides, and perhaps I *do* have a soft and bleeding heart; perhaps I shouldn't protect her right now, but I also cannot help it. She is my sister, and she will always be my sister. I never want to see her cry. Michal and I move closer to them. Closer to the veil. "Just think about it, Filippa. Your life has been hard, but it didn't always need to be. Let us help you."

She still does not answer, however, as if paralyzed by emotion.

I look away to give her distance, focusing on the shredded veil, and Dimitri does the same, the wheels spinning inside his head. He studies his hands then, suddenly rapt in thought. "If we returned to our original bodies when we entered this realm," he begins slowly, "what would happen to Death if he followed us?" His gaze snaps abruptly to Michal. "Perhaps we have a third path before us. One that doesn't involve the end of the world *or* the two of us crossing that damn river again. Permanently this time."

Michal raises a brow, intrigued. "You think Death would return to his original body too."

"I think it's worth exploring."

"What does Death's original body even look like?" I ask.

Seconds stretch between us, wrought with tension, apprehension, even the smallest flicker of hope, until at long last, Filippa speaks. "He doesn't have one," she says quietly, refusing to look at any of us. "He came to me after Morgane finished her torture, but I couldn't see him. I felt his presence instead—like a gentle night settling over me. I simply closed my eyes, and when I opened them again, I was here. Death isn't meant to be a villain. He is meant to be . . . *Death*."

"Yes, well, that's all very good, except—" A bite of impatience sharpens my words. Not at them, but at this wretchedly circular conversation. "Look, we've already failed to lure Death, the *villain*, here once, and even if we hadn't, we have no way of mending the veil to trap him—not without you crossing the river and dying all over again." Filippa doesn't look surprised by this information. Instead her emerald gaze glitters with cunning. She already knows all of this—three steps ahead, as usual—yet she still refuses to share anything else.

We stare at each other, both refusing to budge.

"If I return," Michal says after another moment, "you won't even be able to try. Perhaps my resurrection will not bring down the veil completely, but it will tear another hole, create another maelstrom. Potentially it could even trigger the end of the world as we know it."

I resist the urge to stamp my foot in refusal. He still doesn't seem to understand that I will not—cannot—live without him. I would rather cross the river myself than return as Death's Bride. "We've been over this too," I insist. "How many times have you watched me do it? I can mend any tear I create. I can *stop* the sickness before it becomes permanent, which means—"

Which . . . means . . .

I can mend any tear I create.

Any tear I *create.*

Realization strikes like a fist to my ribs, and I nearly double over with it. Whirling to face Filippa, I say, "You can close the door."

Dimitri leans closer, unable to hear over the roar of the waterfall. "What?"

"You created the door," I say louder, clearer, staring at her in shock. In slowly burgeoning hope. It grows from a flicker to a flame in a single breath. All this time, I've been searching for a solution to save my sister, but could it be that—that she *is* the solution? Not her death after all, but her life. Just—*her.*

Filippa knows how to manipulate the veil; I've watched her come and go through it, watched her tear it apart as she pleases. She has never died to mend it, and she needn't die now either. Breathless with the revelation, I dart forward to seize her hands. "You created the door, Filippa, so you can close it. You've been able to close it all along."

She needn't die.

Again, Filippa does not react, instead staring back at me with that same unerring cunning. "Yes," she says simply. "I know."

CHAPTER FORTY-SIX

The Tide Changes

Filippa and I return from the garden alone.

We also—somehow—return human.

When we swim into the grotto, everything remains just as we left it—Lou and Reid sit on either side of my mother, while Odessa stands sentry between them and the revenants. Death waits at the shore impatiently, tapping his foot like a petulant child, before splashing out to meet us in the shallows. Seizing first Filippa's arm, then mine, he wrenches us from the waves before turning to search for Michal. "Well?" he snaps. "Where is he?"

I collapse to the ground at his feet, struggling to breathe after navigating the vicious current. My limbs tremble with exhaustion, and my lungs ache; my throat is blistered and raw. "He—he refused to come back with us."

"Excuse me?" Death asks sharply, his eyes widening. "What did you say?"

Sensing the danger, Odessa urges Lou, Reid, and my mother toward the stairs, bending down to snatch up Jean Luc and Brigitte at the last second. They remain unconscious. Though the revenants silently follow, circling them, Death doesn't seem to notice; his attention remains fixed upon me, his silver eyes darkening, swirling, building like a storm on the horizon. *Good.*

"Has your hearing deteriorated since we left?" I ask him. "Michal didn't come."

I refuse to flinch—to reveal anything—as Death crouches, seizing my collar and bringing my mouth to his ear.

"Say it again," he snarls.

"He said *no*." I gesture between myself and Filippa, who has managed to remain standing despite her heaving chest. Eyes narrowed, she does not move to defend me, but she doesn't move to join the revenants either. "We dragged him from the river, but Michal knew if he came back the veil would fall. I couldn't force him." Lip curling, I gesture down at my own human body, soaking wet and slight—much too slight to overpower Michal, even if I'd tried.

I couldn't force him.

And that is perhaps the worst part of all—that I could not convince him, that he would not listen to my pleas. Michal chose to stay in the garden to save the world, and how could I ever take that choice away from him?

"He . . . said no," Death repeats silkily.

And—without any further warning—he erupts.

Exploding to his feet, Death throws up his hands before dragging them through his hair, tearing at the strands and screaming with rage. Startled, I fall backward before clambering into the shallows to escape him. "IT SEEMS I HAVE NOT BEEN *CLEAR*"—he sweeps the contents from Michal's desk—"IF YOU THOUGHT *NO* WAS AN OPTION!" He upends the desk without ceremony, but—apparently unsatisfied—next picks up the mantel clock and launches it across the grotto at Odessa. The revenants part like puppets, and it shatters against her back as she spins to protect the others, to *shield* them, and wood ricochets in all directions. "Do you not understand the *consequences*? Do you think this is a *game*?"

He hurls the entire desk at *me* now, and I just manage to flatten myself upon the rocks as it hurtles overhead. Panic claws up my throat as I roll to avoid the matching chair, then a bedpost, which Death has wrenched from its frame; it streaks into the maelstrom like a javelin. And this—*this is bad.* Scrambling for the desk chair, I dive behind it for cover, unable to catch my breath. My limbs threaten to fold at the burst of movement, still exhausted from fighting the maelstrom.

I'd forgotten just how *feeble* my body could feel, but this isn't the time or place for weakness. Though I knew Death would react like this, I failed to distract him long enough for the others to escape. Now they crouch halfway across the room, trapped by revenants, while Odessa snarls and knocks aside another bedpost. She cannot protect five people by herself, however—not with two unconscious and two more on the verge of collapse.

My mother screams as Death advances—shunting aside his precious revenants when they don't move fast enough—his skin flushed, mottling with rage. "I *told* you this would happen! I *warned* you—"

"*Filippa!*" Desperately, I lunge toward her, stumbling to where she stands by the shore and watches in silence. "Filippa, PLEASE—"

Death snarls again at that, whirling abruptly—changing tack unexpectedly and charging toward us instead. He mimics my voice in a terrifying shriek. "Yes, Filippa, *please*! Please, PLEASE, tell me *exactly* how I should fillet your mother and sister because of your incompetence, your *failure.*" He bares his teeth in a truly crazed smile. "Tell me *exactly* how I should—"

"I did what you asked." Filippa lifts her chin at his approach, unflinching, and meets his maniacal gaze without fear. "I guided my sister to your realm, and I brought her safely back again. Where is my daughter?"

"What I *asked*?" Death's eyes bulge incredulously. "You are willfully— You have *not*— I WANT THE VEIL DOWN, FILIPPA," he bellows into her face. "HAVE YOU BROUGHT THE VEIL DOWN?"

"You are clearly overcome"—her voice drips disdain—"and unable to control your emotions." Sneering, she shakes her head. "I should've realized it sooner, but I didn't—or perhaps couldn't. I foolishly agreed to help you, to obey you, in exchange for my sister's protection and my daughter's return. You broke the first condition without hesitation, but I will not allow you to break the second. Not after everything I've done." She draws herself up to her full height now, squaring her shoulders and glaring at Death like he is not a primordial entity but an unpleasant little boy in need of scolding. And despite everything, I cannot help but admire her for it.

I have always admired her for it.

As if I'd ever let anything happen to you, Célie.

"Now," she says coldly, "allow me to repeat myself—*where is my daughter?*"

Death actually spasms in response now. Then his fingers curl around Filippa's shoulders, and he says, "I could not give a single *fuck* about your daughter. If she was still in your belly, I would throw you both into that maelstrom just for the pleasure of watching you drown."

And there it is—the truth we've all tried to speak gently, now spoken with cruelty instead. Unimaginable cruelty. *Despicable* cruelty. I never wanted her to hear it, never wanted her to break, but now she knows the depths of Death's depravity, the lengths to which he will go. She knows Death does not care, that he never cared, and he will never bring her daughter back either.

Filippa stiffens beneath his touch as she realizes it too. And though Death clearly feels no remorse, I still do; it tightens my throat as her eyes lock with mine and fierce understanding passes between us.

A look that doesn't go unnoticed.

"Whatever idiotic scheme you've concocted"—Death's fingers tighten on Filippa with brutal force—"I suggest you reconsider. As your sister has pointed out, you're both quite soft again, darling. Quite vulnerable."

Though Filippa opens her mouth to answer, he squeezes harder—*too* hard—and she cries out in pain as her clavicle snaps. He doesn't stop there, however. He continues to squeeze, and though I leap at him—horrified, panic-stricken—he catches my arm and launches me into the sea, where I plunge straight into the bands of swirling water. Choking now, I struggle to keep my head aloft—my legs spasming, cramping, *seizing* against the tide—as Death throws Filippa in too, and she screams before plummeting below the surface.

"*Filippa!*" Frantic now, I dive toward her because she cannot swim; he broke her *bones*, and the current—it's too strong, too *fast*—

My fingers catch her wrist as Death careens into the shallows after us, but I cannot focus on him. I cannot focus on anything but

Filippa. *Filippa.* She flounders in my hand, clawing up my arm, and I heave her forward with all my might. I fling her toward the islet with the next sweep of the current, and she understands instantly, grappling at the rock with her good arm. Her fingers catch a dip in its surface. When she hooks a leg over the ledge, however, the same current tows me away again, and I hold my breath—lungs splitting—as it pulls me back under. As it pulls me down—

Down.

Down.

And somewhere above, I hear another scream, followed by an abrupt slipstream as something—*someone*—plunges into the depths beside me. My heart sinks as large hands thrust down upon my shoulders, my head, pushing me deeper in an effort to catapult themselves upward. Gritting my teeth, I catch their waist at the last second, and we burst through the surface together.

Death.

He snarls, attempting to disentangle himself, but I will not drown in this wretched place. I will *not.* Clamping my limbs around him, I climb up his body and refuse to let go. Though we thrash like a pair of eels—Death cursing and spluttering and wrenching my hair until lights pop across my vision—my mother stands stricken in my periphery, in the *shallows*, her hands still outstretched as if she—

As if she *pushed* him.

Revenants descend on her in the next second, and my grip on Death loosens. Before he can break free, however, we spiral downward in the treacherous current—deeper this time. Closer to the heart of the maelstrom. And this wasn't part of the plan, not with Michal and Dimitri still down there, still *waiting*, but I bring my knees to my chest and kick outward at Death. I *strike* at him, and I pray it'll be enough. Though he tries to seize my wrist—still snarling, determined to take me with him—I twist at the last second, and he catches my sleeve instead.

When the fabric tears beneath his fingers, I slip from his grasp, and the current rips him through the veil. *We did it.*

I cannot stop to celebrate, however; I cannot even pause to check on Filippa.

I can only pray she'll be ready when I return.

And—without waiting another second—I take a deep breath and dive after Death.

CHAPTER FORTY-SEVEN

A Candle and Its Shadow

Nothing has changed when I land in the garden—not the blues and not the greens, and certainly not the sunshine. The same grass ripples in the same mild breeze, and the river—it moves just as peacefully through the languid afternoon. Indeed, after the nightmare of the grotto, this pastoral scene is almost . . . chilling.

I lurch to my feet in search of any sign of Death, but he seems to have vanished without a trace.

The thought brings little comfort.

"Michal?" I whisper his name as I tiptoe toward the riverbank, peering through boughs of orange trees and glancing behind topiaries for anything unusual. Surely *something* should look different after Death's return? Withered roses, perhaps? Blackened snowdrops? Perhaps the wind should erupt into a gale, yet all remains still—perfect, just as we left it. "Michal? Dimitri?" I raise my voice a little louder, wincing as it cuts through the tranquility. "Are you here?"

No one answers. Michal and Dimitri agreed to wait near the water for as long as they could, yet I don't see either one of them. And those shadows—my gaze snaps toward the orange tree above me—they seem longer than natural, darker, as the wind begins to blow harder. As the river starts to swell.

Dimitri and Michal have been here too long. If I don't find

them soon, we could all be doomed. I glance around helplessly—until Michal's arm snakes around my waist, dragging me behind the nearest tree. With a panicked cry, I nearly leap from my skin, but he claps a hand against my mouth. At my incredulous look, Dimitri whispers, "He's here."

And the entire garden explodes with darkness.

I clutch my head as pressure spikes through my skull and Death's laughter rumbles around us—through the pitch-black, through my very bones—until I crash to my knees, unable to move. Unable to *think*. Unable to see, hear, or even *feel* Michal and Dimitri, who might never have been here at all. Who might never have even existed—for who can exist in this deprivation, this *dearth*?

Perhaps I cannot exist here either.

When Death speaks at last, I sense rather than hear him: "Who did you think I was, mon mariée?" And his *voice*—it feels like a hundred voices now, like a thousand, no longer filled with the warmth of humanity but cold and ancient and strange. Still familiar, however, as if the Death from our realm still exists within it, desperately clinging to existence. "Who am I but an absence? Who am I but the want of creation?"

No. I shake my head without a mouth to form the word, without a voice to speak it, and splitting pain cleaves through my being; the pressure is too much, too soon—

"I was the darkness in your sister's casket." Death constricts around me, *suffocating* me, and I search blindly for Michal, for Dimitri, for anyone or anything with which to ground myself. There is nothing, however. *Nothing*, and now I am falling, my stomach swooping sickeningly. "I was the void in your mother's chest, the disappointment in your father's. I am the hollow inside your sister. I am her sickness too, her hunger, and I am also your fear—and such *fear* you harbor, Célie. I have known and nourished you for so long."

"I—I am not afraid of you."

"Are you *sure*?" Death shifts with the words, and the darkness presses closer as a shape emerges at last—a long shape, a cold one, with a leering smile of white teeth and half her cheeks rotted, her hair like a cat-o'-nine-tails upon my skin. Slick with my blood, with her own fetid flesh. *Filippa.* And there is no Michal this time, no candles to light the way. There is only me—alone—and there is only Death, who wears the face of my every nightmare.

No.

Focus on just one sense, one detail.

The grass. I can still feel it beneath my knees, soft and warm from the eternal sunshine. It does not know this darkness; it tickles my fingers as I flex them into the earth, forcing myself to breathe, to expand my consciousness outward. The river. I can still hear it flowing. Salt. I can still taste it on my tongue.

It all means I am alive. I *exist*, and— "I am not afraid of you."

The words burst from me like a fire in the darkness, illuminating all those parts of myself I felt too ashamed to see—that I *can* be porcelain, and a martyr, and spoiled and soft and selfish too. That I can be incompetent. That time and time again, I have failed—both my loved ones and *myself*—and will continue to do so often. I can be flighty and fickle, and I sometimes care too much when I shouldn't—about society and its pressures, its rules, its people.

I am also loyal, however, and empathetic and curious and kind. My mind remains open and free of judgment. Despite everything,

I have never hardened myself, even when threatened—even when scorned—because there is strength in my softness; there is courage in my vulnerability. I have *never* given up. I have always seen the light in the darkness.

No.

All this time, I've been looking for someone else to lead me, to banish the darkness of my past, without realizing the darkness is part of me too. I cannot outrun it. I no longer want to, no longer need to—I am both the candle and the shadow it casts.

I *am* the light in the darkness.

And I am the darkness in the light.

Pushing to my feet, I stretch out my hands anew in search of Michal, and this time, I find him almost instantly. He has been here all along, searching for me too, shouting— "We need to go! *Célie*—" His hand catches mine, locking around it, and I drag him forward as Dimitri crashes into us with a curse.

"*Fuck.* What is *happening*—" His limbs tangle with mine, but I seize him with my free hand, refusing to leave him behind. Instead I pelt through the flowers and force them to follow—crashing into a topiary, another—as the darkness begins to recede. To *move.* It sweeps ahead of us with the rising wind, and a shard of dread pierces my heart because—

Because he found it again—the way back, the tear in the veil. Because he is *racing* us, and if he gets to the door first, we will never defeat him.

Both Michal and Dimitri seem to realize it at the same time. "Keep going," Michal says fiercely before lengthening his stride and pulling away from us, *ahead* of us, but even he cannot catch Death. That shard of dread twists deeper. What are we going to *do*?

The wind whips violently through my hair now—frantic, almost crazed—as the river rushes behind us in a fast, roaring torrent. "What if we don't make it in time?" Dimitri asks desperately.

"I—I don't know—"

Snarling, Dimitri tears an orange from a branch overhead and hurls it at Death's shadow. He overshoots our momentum, however, and before I can do anything to stop it, the two of us tumble head over heels to the ground—and straight into Michal's knees.

Though Dimitri and I flail in a tangle of limbs, Michal uses the collision to propel himself forward, launching back to his feet and diving toward Death. And from those fluttering ripples in the veil, Odessa's garbled shout drifts toward us. "Célie, hurry! *Hurry!*"

But now Death is contracting, folding, *squeezing* into himself—into the ripples—and Michal cannot stop him. Michal cannot even see the exit to pass through it. *I* am the Bride of Death. Michal and Dimitri cannot return without me, so I leap, I *slash*—

I tear through the darkness like I would the veil, and it shudders in response.

It recoils.

"Don't fight the current in the maelstrom," I tell them, "and don't look back." Tackling Michal around the waist—dragging Dimitri behind—I careen through the ripples and into the grotto before the darkness can re-form.

Instantly, the ocean rips us apart.

It turns the world upside down, turns *us* upside down, but I've done this before. *I am not afraid.* Relaxing into the current—and praying fervently Michal and Dimitri do the same—I allow it to spiral my body down, then up, up, *up* until I break the surface.

"They're here!" Odessa's shout splits the air as Michal resurfaces beside me, then Dimitri. Diving past three revenants, she reaches for us from the shore. "Come on! Swim, *swim*—"

Instantly, I know something is wrong. The air is too thin, too cold, and the world is too gray—all color has leached from the grotto entirely, spreading beyond it in a silent and suffocating wave.

"What is *that?*"

Reid's eyes widen as fresh blood trickles from his tear ducts—bright scarlet amidst the gloom—and he stumbles back a step, grasping his chest. Lou collapses in front of him. And the storm winds—they must've followed us through somehow, because the broken bedpost spirals high in the air. Pieces of the splintered desk hurtle toward us.

No.

Toward *it.*

Lungs burning, I inhale sharply at the enormous waterspout rising beyond the maelstrom. It spins viciously, sucking the debris of the grotto into its vortex as the veil around us trembles. Oh God. *The veil.*

In resurrecting Michal and Dimitri, I have created— I have *broken*—

Everything.

Reid faints in the split second of my realization, and Dimitri pulls himself from the heaving depths and onto the shore, sprinting to Reid's side. To Lou's. He drags them both away from nature's wrath—from its last great retaliation at the damage I have caused. Not everyone is so lucky, however; everywhere I look, revenants are clawing at the ground, the walls, anything they can reach to remain standing, yet the wind sweeps several—sweeps most—high into the air. The waterspout rips them apart. Their viscera rains down upon the grotto, but I cannot dwell on it—not as the water whirls higher, deadlier, and shrapnel flies in all directions.

"I have to close it!" Waves crash into my mouth—no, *blood*—as I swim for the islet, as the winds tug and pull me closer. Closer. I need only to mend my tear. I kick out, propelling myself forward, allowing the riptide to speed me along. *As soon as I close it, it'll—*

Death's icy fingers close around my ankle, and he drags me under again.

He's re-forming.

Frantic, I kick out blindly, connecting with his face. When his grasp loosens, I wrench *his* hair this time, and I hurl him headfirst into the waterspout's vortex—into the door.

Without so much as taking another breath, I dive after him into the heart of the storm. *My* storm. Wind pummels me, water battering my skin like fists, but I do not concern myself with the bruises. I *will* close the door.

I *will* stop Death.

Clutching the veil with both hands, I fight the tumultuous weather and begin to mend the rip. I focus on the emotions flowing through me, find strength in each one—fear of losing my loved ones, anger at sparring with Death, *hope* that we can still fix this—and allow them to thread from my fingers as if I'm in my nursery once more, sitting beside Filippa and cross-stitching snowdrops and roses onto pillows and handkerchiefs.

All at once—or perhaps it is slowly, time losing its meaning as I grapple with the waves, with Death, with the balance of our very world—the veil mends. The waterspout dies. The deep blue of the ocean gradually returns, along with the silver specks of mica in the grotto walls. And I—I did it.

I did it.

Death's presence vanishes with the disaster, the water and debris crashing back into the sea, but this isn't over yet. Filippa still needs to mend the hole in the maelstrom, or Death will return—and *soon.* Shouting my name, Michal crouches on the shore and reaches for me, while beside him—

"Get a move on, girl!" Mathilde gestures weakly toward the maelstrom, toward the islet, and tears well in my eyes at the sight of her. *She came back.* Despite her attitude, her scowl, her parting words—she came back. She is *here*, and— "Your sister seems to be experiencing performance issues!" She jerks her warty chin toward Filippa, who stands on a shelf near the islet, wringing her hands hysterically. "And *that*"—she points to the tendrils of darkness already creeping from the maelstrom—"does not look promising."

Fuck.

Changing directions abruptly, I throw myself toward my sister as Mathilde lifts her hands with a determined expression, shouting, "I cannot hold the bastard for long! One way or another—no matter the cost—we must close that damn door!"

"Filippa!" I heave myself onto the shelf, gasping and shaking. "You need to—to close it. Do it *now*—"

Filippa drops to her knees, reaching into the water and attempting to hold the veil, to force it together in her hands. Her movements are jolting, however, almost convulsive. With each thread she mends, another splits apart. And this tear—it spans larger than the grotto, larger than life itself. It'll take more than her anger to mend it.

Did Death even teach her how to wield her power? How *could* he have? He never learned to control his own emotions, and Filippa has always fled hers. As if realizing the same, she whispers, "I can't do it."

"Yes, you *can*." I sink to my knees beside her. "Channel your emotions—all of them this time. You cannot manipulate the veil—you cannot mend this tear—while still acting like you do not feel." When she thrashes her head in denial, I say fiercely, "I *heard* you, Filippa. While I was drowning in the garden, you begged me to live, and when Death threatened our mother, I *saw* the look on your face. I saw your fear, your anger, your *love*. And you do love us—all of us, including your daughter, which is why you nearly rent the world apart to meet her. Everything you've done has been out of love, and of *course* it has. You are human, Pip, and you feel just as deeply as the rest of us, if not more."

Her hands clench into fists. "I've never been like you. I've never been able to do this—never *wanted* to feel this—"

"Aren't you a little old for pretend?"

"ANY MOMENT NOW!" Mathilde strains on the shore, her own hands twisting as blood begins to trickle from her ears and the grotto shakes with Death's roar.

Filippa laughs harshly, the spray of the sea hiding her tears. "Perhaps we should just be done with it." She glances at me, her eyes hard as ever. "If I jump and cross the river, this ends. Save the world, right? That's what this has all been about. We know how to do that, Célie."

I glare at her, guiding her fists back toward the water, toward the veil. "Don't be ridiculous."

Though her grip remains stiff, almost immovable, I manage to unclench her fists and smooth out her palms, just as Death's hand shoots from the maelstrom. Mathilde collapses with a hiss.

True panic rears within me now. We do not have time for this moment, but it is perhaps the last moment we will ever have.

"I lost her," Filippa says, quieter now but no less cold. "I lost Frostine. I lost Frederic. I lost . . . *everything* that I considered for my future. What else is left for me?" She turns her gaze to the maelstrom, and her fingers seem to stroke the tear. They seem to beckon it forth. "If I mend the veil, what lies ahead except a life of torment? Of *grief*?"

Pain laces the last, and for the first time since our youth, Filippa's icy facade falters. I move my hands to her arm, squeezing tightly so that she will feel it—feel *me*—and know that I am here.

I am here, and I am not leaving her.

I will not let her die.

"I can help you, Pip. We—we can *all* help you. The grief you feel over Frederic and Frostine . . . it will not vanish, but it will fade. Little by little, you *will* overcome it. Please, Filippa." My voice breaks on her name. "*Please* don't give up now. If not for me or Maman or the life we might share together, then . . . then stay for *yourself*." I guide her hands closer to the heart of the maelstrom, where Death snatches the air wildly, desperate for leverage. Mathilde groans. "You aren't alone. We can do this together."

She shakes her head. "That—that isn't how mending the veil works—"

"So do it yourself." Desperation sharpens my voice, all my hope and my fear colliding within my chest and exploding outward as my fingers dig into her skin. "Do it yourself, but know that I am here beside you—that I will *always* be beside you. I will be here, Pip, because I love you. *I love you.*"

Her hands tremble, and her lip quivers. Though her gaze widens like she's listening—like she's really, truly *hearing* me—she does not yet move to close the veil. "You should hate me, Célie. The things I've done . . . the person I've been . . . you should shove me inside this stupid fucking maelstrom without a single regret."

"Funny, that." I lift my chin, conviction pulsing a steady beat in my veins. "I no longer care about what I should or shouldn't do. You are my sister, and I *want* you to live. I cannot make you, however; *you* need to want to live too. The choice is yours, and the clock is ticking." Though I release her at the last, I remain near her side, willing her to feel my warmth.

I will not leave her.

Filippa has been awful.

She aligned with a murderer, she killed Dimitri, she kept the souls of her ex-lover and our nursemaid trapped inside her ice palace, and she has threatened me more times than I can count. But life does not work in absolutes. *No one* is wholly good.

I once called a young woman a whore, and she soon became my dearest friend. That same young woman set her own best friend on fire, but they reconciled just as quickly—in the flash of a single spark.

That same spark resides in each of us, that glimmer of light and that touch of darkness. The propensity for good, yes, but also the potential for great evil. Filippa is no different. Both exist within her as well.

She *can* change. She can decide to do better, to do good, so long as she makes the decision for herself. Filippa glances at me, at our mother, at Mathilde, then at Michal and Dimitri and Odessa. She even glances at Lou and Reid, who slump beside Jean Luc and Brigitte. Our family. My friends. People she will someday know too, hopefully, if she dares to imagine that future for herself—if she dares to reach for happiness.

Without another word, she turns to Death, and she slaps his hand away.

A cry passes my lips, unbidden, as she clutches at the seams of the tear—as much of them as she can hold—and leans forward, pressing the ragged edges together. *Her* edges. Her tears fall faster now, dripping into the storm that her rebirth created.

"I never want to smell another revenant again," Filippa says.

And then my sister closes the veil.

CHAPTER FORTY-EIGHT

A New Beginning

I expect thunder and lightning, a tidal wave—anything to signify Death has gone and the world has righted. None of those things happen, however.

Instead it's just us.

My sister and me crouching on the islet, and the others gathering on the shore. Odessa resting her head on her brother's shoulder—her arms tight around his waist, refusing to let go—while Lou and Reid stir at their feet. Jean Luc and Brigitte are rousing now too. Mathilde is turning to murmur something to Dimitri, who chuckles and glances at Michal.

Michal.

Our eyes meet across the grotto, and he wades into the water as the maelstrom gradually slows, as it stills, and the gentle tide returns to lap against the rock. Though my mother follows, there will be time for reunions later—an entire lifetime, which is all the more precious than eternity. They both seem to sense as much, waiting in the shallows as I help Filippa stand. As I pull her into a fierce embrace and whisper, "I knew you could do it."

I knew you would stay.

She trembles in my arms.

"I shouldn't have ever climbed out that window." Voice low, she fixes her gaze upon the sea, as if waiting for Death to somehow reappear, to pull her back under. I hold her even tighter in promise, and slowly—tentatively—she returns the pressure, murmuring, "It felt like I was suffocating in our nursery, watching your life unfold when mine hadn't even started. I didn't know what to do—how to get *out*—and Frederic—he promised a fresh start." She shakes her head before resting it upon my shoulder. Fresh tears trickle down her nose. "Sometimes I wonder how different things might've been if I'd simply confided in you rather than running away."

"How fortunate that we both get a second chance."

"You've always been too good for this world, ma belle." Pulling away abruptly, she wipes the tears from her cheeks, smooths her soaking-wet gown, before inhaling deeply and straightening her spine in the spitting image of our mother. And just when I think her defenses have slipped fully back into place, she adds, "Too good for *me*."

I bump her hip, a smile tugging on my lips. "For your information, I'm not as good as you might think." I lift my chin for dramatic impact. "I've killed a man, you know . . . and I've also *lain* with one."

Filippa laughs out loud at that—unexpected and uninhibited—and her smile cracks my chest wide open. I'd almost forgotten what it looked like. I'd almost thought to never see it again. *Almost.* "Only *you* can make murder and sex sound whimsical," she says.

I blink at her in feigned innocence. "Was yours not?"

Though Filippa rolls her eyes, it is our mother who calls sternly, "If you're *quite* finished with that sordid talk, perhaps you'd be so kind as to greet your dear old mother. It is rude to keep me waiting!" She sounds impatient, anxious, but when I glance in her direction, her eyes shine with exhilaration too—to have her daughters back again, to have her own new beginning.

Still smiling, I take my sister's hand, and we do just that.

We start over.

Together.

"Ho-*ly* fuck," Lou says slowly a half hour later. Whistling in appreciation, she circles me in Michal's study before tossing her bloody handkerchief atop his desk. Though he glares at it pointedly, she ignores him. "I didn't think such a thing was possible, yet here you are, all bright and shiny and new again. And *human.*" She glances at Filippa, who stands in the corner with our mother, talking quietly among themselves. "Both of you—all *four* of you," she adds, her eyes wide with wonder as she points a finger between Michal and Dimitri. "Incredible."

"Your refuse is on my desk," Michal says.

Shaking his head apologetically, Reid plucks up the bloody handkerchief. "How does it feel?"

"Like yesterday I would've gnawed off your hand to eat that handkerchief," Dimitri says cheerfully, "and now I won't."

With a grimace, Reid shakes the handkerchief, and the blood vanishes instantly. "A definite positive, then."

"It feels wonderful," I say in earnest, squeezing Michal's hand. We sit together in a chair by the fire—or rather, *he* sits in the chair, and I sprawl across his lap, heedless of anyone else in the room. "Like I'm finally myself again. Not that there weren't benefits to being, well—"

"Supernaturally strong?" Lou pauses in rummaging through his desk drawers to look up at me with a sly grin. In her hands, she holds Michal's skull-shaped wax seal. "And fast? And graceful?

And *impossibly* beautiful? Yes, I can see how that would weigh heavily upon a person." Then, to Michal, "This is a little on the nose, isn't it?" She waves the wax seal in distaste before dropping it back in his drawer.

"I almost ate you, Lou," I say flatly.

"And I would've enjoyed it, I'm sure." She goes back to her investigation, cackling and pulling out Michal's thumb claw next. "Much like I assume the two of you enjoyed . . . *this?* Whatever it is? Some sort of blood play—"

Reid shuts the drawer with a snap, shaking his head again. By the door, Jean Luc coughs awkwardly while Brigitte scowls at all of us, her arms crossed and her jaw tight. They haven't spoken much since the grotto, since we explained all about Death and the maelstrom, the garden and the river.

To be honest, they seemed unimpressed that we allowed it to go that far—and even less impressed when Mathilde waltzed out of the grotto without returning them to Cesarine. At least they missed Guinevere's prying questions—*Who is* he*? Did you love him? Does he love* her?—because no one can see her anymore, or any of the other ghosts either. No one except me, Filippa, and Mathilde, who is probably drafting demands for her new cottage at this very moment.

Like the veil, the spirit realm is healing. And so is the isle. The *world.*

Odessa left the grotto shortly after Mathilde to address her sentries, and the scent of Lou's magic still lingers upon the door, which she spelled to be impenetrable to vampiric senses. For now, they cannot hear or scent us, but that doesn't solve the problem of how to leave.

Because we must leave eventually. Requiem is no longer safe for us—not for me and my mother, not for Michal, not even for Dimitri anymore. "Do you think Coco and Beau are all right?" I ask quietly after another moment.

Lou opens another drawer, pulling out a pouch of Michal's coins and weighing it in her palm. "I assume Coco and Beau are fine—probably enjoying some well-earned alone time. Talon would've found me by now if not, and more than that"—she pockets the pouch without a word—"I suspect that our revenant problem is at an end."

Michal glares at her, his hands twitching slightly, but makes no other move to stand. "I suspect the same."

Lou grins. "*Do* you?"

Dimitri chuckles at Michal's black expression, leaning back against the desk and musing aloud, "I'm not a witch, but I suppose it makes sense. . . . When our darling Pip closed the veil, she ended the ritual that resurrected them."

My sister snaps to attention, her face whipping toward his. "What did you just call me?"

He leans back farther, gazing up at her through his lashes. Splaying his hands wide across the desk. "Did you really not hear me?"

"Apparently not," she says through clenched teeth, "as my name is *Filippa*—Mademoiselle Tremblay to you."

"Hmm. I prefer Pip."

Our mother blinks at him in shock. "Monsieur Petrov, I am *astonished* by this lapse in decorum—"

"She did stab him in the heart," Brigitte points out.

When we all stare at her, she shrugs defensively—her cheeks

turning pink—and Lou lifts a finger in acknowledgment. "Fair point, well made."

Dimitri dips his chin. "Thank you."

"In all seriousness," Lou says, "my magic feels—better now. Whole again, which tells me the natural order has been restored." She pats Dimitri on the back, then Reid. "Good job, everyone. A real team effort. I especially enjoyed the part where I lay on the ground for all of it."

Filippa and Dimitri both snort.

Rolling his eyes, Michal brushes his nose along the curve of my neck before pressing a kiss there. Silence descends, but it isn't tense any longer. It isn't panicked or strained. Instead it feels . . . comfortable. Safe. I toy with Michal's fingers, relishing their warmth; he runs much hotter than I expected, and I burrow deeper into his lap. "What happens now?" I ask after another moment.

Though we all look at each other, no one seems to have an answer—no one except Michal, who absently coils a strand of my hair around his finger. "Whatever we want, pet. We can do whatever we want."

CHAPTER FORTY-NINE

Happily Ever After

As it turns out, Odessa cares very little about ousting Michal to the island—perhaps because she informed the populace that she single-handedly disposed of the revenants, healing the isle and saving their lives in the process. Or perhaps because Lou affixed a mustache to Michal's lip, and the two proclaimed him properly disguised.

Or perhaps because Michal's heart beats steadily in his chest, and the vampires who've gathered to watch our departure seem more puzzled than outraged. They watch us warily from the shadows of the dock as our strange entourage, including Jean Luc and Brigitte, descend from the carriages. Odessa's sentries surround us, first to act as protection, and second to carry our luggage across the gangplank. They do not speak as they load trunk after trunk onto the ship—and even an enormous portrait of Mila, which Dimitri insisted on bringing.

"I'm not sure the mustache is working," I murmur to Odessa, who follows my gaze to where Léandre and Violette linger in a nearby alley, their eyes narrowed upon Michal. Upon *me.* Unease skitters down my spine, but Odessa merely scoffs, unbothered, and commands them to come closer.

"Wait," I hiss, incredulous. "We shouldn't—"

"Léandre, Violette"—Odessa gestures to Michal, who pauses

in his conversation with Dimitri—"meet Panteleimon, my seventh cousin, twice removed. An uncanny resemblance to our late king, is he not?" She looks them dead in the eye, daring either one to challenge her. After inhaling subtly, their noses wrinkle at our human scent, and their frowns deepen. "Greet him," Odessa says pleasantly.

Michal regards them with cool indifference as they gape at her, torn between disbelief and confusion. "My queen . . . ?" Léandre asks slowly.

"Yes." She bites the word, still maintaining her smile. "Your *queen* has issued a direct command, and she does not like to be kept waiting. Now I suggest that you *bow*."

Something in her expression sharpens at the last, and at once, Léandre and Violette mumble their apologies, dropping into a bow and a curtsy respectively. And—remembering their threats at the black soirée—I enjoy the sight of them prostrate. I enjoy it every bit as much as I should.

When Léandre finally rises, lip curling, Odessa orders him and Violette to carry Michal's luggage to the ship. Jean Luc and Brigitte follow. Though the former nods—looking grudgingly impressed—his hand hasn't left his Balisarda since we departed the castle. Still, however . . .

"That went surprisingly well," I murmur to Odessa.

She lifts an elegant shoulder. "And why wouldn't it? I am a better queen than Michal ever was."

"Easy to do." Dimitri chuckles as Michal rolls his eyes to the sky, peeling off his mustache and dropping it at our feet. "Though imagine how *fabulous* he would've looked in one of your gowns." He lifts a hand to ruffle his sister's hair, but she catches his wrist midair. Startled, he blinks before remembering she is still a vampire, and he is not. For just an instant, wistfulness flashes in his eyes—there and gone again before his sister notices—but I think I understand.

Dimitri's and Odessa's lives have been intwined since birth. Before it, even. Everything they have done, they have done together, but now . . . they cannot be together anymore. Their lives must separate; they must part, and everything is about to change.

He shakes his head ruefully. "Damn, Des. You're quite a bit stronger than I remember."

She releases his wrist to pat his cheek. "And I will happily break your arm if you ever touch my hair again."

Behind them, Filippa snickers.

Dimitri pretends not to hear it, instead pulling his sister into a hug and resting his chin on her head. The gesture is intimate, even childlike, and I can almost picture the two as such—much younger, much smaller, with long and bright futures ahead of them. "You were born for this, Des," he murmurs, squeezing her tighter. "If anyone can wrangle this island into order, it's you, and I could not be prouder to call you my sister."

"No." She shakes her head abruptly, pushing him away with much greater care than usual. With gentleness. "*No*, do not say another word. This is starting to sound suspiciously like farewell, but that *cannot* be the case when there will always be a ship in Cesarine to bring you back. And if there is not, I will send one; I will send a hundred boats if that is what you require." Sniffing, she steps backward and turns away, but I still recall her at the grotto, clinging to Michal and screaming her brother's name. His absence will pain her more than she'll ever admit.

I catch her hand as she brushes past us to speak to a nearby sentry. I squeeze it, and she returns the pressure without a word. "Take care of him, Célie," she murmurs. "For me. Please."

"You know I will."

She smiles at that—small and perhaps mournful—before giving her undivided attention to the sentry. I loop my arm through Dimitri's next. "What about Margot? Will she be joining us in Cesarine?"

He heaves a dramatic sigh. "She wants to stay in Requiem." At my confused look, he adds reluctantly, "I snuck out to the flower shop earlier, hoping to surprise her, but she—she didn't know what to say. It isn't that she *doesn't love me*"—he scoffs at the trite excuse—"but that her life is *here*, and my life . . . cannot be here anymore. She never admitted it, but I think she hoped I'd someday change her into a vampire."

"I'm sorry, Dima."

He slides his free hand into his pocket. "Don't be. I probably would've killed her, and I—I *think* I'm excited about Cesarine." Tilting his head in frank consideration, he says, "You know, perhaps it won't smell so foul now that I'm human."

"It still will," Lou says.

She passes us now too, slinging a satchel of food over her shoulder. Though she moves to chomp into an apple on her way to the gangplank, Dimitri snatches it from her at the last second. He tosses it between his hands experimentally before taking an enormous bite. "Oh my *god*," he says with his mouth full, staring down at the apple in blissful wonder. "I think I'm most excited about the *food*."

"A bore *and* a brute." Hitching the basket of kittens higher on her hip, Filippa rolls her eyes as she follows after Lou. "How shocking."

His eyes spark, and he abandons the rest of us to follow hot on her heels. "A *bore*? Tell me, are you aware of what that word means? Out of the two of us, I can assure you, I am not the bore. You even walk like you have a stick up your—"

Madame Tremblay snaps her gaze to him.

"—corset," he finishes humbly, catching her hand to help her onto the gangplank without missing a beat. Madame Tremblay nods in approval as Filippa tries to crush his fingers. "Excellent posture. Really, truly excellent."

Filippa hisses something in return, too low for me to hear, and Dimitri laughs, releasing her hand and assisting Madame Tremblay next. "You mustn't judge the state of the town house when we arrive. I did not know I'd be receiving guests—"

"Do not inconvenience yourself for our sake," Dimitri says. "Michal and I are indebted to you, madame, and we promise to trespass upon your hospitality only until we procure our own lodgings."

"And *I* am hardly a guest, Maman," Filippa says over her shoulder. "I assume the nursery is right where I left it."

Madame Tremblay hesitates on the gangplank, looking suddenly nervous. "I think . . . well, to be quite frank, I think the time has come to retire the nursery." Then—as if realizing every eye in our party has turned to her—she clears her throat, hastening to look down her nose at us. "Perhaps, Filippa, you would rather claim your father's room instead?"

Filippa blinks at her in perplexity. "What do you mean? I will not be sleeping with Pére—"

"Oh, of course you won't." Our mother waves a hand, interrupting in an unusually loud voice. A shrill one. "Because I—I have kicked the wastrel out. He is not welcome in our home any longer, though, of course, I will respect your decision to see him again if you so wish." An uncertain pause. "I do apologize for not telling you sooner," she adds, softer now, "but we had rather more important things with which to deal."

Filippa's eyes catch mine, and we stare at each other in shock. In *awe.* Before I can congratulate our mother, however, Filippa says, "Good riddance."

And I couldn't have put it better myself.

Beaming at them both—at Dimitri too—I bounce a little on my toes, unable to contain my excitement. It courses through me like a salve, healing the horrors of the last several hours, the last several *weeks. Years.* I wrap my arms around Michal, pulling him toward the gangplank. "This really will be a new start for all of us. A new *adventure.*"

"Ah, yes." Dimitri shakes his head and leads my sister and mother onto the ship. "Three single women alone in the city. What mischief could possibly await?"

"Or not so single." Michal pulls me aside before we step onto the gangplank, black eyes glittering with anticipation. He brushes my hair back, cradling my cheek in his palm, while his other hand slides around my waist. "All the pieces are falling into place," he murmurs, "but is this what *you* want? To return to Cesarine? To walk under that orange tree and sit at that nursery window?"

I breathe a soft laugh. A rueful one.

"If you'd asked me those questions a year ago, I would've said no." I turn my cheek into his hand, and if any tension remained in my body, it leaves me now. *Is this what you want?* Such a simple question should not have such a complicated answer, yet it does. Once upon a time, I wanted to be a dutiful daughter, then a wife. I wanted to be a huntsman—no, a hunts*woman*, the first of her kind. I envied witches; I coveted magic; and I longed to live within the pages of a fairy tale—to be the heroine vanquishing evil, the princess falling in love. Their stories seemed so preferable to my own. Their stories seemed so important.

I was forgotten by my parents.

I was abandoned by my sister.

Even my first love left me—as did my second, in his own unique way.

No. Perhaps what I really craved from those fairy tales had little to do with saving the world—with proving my worth, with leaving a mark—and everything to do with what came after. The happily ever after. The *hope*.

Pressing a kiss to Michal's palm, I murmur, "Death has a way of changing our perspective. Those things sounded so mundane, but now . . . now I do want to sit at that nursery window, and I want to sit at it with *you*. I want to walk under that orange tree together—want to kiss you with pulp on our lips—and I want to listen to our families bicker. I want to laugh with my mother. I want to braid my sister's hair. I want to watch Dimitri taste a chocolate éclair, and I want to drag you to Chateau le Blanc, where we can dance around the mayflower pole every spring. I never appreciated any of it before, but now . . ."

Michal seems to be holding his breath. "But now?"

I stand on my toes to kiss him—just the breath of a touch—before whispering, "Now I want it all, Michal. I want *you*." Still, I force myself to acknowledge the city around us, the island, even Odessa, who stands a discreet distance away while pretending not to eavesdrop. "Unless—unless you'd prefer to go back to how we were? Odessa could still turn you." I draw back to look at him—to *really* look at him, and to ensure he looks at me too. To ensure he hears this next part. "She could turn me too."

He blinks, frowning slightly. "You would do that?"

"I would do anything for you."

At *those* words, however, a broad grin splits his face. As if unable to help it, he spins me toward the gangplank before drawing me back again, brushing my hair from my nape. He nips my skin playfully, his voice rough against my ear. "As much as I'll miss biting you, Célie, there are an exceptional number of things we can do instead—things I'd much rather do, but things that'll prove quite difficult while living with your mother and sister."

"And Dimitri," I add breathlessly, arching into him.

He kisses the spot he nipped, his tongue soothing the hurt, and I sink my teeth into my bottom lip to keep from gasping. *God*, I love him. I love him so much.

He chuckles under his breath. "I'd rather not hear my cousin's name right now."

"Fortunate, then, that my sister will kill him within the week."

"Oh, I don't know." He gazes past me toward the ship, where their raised voices already carry to us. Lou laughs loudly at whatever Filippa said. "I think there might be something there."

I crane my neck to peer up at him through narrowed eyes. "And I stand by what I said—though if Filippa doesn't kill him, my mother will kill them both. If we want any privacy at all, we'll need to find our own place soon—" The words slip out before I can stop them, but I cannot take them back either. My blush deepens. "I mean, if—if you *want*—"

"Mademoiselle Tremblay," Michal says with feigned outrage, spinning my hips around and pinning me against his hard body. Heat spikes through me, just as sharp and needy as before—better, even, because now we are free. "Are you . . . *proposing* to me?"

I lift my chin and scowl at him. "I am proposing you stop telling me about those *exceptional number of things* and start showing me instead, preferably somewhere far, *far* away from listening ears."

"Why?" He cocks a brow, his hands sliding around my back and hooking my corset strings. He pulls them tight. "Are you going to moan, pet? Are you going to scream?"

Leaning into his lips, I exhale softly. "Maybe I will."

From somewhere behind us, Odessa sighs loudly. "I feel compelled to point out *this* is not that place." At the sound of her exasperated voice, I spring away from him, flushed from my head to my toes. Though I grin sheepishly, Michal grins without remorse—wide and unabashed and beautiful. He snakes an arm around my waist as Odessa prods him in the back. "Get off my isle, cousin." To me, she adds, "I shall see you again at Yule, but—public displays of affection notwithstanding—you're both welcome here anytime. My home will always be open to you."

Home.

Warmth spreads through my chest at the word, like the first rays of dawn after a long night.

"Thank you, Odessa." I place a kiss upon her cheek, infusing every ounce of my incandescent happiness into that kiss. Every ounce of my eternal gratitude. "For everything. I wouldn't have survived Requiem without you."

"Yes, you would've." Smiling, she inclines her chin toward the ship. "Now go forth. Your family is waiting for you."

I take Michal's hand, and together, we stride across the gangplank to the ship. Waves lap upon the keel, and the wind picks up in anticipation as we join that family; it tousles our hair and caresses our cheeks. Though the island remains shrouded in shadow, I can almost see the sunlight on the horizon, waiting for us. *Life* is waiting for us.

And I am not alone.

EPILOGUE

Yuletide dawns cold and silver-white this year, and my mother insists on hosting all the festivities—though to her, of course, we're simply celebrating Christmas three days early. "You missed a spot, young man," she says now to Reid, pointing her sharp finger at the very top of the tree. "Just there."

With a pained glance in my direction, Reid stretches to his tiptoes to untangle the tinsel. It drips from the boughs—from the mantel, from the windows, from *everything*—like melting icicles, interspersed with shining baubles and golden bells. Poinsettias. Garlands of dried oranges and velvet ribbons and white berries, candles, and enough mistletoe to make the town house a veritable tinderbox of awkwardness.

Filippa and I might've gotten a little carried away.

Still, exhilaration tingles from the top of my head to the tips of my toes as I gaze around at them—my loved ones, my family—all gathered in my childhood sitting room. Never in my wildest dreams would I have imagined such a happily ever after for us: humans, witches, and a vampire queen celebrating together on a perfect winter evening.

I hasten to distribute their gifts: one present for every person in attendance, each chosen anonymously and placed under the tree in secret.

When I stumble on the edge of our festive scarlet rug—a gift from Odessa—Michal catches the wrapped packages that spill from my arms. Whereas I've lost my immortal grace, he seems to have retained his entirely, and I am not at all sure that's fair. To Reid, he says in a wry voice, "If you can't reach the top, I'd be happy to offer my assistance."

Reid scowls at him, but in his eyes, a glimmer of mischief sparks. With a snap of his fingers, the tinsel winds around the last branch before twining upward, past the boughs, and twisting around the chandelier where it glitters in the candlelight. Reid smirks at my mother's delighted gasp. "Thanks for your concern," he says dryly, "but I think I can handle it."

Lou cackles, sitting cross-legged by the hearth and braiding Coco's hair while Beau attempts to light the ceremonial log. He shoots them an aggrieved glance. "Either one of you could do this with a wave of your hands, you know."

"Oh, we know." With a serene smile, Lou weaves a strand of tinsel through Coco's braids too. "But it's much more entertaining to watch the king do it."

"Ingrates," Beau mutters. "I didn't escape the castle this evening to put up with this kind of harassment—"

"That is *exactly* why you escaped the castle this evening," Coco says sweetly. She plucks a marshmallow from her mug of hot cocoa and flicks it at him. He dodges at the last second, and it soars into the hearth. "Would it help if I say you look extra dashing tonight?"

A grin tugs on his lips as he straightens his brocade vest. "It would, actually."

"Are we sure Beau should be in charge of lighting anything?" Reid drops to the floor beside Lou, stretching out his long legs and stealing a sip of her cocoa. "He nearly burned down the city the last time he played with fire."

Beau shoots him a narrow look. "By *played*, I assume you mean *attempted to save your ungrateful lives*—"

"Is that what you were doing?"

Coco leans forward to press a kiss to Beau's cheek before he can retort. "And we're all very appreciative." Slightly mollified, Beau closes his mouth once more, and his dark eyes burn with fervor as he watches Coco settle back upon the rug. No. They burn with *love.* If I'm any judge of character, I know exactly what he intends to give Coco for Yule this year.

The only question is *when.*

Unable to contain my giddy smile—shooting them both covert glances every few seconds, just in case—I do my best to distribute the rest of the gifts without giving his secret away. When I extend a brightly wrapped present to Odessa, she inspects it with keen interest, turning it round and round before shaking it abruptly.

"Stop that!" I snatch it away from her, clutching it to my chest indignantly. "It's supposed to be a *surprise.*"

"I am not trying to learn what it *is.*" Odessa leans forward in my mother's favorite high-back chair, clad in an opulent gown of crimson and emerald silk with an enormous crown of poinsettias atop her sable hair. The entire ensemble should look completely ridiculous, but instead, she looks like some sort of Christmas angel thanks to her preternatural beauty—or she would, if not for the goblet of blood in her hand. "I am trying to learn who it's *from.*"

"Which is also against the rules." Whirling, I hide her gift under a pillow across the room—safe from her prying eyes—and offer Michal the last remaining present, this one wrapped in silver foil with deep emerald stars. Odessa peers at it for the briefest of seconds before swirling her goblet in smug satisfaction.

"*That* one is from Reid." When I scowl at her, she shrugs delicately. "Look at those corners—they're sharper than a Balisarda. I am not entirely sure he didn't steam the paper before wrapping it."

"He did." With a chortle, Lou ties a ribbon around the end of Coco's braid. "I watched him do it. And it took him *weeks* to pick out your gift," she adds to Michal, who laughs and sinks into the settee, completely at ease as he spreads a broad arm across its back. Heat infuses my cheeks at the sight, at the memory of him on a very different settee, and when his black eyes cut to mine—darkening slightly, his lips curling into a smirk—I know he remembers it too.

A different sort of heat spreads through my belly as I hold his gaze. So similar, yet so different from the vampire I knew. Once, I would've attributed the softness in his eyes to becoming human, but now I know I would've been wrong; that softness has always been there when Michal looks at me.

Somehow, this beautiful and breathtaking man—this man who held true power in his hands, who wielded it, who might've lived forever on an unbreakable throne—has chosen to be here instead. *Here.* In my mother's threadbare sitting room, surrounded by tinsel and mistletoe and cats.

Toulouse darts across Lou's lap, and Reid grimaces as Melisandre pounces after the kitten, her claws catching on his trousers. "It didn't take *weeks*—"

"The game, as you all remember, is called le secret du Père Noël." I plant my hands on my hips, glaring at everyone despite the brilliant smile on my face. I cannot help it. Not with Michal watching me like this—like he is seconds away from pouncing, from dragging me into a dark corner to have his wicked way with me. His rapt attention makes my smile all the brighter as I pretend to ignore him. "Emphasis on *secret.* Are you all trying to ruin Christmas?"

"Yule," Coco and Lou say simultaneously.

"*Christmas.*" Voice tart, my mother strides back into the room carrying a tray of rich, chocolaty bûche de Noël, along with sugarplum pudding and spiced pear pies. My stomach rumbles at the decadent scents. "Though if anyone else is trying to ruin this holy day, I fear you have competition."

As if on cue, Filippa's and Dimitri's voices rise from the kitchen, where they sound like they're doing their best to kill each other. "That is *salt*, not sugar!" Filippa snarls, and an ominous crash follows, rather like Filippa just launched the saltcellar at Dimitri's head. He curses viciously.

"Salt enhances the flavors of the dish!"

"Not four *spoonfuls* of it—"

Beau eyes the food on my mother's tray dubiously. "While I, er—admire Dimitri's newfound interest in the culinary arts, I shall allow everyone *else* to sample these delicacies first—"

My mother thrusts the tray under his nose with quiet menace. "Nonsense, Your Majesty. Monsieur Petrov made the pudding especially for you."

Together, our gazes fall to said pudding, which looks a bit—

Congealed.

My stomach churns as Beau swallows hard, accepting the knife from my mother and moving to scoop up a piece.

"Wait." Sighing heavily, Reid climbs to his feet and nudges his brother aside before choosing a pie instead. These, at least, appear fully baked, and when Reid takes a tentative bite, he manages to swallow with little to no chewing. *A blessing.* I lift a hand to take one too—for Dimitri's sake. Since turning human and moving to Cesarine, he has truly cultivated a passion for food. Pastries, meats, and last week, even a vaguely edible herring soup.

To his credit, he has only poisoned us once.

As if remembering that miserable night, Michal places light fingers upon my wrist, shaking his head slightly when I move to take a bite. "Don't eat that."

My mother scowls at him.

Filippa and Dimitri burst from the kitchen in the next moment, however, and Michal uses the distraction to flick the pie into the fire. "Oh my *heavens*." My mother's eyes widen at the flour dusting Filippa's entire face, at her murderous expression, and Dimitri's self-satisfied grin. His velvet collar is sticky and stained with the jam still on Filippa's fingers. "What in God's name just happened?"

"When I took the salt from him," Filippa says through clenched teeth, "he threw flour at me. *Flour*—"

Dimitri bristles instantly. "You knocked the salt from my hands and proceeded to *attack* me with a jar of apricot jam. A terrible flavor, by the way—"

"You are *lucky* it was just jam—"

"It's true, Dima." Lou nods cheerfully from the floor. "There *is* a set of carving knives on the table."

"And a frying pan," Odessa adds.

"Flinging food." Mouth pursed in exasperation, my mother drops the tray of desserts onto the sideboard with a ringing *clang*. "Honestly, if I must separate the two of you, I will—"

"*Please.*" Filippa stalks across the room to the foyer entrance—away from everyone—and leans against the threshold, crossing her arms tightly, while Dimitri strolls over to sit next to Michal. When he opens his mouth to goad my sister further, I step between them, just like I always do. My lips twitch as I clap my hands together.

"Presents! Who wants to go first?"

To my surprise, it isn't Lou or Coco or even Michal who answers, but my sister. Still scowling, she reaches into the darkened hall behind her to pluck a present I must've missed from the entry table. Sturdy and square, wrapped in paper of palest pink, the package shines incandescent in the candlelight as she extends it to me. "For you," she says simply, not quite meeting my gaze.

My hands reach for it of their own volition. "You drew my name? I never even suspected."

"Le *secret* du Père Noël, remember?" She crosses her arms as if unsure what else to do with them. "We all took great pains to ensure you didn't suspect."

"And it was quite difficult too," Dimitri adds, though not unkindly, "as you're a bit of a busybody, Célie."

Rolling his eyes, Michal pushes him to the end of the settee. "Pot, meet kettle."

Before Filippa can protest, I seize her hand and drag her toward them, pushing her into the seat between Michal and Dimitri. The latter laughs out loud at the sour expression on her face. And perhaps I should apologize, yet I cannot possibly sit in her place; I'm much too excited. Though I did in fact suspect my sister drew my name—there'd been far too many clandestine conversations between her and Lou for anything else, as my sister doesn't even *like* Lou—my hands still practically vibrate in anticipation as I shred the beautiful paper, mourning its loss for only a second before inspecting the simple wooden case beneath.

My breath hitches as I open the latch.

Inside the case sits my perfectly repaired, perfectly *beautiful* music box. As if sensing my elation, Michal reaches for the case before I hastily discard it, his fingers gentle as he helps shimmy the painted fairies into view. I lift the music box into the air to examine it from every angle, my chest tightening as my mother gasps behind us. "I thought it was broken," she whispers, drawing closer to examine it too. Even the cracks from my childhood have somehow vanished, as if they never existed at all, as if Filippa and I never touched this music box. Never loved it. The thought leaves me unexpectedly breathless. Indeed, as I gaze into the pristine faces of its fairy dancers, my chest constricts further with . . . not regret, perhaps, but sorrow.

When my mother reaches for it in the next second, I hand the box over reluctantly, and she murmurs, "How extraordinary. I saw the pieces myself when I came to Yew Lane—I thought the damage irreparable."

My eyes snap to my sister, who looks deeply uncomfortable but forces herself to meet my gaze at last. Her green eyes gleam overly bright in the candlelight, even tense, as I fix her with a curious look. "When Louise mentioned the music box," she says, "I asked her to let me have it. I couldn't stand to see the pieces in the bin, but if you don't want it—"

"I want it."

"You do?"

Green eyes flick to mine as I nod, and something hopeful shifts within them. Something vulnerable—there and gone again before anyone else can see. Moving forward to clasp her hands, I kiss her cheek and whisper, "Thank you. Truly. I've always loved this music box."

She pulls away awkwardly, pink creeping up her throat. "I know."

The rest of the exchange passes in a dreamlike haze, my friends' grins and sparkling eyes softened somehow, almost magical, in the golden glow of the candlelight. Odessa unwraps the mechanical puzzle I bought her while Michal carefully lifts his own gift—a blown-glass oil lamp from Reid—to examine its silver trim. "A housewarming present," Reid says from the carpet, resting easily against the leg of Odessa's chair. "Célie gave us a tour of your town house last week. The renovations are impressive."

"And right across the street too." Leaning back against Reid's chest, Lou arches an impish brow at Michal and me before—incredibly—*winking* at Filippa and Dimitri, who both pretend not to see. "Such close proximity must be incredibly convenient for all parties involved."

Michal ignores her, his brow furrowing as he considers the glass lamp. "You have . . . unexpectedly good taste, huntsman."

"Of course he does." Lou beams down at the slip of parchment in her hand. Apparently, she drew her own name in our secret exchange, and she gifted herself the deed to a local tavern, Les Pêches—a tavern rumored to have been owned by a very well-endowed barmaid named Lydia. "Just look at me."

Though Michal shakes his head, his chest rumbles with suppressed laughter as Dimitri opens an envelope containing a certificate for baking lessons with Johann Pan, courtesy of Coco, and Reid unwraps a leather journal from my mother, who stares down at the jewelry box in her lap with a stricken expression.

A gift from Michal.

His laughter fades as she turns wide eyes toward him. "Open it," he says softly. And if the box itself weren't enough—gilt and ornate, its carved roses set with rubies—the pieces within seem to render my mother speechless. Not because of their fabulous cost—though the diamonds, pearls, and emeralds once fetched a small fortune—but because she recognizes them. *I* recognize them too, as does Filippa, who goes very still beside me.

Maman trails trembling fingers across a pearl-encrusted hairpin. The same hairpin my grandmother gave her for her eighteenth birthday.

The same hairpin she sold five years ago to disguise our father's crippling debt.

Swallowing hard, our mother tears her gaze away from it. "But how—?"

Michal leans forward in his seat, and I don't think I've ever loved him more than in this moment. Though he told me about her gift weeks ago—even asked for my help in confirming the pieces—it is quite different to know than to *see*, and the sight of my mother gaping down at her old jewelry, her eyes filling with tears, nearly causes my heart to burst. Abruptly desperate to touch him, to hold him, I seize his hand, and Michal squeezes my fingers gently before saying, "You'll notice one or two pieces are still missing from the collection. I'm hoping to procure them by the end of the month."

Maman still seems unable to speak, opening her mouth before closing it again in helpless defeat. At last, she straightens her shoulders and pretends to push back her hair, wiping her eyes discreetly in the process. "This is— Young man, I cannot—cannot *possibly* accept such a gift. Really, Monsieur Vasiliev, the expense alone—"

"Joyeux Noël, Satine," Michal says firmly. "You deserve a bit of happiness."

Odessa skewers Beau with an odd, pointed look at that. "And in the spirit of pursuing happiness, I would get on with it if I were you." She lifts her chin toward the bottle of absinthe in his hand, toward the note she attached around its neck written in bold script: *For courage.* Beau has been staring down at it for the last ten minutes, his thumb sweeping reflexively across the green fairy on the label. His throat working as if unable to remember how to breathe.

"What is she talking about?" Coco asks curiously, still lounging on the rug beside him, Lou, and Reid. Discarded paper litters the floor around them, and lilac ribbons glint in Coco's long plaits as she turns to grin at Beau, the firelight casting her in a warm and lovely glow. Indeed, when Beau finally glances up at her, it looks like someone has clubbed him over the head. She raises her eyebrows at his dumbfounded expression. "Beau . . . ?" she asks slowly. "Does she mean my gift? Did you draw my name?"

Though Beau coughs to clear his throat, his voice still comes out hoarse. "Yes."

Coco's smile falters slightly as she sits up. "What is it? Are you all right?"

He gives a strangled laugh in response, refusing to look at anyone, and I resist the urge to leap forward and drag the ring from his pocket myself. *Honestly.* Lou and I exchange a long-suffering glance, her turquoise eyes bright with anticipation. Because if Beauregard Lyon still thinks there is even a *possibility* Cosette Monvoisin will reject him, he is clearly the most oblivious man alive.

"What is this?" Coco's gaze narrows as it sweeps from Beau to the room at large, all of us waiting with bated breath for him to do it. To *ask* her. As if to bolster his brother's nerve, Reid surreptitiously flicks a finger, and the candlelight dims; the pianoforte in the corner begins to play a soft, crooning melody the next second. Coco stares at everyone, bemused. "You're all acting very *odd*, and if someone doesn't tell me why in the next three seconds, I'm going to— *Oh*."

Her threat ends on a sharp exhalation—her mouth falling open—as the explanation becomes clear the instant she turns back to Beau, who has climbed up to one knee. Face pale yet determined, he holds a small velvet box in one hand.

"I prepared a speech," he whispers in the abrupt silence of the room. "I mean, I've spent the last year dreaming up this exact moment, rehearsing it in the mirror—"

"Of course you did," Lou says with a delighted cackle.

Reid claps an impatient hand over her mouth, his attention fixed on Beau and Coco.

"—whispering it to myself in quiet moments, on long walks around the castle," Beau continues determinedly, ignoring them both. "Typically, in my head, it included your name written in the stars, and also lots of *se*—that is—" He coughs and glances hastily at my mother before turning back to Coco, who snickers despite the tears filling her eyes. His face softens. "I can't remember any of it now. All I know is that, once upon a time, I met a beautiful healer named Brie Perrot who enchanted me from that very first minute. Truly, she shouldn't have paid me any mind. Everyone said so—"

"I didn't," Odessa points out.

Beau flashes her an appreciative glance before reaching out to clasp Coco's hand. "I was a boy when I met you, Coco. An arrogant, stupid—albeit rather dashing—boy. And through you, through my time with everyone here, I've grown into someone I hope can make you proud and happy and . . ." His voice trails away as he releases her hand to flick open the latch of the box, revealing a golden ring with a magnificent ruby centerpiece. Tears spill down Coco's cheeks now, but she does nothing to wipe them away. Instead she simply stares at Beau, and in her eyes, it is clear he need never write her name in the stars.

To Coco, he *is* the stars, and the sun, and the moon; he is her entire universe.

Just like Michal is mine.

As if sharing the thought, he laces his fingers tighter through my own, and together we watch as Beau says, "I want to spend every day with you, Coco. I want your lovely face to be the first thing I see in the morning. I want your laugh to be the last thing I hear every night. I want the big moments with you—a wedding, a coronation—but I want the quiet moments too. I want us to curl up near the fireplace while you work on your tinctures, and I read my ledgers. I want to shop at the markets, to bicker about the best kind of cheese for a soufflé. More than anything, I want *you.* Just you." His hands begin to tremble now around the ring box. "I would be honored for you to take my last name, or for me to take your last name. The logistics don't matter. I just . . . I want to spend my life with you, Cosette Aurélie Monvoisin. My whole life. Every single moment. Because you make it better—you make *me* better, and I love you. I never thought I could feel this way, but I love you so much it feels like I might die without you. You are my other half."

In the brief, tentative silence that follows, Coco laughs and leans forward to wrap her arms around his neck. "And that *wasn't* the speech you've been preparing?"

His entire body relaxes as he presses his forehead against hers. "What can I say? You inspire me." Then, quieter still, his voice a breath against her lips, "Every day you inspire me, Coco. Would you marry me?"

Coco hesitates for not even a second.

"Yes. Of course, *yes*." With an incandescent smile, she pulls him into a fierce embrace, the strength of it knocking the ring from his hands. Though it soars through the air, Odessa catches it before it hits the floor. "This was perfect." Coco kisses his cheek as the room breaks into applause, into raucous cheers and congratulations. "More than perfect," she manages, kissing his other cheek too, kissing every inch of his face in between. "You have"—his nose, his forehead, his eyelids—"always undone me, Beauregard Lyon. You have always been the one for me. I love you too."

Odessa passes Beau the ring surreptitiously, and he untangles from Coco long enough to place it on her finger. And then he kisses it. He kisses every finger, every knuckle on each of her hands as she clings to him even tighter. The moment is beautiful, intimate, and I cannot help but throw myself at the two of them along with Lou, Reid, even Odessa, who begins to offer floral suggestions for Coco's bridal bouquet.

"This ruby could chip several teeth," Lou announces, seizing Coco's hand and inspecting it in the light. She winks at Beau. "Fantastic job, brother mine."

Coco beams with unbridled joy, and even my mother comes over to congratulate them. When they kiss again, I shoot her an expectant look—anticipating disapproval—but she simply arches a superior brow. "They're getting *married*, Célie. How else do you expect grandchildren are conceived?"

I gape at her. "They won't be *your* grandchildren—"

She lifts her chin. "Says who?"

Shaking my head incredulously, I turn to make a face at Filippa, but she is no longer sitting on the settee. Indeed—I sweep the room quickly—she seems to have vanished altogether, slipping out during the celebrations without notice.

Dimitri has vanished with her.

"Where are they?" I ask Michal in a low voice, and he tilts his head toward the window beside us. Curiosity burns through all decorum at that; the temperature has been steadily dropping for the last week, and on my walk to Michal's town house this morning, my toes nearly froze from the snow. When he offers no further explanation, merely smirks, I attempt to part the drapes as furtively as possible to see where they've gone. A fool's errand. Nothing escapes my mother's notice for long, and especially not inside her own house.

"What are you doing?" Her sharp voice cuts through the room, startling everyone from their revelry. Even Coco and Beau look back at us, intrigued. "Is there someone outside? Is it the carolers again? I did not hear them knock." She exhales a harsh, irritated breath through her nose at the last. Then—

"I loathe carolers," she and Michal say in unison.

Lou snorts as they glance at each other, startled. "Do you also loathe grandchildren?" she asks my mother politely. "Because based on what's happening outside, you might be well on your way."

The room explodes with movement at that, everyone hastening toward the window to eavesdrop. "You owe me twenty couronnes," Coco says to Odessa, who elbows Michal aside to peel back the curtains.

"Absolutely not." Her eyes narrow as she peers outside into the shadows of a—garden? My lips pull down in a frown. There shouldn't be a *garden* beyond this window, yet sure enough, the earth looks freshly dug, inexplicably green amidst the snow. Two silhouettes stand stiff and awkward beside it. *Filippa and Dimitri.* He must've drawn her name, and this—*this must be his gift*, I realize in dawning comprehension. Even Odessa cannot disguise her interest. "You said Filippa and Dima would be kissing by Christmas, yes, but there must be an explicit exchange of saliva—"

Beau protests at once. "We never specified tongue!"

"You watch your tone, Your Majesty." My mother pushes through everyone, craning her neck to see through the clouded glass. "I cannot hear them! I cannot even *see* them—"

Before Lou can react, Reid flicks his wrist, and quiet voices drift through the windowpanes. Everyone stills to listen. To *watch.* The bitter wind lifts a tendril of Filippa's hair as she stares at the white flowers carpeting the ground at her feet. "Snowdrops," I whisper in awe. Michal and Lou exchange conspiratorial grins, and I point an accusatory finger between them. "Did you two know about this?"

"Perhaps," Michal says.

"And you didn't tell me?"

Looping her arm through the crook of my elbow, Lou bumps my hip. "Le secret du Père Noël, right? Emphasis on *secret.*"

"Quiet, all of you," my mother hisses, practically pressing her nose against the glass now. "I'm trying to listen." When Dimitri steps forward outside, lifting a hand as if to tuck a strand of Filippa's hair behind her ear, we all obey instantly, the entire room holding its breath.

He drops his hand at the last second, however, his fingers curling into his palm. "For your daughter." At Filippa's stricken expression, he adds gently, "They'll bloom each winter in honor of Frostine."

Though Filippa stiffens slightly at the name, she does not snap at Dimitri. She does not flee either, or fold into herself as she so often does. Instead, she slowly bends to trail her fingers over the nearest buds, as if checking to ensure they're real, before staring up at him in equal parts disbelief and accusation. "But they—" She swallows. "Snowdrops have always been my favorite."

His dimples flash. "So you've mentioned."

"And you remembered?"

"I remember everything you say, Filippa."

She flinches unexpectedly at that, staggering back a step as if his kindness is somehow a weapon, as if it *hurts.* "I—I don't understand. I *killed* you."

Dimitri chuckles low, sliding his hands into his pockets and matching her step for step. Refusing to give her an inch. "Strangely enough, I remember that too. Stranger still is that I've chosen to forgive you." A meaningful pause. "Everyone has."

Her face crumples, and all at once, she stops trying to escape, instead turning away to hide her face. "Thank you, Dimitri," she breathes after another long, painful moment. "They're . . . beautiful."

He touches her shoulder before gesturing toward an upstairs

window, and we all duck swiftly before peering back over the windowsill, unable to help ourselves. Fortunately, their attention has already returned to each other, and we shamelessly and simultaneously rise; even Odessa, with all her vampiric grace, flattens her ear against the glass.

"You'll be able to see them from your window as you write," Dimitri says softly. Hopefully. And now he does tuck that errant strand of hair behind her ear, his fingers lingering for just a second too long. She almost leans into the touch—*almost*—and his gaze falls to her lips.

"It's happening," Coco whispers gleefully, bouncing on her toes behind me.

Odessa shakes her head, opening her mouth to argue, but I hardly hear her—not as Michal slips his hand through mine, bending low to murmur in my ear, "We should give them some privacy."

Gooseflesh erupts down my spine.

"An excellent idea!" Before anyone can protest, my mother snaps the curtains closed, and a moment later, Filippa returns to the sitting room with a snowdrop tucked behind her ear, her cheeks flushed from the cold. When Dimitri follows, the entire room hurries to feign disinterest—Lou opens the bottle of absinthe with a cheery *pop*, Beau drags Coco into his lap on a nearby chair, and Reid joins my mother in hastily collecting the discarded wrapping paper. Only Odessa notices, her smile wry, as Michal pulls me away from the flurry of activity, slipping into the quiet of the kitchen. *At last.*

He lifts me onto the counter without a word, stepping between my legs as I drape my arms around his neck. Unable to help it,

I glance back at the door through which we just came. "Dimitri could be good for her, I think. She seems to . . . like him, which is a small miracle because my sister doesn't like anyone."

Michal brushes his lips against my throat. "And what about you, pet?"

Arching my neck to ease his access, I shiver as his hands skim up my thighs, parting my legs farther. "What about me?" I ask breathlessly, forgetting all about my sister. As his fingers dance across my skin, I can hardly remember my own name—and in this moment, it doesn't matter. Nothing else ever matters when I'm with Michal. I'll want him always. I'll love him always. And today—with the holiday festivities and our closest friends exchanging tender promises—it feels like it should be a dream. It feels beyond what I could have ever hoped, what I could have ever imagined. My head tips back as Michal continues his languorous perusal of my throat, and above us—

Mistletoe.

Michal must feel my slow grin.

"Who do *you* like?" Voice purring at my ear, he flicks his tongue against a sensitive spot, and I tip forward again, stifling a moan against his broad shoulder. Those fingers continue their wicked taunt, and I would give anything—*anything*—to be back in Michal's town house. Behind the closed door of his blackened room, atop his silk sheets, with the moonlight spilling onto his bare chest.

"This is cruel." My own hands slide through his hair before curling into the collar of his sweater. I knitted it for him last month, and it looks like a woolen bladder. "You're torturing me."

"Perhaps." His mouth captures mine then, and he kisses me

with all the fierceness of an immortal king, a groan building hot and heavy in the back of his throat. Against my lips, he murmurs, "Is this making it better?" His tongue plunges inside then, tasting of cinnamon and apples and spice, and my legs hook instinctively around his waist before tightening and drawing him closer still. It isn't enough. Never enough.

"My mother could walk in," I remind him with a gasp.

"Your mother is cleaning."

I clench his shirt in my hands, unable to stop myself from kissing him again and again and again. "What about the others?"

"Busy," he says, and I swallow the word. I savor it.

I savor *him.*

"Michal," I whisper, shuddering, and he pulls back with a groan. "We cannot have—*relations* on my mother's kitchen counter."

He chuckles darkly, and I feel that rumble in his chest through to the tips of my toes. "You didn't seem to have a problem having them in the library this morning." Memories flash through my mind's eye at his words: the gilt of a sliding ladder, the scent of fresh paint, the sharp edges of brand-new bookshelves pressed into my spine—and Michal.

Michal against me, on top of me, all *over* me as we christened his gift to me. Twice.

"We'll finish this later," I say against his lips, and he seals the promise with another scorching kiss. When he pulls away, however, his thumb lingers on my empty ring finger, and my entire body goes still.

When he finally looks up again, his eyes burn with fiercer promise still. "Expect more than a library for Yule next year."

Next year. We stare at each other, the words lingering in the air between us, and nothing has ever sounded so sweet. An entire year of courtship with Michal—of stolen kisses and midnight promenades and library trysts. “Next year,” I whisper, kissing him softly. “And then forever.”

ACKNOWLEDGMENTS

Life has this thrilling and often devastating habit of changing on us without notice. One moment, I sat down to write the first words of *The Shadow Bride*, and the next—a year and a half later—I'm sitting down to write its acknowledgments. So much has changed in the moments between, but one thing remains the same: I am so grateful to be here. I am so grateful to write stories for a living, and I am so grateful to each of my readers for bestowing that privilege. From the bottom of my heart, thank you.

To RJ, Beau, James, Rose, and Wren, you are the greatest gifts I've ever been given. I couldn't have written this book without you, or without the love and encouragement of my parents, my family, and my friends. I love you all endlessly. Thank you for being a soft place to land in every season. To Finna, Pippa, and Gus Gus, thank you for keeping me company during all those long hours at my desk. To Pippa in particular—I can still feel your head on my shoulder, and it breaks my heart. I'll miss you forever. I hope there are squirrels for you to chase in heaven.

All books take a village to publish, and this one is no different. I'm incredibly thankful for the guidance and support of my entire team at HarperCollins and Park & Fine, including my editors, Erica Sussman and Sara Schonfeld, and my agent, Pete Knapp.

Thank you for navigating the highs and lows of this industry with me. You are, quite simply, the best.

And lastly, to Jordan Gray, who knows what she means to me. It would take pages and pages to list all the ways you've helped with the creation of these books, so instead I'll just say thank you. For everything.